Praise for
the Dragon Knight novels

"Dickson pulls more surprises out of his storytelling hat than any other writer working in light fantasy."
—*St. Paul Pioneer Press*

"His characters are charming, and the novel uses mythic material in innovative ways."
—*Publishers Weekly* on *The Dragon in Lyonesse*

"An entertaining jaunt through the mists of legend and magic."
—*CNN.com* on *The Dragon of Lyonesse*

Tor Books by Gordon R. Dickson

NOVELS

Alien Art
The Alien Way
Arcturus Landing
The Far Call
Gremlins, Go Home! (with Ben Bova)
Hoka! (with Poul Anderson)
Home from the Shore
The Last Master
Masters of Everon
Mission to Universe
Naked to the Stars
On the Run
Other
Outposter
Planet Run (with Keith Laumer)
The Pritcher Mass
Pro
Secrets of the Deep
Sleepwalkers' World
The Space Swimmers
The Space Winners
Spacepaw
Spacial Delivery
Way of the Pilgrim
Wolf and Iron

THE DORSAI SERIES

Necromancer
Tactics of Mistake
Lost Dorsai: The New Dorsai Companion
Soldier, Ask Not
The Spirit of Dorsai
Dorsai!
Young Bleys
The Final Encyclopedia, vol. 1 (rev. ed.)
The Final Encyclopedia, vol. 2 (rev. ed.)
The Chantry Guild

THE DRAGON SERIES

The Dragon Knight
The Dragon and the Gnarly King
The Dragon in Lyonesse
The Dragon and the Fair Maid of Kent

COLLECTIONS

Beyond the Dar al-Harb
Guided Tour
Love Not Human
The Man from Earth
The Man the Worlds Rejected
Steel Brother
The Stranger

THE DRAGON AND THE FAIR MAID OF KENT

GORDON R. DICKSON

TOR®
fantasy

A TOM DOHERTY ASSOCIATES BOOK
NEW YORK

This is a work of fiction. All the characters and events portayed in this book are either products of the author's imagination or are used fictitiously.

THE DRAGON AND THE FAIR MAID OF KENT

Copyright © 2000 by Gordon R. Dickson.

All rights reserved, including the right to reproduce this book, or portions thereof, in any form.

A Tor Book
Published by Tom Doherty Associates, LLC
175 Fifth Avenue
New York, NY 10010

www.tor.com

Tor® is a registered trademark of Tom Doherty Associates, LLC.

ISBN: 0-812-56272-0
Library of Congress Catalog Card Number: 00-043028

First edition: December 2000
First mass market edition: September 2001

Printed in the United States of America

0   9   8   7   6   5   4   3   2   1

THE DRAGON AND THE FAIR MAID OF KENT

Chapter 1

Jim (Baron Sir James Eckert, Lord of Malencontri Castle and its environs, and also now uppermost-level apprentice in Magick) woke two hours before moonset; and rose from bed, going to the nearest of the Solar windows to look out.

Behind him in their bed his wife, Angie (Lady Angela), slept peacefully. Beyond the window it was still full night, but cloudless and moon-bright. From just under the top of Malencontri's tower, where the Solar's large, single room was, the full moon itself was still up, and everything far below him stood out clearly.

The tall trees beyond the cleared space surrounding the castle blended together in an unbroken wall of blackness; the stubbled ground of the cleared space showed a faint shine on its patches of grass, evidence that the night's rain had stopped only recently.

As he watched, two figures, bent under the loads on their backs, came out of the woods to his right and cut across the cleared space at an angle to enter the woods again on its further side. They walked slowly, heavily, one figure taller than the other, the large bundles riding high on their shoulders.

The prospect of dawn must have roused them, with its hope of sun to dry their worn clothes—for clearly all they owned was carried on their shoulders now—and put a little heat into their bones. So they had roused from whatever forest nest they had made in the rain for the night and were once more moving on; to what they did not know, but someplace better than this, and much better than wherever they had left.

Standing before the six-inch squares of glass that made up the panes in the Solar window, warmed by the blazing fireplace, refueled even while he and Angie slept by the servant who, with a man-at-arms, was always on duty outside their door, Jim felt a chill go through him.

They grew more numerous every day, these drifters. Running from news of the bubonic plague, now in France—always traveling west, always so poor they did not even have a donkey to carry their belongings, and with no real goal in sight—driven on only by the instinct for survival. The chill deepened in Jim. There they trudged, cold, undoubtedly hungry, if not starving. All doors were closed to them out of a fear of the very sickness they fled from.

No community would take them in, for the same fear. Some member of the Church might put out food for them, but otherwise could not help—probably would not help. They had probably given up hope of aid, even from Heaven.

Faith and Love, those two great Pillars of Strength in the medieval world—available to even the poorest—were almost surely lost to them by now. Faith, that offered hope even beyond the grave, would have been drowned in the animal effort to live. Love, in all its meanings of this time—love of wife, children, comrades, community, and country—all the ways the word wove together in the tapestry of medieval society, had once made the fabric of their lives. All gone now.

What was left now was no more than the blind urge to run, and under that instinct, they trudged mindlessly westward, ever westward, like cattle before the driving, level snow in the fierce wind of a blizzard.

Jim remembered how he had lied about being a knight and a baron when he and Angie—now his wife—came to this medieval world, a far different version of the Earth into which he had been born and grown up. He stood here now, warm, protected and fed as what he had claimed to be. It was true he had done what was required of someone with the rank he had claimed. He had followed the rules. He had fought with the proper weapons when necessary, according to the customs here—not well, but well enough to get by. But his attempts to live had been rewarded. Those two out there had not. There was no more fairness in this time and place than there had been in the world of his twentieth-century birth.

The ones he watched might reach the sea eventually—it was not a great distance from them now—and there would be nothing for them there, either. What would they do then? Drown themselves like lemmings in their spring migration? There seemed no sense or reason to their keeping on.

The chill was deep in him now, and he knew what had driven it there: the question that had returned again and again to him the last two years of those few he and Angie had spent in this historic period of a world almost exactly like the one in which they had grown up.

Will Angie and I ever really belong here?

And even as he faced that question once again, Carolinus, his Master-in-Magick, appeared beside him.

"Good! You're up!" he said. His red robe, like all his robes, was worn thin, and would stay that way until, in a less absent-minded moment, he would recollect the fact and make it clean and new again. "Jim, I've only a short time to tell you something important."

"Shh!" said Jim. "Angie's asleep!"

"She will not wake while we talk," said Carolinus, "and, Jim, try practicing at least a little proper respect to senior Magickians. You may need it soon. You may now be in the last stage of apprenticeship, but you're not yet a fellow member to a Magickian—let alone one like me. Must I remind you I'm not only the most senior of Magickians, but one of the only three AAA+ Magickians in the world?"

"Of course not," said Jim. "I never forget. But I thought we could drop formality in private."

"Sometimes. Sometimes not! This is not one of those times. I come to you at this hour in person, that no other Magickian might chance to overhear, and, by the way, with a ward around us now through which nothing could be heard, to privately give you information it is against the laws of the Collegiate of Magickians for a member to share—two laws in particular I, myself, helped write. It was I who woke you just now, I who then gave you some moments in which to become fully awake, so that you would fully grasp the importance of what I have to say."

"Sorry," said Jim. "But look, Carolinus, I was deep asleep just ten minutes ago, and about to go back to it. Wouldn't you rather tell me in the morning—"

"Jim, listen to me! You must tell no one—not even Angie. There are things no apprentice should ever be told beforehand. One is that his Master-in-Magick has proposed him for full membership—until the Collegiate has agreed to consider him. I'm telling you this now—and the other matter that brings me here—because the problem is dire, and I believe I have seen in you a capacity no other apprentice has ever shown."

"I see," said Jim, fully awake to the conversation now and at last impressed by what Carolinus was telling him. He had never heard the elder magickian speak to him with quite this much urgency before. "All right, if it's that serious I won't even tell her—though we generally don't keep secrets from each other—"

"This is not *your* secret!"

Carolinus glared at Jim for a moment. He seemed to grow in stature.

"I understand," Jim said.

"Then engrave this thought in your mind. Whatever must be done to prevent it, whatever it costs you, me or anyone else—the King must not die! *The King must not die!*"

"You've mentioned this before," Jim said. "But never this seriously. Is there some immediate danger—" Jim began to ask, but it was too late.

Carolinus was gone.

Quietly Jim went back to bed and slid carefully under the

covers. Angie did not stir. The image of the two refugees, drifting westward, was still with him; riding on top of it in his mind was what Carolinus had said. The part about his now being considered for membership in the Collegiate was welcome—he had ideas of what he wanted to do with that membership—but it was no great surprise. They would have had to do something about him eventually.

Although he had no direct evidence of the fact, he was sure that no other apprentice-rated magician came within a country mile of him in terms of magical abilities—not anywhere in this world, though that was not really due to his having an innate genius where magic was concerned. It was to do with the advantage of having grown up in a world of scientific method and knowledge more than five hundred years in the future of this time.

Carolinus' unusually powerful concern over the life of the King was something else again. There must be not only reason for it, but reason that deeply concerned the worldwide Collegiate of Magickians itself. According to the history that had been his undergraduate and graduate study where he had come from, Edward IV was not due to die for years yet.

But—he reminded himself—events here often did not exactly match what he had learned in the world of his birth.

This last thought gnawed at his mind, colored by the emotion of seeing the drifters. He was tired, in need of sleep, but sleep seemed impossible.

Thought succeeded thought. Possibility followed possibility. Mental scenarios in which he dealt with one wild situation after another. . . . The night-duty servant quietly came in several times to replenish the wood in their fireplace. Each time Jim pretended to be asleep.

At last, he did sleep—but not well—waking to find predawn looking in the windows and Angie gone. He got up, dressed, called in the room servant to make up the bed, and lay down on it.

He fell asleep again. This time he dreamed—until the sound of the door opening woke him a second time, as surely as if it had been an alarm.

"Jim!" said the Lady Angela Eckert, to the further sound of the door closing sharply behind her. She came in, lit now by bright morning sunlight through the Solar windows, moving swiftly to his bedside to stare down at him. "You're as white as a sheet!"

Jim looked up at her from their big bed and answered without thinking. His voice did not come out right. He had meant it to sound humorous. It did not.

"Someone just walked over my grave," he said.

Angie continued to stare at him, her face showing a mixture of expressions: alarmed concern, near anger.

"What on earth do you mean saying a stupid thing like that?" she said finally . . . but gently now, her face showing only concern as she sat down on the edge of the bed. "Here you are, all dressed up and lying there on a made-up bed."

"Dressed up?"

He glanced down at his body. He had forgotten he had dressed—dressed up—in his finest clothes, and had forgotten that the bed beneath him was made up. The dream came back to him.

But Angie was going on, talking almost automatically as she stared at him with still deeper concern.

"—When I let you oversleep it was because I thought you looked so tired. But everyone in the castle is going to have to work like beavers today—"

"No beavers," he said, still stupid. "Fourteenth century. England. No beavers here."

"Bees with their little tails on fire, then! If we're going to get the castle ready in time for Geronde and Brian's wedding—"

"The servants'll do all that," he said, and once again his voice came out wrong. "They won't let me do any of it."

"That's not the point and you know it. They've got to

see you looking furious, as if you'd have to do it yourself if they don't. They want you all worked up and involved, so they know they ought to be all worked up and involved, too—they're our two best friends, after all, and everybody knows it. All worked up because the banns had to be read again to have it here by extraordinary Church permission and our dirty old chapel cleaned and refixed in no time at all so that Geronde can have the Mass she wants following the wedding—and everything else."

There was no good answer to this. It was all true, so he said nothing.

"And here you lie," she went on, "three hours past sun-up, in visitor-greeting clothes, doing nothing!"

He could hardly deny his clothes or the fact he was doing nothing. So he said nothing. Angie would change gears in a moment. She herself was wearing an old, mulberry-colored gown . . . everyday clothes—

"Jim," she said, firmly, "what is it? First the dress-up. Now you scare me half to death saying what you did."

He had to give her a reasonable answer. The truth.

"They're both part of the same thing," he said. He sat up, swinging his legs over the edge of the bed so that he sat beside her. He put an arm around her shoulders. "Carolinus came toward the end of the night. He had something to tell me. But he made me promise not to tell anyone else—even you."

"Well, that was good of him!—No, cancel that. I know he wouldn't do anything like that without a good reason." She turned her head to look up into his face. "And that made you have some crazy dream?"

"Maybe!" said Jim. He did not really know. "But when he came, I'd just been looking out the window and seen a couple of drifters—a man and a woman, I think. One was a full head taller than the other. I couldn't get them out of my mind. So, I lay awake a long time, then went back to sleep and had this dream."

"And made the bed yourself, and got dressed up like this while you were still dreaming?"

"Of course not. I dressed, thinking I'd stay up, called in the servant to make the bed, then lay down on the made-up bed—and had the dream."

"Some dream, to affect you like this!"

Again he had no easy answer.

"Tell me what it was about," she said.

He put his arm around her and took her hand, laying it out palm up in his own open palm. They both studied it for a moment—Angie's looking fragile against his broader, thicker hand, with its longer fingers, callused now by tight-held reins and hours of weapon practice with Brian. Then he brought his arm back and covered both hands with his other, holding her hand within both of his.

"I meant what I told you earlier, literally," he said, as gently as he could. "I dreamed they were walking on the ground over me. I dreamed I was dead."

"*Jim!*"

"I'm sorry," he said. "I wasn't going to tell you. But you had to know. That's how it was."

There was a moment when neither said anything.

"I believe you," Angie said gently. "But you know, none of what you've told me makes me understand why there was this business of walking over your grave."

"In the dream," he told her, "it was an experiment. I was thinking of all sorts of things after Carolinus left and I didn't think I could go back to sleep, and one of the things I was groping for was a hunch about what was behind Carolinus' visit. You know how I do things. I don't ignore my hunches—so I was reaching for one, and about that time I must have fallen asleep."

"You think just a hunch could give you a dream like that?"

"Maybe. Remember, in this magic-filled world hunches could be more than hunches."

He shivered, remembering the reality of his dream, then cursed himself for putting it into words, because he knew she must have felt the shiver in his hands as he held hers. "I just mean that in this world, hunches can be more than hunches."

"I won't believe that!" said Angie. "Did Carolinus ever tell you hunches were real here?"

"No. But he's never told me much about magic. What I've picked up from him has mainly been through watching him, listening to his talk generally, and adding two and two together."

"Did you ever add things up to come up with this hunch idea, before last night?"

"No, I never did before."

"Then any hunches that made your nightmare were just that," she said. "It could just be your imagination making everything bigger than it is. What did Carolinus tell you to trigger all this off?"

"Just reminded me the King must not die."

She stared at him.

"Why should he die? How could it be any business of yours if he did?"

"I don't know," he said. "Carolinus was gone without telling me. He's said the same thing before."

"Well, it could all be coincidence. Or it could have been just as you remember it and still be wrong. Now what's all this got to do with putting on your good clothes?"

"That was another hunch after I got up."

"Well, change to everyday clothes, then. Spit in the eye of the Devil!"

She was trying to help him forget, and he loved her for it, but the reality of the dream was still with him. He would have had to tell her about it anyway, but he had made a clumsy mess of it, diving into the telling as he had.

"No, I think I'll leave them on. Remember, it's an experiment."

"Then leave them on! It doesn't matter. But come help me fire up the staff and maybe you can forget about it!"

"Here I come," he said, more cheerfully than he had said anything since she had come in and found him on the bed.

But late in the afternoon, the Bishop of Bath and Wells, with his customary entourage of chaplain, clerk, personal servants and a dozen stout men-at-arms, came visiting, and Jim had to play host to him alone, while Angie hastily changed into more formal apparel.

The equivalent of afternoon tea was set up immediately, and they all settled down (or up, rather) in the Solar for a leisurely exchange of news and views until the formality of supper. Meanwhile, outside, the afternoon waned, to the point where the Great Gates of Malencontri were closed against the oncoming night.

To the west of the castle, the red, late-autumn sun was still visible, but already beginning to lose its lower edges behind the tops of the thick belt of trees out of which the drifters had come the night before. Still, the fading, late-fall twilight continued to give illumination to the end of the day. Only now, only a few moments past, two riders had come out of the ruddily tipped trees, heading for the already barred Great Gates of the castle.

Already, however, several senior men-at-arms were gathered on the catwalk, looking over that part of the castle's curtain wall to observe and leisurely discuss the newcomers. They would most certainly not be let in now, after gate-close.

Other men-at-arms were joining them as soon as they were off duty. Men-at-arms only, for the defensive catwalk below the battlements clear around the castle wall was territory of the men-at-arms alone—ordinary Castle servants were allowed up on it solely when their added numbers were needed to repel an attack on the curtain walls.

Regardless of this—though they could hardly have failed

to understand the situation—the two now walking their horses toward the gate came on.

It was not merely Malencontri's orders that would bar entrance to them, of course. Cities, towns, castles, even private dwellings with anything that could be stolen inside them, barred all entrances, locked all shutters and put themselves in a defensive position every eve until daybreak. It was common sense against any night attack when most inside would be sleeping. More than that: it was the custom.

Custom, of all holy things, rating just below Faith and Love, was not there to be treated lightly in this society and time. Faith simply *was*, of course; Love—here in its full sense, stretching all the way from duty to a superior or an ideal, to the child who could be gotten at only over your dead body—could not be questioned. But Custom endured because what had always been must always be. Custom, sworn to in court, could make even a lord back down to a demand by his tenants. So the men-at-arm discussed the two approaching with the distant interest given to something that would have to wait until the morning to be resolved.

The taller of the two was clearly a knight. He wore the weapons, the swordbelt. Moreover, his spurs, which might even actually be gold, glinted occasionally in the light that remained. The other, smaller rider, also weaponed but without the swordbelt, was undoubtedly his squire. It was even possible that the smaller was a younger brother or otherwise related. The two wore visorless helms and looked more than a little alike.

But what really interested the more experienced men-at-arms was not the pair themselves so much as the armor worn by the knight. Dulled as it was by the soil of travel, it was obviously beautifully made and fitted him like a set of court clothes. A suit of armor almost beyond cost for the person who had paid the original price for it. But since he was so poor or unimportant that he traveled with none but his squire—and probably a family member at that—that person could not have been him.

So how had it come into his possession, fitting him as perfectly as it did?

They all turned with expressions of interest as they were abruptly joined by Theoluf, a former chief man-at-arms himself, now elevated to the rank of being their lord's squire (and now therefore officially a gentleman), but one who would still unbend to the point of speaking more on a level with his men than most squires would.

They pointed out the stranger knight's armor, even as he and his companion reached the gate and the knight began to hammer on it with the shaft of his lance.

"Open!" his angry shout came up to them. "Open, I say, for Edward *Le Captiv!*"

Theoluf's normally good-humored—if wound-marked—face flashed into an expression of fury, terrifying behind the scar that almost split his face from right chin-point to his left forehead. Instantly he leaned over the battlements and shouted back.

"At once, Your Grace! At once!"

He swung back to face his men-at-arms.

"Bone-heads! Privy-wits!" he snarled at them. "Were none of you with me on our first visit to France when we rescued him from the Rogue Magickian, Malvinne?"

Silence. White-faced, none of them answered. The wrath faded from his expression. None had been with him in France. There was always considerable turnover in the manning of the establishment's men-at-arms, for numerous reasons. His voice became a little less outraged—but still sharp enough.

"What do you wait for? That is the young England who asks entrance, Edward, heir to the throne! Dolts! Run!"

They ran.

Chapter 2

The Bishop of Bath and Wells was a burly, pugnacious man in his early middle age who could be very powerful and demanding in his speech, but at the moment he seemed on his warmest and most congenial behavior. This, in spite of what he announced as a mere slightly twisted ankle, but which required him to limp and use a walking stick.

He had come, with a small gold crucifix to be a present of his own, to thank them for the white Chinese silk altar-cloth material Angie had been able to get through Carolinus' eastern Magickian connections. The cloth itself had been a thank-you gift from Angie for the Bishop's help in getting the English King to give Jim ward of the orphaned baby, Robert Falon.

Today, the Bishop had brought part of the silk, already made into the frontal of one altar cloth, to show it off—so went the intricate business of gift-giving in the high Middle Ages.

". . . I have just had word—" the good prelate had begun by saying, once he, Jim and Angie were safely private below Malencontri's tower top in the Solar apartment. He had reached for another small cake. "—that the plague has reached London."

"But it's too early!" Jim almost said aloud before he caught himself. In the history of his world and Angie's, the plague had only just reached Genoa in a rat-infested ship, sometime between the years of 1347 and 1349.

The times of their world and this were out of whack. They were not just off by a set number of years, as the early Julian calendar and the later, modern one of Jim and Angie's future century had been found to be. Various important incidents, like the deaths of kings or the year of a decisive battle, seemed to be taking place here at unexpectedly different times.

Meanwhile, having stunned his two listeners with his news, the good Bishop took up his wineglass and sipped from it.

"Yes," he went on, "it moves swiftly. Already, there are villages in France where not a soul has survived."

"I thought those were just stories!" said Jim.

"Unfortunately, they are true, Sir James. The Fiend is among us, and it is our duty, not only within the Church but without, to do what we can to deny him at least some of his victims."

These last words came out with a more steely edge than Jim had expected to hear, even from this prelate. The Bishop (Richard de Bisby) came from one of those families of the upper nobility called magnates. Families such as that of the Earl of Oxford; families in which, under the rule of primogeniture, the eldest son inherited everything, and the younger sons were either sent into the Church or pointed toward the military.

In the Bishop's case, this had made him a prelate who might actually have been happier in life with a sword in his hand rather than a crosier. Certainly he was built to take on the duties of a medieval swordsman, from his ruddy, tough-featured face to his meaty, powerful-looking hands.

But this was a new Bishop, a different, fully ecclesiastical Bishop, very much a leader who thought in the long terms of the Church, and the survival of his communicants.

"It seemeth," he was saying now, "there is no medicine for it—no salves to ease the pain of the cruel buboes of those dying from it, so that they are already in Hell before they die. Carolinus tells me, Sir James, that you and the Lady Angela come from a far place. Could it be that either of you know more of this plague and what might be done to stop it than we do?"

Information rushed from the back of Jim's mind. As a graduate student working toward a degree as a medievalist he had done a paper on the plague, and facts jumped forward, only to be pushed back before he could utter them.

He could tell the tough-looking man sitting opposite him nothing that would stop the disease or cure those who had caught it. The medical terms that would explain the known later-day details would make no sense in this time.

"We believed it was spread by the bites of fleas, who'd already fed on rats with the disease in them—but that's all," he said. "The rats that brought the disease to Genoa—from which it's been spreading—must have come on a ship from the Far East, where the plague has been known for some centuries; they've had no cure for it there, either."

That much was an honest answer. The details about its pneumonal form, spread by the breath of those already infected, were not only unexplainable in fourteenth-century terms but could not help the situation. There was nothing else Jim could say which would give the Bishop any assistance.

"—it might be wise," he added, however, "to clean your church property and people as much from fleas and rats as possible."

"I will remember that," said the Bishop; and Jim, knowing the medieval memory, even in an educated literate man like the Bishop, knew the other would.

"—And Your Lordship is undoubtedly aware of the penny-royal? That small mintlike flower that fleas do not like and which therefore repels them? We'll be putting it all around the castle here generously, ourselves," said Angie.

"Thank you, my daughter," said the Bishop. "I was aware of the plant, of course, but I had not thought of it in connection with this."

Jim, meanwhile, had stolen a glance at Angie, who had returned it briefly after the Bishop answered. The one thing they had both feared for themselves, stuck in this early historic period, had been sickness—for either one of them. Magic could close and cure wounds. It could not do a thing for any kind of physical malady.

"I have been in contact by fast rider with my Brother in Christ, the Bishop of London," announced the Bishop, who had intercepted the glance between husband and wife and was beginning to fear that the shock value of his news might be fading in his audience, making them less likely to fall in blindly with the request he had come to Malencontri to make. "I am aware, of course, that magick has no cure for sicknesses—except on the lips of charlatans. Nonetheless, Sir James, your Master-in-Magick and I, both feel that talking the problem over together might be of aid—but there is a difficulty in doing that."

He took a sip of his wine.

"Unfortunately—as two like you might understand more quickly than most—for a Lord of Holy Church like myself, appearing to consult with even perhaps the greatest Mage might be misunderstood if generally known. As a result I can hardly ask Carolinus to visit me for privy talk at Bath or Wells—much less risk having it known that I had made visit directly to him."

He cleared his throat. He was not usually in the position of asking favors from others.

"As a result," he went on strongly, "it occurs to me to ask you if you would be contemplating inviting Carolinus to Malencontri during the few days I can be here. If so, it would be a convenient time for me to speak with him."

"Of course!" said Jim. "You are now here, my Lord Bishop; and as for Carolinus, he needs no invitation, but I confidently expect him—possibly as early as tomorrow. I could just visit him, no problem if I fly to the Tinkling Water, as I so frequently do, and ask him to come."

"No, no!" said the Bishop. "It must be known that he was

invited separately—a day or so before I was—so that our meeting here was entirely by chance—"

A scratching at the Solar's hall door interrupted him.

"Come!" said Jim, and Theoluf stuck his scarred face into the Solar.

"My lord, may I crave your kindness to leave for a moment, on a matter of greatest seriousness?"

"Would you forgive me—" Jim looked questioningly at the Bishop.

"Certainly, my son."

"It's all right," said Jim to Theoluf, getting to his feet. "I'll come. But I'll be right back—won't I, Theoluf?"

"Indeed, my lord! Indeed! A moment, only."

Jim went out, carefully closing the three-inch door, built as a final barrier against any attackers who might have driven Malencontri's defenders to their last and stoutest defensive position.

"What is all this, Theoluf?" he asked.

"My lord, I am bade to tell you that the Count of Woodstock and the Countess of Kent are at the High Table in the Hall, being cared for and wishing to speak to you and Lady Angela as soon as possible."

"Countess of Kent?" The Countess of Kent was the highborn woman otherwise known as "the Fair Maid of Kent," reputedly the most beautiful woman in England. She had her title by right of birth, but she was also the Countess of Salisbury by marriage with her present husband.

"The *Countess of Kent,* m'Lord," repeated Theoluf with particular emphasis—and the Count of Woodstock, *le captiv!*"

"Oh!" said Jim. The Count of Woodstock, eldest son of King Edward and heir-apparent to the English throne, had sometime since been given a higher title, that of the Prince of Wales—the title for the King's eldest son, heir to the throne. But he had been just "the Prince" when Jim, Brian, and Giles de Mer, with Dafydd and Aargh, the English

Wolf, had rescued him from captivity at the hands of Mal-vinne, a rogue Magickian. Clearly the Prince did not want knowledge of his presence spread around the neighborhood.

Jarred back to a more general appraisal of the situation by realization that England's Crown Prince was suddenly a guest here, along with someone else's wife—at the same time as the Bishop was in residence—Jim found his usually nimble wits had no quick decisions to offer.

"Tell them I'll come to them as soon as I can—my apologies, of course. Don't stint on the apologies. Is Mistress Cinders preparing a couple of rooms?"

"All is in hand, m'Lord."

"Good!" Jim went back into the Solar with a troubled mind.

"Forgive me for this interruption, my lord," he said to the Bishop.

"Of course, my son," said the Bishop. "I am familiar with such in my own establishment. So, I take it you are not adverse to my guesting here for the next few days. It would be a kindness to find out for me if Carolinus plans to visit in that time—I understand he lives not far from here."

Jim knew that the Bishop knew full well how close Carolinus lived—but he was being polite.

"No distance at all," said Jim, getting up again, "and no trouble. Also it is a pleasure to us always to have you under our roof. If you'll forgive me for leaving, I'll go right now."

He was only too aware of how Carolinus suited time to himself. This world's leading Mage could easily interpret "a day or two" as meaning "whenever you feel like it." Jim closed the door to the corridor behind him before the Bishop could offer any more polite protests, and headed toward the stairs to the tower roof.

"Stand back, William," he ordered the man-at-arms on watch, once he was up there—this being the standard warning to one of his retainers that he was about to change into his dragon form. William was already a good twenty feet away. Nonetheless, he backed clear to the battlements on the opposite side of the tower top.

It was prompt obedience to orders, but it was also prudence. The full spread of Jim's dragon wings was a good deal more than the width of the tower top.

Then Jim had changed and was gone, almost straight upward on the thunder of those enormous wings. In moments he was high above the ground. He found a current of air in the ocean of the day's atmosphere, one heading roughly toward Castle Smythe, Brian's residence, and ceased climbing, spreading his wings and holding them outstretched, to coast gently downward in the direction he wished to go, without effort.

The pleasure of that effortless flight took him over again, as it always did, and soothed him. Dragons were not given to wrestling with mental problems, and for the movement he was as much dragon as human. But gradually the tangle of the present situation at Malencontri crept back into his mind.

Getting the invitation to Carolinus was no real problem at all; the only possible sticking point would be to get Carolinus to openly promise he would be there tomorrow. If he actually said out loud he would be there, they could count on him.

It was ridiculous, when Jim thought about it. Carolinus was always preaching to Jim about being as thrifty as possible with his available magickal energy—and admittedly there had been incidents that seemed to justify those warnings.

But the Mage himself could appear at Malencontri without even winking, and seemed to think nothing of hopping from wherever he was to as far as World's End (than which there was no farther) and back, even taking people like Jim and Angie along with him, and never counting the magickal cost.

At the same time, his home at the Tinkling Water resembled nothing so much as a pleasant little fairy-tale cottage. But it could somehow make its ordinary-sized door admit, and its inner space accommodate, a dragon Jim's size—which was large, even among that species. Meanwhile, ever-blooming flowers bordered each side of the evidently self-raking gravel walk to that door, and at the walk's outer end were shining pools of water on each side, from which what looked like tiny golden mermaids leaped into the air periodically . . . but they did this so fast that it was impossible to be sure if they really were mermaids or just golden fish.

The whole establishment, circled by greensward with tall trees beyond, was an isle of peace that Jim's troubled mind looked forward to right now.

Even as he thought this, he spotted the clearing that held Carolinus' home, and altered his flight pattern to bring him down with a heavy thump on the gravel walk to its front door.

As he did so, the door opened, and the small, green, fairy-beautiful figure of a sibyl slipped out—and she was crying.

The sight of something as small and vulnerable as a sibyl—most people mistook them for butterflies from a distance—in tears, was so moving that it was hard to imagine anything that lived being untouched by it. A heart of stone would instantly offer to throw itself into a ten-thousand-degree melting pot, if only she would give over being sad and smile again. Jim, despite his other lacks, had a heart considerably softer than stone.

"Why, Ecce!" he said. "What's wrong?"

But she was already gone, with a skill at disappearing that would have put to shame even that of Aargh, the English Wolf; who, with no magic at all, made a practice of seeming to disappear while right before human eyes.

From the still-ajar door, politely and magickally waiting for Jim to enter the cottage, came Carolinus' voice, evidently raised in some sort of diatribe. Jim took a step toward and stuck his dragon head on its long dragon neck through the open doorway.

"—and there's no excuse!" Carolinus was almost raving. "I'm gone for just a few days—"

"*Carolinus gone six weeks, Carolinus very sick*"—sang the teakettle on Carolinus' hob, sending out a dutiful puff of steam, to show it was on the boil and ready to make a soothing cup of hot tea in a instant.

"Weeks, days—what difference does that make?" cried Carolinus, waving his long, skinny, red-robed arms. "Everyone piling up to talk to me—no order to who came first—"

He apparently ran out of breath. Taking advantage of the moment of silence, Jim spoke.

"Oh, Carolinus," he said, speaking in as calm and reasonable a voice as he could manage, "something very serious has come up. We need you at Malencontri early tomorrow for a few days of visit—"

"Impossible! Absolutely. impossible! Dozens of beings ahead of you. No, no, it can't be done! You'll have to wait your turn like everyone else ... as soon as I figure out whose turn is before whose!"

Chapter 3

"No, no—" Carolinus was going on "—impossible! I'll see you later—"

"Carolinus!" said Jim loudly. "Stop babbling and listen to me for a moment!"

"*Babbling?*"

Carolinus, who had gone right on talking in no more than a bothered voice until that word, broke off suddenly. His voice rang through the cottage, which was abruptly vast and full of shadows. He had grown six inches, and his worn old robe was rich and more than heart's-blood new and brilliant.

He was no longer old and stooped, but upright and looming above Jim in a room that was held in a new and utter silence. Even the kettle no longer made a sound.

There was only the echo of that single word in Jim's ears—until other words came like the freezing wind off a mountain glacier.

"YOU DO NOT SPEAK THAT WAY TO YOUR MASTER-IN-MAGICK!"

In spite of some years of friendly interchange with Carolinus, for the first time Jim felt a chill. But in the same moment that feeling touched off his inborn stubbornness.

"Forgive me," he said stiffly to the towering figure before him, "but I had to get your attention. The plague's reached London, and the Bishop of Bath and Wells is at Malencontri right now, come to talk to you there about it privately."

"Already?"

Carolinus was abruptly his normal self and size. He sat down heavily in a padded chair that scooted over just in time to catch him. The cottage was also back to being its usual self again.

"It was in France but little more than three weeks gone," the Mage said emptily to Jim, the kettle and the cottage. "I'll come at once, of course."

In the silence the voice of the teakettle steaming on its hob filled the cottage.

"Tomorrow would possibly be better," said Jim. "The Bishop wanted it to seem as if you just happened to bump into each other by chance."

"Of course," Carolinus said. He looked at Jim. "Forgive my abruptness when you found me here."

"Granted, naturally," said Jim. "It was just that—"

"But—" for a second, the Mage, the robe, the cottage seemed to threaten a return to what they had momentarily been "—I must warn you never again to say that sort of word you used to me, and above all never in public. In public I would have no choice in how I answered you. Such language to one's Master-in-Magick cannot be tolerated—"

"Of course not. I understand!" said Jim, regretful now that he had a moment to cool down himself. "But I'd just met Ecce at your door, going out as I was coming in, and she was crying—"

"Ecce? Crying?"

Carolinus was suddenly on his feet, completely back to his normal self. He all but leaped toward the door.

"Get that wagon-sized head of yours out of my way, can't you?" he snapped at Jim as he went by. "Ecce! *Ecce!*" he called to the gravel path, the pools and the flowers, "Where are you, dear? I didn't mean—whatever it was I said!"

Nothing happened.

"Oh, Jim!" he said, looking despairingly at him. "I don't know what's got into me lately! I'm become a cantankerous old man nowadays!"

In spite of having completely forgiven Carolinus, Jim felt a strong urge to tell the older man that he had always been a cantankerous old man—at least as long as Jim had known him. But Jim held the words back.

Then Ecce was suddenly there, in front of Carolinus, hovering in midair. She kissed Carolinus' dry lips as lightly and briefly as a blown flower-seed.

"Oh, Ecce!" Carolinus said. "But how can you forgive me? What was it I said?"

She shook her head and laid three of the tiny, green fingers of her left hand, like the tips of fern fronds, on his lips.

"Very well, but I don't intend to lose my head like that again. Oh, Ecce, you know a matter occurs to me. The plague has come into England—no, you needn't worry for your friends, or the flowers, the trees or anything. Only humans can catch it—"

She suddenly flung herself at him, her small arms stretched to their limit to embrace as much of his chest as she could reach, the left side of her face turned to press as hard as it could against the rough surface of his robe.

"Now, now—nonsense—" he looked helplessly over her head and spoke to Jim "—I don't seem to be able to say anything right today. Ecce! You don't suppose for a moment something like that could bother *me*? I'm a Mage, a Magickian!"

He winked at Jim. But as if Ecce had felt that tiny movement of his eyelid, she lifted her head to look hard at Jim.

"No, no, you don't need to concern yourself about him, either," said Carolinus, "and in any case, very soon now— well, he and I are going to talk about that later. But Ecce, a thought just came to me. It seems I must leave here early tomorrow for several days, and there're all these beings who've been waiting to see me. But if you could help? We could sort out together the order that I'll be seeing them in. That should make them feel better about waiting. Now, I could make the decisions, and you could stop me if I forgot anyone. . . ."

She flung herself up to his face and kissed him again.

Soaring homeward under a half-full, lopsided, but rising moon, and with an increasing feeling that he was doing exactly the wrong thing by heading there right now, Jim tried to think of what he had overlooked.

Then it came to him. Of course. The last thing in the world he needed or wanted among these guests of his were sparks flying between the Bishop and the Prince.

The Bishop, he knew from experience, was nothing if not outspoken. Happily, he also was not given to sneaking small sneering comments into the conversation to kindle argument while still maintaining the forms of politeness at meals— his weapon was the mace rather than the dagger.

But in that outspokeness, the Bishop would be feeling it his episcopal duty to be plain about the attitude of the Church toward the heir to the throne of England gadding about the countryside with the wife of another man. The wife of a Count, and no inconsiderable one, either.

But the Prince, who, even in his teens, had showed no hesitation to clash head-on with people as tough as the Earl of Cumberland, would not be likely to back away from anyone who seemed to be casting a slur on either his companion or himself.

At meals *courtoise*—the rule of manners among the ruling class—would keep an out-and-out explosion from the conversation. The tabletop language might be more than a little on the formal and frigid side, but that was a cheap price to pay for peace.

But what was really needed was something that would keep both sides from bringing the subject up in a face-to-face moment away from the table. What was needed was some kind of permanent buffer between them. Perhaps yet another guest in the castle before whom the two potential combatants would not want to air their differences of opinion?

—Of course! Brian would make the ideal buffer. Brian was part of the same Somerset neighborhood as Jim and Angie and, for all Prince and Bishop knew, equipped with eager ears to record every combative word said in the heat of their conflict for gossip in that neighborhood—from which it would soon spread all over England.

They would have no way of knowing that Brian was the soul of reticence itself. Jim pumped his wings with sudden energy, searching upward for a higher air stream that would point him more surely in the direction of Brian's Castle Smythe. He found what he wanted and was on his way immediately under the cloudless but rapidly cooling night sky. Luckily, in his massive dragon body he found the chill more refreshing than otherwise.

Castle Smythe was poorly lit when Jim finally reached it—it was always badly lit, after nightfall, even tallow candles had gone up in price recently—but the gloom hid much of the disreputableness of its decayed outworks, so that it

did not look—at night—as vulnerable as it actually was.
Brian was hoping to start strengthening it, once he and Geronde were actually married and he had a wife in residence.
Bachelors could take their chances, but the wife of Sir Brian
Neville Smythe was not going to, however fiery, pugnacious
and experienced in defending her own castle of Malvern,
little Geronde might be.

But Jim knew the state of its decay well from previous
visits, and made his landing, accordingly, at what had once
been the wall that backed up part of the castle's warming
room. There was a hole there big enough for even his
dragon body, through which he could enter and reach the
remains of the rather small Great Hall.

To his surprise, he found Brian already there where the
wall had been, digging in the darkness in the earth at his
feet.

"Oh, it's you, James," he said, familiar with Jim in his
dragon body. He leaned on the tool he had been using and
wiped his forehead. "I vow you gave me a start, though.
Nothing but a dagger with me—and this spade. Not that a
spade, of course, cannot be an effective weapon, properly
used—but James, what brings you here in dragon form, just
at the supper hour?"

He checked abruptly, and Jim could almost feel the
warmth of his embarrassment through the darkness.

"—Not that you are not most heartily welcome to my
table, now you have arrived. I have a guest at the moment.
A gentleman you met at the Earl's last Christmas party—"

"I'd be glad to meet him again," said Jim, "but I only
flew up here to invite you to be my guest for a couple of
days, since Geronde isn't with you at the moment—"

"No, we were to meet the end of this week at Malencontri. But my guest—"

"He must come with you, of course."

Any other response was unthinkable. Jim's mind spun
madly over the question of finding sufficient guest rooms.

If Brian's guest was simply another simple knight like himself, he and Brian could be decently asked to share a room, of course. The guest would understand at once on seeing not only a Bishop, but the Crown Prince already there. Indeed, he would undoubtedly be overjoyed to rub shoulders (metaphorically speaking) with the great of the land. A feather in his cap.

"Well, I've got to be getting back to Malencontri," Jim said hastily. "Tell you more about this when you get there. Why don't the two of you come tomorrow—come early, for breakfast if you like. Give you good night, Brian."

"And God give you good rest also, James." Brian went back to his digging.

Jim flew home to Malencontri.

Unreasonably, almost unbelievably, once he had got there, and had changed back into his ordinary Jim-body after landing in the courtyard, he entered the Great Hall through its main door to find no guests impatiently awaiting him so that they could graduate from wine and tidbits to the meal proper. All he saw was Angie supervising the clearing of the High Table.

Ready for nourishment himself, now, Jim almost ran down between the two long, lower tables, grabbed a cake from one of the few platters remaining, snarled at a servant who was carrying off the last pitcher of wine, and filled himself a mazer of the red liquid.

"Oh, there you are," said Angie.

"What happened? They ate without me?"

"Of course not," said Angie. "—May Heather, go tell Mistress Plyseth supper for my lord and me is to be served up to the Solar." She turned back to Jim.

"The Bishop sent down word religious duties would keep him from joining us; he would have a bite in his room. And the Prince came down but only to tell me he and the Countess were very tired after an unusually long day's ride; they'd eat in their room. But he also almost whispered in my ear he wanted to talk to you as soon you came in—whenever you did."

"As soon as I came in?" echoed Jim, snatching despairingly at another of the small cakes.

"Don't worry—you can get some supper into you in the Solar, before you go hunting him. He won't melt in the meantime. Remember, he said *whenever*."

"That's right," said Jim, brightening but taking a third cake anyway.

Nonetheless, he was feeling a great deal better forty minutes later, as he politely scratched on the door of the room that had been assigned to the Prince and the Fair Maid. Angie had assured him that, if necessary, separate rooms would eventually be available for everybody—only to meet protests that the two of them were perfectly happy where they were. But it had been necessary for her to mention it—for propriety's sake.

In fact, the separate rooms would be needed, anyway, when Geronde, herself, showed up at the end of the week— and a double room could be provided now for Brian and his guest. There were, as well, storerooms in the tower that could be cleared, cleaned, and furnished. But right now the door Jim had scratched on was opening—though it only opened a crack and a slice of the Prince's face became visible.

"Ah, there you are, James!" he said in a low voice. "A moment."

The door shut again. After a moment it reopened enough to let the Prince slip out. He closed it softly behind him.

"Dead asleep, the angel," he said. "Where can we go to talk privily? Your Solar?"

"My wife is there, Your Grace," said Jim stiffly.

"Ah, I see. I don't suppose she could be sent elsewhere for a time?

"She could not."

Chapter 4

"Of course," said the Prince immediately, but a trifle stiffly, himself. His position in life had accustomed him to giving orders in situations like this. Orders like, "Tell her to go elsewhere until you send her word to return!" A flat denial to a request made as politely as he had made it—and from a mere baron at that—did not ring pleasantly in the ears of the heir to the English throne.

But Jim was his host, and had not invited him here in the first place.

"Ah. Then perhaps you have some other place where we could speak in perfect privacy?"

"Certainly," said Jim. "It won't be as comfortable, of course—"

"Hah! Am I not accustomed to campaigns where a tree to sit on, and a piece of tarred canvas to keep the rain off, were luxury?"

It was no less than the literal truth, as Jim knew.

"Still," he said, "I must apologize, Your Grace—"

"Let us hear no more about it. Conduct me to this other place."

The royal feelings were obviously reassured by the Prince's last two decisive statements. The sticky social spot was being glossed over. A further small touch of apology possibly could cover it completely.

"It's kind of Your Grace," said Jim, "to accept such uncertain hospitality from us. I'll need to send servants ahead to make sure it's fit for use—Howard!"

The man-at-arms posted at the door of the room occupied by the Prince and the Maid—a mere courtesy, but handy in moments like this—came running; when Jim had approached the door he and the servant stationed with him had discreetly retired down the hall.

"Howard," Jim said now, "send the servant to get me Mistress Cinders—no, wait. Have her get me May Heather instead. She's faster. And the servant you send should go as fast as she can, too."

"Yes, my lord," and Howard was running himself, back the way he had come.

There followed a little period of waiting, which might have been awkward if the small, unspoken disagreement had not been settled. They filled time with polite conversation. Jim asked the Prince how the day's ride had gone. The Prince said he had enjoyed it, but the Countess had found it tiring. This led to a short discussion of people who liked nothing better than to spend the whole day in the saddle, while others did so only when necessary—which was beginning to be interesting when it was interrupted by the appearance of May Heather, a little out of breath.

"Mistress Cinders would need to have borrowed you and some of the other Serving Room servants to help her prepare the extra bedrooms," Jim said.

May nodded, still breathless.

"So," Jim went on, "take us to the biggest and freshest one—of those *bed-rooms*—and bring an extra chair—" Jim fixed her with an warning eye to make sure the message was understood. The last thing he wanted was to escort the Prince to a clean, washed, but obviously empty, storeroom "—to the best *bed-room!* You can do that?"

"Yes, my lord—my Grace Prince," answered May with hardly a gasp and a slightly less bobbing curtsy than she had been managing the last time Jim had seen her try it.

"One title at a time is sufficient, lass," said the Prince, almost kindly. But as May turned to lead the way, he went on speaking to Jim, making no attempt to keep his voice down, as he customarily did not, acting as if servants did not exist or were deaf.

"Young, isn't she?"

"For some of her duties, perhaps," Jim answered, equally loudly. "But remarkably willing and learns quickly." He and the Prince went on in contented silence.

As it turned out, Jim need not have worried. The room to which May took them was the furthest from the stairs on the second tower floor below the roof, and half again as large as the usual guest rooms. May had also been showing remarkable initative, Jim saw with approval. Candles already lit, two pitchers—one of wine, the other of water—two mazers and a single platter of finger food sat on the small, square table. He had not needed to emphasize "bedroom."

But how had she known a room like this was what he would be asking her for? Of course—the servant network. The man-at-arms would have overheard the Prince's request for privacy, passed it on to the servant who told May, and May—was it possible this youngster was already ordering around her fellow Serving Room servants?

"Very good," said Jim to her now. "Go."

"Yes, my lord."

The door closed behind her, shutting out sight of Howard and the servant with him—the one Howard had sent with the message for May—both having dutifully followed the Prince to this new location.

Jim sat down on one of the chairs at the table and poured wine into the two mazers.

"Water in your wine, Your Grace?"

"I think not," said the Prince. He had paced over to gaze out one of the room's two arrow slits, which from where Jim sat now showed nothing but night darkness. The Prince went on without turning around. "The plague has reached London."

"So the Bishop of Bath and Wells told us earlier today."

"The public inns light braziers before their doors, to burn up the sickness before it can enter their houses with each person who comes in," the Prince said to the arrow slit. "It is a foul ill to befall any man, woman or child . . ."

He turned from the arrow slit and paced back. He did not, however, pick up his mazer; he seemed, in fact, about to turn away again from the table, when there was a scratching at the door.

"Come!" called Jim.

The door opened enough to let Angie look in.

"Forgive this intrusion, Your Grace and my lord," she said. "But there has been a small dispute of sorts between one of the Bishop's men-at-arms and one of ours, and both are somewhat hurt. I must oversee the binding up of their wounds. This will keep me busy for some little time. It occurred to me you might prefer to talk in the Solar—"

"A most generous offer, my lady!" cried the Prince. He looked at Jim, however, as manners required. Jim met Angie's eye briefly and had his suspicions confirmed—she had learned of the Prince's early request-cum-command to talk in the Solar by the same network that had alerted May. In fact, it was probably May who had warned her. Most servants kept the network strictly to their own class, but May was not afraid of anything on Earth—or Heaven or Hell, for that matter.

Damn servants! Jim told himself. *They'll be trying to think for us, next!*

He stood up.

"If his Grace would still prefer—"

"Of all things, I would enjoy it!"

They went to the Solar. Howard and the servant with him faded away, replaced by the man-at-arms and servant who were already on Solar duty. Angie left them.

"Ah!" said the Prince, luxuriating in one of the padded chairs, mazer in hand. "James, you would have trouble believing how I have looked forward to seeing and speaking to you again."

"And I, you, Your Grace!"

"I am overjoyed to hear it." The Prince took a deep swallow from his mazer. "Good friends—but I get ahead of myself. Ah, perhaps a touch of water would not go amiss, after all . . . thank you. Yes, much better. But as I was saying, James, I have longed to see you again. My true friends in this world are few, and among them all, I count you as one of the truest."

"You do me too much honor, Your Grace," said Jim, warily. He would not have counted himself as that close a friend to the Prince. Could this just be royal court manners, carried a little farther than usual?

". . . A true knight as well, in the real meaning of that word, as is your friend Sir Brian, and I know of almost no others such—except Chandos. In addition, the world knows you are a Magickian without peer."

"As I say, you do me far too much honor, Your Grace!" said Jim, now definitely wary. This was too much praise even for court manners.

"That, I think, would be to try to do the impossible." The Prince smiled at him. "Let me just say that Joan and I— that is to say, the Countess and I—have come to you because you are the only help for us."

Hah! thought Jim, *so that's why they've come here!*

"How can I be of service, then, Your Grace?" he said aloud, his wariness growing to something like real alarm. The Prince was notoriously improvident. He handed out money and his own possessions as gifts right and left. It was considered the noble thing to do—and indeed gift-giving was a mark of the age—but what he handed out had to come from somewhere; and Malencontri was not rich, just comfortably secure.

On the other hand, there was the general belief that Magickians had only to snap their fingers to produce gold, jewels, anything desired. . . .

"That is not a question to be answered in a few short words, James, which was why I was hoping for time in this excellent Solar of yours to explain matters to you. We do indeed have it for our talk now as long as needed?"

"Absolutely!" said Jim.

"Then I will tell you. It is a long story, some of which you already know." The Prince poured some more wine and then water into his mazer and sat back in his chair, the large metal cup in his hand. "You have been aware for some time of how the Earl of Cumberland has sought to make ill feelings between my Royal father and me?"

"Yes," said Jim.

The Prince abruptly put his mazer down and got to his feet. He walked over to the window, gazed out at the unrelenting darkness, turned about and walked back to the table. He did not sit down.

"He has been at it all my life," said the Prince. He turned and went to gaze out again at the night. His back to Jim, he went on talking.

"He has been at this endeavor all my life," he repeated. "A royal court is a place for gossip and people speak privily to one another over the head of a very young child, sure he will not understand what their talk means, but forgetting he will remember every word that he heard before, put it together with that which just touched his ears, and come finally to know what it meant—in his never-ending efforts to understand the world he was born into. By the time I was six, I knew my uncle Cumberland wanted me to like and trust him, but only as a dog trusts his master. Still I did not understand why."

He came back and stood over Jim, looking down at him.

"Wouldn't Your Grace like to sit down and drink some wine?" Jim murmured. The Prince's voice had been dry and matter-of-fact enough, but Jim could feel a strong pain behind his words.

"No, I want to talk."

The Prince went back to the window. His tall, broad-shouldered, upright, horseman's back was perfectly steady.

"Between men there is nothing to say. Only because of my present great need am I telling you all this. That, and because you are from elsewhere, you are the only other man in the world I could tell it to—not even to my confessor. . . ."

Jim drank some wine from his mazer and said nothing. The younger man's effort in saying all this was starkly evident. But there was nothing for Jim to say. The Prince was right. Between men—nothing.

". . . By the time I was ten, my uncle had become aware that I understood him. He yearns to be King—has always yearned to be King—and fancied himself more capable for the crown than any other. But he is a bastard, and England will never accept a King who tries to gain the crown by bastard heritage."

It had taken Jim a few years to learn how much that could be true in this age.

"Moreover," the Prince was going on, "he knew now I would never look up to him alone—not while my father lived. I think I told you how, when I was very young, I once saw my father being fitted with the armor he would later wear at the Battle of Sluys. That great, shining figure of King and Knight stood first before all else in my mind; for all that I knew my uncle was a war captain of repute, Cumberland was only common flesh and blood. My father was King and Knight, beyond all. He was a great King then—"

The Prince whirled about from the window. His eyes glared at Jim.

"He is a great King still!"

"Yes," Jim heard himself saying—and meaning it.

Edward III had come to the throne early. As Jim had known from his graduate studies, for decades he had sat at the center of his court and kingdom, and in those years the ruling of England had gone well. Yet the image of the drunken—and perhaps already moving into senility—old man had become the only one stuck in Jim's mind.

Now it struck him fully that through all those years Edward had kept Parlement and the magnates—the great lords—in balance against each other without usurping their strength. Strength that, along with that of the yeomen and peasants, could always be called upon when he or England should need it.

The Prince had always understood something that Jim had missed entirely. The King was keeping that balance still. True, Cumberland was his chamberlain, dispenser of rights and powers, gateway to the monarch, seeming more powerful than all others in the kingdom. But in practice that power was limited just as much as the rights and powers of Oxford, with his group, and others like them, who if need came to band together with the other magnates, had more total strength, wealth and fighting-power available than even the throne could command. But the King, even now, in seeming drunkenness and other indulgences, had kept them as much at each other's throats as at his.

I'm damn slow to pick some things up sometimes! Jim told himself. Carolinus had told him before that part of his job as a Magickian was to keep Edward on his throne. Jim had thought it a ridiculous statement then—what could he do to keep the King of England in that seat of power? But now, for the first time, he understood why the elder Edward must live to stay in control—perhaps for some years yet. No one else had the experience and skill to keep the combined strengths of the magnates strong and whole, but too much at each other's throats to combine against him. It would be some little time yet before this eldest son of his would have the experience and skill to guide the kingdom.

But the Prince had sat down again, picked up his mazer to drink and was continuing to talk.

"... Recently. Just recently, Cumberland threatened to accuse me of being one with a group to dethrone my father and assume the crown myself—the public accusation would be all that was necessary; people are always only too ready to believe the worst. This he would do unless I would go on exile out of England and have no more to do with England or my father."

Jim nodded grimly. Even in his own world and time, half a millenium later, in spite of law that proclaimed "innocent until proven guilty," much of the public had been all too quick to believe in scandalous untruths.

"But certainly the King—" He broke off, not knowing quite how to word what he would have liked to say.

"—Would never sit quietly if his rightful heir and first son had left England without his permission? And the whole story of Cumberland's action in causing it would come out? Very true, James. But Cumberland would have already given him the false story of how I had mentioned this to him—wishing to become a war captain on my own so that I might be able to raise an army, possibly with French help, to come back and claim either the throne or the place of Regent. He had, he told me, a few Frenchmen to agree with this fable—"

"Agree?" said Jim, startled. Certainly, in any country there might be a few upper-class men who would agree to such a lie. But every Frenchman of whom he knew certainly would not. They could hardly otherwise hold the reputations they had gained by years of living honorably, gained by their proven bravery and the blood most of them had undoubtedly shed to prove themselves the men they were.

"Oh, none of good repute, of course, but that would be beside the point," went on the Prince. "Cumberland need only claim those I had been in contact with had all been ruffians and villains—in search of help with such a scheme."

Jim nodded again.

"I admit," the Prince looked emptily past Jim, "I was ready to yield, at last to go. But first I went to Joan. Salisbury was away in the Low Countries. Joan—the Fair Maid of Kent as she is called, and rightly so—the most beautiful woman in England. But it was not just that which drew me to her."

He broke off to stare hard at Jim.

"You must understand this," the Prince said.

"I'm sure I will." Any noise of agreement would have satisfied the other. The Prince went on almost without pausing.

"It was a love much deeper. We had been children together at court—as an orphan she was often with us. We had played and fought together, but we are first cousins. Her father, Edmund, Earl of Kent, was half-brother to my grandfather, King Edward II. Indeed, we are both descendants of Henry Plantagenet and Eleanor of Aquitaine. But as I say we are first cousins once removed and may not marry. But I hoped she would leave her husband, Salisbury, and go with me—to France or wherever necessary. Some good knights—Audley among them—will follow me, and many of the common sort who have also fought alongside me before. There are kings over the Channel who will have use for such a war captain as myself and those with me— and to be truthful, I am happiest when swords are out. You see, I need her. I can trust her with keeping not only my secrets, but my soul from Hell."

It all made sense, thought Jim, gazing at the still-young face opposite. Youthful as he was, the Prince reminded Jim of his friend Brian in one important characteristic—a love of chivalry—although beyond that they were nothing alike. The Prince was a bundle of nerves and private problems. Brian was a rock and generally as unworried as a day with sunshine.

Jim fought his mind clear of the fog of relationships the Prince had thrown at him. It was customary in these times to explain relationships—sometimes at weary length. They made instant sense to someone brought up in this period. But in Jim's case, it was like being handed a tangle of wire to unravel. He put them all from his mind. Not for him to pass moral judgments on the Prince and the Fair Maid.

"So," he said, "the two of you are headed for the continent now?"

Perhaps the Prince simply wanted to borrow some money from him—which he might or might not ever repay—to help them get to the French court. That would be expensive, but not as bad as some of the requests Jim had been envisioning.

"No!" The Prince's face lit up. "Because she—always the brave one—agreed to come with me only long enough to fight back and make sure I remain in England. 'Stay away from the Royal Court,' she told me. 'Delay answering Cumberland on whether you will exile yourself or not, and meanwhile both you and I will ask those we know for any information that may be useful.' "

The Prince smiled tenderly, his mind for the moment in another room, where Joan of Kent slept.

"Also, however," the Prince went on, his face becoming hard once more, "she reminded me that Cumberland has become so deep in so many schemes at once that he may be vulnerable in one of them. 'If so,' she said, 'you may be able to bargain with him, or even defy him with impunity. One way or another, opportunity will open for you. Meanwhile, in any case, we can find out just how, and with whom, he planned to accuse you of plotting against the King.' "

"Good advice," said Jim, "if you will forgive my opinion, Your Grace."

The Prince had always shown a tendency to act immediately. A good trait often in a war captain, but not necessarily so in an intrigue.

"Indeed, it has proved so," said the Prince. "For with but a little inquiry I found there was a group of gentlemen already seeking me. A group headed by a sterling knight who just happens to also be a member of the gentlemen of Cum-

berland's wardrobe and, revolted by what he has seen of
Cumberland's twisting and using of my father, has determined to do something about it. His idea was to bring me
better friends with my father. I would then be able to show
how Cumberland has been using him. A golden opportunity
has arisen, if I work with them. I do not see how it can
fail!"

"Who is he?" asked Jim, forgetting his medieval courtesies of address entirely.

"I doubt you would know him," said the Prince. "He,
himself, though English by birth, is an exile from France,
and has been seeking some place at court to keep him while
he is here. Unfortunately for him, but fortunately for me,
the best he could do was that place in Cumberland's wardrobe—he shall be repaid by me, if he can help me in this.
A man of great parts, a gentleman in the true meaning of
the word, descended from royalty himself and showing the
finer feelings of a man of such blood. Just the one for such
an endeavor as this. He is the Viscount Sir Mortimer Verweather."

Oh, Hell! said Jim silently to himself.

For at that name the whole scene had come sharply back
into his mind.

Chapter 5

Viscount Sir Mortimer Verweather—

A tall, thin, gangling man, either in his early thirties or
about to enter them, with a small fashionable mustache, unrealistically black, at odds with the mouse-brown of his hair.
A tanned face with a long nose that seemed about to be
catching a whiff of some unpleasant odor.

It had been on Jim's first trip to France, on what—he was
about to discover—was a secret mission to rescue the Prince

from the rogue Magickian Malvinne. Brian had brought both Jim and Sir Giles de Mer to the inn that had become the embarkation headquarters of Sir John Chandos.

The scene came back to Jim with startling clarity—

The ground floor of the inn had been standing room only with knights waiting to see Chandos. But Brian, following the errand he had been sent on to find Jim and Sir Giles de Mer, was just starting to lead the other two up the broad stairway to the floor above, when his sleeve was suddenly caught by one of the brilliantly dressed men there.

"Hold, fellow!" said this individual. "Keep your place. Speak to the steward when he comes by, and if it so be you have some business here, speak it to him!"

"Did you call me 'fellow'?" flared Brian. "Take your damned hand off me. And just who the bloody hell do I have the dishonor of addressing?"

The other's hand let go.

"I am Viscount Sir Mortimer Verweather, f . . ." the other trembled once more on the edge of repeating the word "fellow," but evidently thought better of it, "—and not to be spoken so by any hedge-knight! I can trace my lineage back to King Arthur!"

Brian told him in fulsome scatological terms what he could do with his lineage.

". . . As for me, m'lord," he concluded, "I am of the Nevilles of Raby, and need look down in the presence of no man. You will answer to me for this!"

Both men were now grasping the hilts of their swords.

"Willingly—" Sir Mortimer was beginning, when a stout, very well-dressed man with a heavy silver chain around his neck and some sort of medallion hanging from it pushed his way between them.

"Stop this at once, gentlemen!" he ordered fiercely. "What? Brawling in this, of all chambers—" He checked himself suddenly. "Sir Brian!"

His eyes had rested on Brian's face.

The change in his tone of voice was surprising, although the sternness remained. "You left us but an hour since. I did not look to see you back so soon—"

"As it happens, Sir William," answered Brian, letting go of his sword and speaking in a calmer voice, "I already found and have with me both the gentlemen that were spoken of."

"Excellent!" said Sir William, smiling. "Sir John will want to see you immediately. Come with me."

About to leave, he turned back to look at Sir Mortimer.

"As for you, m'lord," he said, sternly, "it would not bear you amiss to remember to mind your manners in this place. Sir John will see you when he sees you."

He turned back to Brian. "Come, you and the two you bring." He led the three of them to and up the staircase, with the gaze of all eyes in the room following.

That episode, as Jim, Brian and Giles had been on their way to France, had left Jim with anything but a high opinion of Sir Mortimer Verweather—and this was the man who headed a group and had felt for the Prince and the King? He who had set out to bring royal father and son together once more?

Happily, Jim was not being called on to say anything at the moment to applaud the Prince's high opinion of the man. Edward, all his earlier hesitation drowned in enthusiasm and excitement, was now talking his head off.

". . . it was the plague arriving in London that made the opportunity!" Edward was saying. "Cumberland himself was all for withdrawing from the city—as all who were of gentle blood or could afford to do were so doing—and of course, as chamberlain he said that the King and all the chief functionaries of the court must go with them to set up a government in country exile, so to speak, so that the many royal duties of ruling the land could continue unhindered."

Jim nodded. That, at least, made sense—particularly the business of taking the King away from a center of infection. He was about to volunteer the same advice he had given the Bishop—about clearing wherever they could of both rats and fleas—but Edward, eager to tell him the full story now, did not give him a chance.

". . . As it happened," the Prince was going on, "Cumberland already had in mind a particular castle in his own possession. A castle named Tiverton, in Devon, ordinarily occupied by the Earl of Devon—but he is not there at present. It is a castle already fully staffed with an unusually able staff—my father could look for all court comforts and the best of service. It has a cellar of unmatchable wine . . . and so forth. Cumberland brought the King to a high degree of willingness to leave court. But then, a difficulty arose."

Edward beamed at Jim.

"It was a blow to Cumberland himself, for he had already set in action the plans for his own removal to Tiverton, and of course my royal father was now determined to go. The problem was that Cumberland found he could not go also—at least for the moment. The biter, bit—how do you like that for the shrewdness with which he is too often given credit, James?"

"Forgive me," said Jim. "But why couldn't Cumberland go?"

"As I told you, but a second since," said Edward, casually riding over his own failure to have done so, "it turned out that the moving of all the necessary high functionaries Cumberland needed close at hand for matters now in process required taking more people than the castle—it is a good-sized castle, but too small for the number of people he had picked for the retreat—could crowd in, with all their necessary clerks, papers and other necessities!"

He stopped talking to stare at Jim.

"Ah-hah!" said Jim, feeling some comment was required from him, and hoping that would do.

"Exactly!" said Edward. "He should have made sure there was room for all before he made my father eager to go—he had not been at all of a mind to leave his familiar apartments at court when Cumberland first spoke to him. But there the Earl now finds himself, with no great choice in the matter. My father must certainly go; Cumberland, himself, must as certainly stay, for some little time at least. Joan had been right. Opportunity had been found for me. You do not see how?"

"No, Your Grace."

"I am surprised at you, James, who also have something of reputation for quick wit. My father is King. No one can deny him if, in exile, it is his choice to admit me to his presence—something Cumberland and his people had been keeping me from with no end of lies and excuses. Also, now I had a friend, Sir Verweather, on the inside to help me frustrate those functionaries and spies Cumberland had sent with the King's entourage."

He stopped talking, drank from his mazer—stopped drinking to pour in a good quantity of wine—and drank again, deeply. He sat back in his chair, smiling.

"To make a long story short," he said, "I have since seen my father several times, and things progress. Not apace. But they progress!"

"Then everything's taken care of for you," said Jim, relieved.

"Not everything."

"Not everything?" Jim looked at him cautiously. What was to be proposed now, which might involve him, Angie, Malencontri or their friends?

"There is a small problem yet remaining. Only a small one, but I assure you it means a great deal to me. It is necessary that at frequent intervals I discuss matters having to do with my meetings with my royal father privily with Sir Verweather. But the servants in this castle where he now is were spoken of to Cumberland as being excellent beyond description. It is only too true."

Jim frowned at him.

"Only too true?" he said. "How can they be excellent beyond description?"

"How, I do not know, James," said the Prince, sobering. "But I assure you they are. Never have I been served with such excellence. They must all have fairy blood in them. You open your mouth in your room to call for one, and he or she is scratching at your door before the words are hardly out of your mouth. At table they are always at your elbow. It breeds an uneasiness both in me and in Sir Verweather. If this excellent staff can do so much, perhaps it also has ways of listening in through closed doors and stone walls in Tiverton Castle."

"Yes," said Jim, "it could make things difficult—if they actually can, of course." Perhaps this was what the Prince had come to him for. He wanted Jim to use magic to see whether the staff actually could do such a thing.

"—and, as I say," Edward was going on, ignoring him, "we must, Sir Mortimer and I, confer privily. But the slightest whisper in my father's ear that there might have been a secret arrangement made to bring the two of us together would confirm in my father's mind all the evil that Cumberland has been at pains to place there."

"I see," said Jim, beginning to take this situation more seriously.

"I knew you would. That is why we have come to you— Joan and I—with a simple request. There is no safe spot in that castle for conversation between me and Sir Verweather."

"It doesn't sound like it," said Jim, perhaps more frankly than was polite. What kind of magic was the Prince about to demand of him now?

"It is not safe. Therefore I would wish, with your good consent, of course, some other place. Tiverton is hardly more than half a day's brisk ride from where we are now. I propose to hold my talks with Sir Verweather in Malencontri. That would also give me opportunity to see Joan, since I had no choice but to accept my father's offer of quarters for myself alone, as he believes me to be, in Tiverton."

Jim stared at him.

"You would oblige me much by permitting this, James," said Edward, smiling at him, "and it is a small request, after all."

"ER-hum!" said Jim, clearing his throat more loudly than he had meant to do.

"There is some small difficulty?" said the Prince, his smile vanishing.

Jim's mind was racing. Was it possible Edward did not realize what he was asking his host? Or was he either so obsessed with solving his own problem, or so used to having his way without counting the cost to others, that he had not even thought of what agreeing could cost Jim, Angie and everyone connected with them?

It would tie Verweather's scheme to Malencontri. Cumberland could charge (undoubtedly successfully, given his power and money for bribes) that they had all been in a plot by the Prince to control the King. The Prince might be driven into exile, after all. Perhaps not; but most certainly the rest of them would be tortured to make them confess to treason, and afterwards hung, drawn and quartered.

"Forgive me, Your Grace," he said now. "But I'm afraid you just happened to run up against an unexpected and unusual difficulty. As you probably know, I am a member of the Collegiate of Magickians—" That was stretching things a bit, since Carolinus had hinted he was being considered for membership, but this was no time for half measures. "As a member, certain laws unknown to those outside our mystic Body are unyielding upon me."

"It is forbidden to allow your Prince a room in this castle

of yours where he can discuss privy matters with a friend?" said Edward. "What law would keep you from agreeing to a simple request from an old friend? Tell me!"

"I regret, Your Grace, I may not speak of our laws with any but another Magickian. It is like," said Jim on sudden inspiration, "and fully as important as the vows you and I took when we were made knights."

The Prince was definitely not appeased.

"Surely the rules of some small secret society must yield before your duty to your King and his well-being? No voice in England speaks louder than the duty to the Crown."

The Plantagenet firecracker temper—to say nothing of Plantagenet unreasonableness—was beginning to sound in the Prince's voice, though just at that moment a booming noise penetrating the rocky ceiling somewhat obscured the Prince's words.

"In all ordinary matters you are right of course, Your Grace," said Jim. "But there are special areas of exemption." He was trying to keep his own voice calm and level. "Areas only, of course. But as in Holy Church—"

"Do you dare to compare your little secret society to Holy Church?" half-shouted the Prince—just as the Solar door behind him scraped open and an even more powerful voice boomed behind him.

"Of course my lord Sir James means no such thing!" the new voice roared, overriding even the booming from the tower—a voice trained to be heard by audiences in large churches. "Like all good men he knows that Holy Church speaks above all, even the voices of Kings, who are only of this earth. Over all, it speaks above the voice of a youth whose wayward and disgraceful actions have become a reproach in the face of the father whose power he cites!"

Angie, followed by the Bishop, had just walked in.

"Er—" began Jim, trying to get into the conversation, but frustrated by the combination of the Bishop's powerful voice and the booming overhead which united to drown him out. The Bishop was only making things worse. Left alone, Jim told himself, he might have been able to smooth things over with the Prince.

". . . And such a son owes a double duty when his father and King are one and the same! A duty to father and a duty to King. Hast thou honored thy father as required in the Gospels? If so, I do not know of it! And now you slander a body of dutiful men and women, permitted by our Lord to do much good, and who have committed their lives to so doing. They have healed the wounds of those who suffered! They are loved by man and beast alike! They have stood between all of us and the creatures of Darkness—and you, callow young man, would sneer at their duties and rules that may conflict with your own selfish wishes!"

"Proud Bishop!" cried Edward, "do you think to preach at me as if I was one of your common communicants, hands still soiled from the plow? I tell you—"

"Excuse me a minute!" Jim finally managed to shout over Edward's voice. "I'll just step upstairs and see if I can't put an end to the noise there, so we can hear each other talk—"

He broke off before the Prince could say anything, and without waiting for agreement from any of them, he got to his feet and bolted from the Solar.

But before he put his head up through the rectangular opening where the stairs to the tower top ended, he knew what was making the booming noise—in fact he had known from first hearing what it would be.

It was the voice of Secoh, the little—by dragon standards—marsh-dragon who had been one of his companions at the Loathly Tower fight, where they had first managed to rescue Angie from the Dark Powers.

Secoh it was, his back to Jim and speaking thunderously in his normal dragon voice as if to another dragon. But in this case the one he was speaking to, the man-at-arms on watch, had never been face-to-face with a dragon in his life. He was a young man, still pimpled and with a tic in his right eye, named Wink Millerson, and had joined Malencontri only recently. Now, white-faced—but with his halberd held manfully edge-out before him, in battle position— he was backed up as far from Secoh as the limits of the tower top would permit.

There was only one cure for this situation, where Jim's own human voice would not even be heard. He vaulted up the three last steps so that he would have room, and put on his own dragon shape.

"*Shut up!*" he roared at Secoh—a full octave lower from his much bigger dragon lungs and throat.

It was the wrong command. He should have ordered "Silence!" in understandable fourteenth-century style. But Secoh knew his voice, and had no trouble interpreting the meaning of the dragon tone which had just bellowed at him. He closed his mouth immediately and spun around just as Jim turned back into his human body. In the closest approach a marsh-dragon could make to a human whisper he replied.

"Very sorry, m'lord. Is this better, m'lord?"

"Yes," said Jim, speaking in his ordinary voice. "Secoh, you know you're welcome here at any time—" he could hardly say anything else in this time and world to someone who had fought at his side "—but I've always asked you to keep your voice down when you're inside."

"But we're outside now, m'lord!"

"No," said Jim.

"No?" whispered Secoh.

"No," said Jim. "Here, the courtyard—anywhere encircled by Malencontri's outer wall, and always when humans are nearby—you're to keep your voice down!"

"Yes m'lord. I won't forget, m'lord—"

"Never mind, what brings you here?"

"Forgive me of your grace and kindness, my lord," said Wink, speaking fast, and the tic in his right eye that had earned him his name had him winking furiously to keep up with the nervous speed of his words, "but the dragon was between me and the alarm bell. I was just about to try what I could do to him with this—" he hefted the halberd, "but his voice was so loud it fair stunned me at first; it did indeed, my lord!"

"That's all right," said Jim. "He's an old companion and friend. Always welcome here. If he booms at you, just wave him down. Now, Secoh—"

"M'lord!" Secoh drew himself up stiffly, almost exploding from the need to deliver his message in a whisper and still give it the proper ring of importance. He added, "I have the honor to report that the Young Dragon Patrol is now on duty and will continue to sweep the skies from here to Castle Smythe in the west and to Castle Malvern in the east. You need never fear being surprised by foes again!"

Jim closed his eyes and breathed deeply. *Be calm*, he told himself. *When things come too thick and fast, be calm, and take each point calmly, one at a time.*

Chapter 6

Jim opened his eyes again, took another deep breath and charged into the cross-examination he was used to giving to Secoh on these occasions.

"Do their parents at the Cliffside eyrie know about this?"

"Oh, yes, m'lord."

"And they approve?"

"Yes, m'lord."

Secoh would not be lying, but this was almost too good to be true. Ordinarily, a marsh-dragon—a tribe shrunken and weakened by evil effect of the Dark Powers' occupation of the Loathly Tower—might ordinarily have been lucky to have any attention paid to him at all in the eyrie of the Cliffside dragons. But Secoh had been transformed from the timid marsh-dragon he had been for a hundred and thirty-three years of living on crustaceans and fish, by joining Jim and the others in rescuing Angie from the tower.

He had become, in effect, a bully; the result of a discovery that he could fight any other male dragon, regardless of size, with nothing to lose—while on the other hand the larger dragon's winning could never redound to *his* credit. Of course, any dragon would fight anything if he lost his temper—a dragon failing. But if the larger dragon did well—after all, the other dragons told each other, what did you expect him to do but win against an opponent that small? On the other hand, if Secoh even barely survived such a conflict, he was obviously a hero-dragon who feared no one and no thing.

Dragons are a pragmatic people. If there is nothing to be gained, why bother with it? So, no Cliffside male wanted to put things to the test. Why get yourself torn up at all for nothing?

Besides, Secoh undeniably had been with Jim at the Battle of the Loathly Tower—where Jim, in dragon body, had slain an ogre—and no dragon had ever done that. Secoh, too—admittedly with the help of the legendary Smrgol, by then aged and recently crippled by a stroke—had also performed like a hero in that battle. Secoh had helped to slay Bryagh, the large and powerful rogue dragon who had stolen Angie away to the Dark Powers at the Tower.

To the dragons of Cliffside, the important thing about that battle was that a *dragon*, in fair fight, had met with and destroyed an ogre, and the dragon—Jim using the body of a Cliffside dragon—was a *Cliffsider*! The glory of that victory shone on all of them, and if Secoh had been there too, he also deserved some glory, as well.

The result was that Secoh had become a fixture at Cliffside. The younger dragons (none of them over eighty years old) worshipped him. He told them tall tales about Jim's exploits—with himself mentioned whenever possible—and he led the youngsters into some wild situations.

It had taken their mothers to save them from eventual and certain disaster. Secoh had learned it did not work to bully dragon mothers, so the young ones were saved from the worst dangers.

Therefore—Jim told himself now—if the mothers knew about this patrol and allowed it, it could not be too dangerous.

"Safe from all my foes?" said Jim, picking up on what Secoh had first announced. "But it's night, now."

"The Young Dragon Patrol is on wing and watch day and night both, m'lord. Just like your watchman here on the tower."

"All night?" Jim stared. "And you say their mothers stood for that?"

"The youngsters have to take turns—they argue a lot about that," said Secoh. "One night a week only for each one. Besides, you proved to them, just lately since you fought King Arthur, that we dragons don't sink in water but float, and now even the older Cliffsiders aren't afraid of landing in a lake or river in the night-dark."

"*Fought King Arthur!*" Jim had not thought even Secoh's tales would distort the truth that much. Of course, it would make a better telling to dragons than his fighting alongside the King. Wink, still holding up his halberd, watching and listening, was looking shocked.

"—Fought *together* with King Arthur—crave pardon, m'lord," said Secoh hastily. "Slip of the tongue. Er—also, the patrol is, of course, guarding Cliffside, at the center of the watch."

That explained a lot. The father dragons would be all for it—"Good practice for the youngsters!" Jim could imagine the fathers booming.

"Oh, well," he said. The novelty would soon wear off for the young dragons and no harm would have been done.

"Good, then. Have the patrol keep an eye out for Aargh

now, and if they see him, tell him I'd like to talk to him, when possible."

"At once, m'lord," said Secoh. "I'll just finish explaining the patrol to your george on watch—"

"I think he understands fully, now," said Jim.

"Oh?—oh, yes, m'lord. I'm on my way."

Secoh took to the air. Jim went back downstairs.

When he stepped into the Solar, there was only Angie there. The last wine cups and food had been cleared away by servants. The room, large as it was, seemed to have grown half again larger without the noisy presences of the Prince and the Bishop.

"What happened?" he asked Angie, who was laying out some of his armor and warmer clothes on the bed—with its curtains pulled back to give easy access.

"Oh, after the Prince lost his temper and stormed out," she said, "the Bishop waited for you a little while and then said he had to get back to his retinue and make sure everything was packed. He came to ask if you couldn't lend him four extra men-at-arms for the trip—since they'd be riding the woods by night and he's lacking one of those he came with: the one that got in a fight earlier with Frank Short."

"Four of our men-at-arms? What's going on here—put that thing down, Angie, and talk to me."

Angie deliberately finished laying out his triple-woven riding cloak with the leather waterproof outer layer. Then she turned and faced him.

"The Bishop's determined to go back to his seat at the cathedral in Wells tonight," she said. "When you were some time getting back from Carolinus—"

"Turned out I had to fly up to Smythe Castle and invite Brian. He and a knight who's guesting with him. They'll both be here for breakfast tomorrow—we can probably give Brian's guest a better breakfast than Brian can."

"Two more. That's Brian, all right, up and about two hours before dawn—I wonder how his guest likes it?"

"Probably not much—but Angie—"

"Also, the Bishop's left some empty rooms for new guests now—but as I was about to say, he took our advice about rats and fleas to heart. Remember, I told you he didn't come down to dinner? Anyway, he prayed and decided his duty was back at his bishopric, getting the rat-flea cleanup there started, no matter if he had to ride immediately by night or day. That's why he and his retinue are packing now."

"It wasn't anything to do with the Prince?"

"No. The Prince just lost his temper and stormed out first, as I said. Joan was up a little while ago—"

"Joan? Joan?"

"The Countess of Kent—and Salisbury. The one who came with the Prince. She told me he'd be all right in the morning. She's quite nice, actually."

Jim digested this last statement. Angie was not ordinarily so quick with her opinions.

"So what's all this with my foul-weather traveling outfit?" he asked. "I hope you don't think I'm going with the Bishop?"

"I thought you might want to."

"Of course I don't want to," said Jim. "It's his decision to take off in the night, not mine!" He prowled up and down the room. "Where's that French brandy?"

"In the bottom of the wardrobe, as always. A cup of tea would be better."

"I don't like tea! I like coffee, but we can't seem to get it in this damn, primitive world where everybody goes around risking their lives for some sense of duty! Dealing with them all's like handling dynamite. . . ."

With his hand on the knob of the tall wardrobe door, Jim dropped it suddenly, leaving the wardrobe unopened, and turned to walk heavily back to the bed. He sat down next to the riding cloak.

"No," he said wearily to Angie, "you're right. Of course.

I've got to go with him. A night ride through the wilds of Somerset—crazy! Outlaw gangs, night trolls . . . God knows what else! But I'm his host, and it was my suggestions that got him going."

While he had been talking, Angie had gone to the fireplace, swung the kettle in over the flames, and went on to get the tall, narrow bottle of brandy out of the wardrobe.

He watched her in silence as she made the tea, spiked it with brandy, and brought it to him. The first sip he took tasted hot and good. He looked up at her.

"I've got to go," he said simply.

She bent down and kissed him.

"Dear Jim," she said.

Dressed, armored and otherwise equipped, Jim stepped down at last into a courtyard that looked something like a small portion of Hell and a large portion of an army headquarters facing instant battle. The air was heavy with smoke from wood burning in the overloaded cressets that gave the courtyard light for this unusual readying. In the cold air, the smell of steaming horses brought from their warm stable and the smell of excited men mixed with the odor of the smoke.

In the midst of all this the Bishop bulked even larger and more pugnacious than usual, in a mail shirt over his outer clothing and a helmet with a nasal guard—neither in disagreement with his usual authority, since the only thing about him that could possibly be considered to have potential as a weapon was his walking stick, and that had no edge to it. It was the use of *edged* weapons—the shedding of blood—that Church teaching forbade those committed to its work.

He stood leaning on that stick now, grimly watching what was being done. The red light of the flames from the overloaded cressets in the surrounding walls glittered on his mail shirt, but he said nothing. Not for him to give the orders. His leading man-at-arms had the responsibility for that. But if any man of God had ever looked ready to meet the armies of Evil, it was he.

He broke his silence, however, at the sight of Jim, equally bundled, equally armored—but with sword and dagger at his knight's belt.

"Sir James!" The Bishop opened his arms wide in welcome. "They told me you would go with us! I could ask for nothing more in this hap—" and Jim found himself enfolded by a pair of powerful arms and his cheek impressed by an equally powerful kiss. "By the by, Sir James, I found time to bless your chapel before you returned, today."

"My deepest gratitude to you for that, my lord," said Jim. He *was* grateful. He and his people had been working to refurbish Malencontri's chapel, which the previous occupant of the castle, Sir Hugh, had befouled, and the local people would now be very relieved by the Bishop's action.

Jim did his poor, latter-day best to return the customary osculatory compliment, although aware he fell short of the Bishop's energy and determination. Something nuzzled at the back of his neck. He turned to look and saw his warhorse, Gorp—saddled and ready, right down to the lance standing upright in its boot—and at the same time felt something else slither down past the back of his neck and end up in between his shirt and his undershirt. Only one creature in Malencontri could make himself so paper-thin.

Hob!" he said sternly. "You're to stay here—to take care of m'lady, and everything else!"

"Theoluf can defend the castle and m'lady as well as I can," said the breathy little voice of Hob in his right ear. "My duty is with you, m'lord!"

Jim sighed inside himself.

"—my lord," the Bishop's chief man-at-arms was saying, "all is ready."

"Then we ride!" shouted the Bishop, and together, with the bishop leading, Jim at his side, but half a horse's length behind him . . . and all of the rest following after, they rode out of the light of the cressets, through the unusually open great gates on to the briefly noisy drawbridge, and into the darkness and different sounds of the late fall night.

Jim was not superstitious in the sense of fearing some evil beyond the norm for these times that the darkness might confront them with. The Bishop certainly was not superstitious (in Jim's modern sense of that word), and possibly those in the service of the Church with him were not either. But almost everyone else in the entourage, particularly those of the common sort among the latter riders—for they were all mounted, necessarily—showed a tendency to crowd together.

But still, as their eyes adjusted to the night and they were able to consider the numbers and the strength of their party—to say nothing of the fact they had not only a Bishop with them, but a heroic Knight-Magickian as well, the gloom ceased to be quite as fearful. They relaxed, spread out and began to talk together in low voices, all but covered by the jingle of horse-harness.

Jim spoke to the Bishop, in case the other should be feeling like conversation. But the Bishop's answers were short and showed no such need or desire. His attention was clearly all on his own thoughts and what waited to be done once he was at their destination.

Jim reined Gorp back a few feet from the prelate and lost himself in his own thoughts.

At the pace the Bishop was setting—a sharp trot—they would have to stop at intervals to rest their horses. Still, they should reach Wells in about eight hours. He could grab four hours sleep, get up, eat something and, hopefully, be back at Malencontri in another eight hours.

With luck he could be home by late afternoon the next day. Out on his feet, of course, but alert enough to do what he should have gotten done already: starting the staff at the job of hunting down every rat and flea on the premises, and setting up a quarantine on anyone wanting to enter the castle in the future.

Also, they would need to set up some exterior shelter to quarantine anyone arriving, once the plague became active here—Angie's suggestion about fleas and pennyroyal had been a good one, if there was any quantity on hand or in the castle. Maybe Angie would already have set all these necessary projects to work by the time he got back. . . .

In any case he was stuck with his Bishop delivery first. Actually, they were now too large a body to run into much in the way of trouble. It was true most of their way was by narrow forest paths—and sometimes no path at all—but the moon was now up, a full moon already on the wane, but bright enough in a night sky with few clouds. Few outlaw bands would be foolish enough to attack.

There still remained the night-trolls, who could and would band together swiftly for a sufficiently large prey.

But already they had left behind most of the thick, continuous forest of the territory surrounding Malencontri and were passing through more open land—natural meadows interspersed with no more than brief patches of trees. In the bright moonlight such terrain was much less favorable for trolls, who liked the cover of darkness. Jim relaxed and his mind wandered off onto other problems.

With an extermination policy on the fleas and rats in the castle, quarantine on those from outside—and a ward he could set up around the whole castle's perimeter, to block any cracks or holes by which more fleas and rats were getting in—they should be about as safe from the plague as was possible in this world.

He thought briefly about offering to set up a ward around the Bishop's seat at Wells, and dismissed the idea. The Bishop undoubtedly would not—could not—accept such unchurchly aid. In addition, such a warding, plus Malencontri's, would almost certainly call for more magical energy than Jim's account with the Auditing Department could supply.

In any case an offer like that would be better to come from Carolinus . . . an image of the excruciatingly painful buboes that would swell on the naked bodies of plague victims until they burst came to Jim's mind, making him briefly sick inside, until he managed to forcibly jerk his thoughts to other things.

First of these, and touchiest, was the matter of the Prince's request to use Malencontri as a private place to discuss his plot concerning the King with Sir Mortimer—

Jim woke suddenly to the fact that the Bishop had held up an arm, signaling a rest halt. Pushing their horses at this rate made such rests necessary, unless they were going to ride the animals to death.

But, Jim saw, the Bishop could not have chosen a better spot.

It was a small rise—hardly more than a knoll—with half a dozen tall elms on it, the shade of which had evidently killed off anything much in the way of underbrush between them. But its greatest recommendation was the fact that all around it was a belt of grassy open ground, and only beyond this, at distances of at least half a bowshot, were there trees thick enough to hide any attackers who might want to creep up on them.

A hum of pleased conversation broke out among the retainers as they obeyed the order of the Bishop's chief man-at-arms to dismount and lead their horses in among the elms—a routine precaution in case they were being followed by outlaws with bowmen among them, waiting for a moment when they would relax their vigilance. A man wounded by an arrow could always ride, even if he would need to be tied on his steed. A horse in the same state had to be left behind—and they had no spare mounts.

But the hum broke off as the howl of a wolf rose from the wood they had just ridden out of a moment past.

The Bishop opened his mouth to order them all back to courage.

"It's all right," said Jim quickly, keeping his own voice down, "I know that wolf."

He raised his voice.

"Fear not!" he told the rigid members of their group. "You all know Magickians can talk to animals."

That was not quite true, of course. Jim could talk to Aargh only because Aargh could talk in human language to him. Carolinus seemed to manage the skill all right, but so far Jim had had only limited success, and that only with horses. The trouble seemed to be that most animal communication was in no way verbal but in body language. "I'll go have a word with the wolf," he added.

Surrounded and followed by a dead silence, he headed Gorp off toward where the howl had come from. Gorp went without protest, being by this time almost as familiar with that particular howl as Jim was—though the other horses were white-eyed and having to be reined in by their riders.

But as he had expected, he had hardly ridden deep enough into the trees to be hidden from his watchers when he heard a harsh voice behind him.

"So, now it's half-grown dragons you send to say you need me! What is it this time?"

Jim turned Gorp about and faced Aargh, the English Wolf, bulking larger than ever in the moonlight penetrating between the two large elms on either side of him.

"There's a sickness called the plague in England now—"

"I've heard talk of it. It's no matter to those of us who go on four legs."

"No, you animals are immune. I'd forgotten I'd sent a message for you. What I had in mind then was that you might be able to tell us if it'd reached this far west and was maybe making people sick anywhere in Somerset. But now something else has come up. The Bishop needs to get home as soon as possible—"

"And you were hoping I'd guard all you two-legs through the fearful night to where he wants to go?"

"Not exactly," said Jim—Aargh had a knack for getting under his skin. Jim sat hard on the temper beginning to simmer toward a boil within him. "I was thinking of something a cautious wolf might not mind doing—like going ahead to see if there're any outlaws or night-trolls waiting ahead to jump us, and then bringing back a warning."

"You did, did you? Well, this cautious wolf has better things to do—except in the case of what you want happening to tie in with what he wants to do anyway. As it happens there's something—lots of somethings—that I don't recognize afoot here in my territory; they act almost as if they're gathering around this little army of yours. In short, I'm going in your direction, anyhow."

I'll bet that's all there is to your being here! thought Jim, ironically, a sudden warm wave of affection for the grim-voiced wolf washing away the irritation he had felt a moment before. Aargh had always been more assistance than he would admit. Then part of what Aargh had just said came back to him. "What do you mean—somethings you don't recognize?"

"I mean they act like nothing I know. They come to the top of the earth, then go away again. But they're somethings I never scented before. It's as if it was more than one scent mixed with another—or more than one other. My nose has never tasted the like before. But they're in my territory and I gave them no leave to come here. I'll find them and have them out—the scent's been following you."

"Following us? Us? Why?"

"Are you asking me to answer that, James?"

"No, no, of course not, Aargh!" said Jim hastily. Through the single cloth layer of his undershirt, Jim could feel Hob's slim body trembling. "What's the matter, Hob?"

"M'lord? Nothing's the matter, m'lord."

"You're sure?"

"Yes, m'lord. I'm sure."

With the fearless gaze of Aargh upon them both, Jim did not want to question Hob further, as he ordinarily would have done.

"At any rate, Aargh," he said, "will you let us know if outlaws, night-trolls or such are lying in wait for us up ahead?"

"Neither outlaws nor trolls lie ahead of you tonight. If warning of them is needed, you'll have it from me."

—And Aargh was gone, in his usual instantaneous fashion.

Thoughtfully, Jim went back to the silent group waiting with the Bishop on the little rise.

"It's all right," he said when he rejoined them. "That was a good wolf, one I know well. He'll be going ahead of us and will come back to give the alarm if there're enemies up ahead."

"The horses have had enough of a chance to breathe," said the Bishop. "We ride on!"

A man screamed.

Jim looked to see who it had been, but even with the aid of the moonlight through the already leaf-bare limbs of the elms, it was impossible to tell. Identifying the screamer was beside the point now.

All around the small rise, the open, grassy earth that ringed them had become hidden from sight. Where it had been was now a swarming mass of rodenlike bodies: large rats, dead black in the moonlight; each of them carried a miniature, almost humanlike figure, riding it and carrying an equally miniature spear tipped with a gleaming, pointed head that glittered and reflected the moonlight so brightly that the spear shafts seemed tipped with fire.

But that was not all of it. As the first wave of these began to mount the slope, they grew and changed into full-sized, near-caricatures of armed knights—no longer riding the now-vanished rodents. Their shapes were not quite right, their armor seemed to be growing out of their bodies rather than clothing them, and their helmets completely hid their faces.

But the swords they carried ready in their hands reflected the moonlight as clearly as had the tiny spear tips—and they, at least, were real and dangerous.

But the imitation men were not. They were slow and clumsy with their weapons. Jim had more than time to get his own sword out and ward off the awkward blow being aimed at him. His opponent was acting as if he had never used a sword before in his life, and Jim's memory of the long hours in which Brian had tried to drill the rudiments of fourteenth-century sword-fighting into him suddenly filled him with confidence.

He swept up his sword accordingly, to dispose of this inept enemy in front of him—and suddenly discovered that victory was not to be won so simply.

An excruciating pain just above his right ankle made him change what might have been a decisive blow into a clumsy parry of another awkward swipe being made at him by his enemy. Glancing down, he saw the ground about all their feet was swarming with more of the original small rat-riding figures; one of these was just letting go of the spear he had driven into the vulnerable point below Jim's right knee where two pieces of his leg armor came together.

The pain was so piercing he could hardly think, let alone fight. Too piercing, in fact, to be just the ordinary discomfort of something not much bigger than the quill of a porcupine. The point had been poisoned—and with magic. As a knight he was forbidden to use magic to help him fight; but if his opponent dealt in magic—or magick—it was a different story. Jim disintegrated the tiny spear, eliminated the pain and cast a protective ward completely about himself.

He was immune now to the other rodent-riders who were angrily—but now uselessly—jabbing at chinks in his armor, but failing to touch him by a fraction of an inch. Free of distractions, Jim finished off his larger opponent with a couple of heartfelt blows, and went hunting for more to destroy. His blood was up now, but at the same time he saw there were too many of their attackers to win against in the end.

A wild sense of despair went through him, but at the same time came the breathy little voice of Hob almost frantically now in his ear.

"Fire, m'lord! Put fire all around us! They like it warm, but they cannot come through flame as we hobs do."

There was no time to question. No time to count the expense of the magic needed to produce flames with no fuel to feed them. Jim cast a ring of fire around all the humans on the hill.

A high-pitched, but savage, moaning sigh from many nonhuman voices rose—and the overwhelming numbers of their attackers recoiled from them like the wave of a dark sea, seen in the firelight. They still threatened with their spears, but from beyond the flames.

Hob had been right. Left within the magic fire were only the dead—the few men-at-arms able to limp about had quickly and savagely hunted them down and slain them—and the slain, impossibly, sank into the solid ground and disappeared. Jim looked over beyond the leaping flames, but there was nothing to be seen. Their clumsy man-sized attackers had vanished.

"Sir James!" It was the voice of the Bishop. "*Sir James!* To me, I say!"

Jim went toward the voice and found the churchman still on his feet, trying to aid his chaplain to stand against the pain of two spears in him—but with the shaft of one of the same spears projecting from the Bishop's own right calf.

The Bishop was sweating copiously, but remained upright himself. Norman, as well as Christian, courage—and pos-

sibly consciousness of the example he must set those who
followed him—was probably keeping him there. Half the
rest of their party was on the ground—none dead or badly
wounded, but hunched up and rolling around in tight-lipped
silence with the stoicism of their time.

"It was demon-work—" gasped the Bishop, as Jim appeared. "Demon-magic, was it not?"

"It was," said Jim. Looking at the Bishop and around the
battlefield, he decided *In for a penny, in for a pound*—and
used his magic to rid them all of their pains and the spears
causing them, while doing away with the magical fire.
Magic might be no good at curing the slightest illness, but
it worked wonders with wounds. The Bishop looked startled, like all the rest; then, understanding, first frowned severely at Jim, then abruptly wiped his face on a muffler
wound around his neck, and looked away with the innocent,
unconcerned, angelic expression of one who sees no evil.

"Mount up!" he roared. "We ride!"

But here now was Aargh, trotting unconcernedly up to
Jim—everybody else hastily made way for him—looking
as if he had been engaged in an adventure with a porcupine,
there were so many little spear shafts sticking out of his
hairy coat.

"Make yourself useful!" he growled at Jim. "And use
those things you call hands to clean these slivers from me."

"Of course," said Jim, swiftly magicking them away.
"There, they're gone. How do you feel now!"

"Just the way I did a moment ago," said Aargh. "How
should I feel?"

"The pain you felt must have been rough," said Jim.
"Those spear-points were made with magic, you see—"

"I knew that. They smelled of magic. But magic doesn't
work with us who go on four legs any more than your
sickness does—you know that; and it's as true for things
made with magick as it is of the magick itself. You've got
a clear road to Wells, now. I don't think those Naturals—

that's what they are, after all, aren't they?" Jim nodded. "—
will try that again. I must have killed a couple of dozen,
myself. They're what I was scenting. I'll be around on your
way back. Just howl!"

—And he was gone again.

They rode into Wells just as the eastern sky first started
to brighten with the morning.

"You'll be in need of rest now," the Bishop said as they
turned their horses over to the lay brothers at the stables. "I
need not tell you how deep are my thanks to you for mend-
ing our devil-wounds so that we made it safely here. You
will be ready for food and rest, now—"

"Food when I wake," said Jim. "For now, no more than
four hours of rest before I take my men-at-arms back to
Malencontri. We've got to be back there before the daylight's gone."

"I will see you are wakened at the hour of Prime."

Chapter 7

They were in the saddle and out of Wells—Jim and his four
Malencontri men-at-arms—by barely three-quarters of an
hour past the time when Jim had been awakened by a lay
brother with a bowl of hot vegetable soup. It had not been
coffee—not even tea—but Jim had drunk it gratefully, and
felt twice the man he had been when first roused out of a
dead slumber with the hot bowl steaming under his nose in
the chill small stony room where he had slept.

Now, with the fresh, even greater chill of the morning air
laving his face as he and his men settled down from the
initial gallop of their departure to a trot that would leave
some chance of their horses making it home alive, he began
to feel alive himself. His mind ran ahead of the beats of his

horse's hooves, counting up all the things to be done once he was home.

There were all the preparations against the plague to be taken care of, the castle staff to be convinced that getting rid of fleas meant getting *all* of the fleas and other vermin destroyed and swept out—the hunt for enough pennyroyal to scatter in at least the main rooms of the castle—strict new rules of hygiene to be taught—and finding staff who had the courage to man the Nursing Room to be set up for any who actually came down with the sickness. . . .

And how to create some kind of device to circulate a good quantity of fresh air through the Nursing Room to minimize more infection from the pneumonal form of the plague? This he had not mentioned to the Bishop because explanation of that form of the illness could not be convincingly explained in fourteenth-century words to a fourteenth-century mind. . . .

Briefly, questions about their attackers of the night before came thronging into his mind. Resolutely, he pushed them out.

He forced his mind back to immediate necessities. He reminded himself that Carolinus was probably already at Malencontri. Brian and his guest certainly would be. Probably as well, Geronde, and Dafydd and his wife Danielle with their children, for the wedding of Brian and Geronde was to take place at the first possible time now. Then, all the preparations for that day: food, other guests . . .

And, to top off the list of unsolved problems, there was still the Prince's request to somehow be diplomatically turned down—Jim could take advantage of Carolinus' presence to ask the elder man about a magickianly excuse. . . .

But most of these things could not be dealt with until he got home. Only the air-circulating device and the selection of people as nurses might be thought out to some extent as he rode.

He concentrated on those two accordingly for a while.

Somewhere in the servants' area on the ground floor of the castle would definitely have to be the place for the Nursing Room. They could knock out part of an outside wall in some room or space there, large enough to make a good-sized window, which could be glazed with some of the precious spare glass stored against breakage of the Solar windows. The Nursing Room window would have to be able to open so it could let fresh air in . . . then a fireplace added, if there wasn't already one there, to compensate for the coldness of the incoming air . . . storage space for extra bedding, other sick-room necessities. . . .

But his mind would not stay on that subject. It kept wandering off to other matters, like the attractive idea of changing into his dragon body and flying back to Malencontri in less time than it would take him to ride there, leaving his men-at-arms to follow on horseback.

But he dared not take that chance. Malencontri was short of fighting men as things were at the moment anyway. He could not afford to lose the four men he had with him. If he had noticed the use of magic by the little, spear-carrying demons, they had undoubtedly become aware of his ability to use it as well, the minute he got rid of the spear stuck in him.

Flying would only save a few hours, anyway. Besides, as had already occurred to him, Angie would already have begun getting the castle ready against the plague—

But wait a minute. She would also have to be playing the role of hostess to the Prince and Joan of Kent–Salisbury, neither of which were likely to appreciate being abandoned for castle preparations against a sickness thought still to be as far away as London.

The Prince should not be too much of a problem, come to think of it. He liked the company of women, but he also liked the companionship of men—particularly fighting men. Brian was certainly that, and the odds were his royal guest would be occupied with Brian. That only left Countess

Joan—and possibly Danielle—if she and Dafydd ap Hywel had arrived yet—to say nothing of Geronde, due from Malvern any day now, since the fire in Malvern's castle had forced the wedding celebrations to be held at Malencontri.

Hopefully, if the men were likely to gang up and go off together, the women might do exactly the same thing. If so, they might be gathered in the Solar right now. . . .

And—as he discovered when he finally got home—as a matter of fact, they were. The other ladies were just where he had guessed they might be, Jim was informed by three servants. And m'lady had asked that they not be disturbed there unless really necessary. What were they talking about, Jim wondered? He shrugged. Clothes, probably. That was something all women seemed to have as a topic in common.

In actual fact, however, there were other topics for them, for they were sitting around wine and a few small cakes as if there was no such thing as plague. Present, of course, was Angie with Joan of Kent and Geronde, who had just joined them—here ahead of schedule. Danielle alone was elsewhere in the castle, occupied with her youngest boy who was fretful with a runny nose and hot forehead he had developed on the trip here.

Geronde was not in the best of humors. She had bypassed Malencontri on her trip from Malvern, going to meet Brian at Smythe Castle so as to come here with him on the weekend—only to find him gone. She had planned to carry out a personal examination of that estate and castle over the course of the next few days, a thing her long experience in managing such estates would enable her to do with a ruthlessness that would no doubt terrify Brian's aging retainers, long used to their comfortable, long-established ways of managing a bachelor household.

But nonetheless, the Lady Chatelaine of Malvern was, above all things, polite.

"—a great honor to know you, my lady," Geronde had

consequently just finished telling Joan now. "My husband-to-be had much to say about you."

Unfortunately, a little of her present feelings had crept into the tone of her voice: Brian was not yet her husband and would not be until the end of the week, when the wedding would have to take place here at Malencontri, because of the unfortunate fire in her own chapel. . . . But the hearing of Joan was as acute as that of any healthy young woman her age.

"The honor is mine, indeed, m'lady," Joan answered, smiling. As with most Plantagenets—like the Prince himself—she was tall, fair-haired, fair-skinned, with an oval face that would have looked almost childish if there had not been a strength of mature bone under the skin. She had made a remarkably believable squire riding up to Malencontri in armor. She made an undeniably beautiful woman in her deep blue dress, now, and when she smiled, as she was presently doing, it was not difficult for Geronde to smile back.

"—I have talked to your husband only briefly," Joan was saying now to Geronde, "but never have I heard one of our sex so praised by her husband. He could speak of nothing else. I see his praise was justified."

The cruel knife scar on Geronde's right cheek, made by Sir Hugh de Bois when he had conquered Malvern by trickery and unsuccessfully tried to force her to marry him, flushed red. She had just been through a hard week, beginning with that fire in her chapel. Also, she was as quick as Brian to flare up. But equally as quick to flare down; now she was embarrassed. She had as good as challenged Joan with her opening tone and statement. Joan not only seemed to be refusing to take any offense, but to be unusually kind.

As the daughter of a knight bachelor (a knight entitled only to carry a swallow-tailed pennon)—albeit one with a prosperous estate—she was not, strictly speaking, a "lady," except to her castle and estate people. Angie, the wife of a

Baron—the least of the titled ranks—was just barely entitled to be addressed so. Joan, particularly considering their
difference in rank, would have been perfectly correct in addressing Geronde simply as "Mistress." That she had not
spoke of a genuine desire to be friendly and an intention to
put all rank aside and make their present moment merely a
gathering of women together.

"You are kind indeed in all you say, my lady," said Geronde.

"*Courtoise* aside," said Angie, stepping into the sticky
breach, speaking to Joan, "is it possible you and Prince Edward can stay for the wedding, m'lady?"

"M'lady," instead of the carefully pronounced "my lady,"
was a further presumption in the direction indicated by
Joan—this time committed by Angie. Formal barriers were
falling fast.

"I doubt it," said Joan. "Edward only came here to speak
Sir James. I know he expected us to be on our way back to
Tiverton Castle this day with Sir James' answer. Unfortunately, there was this small discussion with the good Bishop
of Bath and Wells."

"I had not heard of this," said Geronde, who had indeed
heard of it, but only in sketchy detail from those of Malencontri's servants she had talked to since getting here.
Brian had been absent with the Prince since her arrival. She
could hardly ask Jim, for all their close friendship, even if
he were here. Aside from the impropriety of such question-
ing, Jim was one of the few people she held in a certain
sense of awe—though she would never have let him know
it.

But now there was no need to question anyone else. The
two other women filled her in on it, except for the Prince's
earlier question for Jim, which Joan kept to herself. By the
time they had finished, they were down to first names, at
least part of the time. This would have been unthinkable
with any other Countess in the land, but Joan had made her

own rules from the time she was grown enough to run around on two chubby legs. Commoner or King, it made no difference to her as long as she got the end she was after.

Also, she was able to charm people, both men and women, and Angie and Geronde, though recognizing this, still fell under her spell to some extent.

"—I know he expected no problem," she was saying now (they were back to discussing the Prince). "But any direct attack will always find him more than ready. He has the Plantagenet courage—and, of course, its rashness, as with this demand by Cumberland that he go into exile. I know how his mind works. He planned to gain a military reputation on the continent and with it make an alliance to reenter England with great force and demand, as a price for peace, Cumberland's dismissal, if not his head. It was too large a scheme to commit to on the spur of the moment."

"And he listened?" asked Geronde, thinking not only of Brian but of her fortune-hunting father. "He must love you dearly to let himself be so schooled."

"Oh, he is level-headed enough to see sense once his temper is cooled. As for his love for me—" Joan shrugged "—I would like to think it is as strong as you say. I hope it is—for certainly he needs guidance at times—and we grew up at court together and there as children pledged our love for the first time."

"And when you were young he aided and protected you with all his bravery when you were growing up, no doubt?"

Geronde, reflected Angie, was a hopeless romantic, in spite of her steel-strong, unsparing exterior. Angie hoped—she really *hoped*—that after their marriage Brian would show some signs of understanding what storms of feeling could go on inside a woman with never a sign shown outside. Brian, good man that he was, seemed to see her as he saw the whole world: like himself, simple and straightforward.

"Protected me?" Joan laughed cheerfully. "No, it was I

who protected him through all those younger years! I was two years older than he was, bigger and stronger until the change came upon him, and I fought less wildly, more to purpose than he, with the other noble children, when the need arose. But my chances to protect him ended early, with my first marriage."

Angie had been pondering how to ask a delicate question; this mention of a marriage seemed to offer it.

"Speaking of marriages, Lady Joan," she said. "Are we to expect some attention here from the Count of Salisbury?"

It was a sensitive question, since in effect it asked why their guest, a married woman, was running around the countryside, dressed up as a squire and with an unmarried Prince. On the other hand it was a legitimate question, since it also asked if they might expect Salisbury to come down on them with a force of men and arms that could level Malencontri.

"No," answered Joan immediately. "There is a question now in the hands of the Pope of whether my first marriage, to Holland, is a legal one; if so, I am still the wife of Holland rather than Salisbury. Given his Eminence's present disagreement with our King—who would back Salisbury— there is little hope the matter will be settled soon, or I be sent back to my first love, Holland. But in any case, Salisbury thinks of me only when he is home, which is seldom. He will be gone for some time yet."

"Was Sir Holland really your first love?" asked Geronde.

"First wedded love. Indeed, in some honesty I must say he was otherwise also, since our marriage was when I was but twelve. No, but I do love Holland dearly. Oh, not as I love Edward, but dearly, nonetheless. This is best since, being first cousins, Edward and I are too close in degree of relationship for the Church to allow us a marriage."

"I, myself, was left alone to run Malvern Castle and its lands at the age of eleven, and have done so ever since," said Geronde.

"Were you!" said Joan, and the two of them looked at

each other for a moment, with sudden mutual respect and something almost like cousinly affection.

"In my case," went on Joan, "I had only a few years of happiness. My marriage to Holland had been perfectly legal—we both spoke the words of the *derba de praesente* form of the ceremony, you will observe—'I do take you for my husband—or wife—' as opposed to the *derba de futuro* form—'I will take you for my husband or wife'—at some time in the future—which indeed is merely a betrothal. And of course we had our witnesses, who could help us prove our words."

"But surely the matter was not questioned?" said Geronde.

"No," said Joan. "But Holland is a soldier, and poor. His only hope of wealth lies in capturing in battle someone able to pay a rich ransom—that is what he has tried to do ever since, and it's what might make it possible to approach the Pope—as is necessary in this case, since I am a royal and that is the only way to have declared my first marriage to him the only legal one."

"Is that the way of it, indeed?" said Geronde, deeply impressed.

"It is. An expensive process, producing witnesses, having writs made up, and all the rest of it. But then Holland was only twenty when we were married and, as I say, without such necessary moneys. I was only twelve, as I have said. The King knew nothing of our marriage, but he was in a rage at many wrongs committed here while he had been captive in Ghent. My relatives, knowing nothing of my marriage to Holland—only fearing such a hap—determined that, among other things, I should straightaway marry William Montagu, who afterward became Salisbury. At our marriage he was only his father's, the Count of Salisbury's, son and heir."

Joan paused to drink some watered wine.

"It is a long story and a dry one," she said.

Both Geronde and Angie assured her nothing could be farther from the fact.

"It is clear neither of you have been forced to spend much time at court," Joan said. "Otherwise you would know this history of mine from others. Well, the King is all-powerful, of course—as well as capable of easily flying into a general rage—and I dared say nothing about the marriage to Holland. So it was I was married to Montagu."

"But some day you will be free," said Geronde.

"With a proper decision by the Pope—which can hardly be otherwise than in our favor, provided we can pay our costs for it. The words were said, the witnesses witnessed. But now you understand why I consider myself free enough to accompany Edward."

"You are not easily thwarted," said Geronde.

"I am nothing compared to Edward. You will see!"

Privately, Angie thought that Edward himself might see something in the unthwartable department when he came up against Jim.

Chapter 8

Finally, the gathering of women left the Solar and went their different ways in the castle, and Jim was able to get at his own bed.

Theory had been fine, but reality had to win sometimes. Jim had begun his ride back to Malencontri full of plans to be put into action beginning the moment he arrived. Instead, he found himself just able to fall into the big bed in the Solar in time to be dead asleep as his head hit the pillow.

So much for heroic actions in emergencies.

He woke abruptly. Angie was moving quietly about the Solar. As he stared at her with a mind still fogged by sleep, she brought him a cup of just-made tea.

He drank it, careful not to fall back to sleep and spill it, continuing to watch her. Gradually he ascended into full wakefulness.

"You're tired," he said to her.

"A little," she said, making another cup of tea.

"You stayed up all night after the guests were asleep to get things done in the castle."

"There wasn't much choice. Besides, it helped impress the servants, who all had to stay up with me, with how important cleaning and fixing the castle against the plague was. I think I scared them silly—move over."

She had come back with the second cup of tea. When he shifted away from the edge of the bed to give her room, she sat down beside him, took a deep drink from the cup she carried, and let her head fall back against the headboard.

"Anyway," she said, "everything that's got to be done is underway, except for the Nursing Room. What do you think of using the lowest level of the tower rooms?"

"No," he said. "I thought about it, coming home. Ground floor, servants' quarters—knock a hole in the outside wall . . ." He reeled off the ideas he had matured on horseback.

They argued amicably for a few minutes.

". . . Never mind," said Angie. "I'm too tired to think up any more answers, and you're probably right, anyway. What are you going to do about the quarantine for people who come to the castle and want in?"

"I thought we'd set up the big tent—the pavilion—with some kind of small tent or a shack the carpenter could construct, where food and water could be set out for them to pick up. But, just in case, I'm going to throw a ward around the whole castle, too."

He grinned at her, reaching across to put his empty cup down on the end table, but saw that her eyes had closed and the half-empty cup she now held was about to spill.

Gently he rescued it from her lax fingers, put it also on

the end table, and rolled quietly off the other side of the bed. She was breathing deeply and did not wake as he undressed her and covered her up. That done, without waking she turned on her left side, sighed once and went back to her deep breathing. He dressed in the same formal clothes he had worn the day the Bishop arrived, and tiptoed to the door that opened on the hall running around the curve of the tower.

Rather ridiculous, tiptoeing, he told himself as he shut the door behind him. A cannon—if there had been such things here—going off next to the bed probably would not have wakened her.

"Where's Carolinus?" he asked the man-at-arms on duty outside the door. "He's still here, isn't he?"

"Think so, my lord," the man answered. "But where . . ." he looked at the servant on duty with him. "But where . . . ?"

"He's in his room—doing terrible magickal things," said the servant, a skinny recent recruit in her mid-to-late teens and eager to be noticed by Authority, so she would be kept on. "Shall I go fetch him for you, my lord, forgive me suggesting it?"

"The suggestion's perfectly all right," said Jim. "But he's a Mage—much higher in magickal rank than I am. I'll go to him. You can show me which room it is."

"Yes, my lord. Thank you, my lord. This way, my lord."

He followed her down two levels and around the curve of the hall there.

"Well, there you are," said Carolinus, who was doing no terrible magickal things at all, but examining a spider who was holding up a couple of its limbs for inspection. "No, no damage done at all. They'll be perfectly all right in an hour or so—see if they aren't. Jim, I thought you were going to sleep all day."

"No need. I'm fine," said Jim. "I'm glad you're still here even though the Bishop's already gone. Sorry about getting you here like this—I didn't know he'd leave so suddenly. But since you are here, I need your help."

"Who doesn't?" Carolinus glanced back at the spider, which was just disappearing over the edge of the table. "Actually, I stayed because I have something I've been meaning to speak to *you* about."

"I'm in an awkward position—" Jim began hastily before Carolinus could get off on whatever he was about to launch into.

"I hope not!" said Carolinus. "Just when I've put your name up—as I just said, that's what I've been meaning to tell you," he broke off to cough, "that is to say, I haven't had time to tell you. I've put your name up for graduation to full Magickian, and you're going to be expected—under observation, of course—to do something noteworthy if you expect to be voted into full membership."

Jim had not originally been expecting ever to be voted into full membership in the Collegiate of Magickians. In fact, in his early days here he had wanted nothing better than to have nothing to do with Magick, let alone the Collegiate. It was his view then that he and magick would be best off traveling in different directions.

But that was before his victory over the Dark Powers at the Loathly Tower while wearing a borrowed dragon body had turned out to have a side effect. Which was that he had acquired an active balance in magickal energy with the mysterious Accounting Office, and unless he learned to use that magick—like breaking a horse to wear a saddle and work with a rider—it would use him.

Now, having learned a great deal about the presence of magic in this world which was developing almost—but not quite—along the same historical lines as the Earth on which he and Angie had been born—five hundred years later—his point of view had come full circle to the opposite opinion.

He had come to the decision that not only must he gain acceptance in the Collegiate, he must manage to grow in it to a place where he was finally one of its important voices.

But not yet—above all, not at this particular, critical time.

"Well, I'm not going to worry about that now," he said, deliberately brushing off Carolinus' announcement. "Not with all the other troubles I've got piling up here—and it's the most immediate of these I desperately need to talk to you about. It has to do with the Prince, and it can't wait."

"Young Edward?" said Carolinus, with unusual agreeableness. "Yes, I noticed he was here. Trouble with his father again?"

"Trouble with Cumberland, you mean?" said Jim.

"Hmm, well, yes. I suppose I do."

"Yes. Outside of a few small explosions, I don't think the two of them would ever have fallen out if Cumberland hadn't been deliberately stirring the pot to keep it boiling over all the time. No, it's something else. Now the Prince has got himself mixed up in a sort of harebrained scheme to win himself back into his father's affection while Cumberland's not around. You won't have known, but the King's been moved from his court at the Tower of London, down to a place called Tiverton, to get him away from the plague in London."

"Of course I knew!" said Carolinus. "Give me credit for knowing at least a few thousand more things than you do!"

"The scheme tries to take advantage of that by setting up a situation where the two can get together and find out they still really like each other."

"Nothing wrong about that," said Carolinus. "Giving human nature a chance to work, that's all."

"Theoretically, no. Anyway, that's not what's giving me a problem. Tiverton's only a short day's ride from here. The Prince wants to use Malencontri for secret meetings with a man named Verweather, to talk over things about his plan that he can't talk about in Tiverton itself—and he also wants to come visiting the Fair Maid of Kent, who came here with him. I've got to find a diplomatic way of turning him down.

I thought of using the fact I'm bound by some rule or other of the Collegiate that gives me no choice about saying 'no'—and I thought you, knowing the rules better—could suggest something."

Carolinus might be bone, flesh, heart and soul a Magickian, but he was not unworldly where the politics of his day were concerned.

"I see," he said thoughtfully. He eyed Jim.

"You've looked for your answer in the *Encyclopedie Necromantic?*" he asked.

"To tell you the truth," said Jim, looking the senior Magickian hard in the eyes as he spoke, "I've found the *Encyclopedie* turned out to be almost completely useless for my purposes. Yes, the directions about the simple spell-forms for beginning apprentices were useful for me at first. But from there on, everything seemed to head off in a different direction from the way I was beginning to use magic."

"But you did get to the *Rules and regulations enjoined upon all Members of the Collegiate of Magickians, their apprentices, familiars and all other dependents for which they are responsible while active in the use of Magick?*"

"Well . . . no," said Jim. The truth was, he had never looked beyond the middle part of that massive tome.

"And here," said Carolinus, "I've just finished putting your name up for a vote on becoming a full Magickian!"

"I thought the rest of the book beyond where I stopped was just more of the same."

"Hah!" said Carolinus. "Well, disabuse yourself of that notion! Cough your copy up—you remember the pattern of coughs to do so, I hope."

Tight-lipped, and without a word, let alone a cough, Jim extended his hand, palm upward, with a minuscule, thick volume, the print of which would require a microscope to read, in the center of it.

"Very pretty!" said Carolinus. "A very pretty little bit of magick to be sure. But I hope you don't think this makes up for your despicable failure to read *and memorize* the rules and regulations in the first place!"

"I merely wanted to show you how I had developed some things," said Jim, still coldly. "In more than one way, my use of magic has gone beyond most of the sort of stuff in the *Necromantic*—including some of the advanced forms."

"Every worthwhile Magickian discovers that. Turn to the Rules. Number one hundred and eleven."

Jim opened his mouth again, closed it. Deeds spoke louder than words. In his hand, the tiny volume swelled to the size of a large wedding cake, but with its forty-pound weight no longer bearing down on his palm—instead, it floated in midair, a fraction of an inch above his hand.

It opened itself at its last page, flipped back several more pages, and lay open to be read.

"*No member of the Collegiate will at any time also be a member of any other organization, establishment or group, but will at all times remain free in allegiance only to our own world-wide association in which any other member who has violated none of these laws will be regarded, if a man, as a brother, and if a woman, as a sister,*" he read aloud.

"Well," said Carolinus, "make your choice—give young Edward the cooperation he asks for or continue being a Magickian. I need hardly add that since your name has been proposed in full assembly, you are already considered to be ruled by the laws written down here. So actually you have no choice but to tell him what he wants is forbidden to you to grant."

A great sense of relief took possession of Jim. If this problem fell so easily, why shouldn't all the others turn out to be so quickly solvable?

But then common sense took over, and he realized turning down the Prince without making an enemy of him was not quite a problem of the size of defending against the plague.

"Thank you, Master and Mage," he said, "for coming to my rescue once more. And thank you for putting me up for full Magickian membership. But can we talk about that later? There's all sorts of things I should be overseeing to protect Malencontri's people against the plague—oh, and it was the plague I think the Bishop particularly wanted to consult with you on. But with him having to go back to Wells—"

"Never mind," said Carolinus, once more in the strangely agreeable tone he had used before. "There are ways—vulnerable to the sickness myself, you know."

"I hadn't thought! You've got to come stay with us here, once we get set up." Carolinus had always seemed invulnerable to anything, but, Jim remembered now, they had seen him sick and helpless before.

"We'll see," said the Mage.

Jim went in search of the Prince and was told that royal figure was in his room with the Countess, so he headed for the room. As host, theoretically he could walk in anywhere in his own castle. But that was theory—this was practice. He knocked.

As he did so, a line from a poem by Kipling that Angie had quoted to him a long time ago came back to him. "*. . . they sought the king among his girls and risked their lives thereby. . . .*" The memory stirred the unease within him at having to break his present news to Edward. But this was a Prince, not an Eastern King, and there was only one "girl" with him. But Angie had said she had liked Joan of Kent, and if that was so, the Countess was likely to be a sensible sort of person.

The door opened and Edward's head looked out.

"James!" he said happily. "I will join you in a moment."

The door closed. Jim waited, feeling even more uncomfortable following Edward's cheery welcome. The minutes stretched out. Finally the door opened again and the Prince stepped out, quietly closing it behind him.

"Well, James," he said, "what word do you have for me?"

"One beset with many problems, Your Grace. Unfortunately, my lady wife is asleep in the Solar at the moment after a full night directing the servants in their preparations against the plague—"

"There is no plague here yet, James, any more than there is in Devon—which was the reason my father was moved there."

"The very reason we are rushing to complete our defenses before arrival of it. But, as I was about to say, the day is not inclement and no place could be more privy than the tower top, once I have sent the watchman away."

"Very well," said the Prince, "though I must say this is much of a coil over a simple matter. If you would lead the way then."

They went up to the tower top, and Jim sent the man-at-arms on duty there down until he should be called back. The day was not, as Jim had promised, inclement. The sun shone brightly, and there was hardly a cloud in the sky. However, a stiff, cold breeze—very noticeable up there in the open—whipped the loose ends of their clothing about them, and Jim was thankful for the cloth linings of his hosen and the medieval thickness of his green cote-hardi. Edward, more lightly—if no less fashionably—dressed seemed to pay no attention to the brisk air.

"You may remember, Your Grace, I said yesterday your small request might conflict with the rules of the Collegiate of Magickians, to which I am bounden in duty—"

"I remember very well, and I—" The Prince checked himself. "But as the Countess later pointed out to me, we all have a number of obligations and duties which may not lightly be put aside. Continue, James."

"What I thought might be a clear and simple answer to the question turned out to require knowledge I had not yet acquired. The matter was like those rules that keep monks from falling into worldly ways. I was forced to consult with my Master-in-Magick, the Mage Carolinus, of whom you may have heard."

"Heard and spoken to, James. Get on with it!"

"He directed me to the relevant passage in our Great Book." Magically, Jim produced his copy of the *Encyclopedie Necromantic*, and the Prince, not easily given to startlement in Jim's experience, widened his eyes and stared at the sight of the great tome floating weightlessly above Jim's palm. Both these solid pieces of evidence seemed to impress him more than anything Jim had said so far.

"And—" Edward said.

"And Mage Carolinus directed me to the relevant passage. I can't, of course, read it to you—the words of this Book are forbidden to anyone not a Magickian. But essentially it's like the rules I mentioned that keep monks from slipping into worldly ways."

The Prince nodded, a little impatiently.

"Briefly, it amounts to the fact that you can visit Malencontri any time you wish—in fact, Viscount Verweather could also visit here if he wished—but not both of you at the same time."

Edward exhaled a heavy breath.

"I can't tell you, Your Grace," said Jim, "how sorry I am that I can't fall in with a wish of yours, but this one is not allowed."

"No, James. I see it can't be," the Prince said with sudden, astonishing reasonableness. He straightened up, squaring his shoulders and taking in as deep a breath as he had breathed out a moment earlier. "Very well. What cannot be cured must be endured."

He turned and started down the stairs from the tower roof. Jim went after him and caught up with him on the Solar floor as the Prince was hesitating at the top of the interior staircase to the lower levels.

"Is it three floors down, or two, James? I didn't think to count on the way up."

"Two," said Jim. "I can't tell you how unhappy I am—" he was just beginning to add as they came to the door of the room the Prince shared with the Countess.

"Have done with apologies!" said Edward. "The fault was mine in jumping to conclusions. I will need to leave early tomorrow to get back to Tiverton well before suppertime. If I do not see you again before we go, farewell, my lord, and thank you for your hospitality—as well for providing for the Countess here while I am away. You—can understand. I dare not take her with me to my father until we are on stronger terms. I'll say farewell myself for the moment now, then."

"Farewell," said Jim. "Would you want some men-at-arms as escort?"

"Hah! I can guard myself—and better I ride into Tiverton alone."

The Prince went in, shutting the door behind him.

Back at the Solar, Jim found Angie still sleeping. But Hob was standing in front of the fireplace, and he stiffened up as Jim came toward him so they could talk with lowered voices.

"My lord," said Hob, standing very straight, indeed, "I need a sword!"

Chapter 9

"A sword?" Jim was startled enough to raise his voice. He looked quickly at Angie to see if he had wakened her, but she was continuing to slumber peacefully. He spoke more quietly. "For you, Hob? What would you want with a sword?"

"To die with it in my hand with those I have slain in a ring around me. They have said hobs cannot fight! They will learn it is not that we cannot, but that ordinarily we choose not!"

Jim looked at the little Natural closely. Was this another of the grandiose speeches he had learned from the strolling player and ballad-singer he had at one time hidden for months at Malencontri? The fellow who promised to teach him how to "talk like the gentry," and who as a result had stuffed Hob full of vainglorious stage speeches.

No, Jim decided, this time Hob was serious. Dead serious.

"I still don't understand," Jim said.

"I own I acted like a usual cowardly hob when we ran into them, last night. I hid down in the back of your shirt, shaking like a leaf. But now I've had time to think things over, and I'm *not* afraid! Also, I'm not any run-of-the-mill hob. I am *your* hob—and you are a paladin! Would the hob of a paladin cower in a corner when his lord fights for his life? No, he would fight alongside and, when the time came, die as a hob should, sword in hand!"

"But who are you going to fight?" Jim stared at him.

"Why *them*, m'lord! You know. Those we encountered when we went with the Bishop to Wells."

"The little Naturals with the spears, riding the ratlike animals? We may never run into them again."

"Oh no, m'lord! With the rats—they *were* rats, M'lord— a herd of plague flea-ridden rats being ridden into Somerset to spread the sickness. They're determined to win this time. They'll kill off as many of you as they can and rule the rest—and kill off all of us hobs, too. It'd be one of them my lady would be left with, instead of me."

"The rats are trying to win? What?"

"Not the rats, M'lord. *THEM!*"

"Hob," said Jim. "I'm not making head or tail of this. Where did you pick up such a wild story?"

"It's no wild story, m'lord! It's the truth. It's history— their history and mine and the history of every hob there is. They're goblins, m'lord, just like we are—only we're a different kind of goblin, and always were. Maybe I should tell you the whole story, right from the beginning."

Jim glanced over at Angie, but she was still sleeping undisturbed. If their voices hadn't wakened her before this, it wasn't likely they would now.

"Go ahead," he said. "But keep your voice down."

"It's an old, old story," said Hob, low-voiced but earnest, "hundreds and hundreds of years old. But once all the goblins were part of the Kingdom of Demons and Devils."

"Including hobgoblins?"

"We weren't called by that name, then. Then, we were just goblins like the rest of them—only now and then one of us would be born different. I mean, we were all part of goblin-kind, but mixed in with the rest, except we didn't want to do mean and terrible things to everyone else. Like the others did. And the other kind of goblins hated us for it. But they weren't doing too much to us about it—at least, not then. But they said we kept giving goblin-kind a bad name among the devils and demons—and they had to bear that because of us."

Jim sat down. This was evidently going to be anything but a short story. Hob remained standing, shoulders squared.

"It was a bad place, that kingdom, m'Lord. A terrible place," he said. "It held—and still does—those like that Ahriman we faced when we brought back Lady Geronde's father. . . ."

His voice softened for a moment, and for that movement his gaze became absent.

". . . it must be wonderful to be a father. A hob almost never is—or a mother. But the other goblins—that's why there's so many of them—"

He broke off, pulled himself together and went on.

"I never thought then, long, long ago, that I'd ever find myself actually face to face with Ahriman—let alone pushing him back the way we did, back into the kingdom. In the early times, he and those with him were called the Great

Demons. Below them came rank on rank of the Lesser Demons, like that djinn we met on the same trip. And then at the very bottom there were us, the goblins, and we were called the Least Demons by all the rest. The kingdom swarmed; earth, water and air filled thick with all those wanting to get out into the world, hurt and kill . . . too many of them to count."

Jim found his mind boggling. That many individual entities with only one wish. It wasn't believable.

"They must have had some other aim besides just doing harm," he said. "That many couldn't all just live for just that alone!"

"Not all, m'lord. There were we few hobs—though not called that yet, as I told you, m'lord. But all the rest, m'Lord—they *liked* being cruel. They lived for it. The Great Demons had very terrible powers of magic. With those they'd work on one man, say, who was very powerful or ambitious among humans—a King or an Emperor, or somebody who just for the moment was able to do great harm. And because of the demon-work, that person would end by doing what the demon wanted to happen, and hundreds or thousands of you humans starved, or suffered and died—so that the demon who made it happen could watch and enjoy what he saw happening."

Oh, my Lord! thought Jim. *A kingdom of sadists? I can't believe it!*

". . . but the moment that was all over," Hob was going on, "the Great Demon who made it happen was all sour and unhappy and upset again as usual, and he'd stay that way until he could do something like it again. And so it was with all the Lesser Demons, including even we goblins— though we were so weak in magic all we could hope to do was creep into houses and play cruel tricks that weren't strong enough to kill, inside. Like making maidservants spill boiling water on themselves."

Hob paused.

"But then trouble came!" he said, and stopped, and Jim realized these were dramatic pauses, not the end of the story.

"—All over the world humans started making shields of what they believed in—whatever their faith was, m'lord. As long as they really had faith in it shielding them—all at once, goblins couldn't creep into houses, anymore. The Lesser Demons began to be stopped, too. Even, finally, the Great Demons found there were places they couldn't go, people they couldn't touch or harm. Some humans could walk right at as great a demon as Ahriman, like we did. Of course, they all had to believe in something. I believed in you and your magic staff, m'lord—and the demon had to back up, just as Ahriman had to when we walked at him on that same trip to bring home Lady Geronde's father—"

I'll be damned! thought Jim. *I knew it was the strength of spirit in each of us holding hands as we walked toward that demon that was pushing him back, not the staff, hard as it was for me to get it. The staff only focused what was in all of us. But never in a million years would I have dreamed Hob could have known that at the same time.*

"—the Kingdom of Demons and Devils was all upset when they found they were kept out," Hob was continuing. "Everybody blamed everybody else for not thinking, and doing something wrong. The Great Demons blamed the Lesser Demons, and all the Lesser Demons, down their ranks, blamed the Least Demons for getting into houses and other buildings in the first place."

Hob paused again.

"And the Least Demons, the goblins, turned around and blamed us hobs!" he said. "That is, m'lord, they blamed those of us who didn't want to do cruel things."

"That's how it usually goes," said Jim.

"So they drove us out of the kingdom, killing those of us who wouldn't go, and there we were, adrift in the world."

"How'd you survive?" Jim asked. "I know you really don't seem to need to eat, hardly at all, but I'd think the loneliness, the cold—all the weather, in fact—"

"We discovered a wonderful thing, m'lord." Hob's eyes all but literally shone at Jim. "All the things that kept the others of the kingdom from getting into human buildings didn't stop us!"

Jim stared at him for a full fifteen seconds.

"Well, of course!" he said at last. "There was no desire to do harm in you—nothing there to be kept out."

"Was that it, m'lord? Anyway, we crept in at first, into some building or other, just to get out of that weather you mentioned. We hid very carefully at first, but finally all of us started exploring the buildings we were in—and we found fireplaces, sometimes with fires in them. Warmth, m'lord! It was always warm to hot in the kingdom, for all the other goblins couldn't stand fire, itself, and now we had heat, and chimneys to hide in!"

"And, of course," said Jim, "in time the people in the house began to catch glimpses of you, and eventually they got to know you, so here you are today."

"Yes, m'lord, and how lucky I am to be your hob! The one thing I'm sorry for is that the only magic we had as goblins was the little magic, and the only part of that they didn't think to strip from us as they drove us out was the one they no longer could use themselves, the ordinary magic for entering strange houses and other places. My regret is I no longer have any magic at all to use in your service, as even a one-time Least Demon should."

"No magic?" said Jim. "What about your being able to ride the smoke halfway around the world—and being able to thin yourself down so much you can go through the crack of a tight-fitting, locked door?"

Hob stared at him for a second.

"Oh! forgive me, m'lord," he said. "But are those truly magic—I mean magick like you do—is that the way I should say the word?"

"You say it any way you want."

"Oh, then I'll say it the way you do . . . magick. Thank you m'lord. But all our hobs can do those things. How would we get them?"

"My guess is," said Jim, "you were used to making magic—small magic, if you say so—and when what you had was taken away, you simply made more in its place. Only, this time it was magic that helped you in your new life, as the magic you had before was built to help goblins in your old."

"You really think so, m'lord?"

"I do."

"I'm magic! I'm magic!" cried Hob happily. *More than you think,* thought Jim, remembering how Hob had warmed the icy heart of the Witch Queen of Northgales, down in Lyonesse. In his excitement Hob was now turning a perfect cartwheel—but then he instantly sobered up.

"Oh! Forgive me, my lord. I'm so sorry—"

"It's all right."

"Thank you, m'lord, but I must be serious. It's so important you understand. To make a long story short, in the end the other demons drove all the goblins out of the kingdom, and persecuted them once they were out. In defense, the goblins went deep—very deep in the earth, where demons and devils don't like to go. There, their only enemies are the gnarlies; though the gnarlies, being so tough and strong, it usually costs them more than they win to fight them. But that's why they're called the deep-earth goblins to this day, and now there's thousands and thousands of them. But their greatest hatred still isn't on the demons that threw them out, or even on us quiet hobs. It's you humans they hate, blaming you for doing things to your houses so they couldn't get in. For a long, long time they've wanted to pay you all back, and now with the sickness to help, they're trying."

He stopped. Jim looked at him.

"But what's all this to do with you wanting a sword?" he asked.

"Last night was just the beginning, m'lord," said Hob earnestly. "But I know goblins. I'm the only one here who really does. They've let us see them; they'd never have done that unless they had at last thought they could finally pay humans back for locking them out of their human places. Either now they can get around the faith that's kept them out before, or they've found out how they can get into houses and buildings in spite of it. We will have to fight them for our lives, m'lord, and I must fight with you. They must see a hob matching them, weapon for weapon. I need a sword—a real sword!"

"You don't know how to use it."

"I will learn."

Jim stared at him. The little fellow meant what he said.

"Come on," he said. "We'll go talk to the castle blacksmith."

"Of course," said the blacksmith, almost cheerfully. He could not quite manage a real cheerfulness, being the kind of person who usually went about growling at people—so much so that the rest of the staff visited his open-sided smithy in the courtyard only when they had to. But it did not pay for the most skilled artisan to growl at his lord. "I'll make him a pretty little sword."

"I want a real sword!" said Hob. "A killing sword."

" 'Course you do," said the blacksmith, winking at Jim.

Jim did not wink back.

"That's right," said Jim. "A sword just like my own, but his size. Harkye, Master Blacksmith, that means a working blade."

The blacksmith, stared, open-mouthed.

"You heard me," said Jim.

The blacksmith literally wrung his hands.

"But, m'lord, I can't do that!"

"You can if I tell you to."

"But I can't—I mean, m'lord, I would do so, right now, right willingly. But I just can't! I haven't the metal. I haven't the Mystery. I haven't the skill in my hands. My lord—it takes a *swordsmith* to make a weapon such as you ask for!"

Jim stared back at him. The man was right, of course. The "Mystery," the exact method by which the blade must be shaped and tempered, was a guarded secret—many guilds had such—and the guild of Swordsmiths would have been careful to keep the knowledge hidden from someone like an ordinary blacksmith. Experts were needed at this point.

"Get me Theoluf!" Jim snapped.

"Get His Lordship his squire—and be quick about it!" snarled the blacksmith to his closest journeyman-assistant, who had been standing by, staring and listening, up to this point.

"At once, m'lord! At once, Master!" The journeyman went off at at a run, still wearing his leather apron.

He was back in no time at all, unexpectedly followed by two others: one was Brian, and the other was obviously the knight who had been his guest and come down to Malen-contri with him on Jim's invitation. They had plainly been out hunting. They both wore the heavy-leather outer clothing useful to men who might need to gallop or run through brush, and both were wearing their poniards as well as their swords.

However, Jim got a jolt on seeing the guest. He was one of the last men Jim would have expected to find visiting with Brian—Sir Harimore Kilinsworth, whom Jim had met for the first time at the Earl of Somerset's castle. He was a little taller than Brian, but moved with the same lean, eager, supremely confident manner. He sported one of the little mustaches that were fashionable at this period, but was otherwise as clean-shaven as Brian.

The two men obviously respected each other for their strict adherence to their knightly vows and military skills—in which they were a class by themselves. But Jim had always understood that otherwise they were at swords' points.

But they came up now behind the panting journeyman-helper, who came running ahead to unnecessarily announce the arrival of Jim's squire, Theoluf—unnecessarily, since in fact Theoluf had already arrived ahead of him.

"No proper metal to make a sword?" demanded Theoluf of the sweating blacksmith. "Don't tell me you have no store of broken swords or other weapons! Get them out!"

"Get them out!" barked the blacksmith at the journeyman-apprentice. "Don't just stand around there all day!"

"Yes, Master—yes, m'lord" gasped the journeyman, and plunged through a door to the back room of the smithy.

There was a grunting and a jangling of metal as the journeyman brought out armloads of old iron in the shape of damaged swords, daggers—from brasards to poniards—spear points, half-cracked halberds, pikes and other damaged or worn fighting equipment, and spilled them up in front of the smithy in the courtyard, along with a broken saw and some reaping hooks—rusty, nicked or otherwise in bad shape.

Brian and Sir Harimore immediately plunged into the pile, searching and examining like boys on a treasure hunt—and incidentally betraying at least one reason why they had followed Theoluf here. The blacksmith and the journeyman stood as they were, making no move to interfere. These two were belted knights; if they chose to take precedence in rummaging through the pile before them, who was to say them nay? But Theoluf, who had been a chief man-at-arms for years before the rare lack of anyone else suitable had raised him to the gentlemanly rank of squire, had dealt with the higher ranks before.

"By your great grace and pardon, sirs," he said, and he did not keep a note of asperity completely out of his voice, "my lord is engaged in a matter of some importance here, and it is necessary that I examine the old iron myself as soon as possible."

Both Brian and Harimore were completely aware of the fact that either one of them could handle Jim with one hand tied behind his back, and the elbow of the other tied to his side—plus a blinding hangover to boot. But they both backed away instantly.

Jim was their host. It was his castle, his iron, and they were here only by his courtesy in inviting them. Theoluf dug into the pile and began to come up with his own choices from it.

"You say you lack the metal to make a sword, Master Blacksmith?" Theoluf said, waving a rust-streaked blade with the last third of it gone near the tip end. "Here in this heap is good striking metal enough to rearm all our castle's fighting men—once it has been recut, sharpened and fastened to a new hilt and hold! But you are not being asked to rearm us all, merely make one good, battle-worthy sword for a hob less than half a man's size . . . and perhaps a dagger and shield to go with it!"

"Well, I doubt a shield, now . . ." began the blacksmith, gathering his courage but sounding remarkably timid in spite of all that.

"Use your wits, man! Shields are not solid iron—if they were, the weariness of shield-arms would make many encounters much shorter than they are. Also, the function of the shield is to turn a blow. To be sure, it is a fine thing to have that well-polished, shining surface on which is a coat of arms. But there is no question of coats of arms here, any more than there would be for one of our common armsmen, and strips of iron, laid close together, will turn a sword edge as well as a solid cover. True, a spear point may catch on the line between two strips, but there is no question of the hob riding with couched lance, either!"

"What you say is true—" began the blacksmith.

"Then get on with it. You may need the help of Master Carpenter and others, but I leave the small parts up to you."

"I'm glad you're here," said Jim to Brian and Harimore. "I was going to find you and ask you about this. Brian, you know our hob well, but of course, Sir Harimore, you know nothing about him—that's him, standing right over there."

He gestured at Hob, who had backed off some little distance so as not to intrude. He had been looking excited, hopeful, worried—and showing half a dozen other emotions in a sort of kaleidoscope of reaction as he listened. He was resisting his frequent tendency to stand on one leg, however, and still had the squared-shouldered, upright stance he had shown Jim in the Solar.

"Indeed, Harry," said Brian unexpectedly. "He has been with James and myself on many a dangerous expedition, and shown great bravery as well as sharp wits. I do not believe there is another hobgoblin living who has had such adventures and carried himself so well."

"It's true. Thanks, Brian," said Jim gratefully. Brian had unknowingly given him the excuse to speak, and now was the time to follow up with the information. "It just happened that today he was able to tell me something that touches all England—perhaps touches the whole world. I can't, unfortunately, tell you the details because it involves magic. But it's the reason we now need him not only armed but able to fight with the rest of us."

"Armed? Fight? A hobgoblin?" Sir Harimore stared at Jim.

"Yes!" said Jim. "As I say, I wish I could tell you more so that you could see the need of it, but as a Magickian my lips are sealed."

Mentally, he crossed his fingers, remembering that Brian had told him Sir Harimore's respect for his knight's vows and obligations were as strict as those of Brian himself. Would they, in this case, tip him toward acceptance of an armed and battle-ready hobgoblin—or against the very idea? Jim could not directly lie to the man, but—he was suddenly inspired.

"As I said," Jim went on, "my lips are sealed. I can only give you my word he must be armed and learn to fight."

"I accept your word of course, Sir James," said Harimore stiffly. "No more need be said."

"Well, there's just one thing more," said Jim. "I was going to try to give him a lightning-swift course in how to use his sword and shield—"

"James, there is no thing such!" said Brian, looking embarrassed. "The art of arms cannot be taught in an hour or a day—"

"I know that," said Jim hastily. "But there are a few necessary things to know, such as how to hold your sword and how to strike with it, regardless of what your enemy might be doing in the same movement. I'd hoped I could at least show that much to Hob." Mentally he crossed his fingers again before going on. "And then—if you will forgive me, sirs—it came to me that two gentlemen like yourselves, learned in the art, might be willing to at least teach such simple things correctly, where I could likely not. . . ."

He let his voice trail off hopefully. Brian, he knew, loved to teach, but Jim had never heard of Sir Harimore Kilinsworth educating anyone in the skills he was so good at himself.

"Hah! No doubt!" said Harimore. "But there must be something of a makings of a man to start with—catch that!"

With the last words, and so swiftly that Jim had barely time to realize the knight had done it, he had drawn his needle-sharp, razor-edged poniard and thrown it tumbling through the air toward Hob.

Hob, looking puzzled, watched the approaching weapon until it was almost upon him, then took one step aside, picked it out of the air by its hilt and started carrying it back to Harimore.

"Hmpf!" said Harimore, in an obvious tone of surprise, then lifted his voice to speak to Hob again. "No! Hold to it! Go back where you were."

"Yes, m'lord." Hob obeyed. Harimore poked through the pile and came up with the amputated handle of a diseased-looking half-pike.

"Come," he said to Hob, and when Hob came, he handed him the handle. "Let me see you cut that—with my poniard."

"Yes, m'lord."

Hob lifted the poniard and brought its blade down edge-wise on the old, dark wood of the handle. A little of the dry, hard wood chipped off, but that was the only result.

"So it is revealed," said Harimore, turning to Jim and Brian, who had drawn close to watch. "Natural speed of eye, hand and body make for a good swordsman, but what is it of worth if he has no strength of body?"

"Forgive me, my noble lord," said Hob in a small voice, "but did you mean you wished me to cut the staff in *two?*"

"Of course."

"Oh!" Hob picked up the ancient half-pike handle with one hand and lifted the poniard. He brought the weapon down again—but this time with a difference. This time his whole body arched to the blow and his feet left the ground as blade met wood. The hard, dry pike handle opened up— not completely, but the handle's two end-pieces fell apart, all but perhaps half an inch of wood clinging to both ends at the bottom of Hob's cut.

Brian and Harimore stared at each other in what was plainly amazement.

You see what he can do if he tries! Jim was about to say, when he discovered there was no need. Brian exploded as Harimore stared. "A drawing cut! He used a drawing cut— you saw it yourself, Harry!" he cried.

A drawing cut was where the blade was pulled along the surface it contacted, so as to make a deeper wound. Brian had mentioned it from time to time, but it was never one of the things Brian had attempted to teach Jim.

"I saw," said Harimore. "I still believe he will make the equal of a fighting man only by an Act of God—" he crossed himself "—but I own you were right, Brian—and my Lord Sir James. The makings of a small fighter at least may be there. If you will adventure, Brian, to teach him some simple matters of weaponry, so will I also."

Chapter 10

Cheerfully, Jim left them all and went on his way. Now, finally, for a look at how they were coming with the Nursing Room—also the chance to get some idea of how the people of Malencontri were reacting to this terrifying shadow of plague creeping upon them. He found the place in the servants' quarters which had been chosen—almost certainly by Angie, who knew these precincts much better than he did.

It had already been walled off to make a large separate room—that was what had probably kept Angie awake and up while he slept. She would have wanted to supervise the work closely until it was done.

The door in the new front wall was wide open, and a considerable din was coming from within. Instead of simply walking straight in, he stepped to one side of the door and peered inside. The room reeked of pennyroyal—the herb that fleas did not like.

The men and women at work there had already knocked out a hole for a window in the stone outside wall of the room, but the glass to put in it had not been fetched from the storage room on the Solar floor, where an eye was kept

around the clock on something so precious and expensive—
and, above all, so breakable.

The eight spare beds Malencontri had had been placed in
a row, along with a number of pallets. The single fireplace
that had existed there before this section of the larger room
was walled in was being enlarged to three times its original
size, with a chimney to match. A sort of platform about the
height of the dais in the Great Hall that held the high table—
but about half its circumference—was being built.

But among all this activity was a strangely merry air. To
Jim's surprise, the workers were responding almost as if
what they were preparing for was the wedding dinner that
was to be held at the end of the week. Nobody was sick
yet, seemed to be their attitude, and this break in regular
routine was an occasion for games, practical jokes and general buffoonery.

Jim stopped snooping and strode into the room.

"What is this, a game of some kind?" he roared at them
in his best autocratic, dominating voice.

There was instant silence, instant stillness. Nobody
moved. All faces were completely sober, completely hu-
morless.

But he was not fooled. In spite of their appearance of
being struck dumb and motionless by the mere appearance
of Authority, he knew perfectly well the moment he walked
back out of the door, the joking and general merriness
would be going full-blast again. The cheerful glint of their
eyes gave them away. They knew him too well. Angie
might not spoil the servants as Geronde claimed, but by now
all those at Malencontri knew Jim's bark bore the same
resemblance to his bite as the gentle mouthings of an ador-
ing domestic dog to the driving fangs of a wild wolf.

He walked further into the room.

"Is this all that's been done so far?" he said in the same
hard voice. "We may have to do it all over again!"

He saw the glints go out in a few of the eyes—but not many.

"M'lord," said the Master Stone Mason, whose graying hair, age and authority gave him something of a license to ask questions. " 'Tis true the plague is in London?"

"Yes!" said Jim.

" 'Tis a great distance London is from here."

"Perhaps not to the plague," said Jim. "Last night, escorting the Bishop home, we were attacked by demons, riding on gray rats and carrying lances tipped with diamonds."

Instant reaction on the part of everyone at the word "demons." Clearly the men-at-arms had been following the custom among the staff of taking an unofficial day off after they had returned from a trip, and had made a suitably spine-chilling tale of their adventures.

But Jim went on quickly before Malencontri's Master Stone Mason could hint at other arguments. "What's this?"

He kicked the edge of the platform.

A number of people who were standing on it decided to get off, revealing the fact that it was completely carpentered, but so far had neither paint nor any kind of superstructure on it. It was simply an elevated platform holding a chair, a small table, two busy women and what looked like a sawn-off lower half of a small wine barrel. Sitting in the chair was the Serving Room Mistress, Gwyneth Plyseth. Standing beside her was May Heather, officially her apprentice—though lately May had been acting more like an auxiliary Serving Room Mistress without title.

Jim stepped up on the platform and strode ominously toward them (just in case one or other of them had been exceeding orders—neither he nor Angie had spoken of this sort of structure). Mistress Plyseth got up—awkwardly, because of her arthritis—and curtsied to him. May followed suit. She had grown a good deal more expert in that polite maneuver lately, Jim noticed.

"Sit down, Mistress!" Jim growled at Gwyneth. With

gratitude plain on her face—her joints as always pained her in the fall—she sat. "What is all this?"

He waved his hand in the general direction of platform, barrel-half and the two of them.

"Please you, m'lord," said Gwyneth, " 'tis for the Chief Nurse, and all the things."

"All the things? What things?"

"Oh, a mort of things, m'lord. The pair of terriers from the kennels—"

Jim had to admit to himself that it had never occurred to him that the terriers, kept for following a small prey down into its den, and feisty as the day was long, would be sure death to any surviving rats that followed their noses toward the smell of food in the Nursing Room. But Gwyneth was going on listing what seemed to be innumerable items.

"—more pallets and bedding, fast as we can make or sew them together, a sandbox to reheat the soup that comes from the kitchen for our sick ones—"

"I take it," Jim interrupted, "you're going to be the Chief Nurse here in the Nursing Room?"

"Yes, m'lord, if you can spare me from my duties in the Serving Room for some hours a day—and if I do say it myself, being older and some wiser than any other for the work. May Heather will take over my place either there or here if I'm gone, if sobeit that meets with your approval."

She started to struggle up from her chair to curtsy again.

"Sit!" said Jim, adding as she sank back with a breath of relief, "Just tell me one thing more. What's this barrel for?"

"Why, for the tar, m'lord."

"Tar?"

"Oh yes indeed, m'lord. 'Tis said when they sicken with the plague they get these great swellings upon them, and there's nothing like heat to take your swellings down. To put hot compresses on a whole roomful of sick and keep they compresses warm and in place would take as many nurses as sick. But a great spoonful of hot—well, not too hot—tar put on each swelling would keep the warm on it for some time, nor be like to slip off as a compress would. So we'll keep this barrel warm and ready for each new one as he comes in. All in all, everything will be kept here on this platform, close to hand, and a nurse can call to me from anywhere in the room, and I'll see we have what else is needed."

She beamed up to him, plainly waiting for a word or two of approval.

Jim cleared his throat. The thought of the stricken patients—or at least those among them who would have the buboes, or "swellings" (not all forms of the plague produced them)—and already suffering from those exquisitely painful lumps in groin or armpit—having hot tar poured on them while trying to endure it with the stoicism of the age, was beyond imagination. It robbed him of words temporarily, and left him without any of the quick excuses that usually came so easily to him.

Gwyneth would have to be stopped from trying that barbarous, useless treatment on her patients, but right now he could not think of a way to do it that would not wound her. Well, he could think about it, and maybe Angie would have a suggestion.

He turned back to the room and raised his voice.

"You've all done well!" he told them. "But we need more done, and done faster! Let's get that window in, and the glass in the window—and remember, I want the window to open so we've got fresh air, too. Get back to work now, all of you. I'll have some beer sent over."

The castle staff considered itself above cheering such an announcement, but a strong murmur of gratitude went through the room as he dropped down to floor level and made his exit.

If Angie had only been awake, it would have been useful to find out from her what she had done while he was gone, and what she had intended to do. But if anyone ever needed sleep right now, it was she. Waking her up was unthinkable. It didn't matter. The servants would tell him what she had done to further her plans—or he would simply have to guess. Somewhere not too far off, she seemed to have located a large supply of the pennyroyal. This room reeked with its mintlike, musty-unpleasant smell.

One thing was certain. Running around to see what had been accomplished, the way he had started to do with this visit to the new Nursing Room, was not the way to get things done. The center of command at Malencontri had always been the High Table in the Great Hall—the servants had taught him and Angie that from the beginning. In situations like this, the procedure for him was to seat himself at the High Table and call for conferences with his lieutenants.

Accordingly, he dropped by the Still Room to leave his order for the promised beer, and headed for the Great Hall by the fast route through the servants' quarters. But when he was halfway through the now-empty Serving Room, he heard the sound of women's voices from the area of the High Table. One was Geronde's—sounding rather fierce at the moment—one was the voice of Danielle, and one a voice he did not recognize.

He stopped, irresolute. It was *his* table, of course; and if he merely walked in, looked surprised and then stood hesitating for a moment, the owners of the voices would take the hint and make an excuse to go elsewhere.

But his early training in twentieth-century manners disagreed with the practical purpose for which he needed the table. So he hesitated where he was, and the words from those at the table came clearly to his ears.

". . . they're all alike!" Geronde was saying, with what seemed to be considerable venom. "Dependable as weather in springtime! He makes agreement, this husband-to-be of mine, that I shall pass by Malencontri on my way from Malvern, to ride up to Smythe Castle for a look at my future home with Brian! But, when I get there he has gone and taken a guest of some sort. I ride hard to get back here and find him and his guest—where?"

She paused, evidently to take a breath, and almost snarled the last word.

"*Hunting!*" She took another breath. "Of all things, with a wedding we've both waited years for—hunting! As soon as he's back and I can say a word or two to him, I'll tell him—"

Jim sneezed.

Damn pennyroyal! he thought. *Maybe I'm allergic to it—*

Then he forgot all about allergies.

There had been nothing he could do about the sneeze—no warning at all, and no time to stop it even if he could have. The voices in the Great Hall had fallen suddenly silent.

There was no way out of this situation now. The faster he moved the better.

He strode the last few steps to the Great Hall as noisily as he could, and stopped there suddenly, staring at those at the table as if startled to find them there.

"Forgive me, my ladies," he said, panting discreetly. "I didn't know you were here."

"Nay, forgive me, James," said Geronde. They were all rising. "I suggested we get something solid to eat down here and we got to talking. You haven't seen Brian, I suppose?"

"Just a few minutes past," said Jim. "In the courtyard. He and Sir Harimore had just come from hunting. Just happened to run into them, while setting up things for the plague—and getting things ready for your wedding with Brian."

"Wedding!" muttered Geronde between her teeth. "Oh, forgive me, James. May I name to you Lady Joan Montacute, Countess of Kent. My lady, this is Baron Sir James Eckert, our host."

"Indeed, I guessed it might be so," said Joan. She made

no attempt to give her voice any particularly warm intonation; but the lightness of it, combined with the young-looking Plantagenet features under the blond hair, gave it a quality of friendliness that Jim could not help feeling. "It is an honor and my great pleasure to know you, my lord, but it is clear you have much on your hands at present. We must make haste to withdraw."

And so they did.

Jim seated himself at the table, which still held several plates of foods and part-empty wine cups. A small mouse of a servant—another recent recruit, looking to be about ten or twelve years old—crept out of wherever she had been hiding to stand beside his chair.

"May I fetch you something, Your Lordship?"

"M'lord can do for everyday purposes," said Jim kindly. "Nothing to eat or drink. But get me my squire—you know Theoluf."

"Oh yes, your m'lordship."

Jim sighed internally. She would learn.

"I want him. I also want my Master of Hounds, my Stable Master, and I want Mistress Plyseth of the Serving Room— no, not Mistress Plyseth, she's needed where she is—get me her apprentice, May Heather. May Heather will help you to get used to things here—tell her I said she was to help you."

"Yes, your m'lordship."

"Run along then." She ran.

Who could tell? In twenty years she could turn out to be one of the most valuable members of the staff.

"At your service, m'lord," said Theoluf, appearing.

"Theoluf," Jim said, "what's our strength of men-at-arms right now in the castle—I mean of healthy men?"

"Frank Short's still not full healed, m'lord—of those cuts he got from his fight with the Bishop's armsman—but they're nothing to stop him if he's needed. Counting him, we've got twelve, counting Yves Mortain as chief man-at-arms."

"If the plague gets this far west and word gets out we're plague-free here, there could be a lot of people outside the castle trying to get in. Maybe even neighbors—perhaps men of rank. We're setting up a pavilion outside for a quarantine station, but those of rank and others may demand to come in directly."

"Very true, m'lord."

"They must be refused, Theoluf!"

"Aye, my lord!"

"Now, should we try to get more armsmen while we can still get healthy ones?"

"I like to watch each one a month at least, before I keep him. Have we that time—pardon my plain speaking, my lord?"

"No. I don't think we have."

"Then no, I'd rather not. In the field, maybe. But we've got stout walls to stand behind and servants who've borne steel cap and spear before. I could drill them some on the way they run up the steps to the wall and take their place there, so their caps and spears make them look like better-trained fighters."

"Do that," said Jim. "Now, I may be gone when you have trouble—or sick myself—"

"God forfend, my lord!" Theoluf crossed himself.

"But I may be. How well will you and my lady work together defending the castle? Speak your mind on this."

"I will, my lord. My lady and I have faced attack here—though they were mostly mere brushes—when you were gone. We are of like mind in such a defense. I would rather have her over me than many a belted knight I've known. She is not rash—and that is a thing of value."

"Good."

"Good it is, my lord; and, if I might be so bold, it may well not come to this. Sir Brian or the Master Bowman may be here when you are gone. Also neither Lady Geronde nor Mistress Danielle lacks some experience to command as I would, or better, should any mischance befall me."

"It's good of you to remind me of that—"

Jim broke off in mid-sentence and rose to his feet, seeing Prince Edward was approaching at a swift pace through the Serving Room.

"Your Grace!" said Jim. "I thought you had left us this morning early."

"I had so planned," said Edward brusquely. "But—James, come down from there, will you, and let us walk a ways. I must talk to you."

"Certainly, Your Grace," said Jim, inwardly grinding his teeth at the interruption. "Theoluf, we will continue our talk later. Wait me here."

He stepped down from the dais and walked off with the Prince through the Serving Room, where he now saw his Master of Hounds, his Stable Master and May Heather, with the mouse at her side, also waiting for his attention.

"Damned nonsense, dealing with the routine running of a castle," said the Prince, noticing the direction of his glance, then dismissing the three waiting in the Serving Room as if they did not exist. "But never mind that, James—let us find someplace privy, in which to talk—"

They had passed through the room, and the Prince turned right toward the foot of the stairs that wound up the inside of the tower. There was no one in sight. Edward stopped and turned to Jim, who stopped also.

"You dealt me a shrewd blow yesterday, James," the Prince said. "I do not blame you for being bound by the laws of your order—but it was a shrewd blow, a shrewd blow nonetheless. Where I had asked for help and never doubted it would be forthcoming, there was none—but enough of that. We Plantagenets know how to take misfortune, James—"

Not without a lot of talk about it, thought Jim.

"—So I was determined and ready to take the horse this morning to Tiverton and look elsewhere for what was needed. But last night Joan—the Countess—made a suggestion at which the very saints would marvel. She has great wits for such coils as this. Much better than mine ever were—though I doubt not she would be sadly lost about what to do with an army on the field of battle. Whereas I—but that is not the point here. It was quite simple—so simple. You will go back to Tiverton with me to meet with my father for the first time! You have never met, I understand—having merely written him for permission to rid the land of the evil in the Loathly Tower—and received his gracious agreement back by letter."

He stopped abruptly.

"You do not see the cleverness of that? Neither did I, James, neither did I—at first. But then she explained—" The Prince failed to notice that Jim had clamped his teeth at that mention of his letter to the King. There had never been such a letter, and the story of it had been a complete fabrication on the part of one or more of the ballad singers who went about the land making their living by embellishing the latest news for entertainment. They had thought it a far more heroic reason for such a deed than the mere rescue of the woman Jim intended to marry.

"Well, then," said Edward, "you are long overdue for a royal audience, and with my father nearby, why not now?"

"Why should my meeting him help you?" said Jim, driving to the heart of the matter.

"Why, once you are known by His Majesty, all but near neighbors, guesting back and forth is natural. Further, it will turn out that I discover one of your guests is my old playmate Joan of Kent, for whom I have a fondness. I can then go back and forth between Tiverton and Malencontri frequently. Sir Verweather may come to you when I am not here to tell you of your audience with my father, and on that trip find one of your castle wenches attracts him. He, too, then, will go back and forth as opportunity presents, but never at the time I do so. As there is little to do for the gentlemen of His Majesty's wardrobe at Tiverton, it may often pass that he and I must cross paths as I come and he goes—or otherwise."

Edward stopped and looked at Jim triumphantly.

"And on those crossings," he said, "we will find opportunity to stop and discuss—what we must discuss! What could be wrong with all that?"

Just the whole practical universe! thought Jim savagely. Clearly, Edward did not take the danger of plague seriously. But changing his mind in that would not be done with an impromptu word or two now. At the moment, the best tactic would probably be to pretend to accept this idea—at least until he could talk it over with Angie.

"It's certainly worth considering, Your Grace," he said, "but there may be some necessary difficulties if the plague moves in on us—"

"Come, James!" said Edward. "It will get no further west than London, and if it does, and this plan matures, I give you my word to get you, your wife and ward and the families of your companions, Sir Brian and that archer fellow, his name slips my mind at the moment—something not English—all to safe haven at Tiverton, where Verweather assures me the servants keep things in such a perfect state of cleanliness that no disease could slip past the gates."

He turned to mount the stairs.

"But now I must dress and to horse, if I wish to be back at Tiverton before deep dark."

Chapter 11

Jim returned to the High Table, along the way collecting the three patiently waiting for him in the Warming Room. He sat down at the High Table, beckoning the huntsman to him first.

"That idea of a couple of terriers to take care of any rats that get into the Nursing Room was a good one, Master Huntsman," he said, sitting down. "Whose idea was it?"

"Mine, m'lord. My father was a miller, and we always had terriers around for the rats."

"How many more have we got?"

"None, m'lord. Craving your pardon for saying it, but it was last March I mentioned there was a litter of at least four more new pups at Sir Hubert's for the having."

"Last March there was no plague in England, Master Huntsman." Jim had learned almost never to admit a failing on his part to any of his underlings. Not only didn't they expect it, but it actually made them uncomfortable. They preferred to think of him as always trustworthy, never wrong. But the Master Huntsman was annoyed at Jim for almost never going hunting, and in addition he had strict ideas as to what was proper in the kennel of a castle this size.

"Where can we get some more terriers now, then? Or could we use the hounds instead?"

"No, m'lord. There are no more terriers to be had now, and hounds will chase, of course, but they rats are so nippy on the turns only a terrier can catch them."

"Very well. You can go. Send the Stable Master to me."

"Yes, m'lord," and the Master Huntsman went back to growl among his charges, who all crowded around, licked his face and tried to calm him down.

"Stable Master," said Jim. "We could end up in something like a six-month siege. How are we supplied for fod-
der for the horses?"

"Six months—aye, twelve if necessary—" said the Stable
Master, who was a small, wiry man. "Harvest hay just in
and granary's full."

"Good," said Jim. "Who'd take over at the stables, if
anything—well, if anything took you away from them for
a while?"

"You mean if I was to catch plague, m'lord? I've two
good lads been coming along for some time now. They
could even do shoe-work if the blacksmith was like-taken.
The great thing for stable-work is to be able to get to know
horses—each horse and its own ways, I mean—and both
these have that now. Would m'lord care to look at them?"

"Maybe later," said Jim. "Thank you, Stable Master.
That's all for now."

"Well, May," Jim said, as the last of those who had been
waiting came before the High Table, "and what do you
think of the Nursing Room?"

"I think it both wise and good, m'lord."

"Have you got any opinion—anything you'd say, one
way or another—about how it's being built?"

May looked a little strange for a moment, staring at
him—a split-second only—then answered firmly.

"No, m'lord. None!"

"Good," said Jim. "You know, May, my lady paid you a
great compliment once, speaking to me. She told me that
I'd always get a straight answer from you. You'd always
tell me the exact truth, no matter what it might cost you to
do that."

"I speaks my mind, my lord. Always have."

"I believe that, and so I'm going to ask you a question.
If you can't answer it, or don't want to answer it, that's all
right. But if you have an answer to give me, it might help
with a problem I've got."

"Yes, my lord?"

"What do you think of the Countess of Salisbury—the Fair Maid of Kent, as most of the world still knows her?"

"She is a great lady, my lord."

"But what is she otherwise being a great lady? What sort of person—what sort of woman is she?"

May hesitated, her face screwed up in thought.

"She's no weakling, m'lord. She's a fighter, and not afraid of getting hurt if she chooses wrong. But she's nice, too."

"Nice?"

"Yes, my lord. You know—*nice*."

Jim pondered. Angie had used that same word to describe Joan of Kent, and it was not a word she used often. Now that he stopped to think of it, he had never heard it used by one woman about another, here in this fourteenth-century world—and also come to think of it, he could not remember hearing it used often, if at all, by women of his and Angie's own original world.

What did the word mean to a woman's mind here? Men did not call each other "nice," and if they had, it might well not have been a compliment—as it sounded as if it was, here. Strange . . .

"Well, thank you, May," he said. "You lived up to what my lady said about you. You can go now."

But she hesitated, her eyes searching his face.

"Was what I said any use to you, m'lord?"

"You were a great help."

"Good!" said May, and went off.

Later on he got a chance to ask Angie. By that time, though the late end-of-summer twilight still lingered outside the windows, they were together, back up in the Solar, getting ready for supper down in the Great Hall, and Angie was slept up and awake.

"You said Edward's Joan was 'nice,' " he said to her without working up to the subject. "This afternoon May

Heather used the same word to describe her. What did you and she mean by 'nice'?"

"What May meant by it—" said Angie muffledly through the gown she was pulling over her head. Her face emerged, speaking clearly, "—I've no idea, of course. I just meant 'nice.' "

"That doesn't help me much," said Jim. "I'd like to know if she's somebody who can control the Prince."

"In some ways she probably can. I think so, anyway. But you have to make up your own mind, and you haven't even got to know her yet. Why not? And why do you want her to control the Prince?"

"I don't want to know if she can do it. I want to know how much of what he's doing is her doing. He and the Bishop blow up at each other, she promises he'll be all over it in the next morning—and he is. I tell him I can't let him involve Malencontri and us in what Cumberland could claim was a treasonable plot. He almost blows up again. But the morning after that he shows up reconciled to it, but with a brand-new plan she suggested to him. She sounds more like an experienced con woman than someone 'nice.' "

"What plan?" asked Angie.

"For me to drop everything here and go meet the King at Tiverton." He told her about it in all the detail Edward had given him.

"What a time to ask you to go!"

"I know."

"Particularly with all this plague preparation, to say nothing of the wedding. If her marriage to Brian gets delayed any more, Geronde is going to go up in smoke!"

"She would, too," said Jim, thinking of Geronde.

"You can count on it," Angie said. "I've already had to tell her it's got to be put off at least one more week, and you ought to have seen her! I think for two seconds she was ready to kill me—if she'd had a weapon to hand at the time."

"Another week? I don't blame her. Why that?"

"The plague preparations, for one. Neighbors from all over Somerset will be coming. If we've got everything in place and finished by that time, it'll give them a chance to get used to all of it ahead of time. They'll just tell themselves we're alarmists, or that maybe they ought to start fixing up their own places against the sickness coming this far west—never thinking of the possibility they might be among the people asking to be let into Malencontri, and finding themselves being sent to the qarantine pavilion instead."

"Well, yes, but—"

"All that to be done—plus the fact no one knew the Bishop was going to come by here and bless the chapel, in the first place. But now he's done that, the place has to be cleaned out and set up properly—and we've got to get Geronde's own priest from Malvern to hold Mass after the wedding."

"She doesn't have to have Mass after her marriage on the chapel steps, does she? Most people don't."

"But not when there's one suddenly available, like this— as if the place was blessed specially for the wedding!"

"Never did understand all that fuss over the chapel being unclean," grumbled Jim. "Nobody ever was able to tell me why it should be. It was just saddles, grain and other ordinary stuff that'd been stored in it."

The fuss he spoke of had arisen during and after the period of Sir Hugh de Bois' occupation of Malencontri. As Jim had just said, the chapel, unused, had gradually become a storeroom. It was only later that stories began to transform it into a place of devilish worship and practice—virgins abducted and raped, black arts indulged in and so forth.

But if the arcane filth of the stories had no basis in anything but the imaginations of the countryside, more than a few years of dirt, grime and ordinary filth had undeniably done its work. Jim could believe the wedding would have to be put off to clean that out—on top of the additional labors of preparations against the plague.

"But about the King wanting you—!" said Angie. "If the Prince just left, and if his father wants to see you—come to think of it, he'll want you there almost immediately! Four hours from now Edward could be telling him to expect you . . . Jim—on second thought, you've got to go right away, as soon as you can."

"Right away? After you just finished reminding me of all the things needing to be done here?"

"I can handle them! It'll be that much more impossible for you to go later on. How can you leave if the wedding's just a few days away—or the day it's happening—or for that matter the next five or eight days while most of the guests make a week-long celebration out of it. Kings don't like it when people dawdle about coming when they're summoned! And that's what you've just been, remember? Not invited—summoned!"

"Yes," said Jim, suddenly remembering. "Also, I wouldn't put it past Brian and Harimore to organize a sort of tournament where the two of them could ride against each other to show how it was done properly. Then all the young squires and gentlemen could try some spear-breakings between them."

It was true. The fourteenth century did not lack for ideas when it came to entertaining themselves.

"—And don't forget," whispered Angie as they finally entered the Great Hall, fully and properly dressed. "Get to know Joan for yourself—there she is," she went on, like a mother coaching her small and bashful son, "you're the host—you're supposed to say 'hello' to her!"

"Hello," said Jim, going up to Joan—and checked himself, "which is to say, in the language of the far-away land from which my lady-wife and I come—forgive me for not welcoming you more properly to our small castle, but I only got back late last night, and of course with this news of the plague there were matters I should have seen to myself, had I been here—which required attention desperately. None of which, of course, excuses my not waiting on you until now to offer you all that Malenconti offers and contains—"

She smiled widely, unself-consciously, at him. The smile went well with the fresh, young face under the blond hair. He noticed it made two dimples in her cheeks, one at each corner of her mouth.

He was not someone who usually noticed dimples, and he had almost forgotten that in this historical period the word "fair" meant blond first, and beautiful only second. Joan of Kent seemed to merit both meanings—or was it her voice, the easy charm of her attitude, that was making him think of her as beautiful? Dafydd's wife, Danielle, was an undeniable beauty—and knew it—but somehow, Jim now found himself sure that if she and Joan were side by side, Joan would win hands down—

He came out of his welter of thoughts with a jerk. She was talking to him.

"There is no need for such an elaborate apology, my good Lord Baron. I know as well as you that it is Edward with his special needs that has multiplied your burdens at this time. It is rather for me to apologize for adding to those burdens by being here myself."

"No. Not at all—"

"Come, come, my lord—and may I speak you simply as Sir James, as all else around you seem to do—let us speak plainly to each other."

"Certainly, my lady—"

"And you will address me simply as Lady Joan."

"I will be honored," said Jim, reflecting for the first time that it would indeed be uncomfortable for someone socially sensible to speak formally to all around her when they chatted comfortably among themselves on a casual level, "—and I agree about speaking plainly, too. That always makes things easier for everyone."

Again she smiled, and the dimples were even deeper this time.

"As for His Grace's special needs—"

"Let us agree not to speak of them." It was remarkable the way she could interrupt like that, thought Jim, without seeming to break in rudely. "I came with him, because my Lord Salisbury is in France for four months yet, and Edward needed someone who had faith he could defy Cumberland. What he has spoken to me about his plans, and what he has said to you may be different parts of a whole. If he had wished the two of us to know the whole itself he would have told us so, I am sure. Since he has not—"

For once, it was she who was interrupted. The last two guests due to meet with the rest of them for dinner had finally arrived. The latecomers were Brian and Sir Harimore.

"You are somewhat late, Sir Brian!" said Geronde with a curiously grating undertone to her voice. Discomfort woke in Jim. Evidently the two had not had time to iron out Geronde's upset even yet. Hastily, he spoke to Harimore.

"Sir!" he said. "The Countess Joan of Salisbury has not yet had the chance of having you named to her. Perhaps I might do that now. My lady, may I name to you Sir Harimore Kilinsworth."

Harimore turned for the first time to look squarely at Joan, and a remarkable change took him over as he did so. He straightened up, took three steps toward Joan and bowed—a bow that might have graced an introduction at court, but so distorted by a sudden stiffness of all his body and a certain jerkiness with which it was performed that it became almost a parody of the polite gesture.

When he straightened up, his face had gone bony and grim.

"A great honor to be named to you, m'lady," he said harshly. "I shall treasure the moment in my memory."

Joan did not seem at all put out. She smiled as warmly

at him as she had at Jim. The smile, however, did nothing to soften Harimore's stiffness and grimness.

"It will be only fair, then," Joan said, "that I treasure it, too," she said. "I know of you by reputation as a famous jouster."

"My lady," grated Harimore, "I have had some small success."

"You must tell me about it at dinner. I love to hear of such martial exercises."

A light went on in Jim's mind. Of course, the two must sit together. That would solve two problems at once: where to place each man to best fit in socially; and how to separate Harimore from Brian, so that the table could avoid hearing the two of them talking weapons all evening long—which might well lead to an increase in Geronde's still lively anger.

"I shall look forward to it, my lady," said Harimore, with the demeanor of a knight just told he was about to be tortured.

"And so shall I." Joan glanced at Jim. "So, perhaps, with all of us being here now, our host—"

"By all means!" said Jim. "Oh, my lady, I did not name to you as well Sir Brian Neville Smythe—of the Nevilles of Raby."

"I encountered Sir Brian earlier in the day, and we are now acquainted."

"And," said Jim, looking at those at the table with hard eyes and no lowering of his voice, "Master Archer Dafydd ap Hywel and his wife—"

"I have not yet met Master Dafydd, but I have already had the chance of meeting for a moment only with his *lady* wife—" there was a delicate but precise emphasis on the "lady" in Joan's clear voice. "I will be deeply pleasured to sit at table with the paladin known as the Master of all Master Archers."

"Then," said Jim, relaxing with a feeling of relief, but

with his eyes still holding those of the other guests, "there is no need for further talk. If you will take this chair here at the top of the High Table, Lady Joan . . ."

And they settled themselves to supper.

However, it was not a very successful dinner, though the quality and variety of dishes served, the promptness of service and the best of high formal manners to avoid contention at table tried hard to make it so. Geronde and Brian were plainly still not back on good terms, and the best efforts of Joan of Kent failed to thaw by a degree Sir Harimore, who seemed to grow even more stiff, grim and uncomfortable.

Jim watched him for a long moment as the last of the meat courses was carried off to make room for the desserts, then swiveled his gaze to catch Angie's attention and raised his eyebrows. She answered with a slight shrug of her shoulders, and with a momentary sideways glance directed his wordless question to Brian.

But Brian was not by nature or training accustomed to deciphering facial signals alone in a delicate social situation. He paid no attention to Jim's attempts to catch his eye.

Finally, the unhappy supper came to an end and the women went off together, at Angie's suggestion that the men should be left to talk about theoretically more important matters. This way of considering it hinted at some special, secret reason for the gathering beyond eating— possibly an explanation as to why Gentlemen and Ladies had found themselves sitting down to table side by side with a common archer and his wife . . . on the other hand, under the circumstances—maybe not.

One thing Jim was sure of was that the odd behavior of Sir Harimore would not be discussed—not with Harimore still sitting at the table straight as an arrow, upright and potentially as deadly as that same arrow shot by the Master of all Master Archers from a table's length away. But as the women disappeared toward the stairs leading to the Solar, Harimore gave a barely audible sigh, and very visibly relaxed. He filled his mazer with wine, ignored the water pitcher right beside him and drank deeply.

"Nothing much larger than a rabbit turned up on our hunt this morn," he announced to the table. "In spite of the fact now is still the season for stags. But I have found them strangely scarce elsewhere as well this year. I venture to say none of you—" His eye checked on Dafydd, who had sat quietly through the meal, having no one to talk to but Danielle, or Jim, who was at the far end of the table from him. But then, Dafydd had never been the talkative sort, anyway.

"—Venture none of you all had much luck this season," Harimore wound up. "Was that not so for you, Sir Brian?"

"What? Oh, stags. More or less," jerked out Brian, whose head was apparently full of things he had not thought of in time to say to Geronde.

"Doubtless, it is all this rain that is responsible," said Harimore, taking another great swallow of wine and stretching out his legs under the table while leaning back in his chair. "It meseems a matter of—"

He became visibly aware, suddenly, that the other three men at the table were watching him intently, none of them drinking, and showing no indication of picking up the conversation. His face stiffened again.

"Gentlemen—" he cleared his throat "—my lord, if you and these others would be kind enough to forgive me, I find myself taken by an old malady for which the only remedy is to lie down. It comes on suddenly and unexpectedly, as you see. So, if you will graciously excuse my leaving you at this time, I would appreciate it."

Polite murmurs of agreement came from the rest at the table. Harimore rose to his feet, looking indeed somewhat wobbly and pale, descended from the dias and walked off unsteadily in the direction of the tower stairs.

"Strange," said Brian, looking at the corner around which Harimore had vanished. "In a lesser man I would have said he was overcome with taking his wine too quickly."

"I believe," said Dafydd, speaking for the first time, but in a courtly voice and with no tinge of deference, "the noble knight may be one of those uncomfortable with women."

"Uncomfortable with women?" Brian stared at Dafydd, then frowned darkly. "Dafydd, I'll have you know Sir Harimore cares—"

"You mistake me, Sir Brian," said Dafydd, "indeed I would believe that he cares for women very much. But the more he cares the more he is afflicted by the curse of not being sure how he should act and speak in front of them—except in certain instances wherein he has learned what to say and do. In all else, he knows not what to do beyond making great show of not caring."

Ah? said the faces of the others.

"But in truth," Dafydd went on, "the greater his care for a woman, the greater his show of uncaring—to the point where he might seem offensive. I am afraid he has been greatly taken by the Countess."

"Indeed?" said Brian. "I have never seen or heard of such a thing. What makes you so sure your thoughts are right?"

"I have seen at least two other gentlemen so afflicted—and one lady."

"A lady?" Brian stared.

"With her, of course, it was different. She wished much for a gentleman who would care for her, but feared all men so greatly, she would never adventure even a close friendship with anyone not a woman. A sad matter."

"James?" said Brian. "Were you aware of such things—and what will cure them?"

"I've run into one or two," said Jim, stoutly backing Dafydd, "but I've never seen a man or woman as unhappy with that curse as Sir Harimore."

"What can be done for Sir Harimore, then, James? He is a highly respected knight and debater with all weapons—but I would see him freed of this strange curse if I could."

"If you mean a magical cure, Brian, there's none I know of," Jim said. "He may only pray to be freed."

"I would not say otherwise," put in Dafydd. "Yet, there are forms of manners in speaking with a lady in which he might avoid uncertainty; and in that way, with practice come to be more at his ease. He could practice easy conversation with a number of ladies until such talk comes naturally to him—it is no different than practicing with bow at a mark, or practice with any weapon. In royal courts, such as the one I have some familiarity with, many such conversations take place as a natural course of things. It only requires the courage to begin."

"I will go surely for his courage," Brian said. Dafydd said nothing.

"I think Dafydd was speaking of another kind of courage," said Jim.

"Nonetheless, if it would please you, Sir Brian," said Dafydd, getting to his feet, "I do not know if he would listen—I am not a man of great estate or of persuasion, look you— but if you think it might aid him, I would venture to ask his permission to speak him on the subject, now."

"Do you think now is the proper time?" said Brian. For while Harimore was a fellow knight and a respected competitor, Dafydd had fought side by side with Brian on several occasions since the assault on the Loathly Tower, some years back now. There was no question where Brian's loyalty lay if it came to a choice between the two men. Furthermore, Harimore had no idea—because Dafydd had asked his friends to keep his secret—that Dafydd was a Prince in his ancestral Kingdom of the Drowned Land, and so Harimore might well dismiss any approach by the bowman offhand.

"Sir Harimore is also among the most skilled in knightly weapons of all I know—except perhaps Chandos," Brian added. "And while no one can touch you with bow and

arrow . . . also he is not likely to be in the best of temper at
the moment—"

"Be not concerned, Brian," said Dafydd, leaving the dais
in the same direction in which Harimore had departed.
"While not a man of great persuasion, as I said, I have some
small skill of words. Our talk should not lead to anything
more than talk, and as we all know, the best time to explain
to a rider what he did wrong is just after his fall from his
horse."

He also walked off, tall and as self-contained as usual,
and vanished behind the corner beyond which the steps of
the tower began.

There was an extended moment of silence at the table in
the Great Hall.

"This is not the place for any further discussion on such
a matter," said Brian to Jim. "And, since supper is now over,
I, for one, will beg forgivess. My Lady Geronde will be
with the other ladies in the Solar—I have not had a chance
to say two words of ex—that is, two words to her—since
she got back here. Come, James, let us go up to my room
where we can sit close and talk as friends should."

At this none-too-gentle hint, delivered in Brian's usual
straightforward fashion, Jim rose when he did.

Chapter 12

ın honor of their status as the soon-to-be newly wedded
couple, Brian and Geronde had had Malencontri's largest
spare bedroom set aside for them by Jim and Angie. At least
in part this had been done with an eye to the number of
guests who would want to crowd in after them when it came
time for them to go to bed on their wedding night.

Angie had been all for ruling out this raucous crowd who
would seek to follow the newlyweds up the stairs to be

witnesses at their bedding. Jim had finally managed to convince her that in fact Brian and Geronde would want those followers along—even though the curtains around the bed would be drawn shut, those people would be the required legal witnesses to testify to the consummation of the marriage vows, which was necessary to make the marriage legal in the eyes of the Church.

With the women who had left the table of course in the Solar now, as Brian had suggested, Brian's room on the floor just below the Solar should be empty. Brian and Jim reached the door—unlocked, of course, like every other bedroom door in the castle—and Brian pushed it open and led the way in . . . and they both stopped.

Geronde was there, after all—alone, standing beside one of the arrow slits that looked out on the same area Jim had seen before sunup that morning. She turned her face to them, then, and it was a face Jim had never seen on her before.

"Geronde!" Brian said, walking toward her. "We—I thought you would be with the other ladies, talking in the Solar."

She held up a forbidding hand, and he stopped. They were only a single long step from each other, but now the distance was marked.

"Forgive me, my lord," she said, in a curiously harsh voice, "had I known you might wish the use of this chamber—"

"It but happened James and I were left, the two of us, alone at the High Table and were merely seeking some other place to talk."

"No doubt. As men talk. I have noticed, my lord, your partiality for the conversation of men all your life, over that of women—or at least of the woman who is myself. But I shall vacate this room immediately for your use. Excuse me—"

"Geronde!" said Brian. "Wait—there is no reason the

three of us cannot sit and talk. James and I had nothing in mind for conversation such as one wanders into after a good dinner. Please . . . join us."

"You are too kind, Sir Brian. But I am sure my presence would only be an intrusion. . . ."

It was an exquisitely painful moment for all of them, including Jim.

"No, I beg you. James, I'm sure, would be not averse to leaving the two of us to ourselves—" Brian suddenly exploded into his full roar—"Damn it, Geronde, what's wrong? Why won't you tell me?"

"Our wedding is put off at least a week!" shouted Geronde. "A lifetime of working, and loving and waiting—I break my neck only to get to Smythe Castle and not find you there so we can go over the grounds together and I can plan how to make the lands pay! And you—you are down here! Out without a care in the world—hunting!"

Without warning, she suddenly hurled herself into his arms, and Jim saw tears rolling down her face, over the ugly scar left by the knife of Sir Hugh de Bois.

"How could you *do* this to me?" she cried.

Jim slipped discreetly out the door, shutting it softly behind him.

Going away along the curving corridor with the sweat cooling on his face, he swallowed, thinking of those tears. He had never thought of Geronde as someone who could cry. This was the woman who had spat in Sir Hugh's face when he had slashed that left cheek and threatened more of the same.

He came to a halt in the corridor. Once again, he had had Carolinus at his side and forgotten to ask the Mage if there was not some magic that would take away that scar completely—it was beyond his own apprentice powers—leaving Geronde untouched and beautiful, for she, too, was beautiful in a delicate, fine-boned way. He had sworn to himself he would get that scar healed if he could before her wedding to Brian.

"Hell's bells!" he told himself. He would do it yet. He would do it now—whatever Carolinus was busy with.

"Carolinus!" he said loudly—and his voice rang enormously, strangely, off the blank stone walls, floor and ceiling of the curving corridor, without as much as an arrow slit on its sheer outer side, forty feet to the ground.

"What is it?" said Carolinus, appearing immediately.

"Sorry to interrupt you—"

"Sorry to *interrupt* me—" began Carolinus, his gray eyebrows flying up his forehead and his voice rising. "Did it ever strike you I might be involved in—well, never mind what I was involved in. You do not call me unless it's an emergency! One you can't handle!"

"Well, it is something I can't handle," said Jim awkwardly. "It's about a scar on someone's face I don't know how to take off, magically."

"A scar? Already? Who do you know with a scar?"

"The same person you do!" said Jim, nettled as he so often and easily was by Carolinus' attitude. "Geronde has one."

"Hmm," said Carolinus, "so she has."

Jim stared at him.

"You never paid any attention to it?" he said.

"I—well, of course I noticed. It's been there . . ."

"Some years," said Jim harshly.

"Some years. Well, there you are. Of course I noticed, but with so many other desperate things, this and that on my mind . . ." Carolinus' eyes avoided Jim's and his voice descended into an unintelligible mumble. "But why call me now, of all times?" he wound up, his voice stiffening—but he still avoided Jim's eyes.

"I think we both forgot," said Jim, feeling much better the moment he had admitted it. "But you see there's that ugly scar spoiling her face, and she's just about to be married. . . ."

"Oh, yes," said Carolinus in more normal tones. His eyes came up to meet Jim's. "Then, of course—just how old is this scar?"

"She was cut by Sir Hugh de Bois right after Angie and I got here. Four? No, five years ago."

"Then I can do nothing with it. Fresh wounds you can handle yourself, of course. But a scar, particularly an old one, is part of the living flesh around it. Maybe a specialist . . . there must be some Magickian in the Collegiate who's taken an interest in working with older wounds, or other disfigurements. Let me inquire."

"Time's short," said Jim.

"How short?"

"A little over a week now, I think," said Jim. "It *was* to be three days away, but it may be put off a bit."

"Thank all good spirits!" said Carolinus. "Well, I'll do the best I can—"

"Any idea what it'll cost?" asked Jim uneasily, remembering the high price he had paid for the white silk he and Angie had given the Bishop, and which Carolinus had got from some Far Eastern Magickian intermediary. It was the first time he had become uneasily aware of the soaring amounts of magical energy changing hands in any deal between Magickians.

Usually the supplying Magickian had a monopoly on what was wanted and intended to make the most of it.

"Never mind that. You've only got an apprentice's resources, and I forgot, too," said Carolinus, vanishing.

Jim went on toward the tower stairs, feeling somewhat lighter of heart—but only somewhat. If Carolinus could have handled it, removing the scar would have been a great deal easier. Now it was surrounded by question. Could Carolinus find the specialist? And if he found him, could the specialist do it—above all, could he be found and do it in time?

But in any case it was out of Jim's hands now. He had reached the stairs and the choice. Up or down? Upstairs, the odds were the other women were still in the Solar. Downstairs one flight was the room of Sir Harimore, but he might not be welcoming visitors just now, and if Dafydd was with him, then the two would be best left alone together for what good Dafydd's words would do him—if Harimore listened to them at all, that was.

In the end Jim decided to return to his command post at the now abandoned High Table and get a status report of how work was progressing from those who had been put in charge of the various jobs of preparing against the plague. By the time he had dealt with that, it would be late enough so he could reasonably go up to the Solar, and by the simple fact of appearing there, hint that it was time for the chamber to abandon its present role as a salon and return to the more private one of being his and Angie's bedroom.

It was a clever thought and he felt rather pleased with it until, halfway down the stairs, his conscience accused him. Angie had little enough opportunity at the company of other women. It was rare that Malencontri held at the same time so many other talkable-to females. The rigid rules of rank of this historic period dictated that it would not do for her to make close friends with those of lower class. In any case, her position as Chatelaine of Malencontri made it unwise for her do anything that would give the appearance of favoring one servant more than another among the staff.

Some years of early-to-bed and early-to-rise habit had made him ready to fold up much earlier than he had once been used to. He came to the bottom of the stairs and plodded on, undecided, to the Great Hall. Perhaps he would just sit there until Angie came to fetch him. It was usually the wives on these occasions who had to look for, find and drag their more-or-less drunken husbands off to bed.

The Great Hall was just as he had expected: clean, with fires blazing in all of its three large fireplaces, and a fresh, white tablecloth on the table, with a few dishes of cold finger-foods at one end, together with a couple of large pitchers of wine, another of water, and half a dozen ordinary wine cups. It was, of course, now doing duty as a *table dormant:* a twenty-four-hour source of food and drink if any guest woke hungry or thirsty in the night, or if some late-comer should arrive, needing sustenance. True, the gates were closed, but this castle was the home of a Magickian and anything could happen.

A whole castle, Jim said to himself, sitting and staring at the far end of the table, with its food and wine—neither of which attracted him. *Here I've got a whole castle with no place in it for me to lie down or no one to talk to. . . .*

He woke up suddenly to the fact he had been sitting here for several minutes and no one had come to see what he wanted—which was unnatural. There was supposed to be someone on Serving Room duty night and day.

Normally there would be a man-at-arms and a servant outside any room he was in, and he could not go out without the word being passed that he was out and about. But the last room he had been in was Brian and Geronde's, and evidently no armsman or servant had been posted there yet.

Still, it was odd.

He got up, descended from the dais and walked into the Serving Room. At first he thought it was deserted, and then he discovered the mouse, curled up asleep in the little niche between the smaller stove and the wardrobe holding the mazers and other tableware. A warm spot—both stoves were banked for the night, ready to be fired up if serious heating of food was required. He stood for a moment looking down at her, so completely childlike, tucked into that small space. Something turned over inside him at the thought of waking her up.

But wake her he must. This was no way to pass a night's

Serving Room duty—particularly with guests in the house and a *table dormant*. She was probably not only the newest but the youngest recruit, and the least able to fight for her rights, and so she had been stuck with the job. But it would have gone hard with her had anybody but Angie or himself caught her like this. He would have to wake her.

He leaned over and gently shook one narrow shoulder.

She did not respond for a long minute. Then her eyes opened sleepily, and she looked up at him with no recognition at all for a long second—until they flew wide open and she scrambled to her feet.

"My—my lordship!" She smoothed her short gown, which had been washed to the point that there was no telling what its original color had been.

"Just 'my lord,' " said Jim, still gently. "If you keep calling me 'lordship' the others will make fun of you. Are you all the way awake now?"

"Aye, my lordship—my lord!"

"Well, you run down to the servants' quarters and get either May Heather or the first servant you see—asleep or awake. Tell whoever it is to get to me here as fast as she or he can—don't tell them you were asleep and I woke you."

"No, m'lord."

"Well, get going, then."

He watched her scoot off. He did not feel like going back to the High Table, so he wandered around the Serving Room, looking at the stoves; the other wardrobes, which held everything from clean, neatly folded tablecloths to certain dried or otherwise cookable-on-short-order foods; and racks holding cooking tools and tableware. It really, he decided, packed a great deal into a remarkably small space.

May Heather came out of the passage to the servants' quarters, looking as if she had been up for some time. The mouse tagged along behind her.

"M'lord?" said May.

"May! There you are!" he said, as if she had just materialized out of thin air with the unexpected suddenness of Carolinus. "I can't have this. This won't do at all—particularly with guests in the house—" He pointed toward the mouse who had started to dodge behind May, then checked herself just in time. "She's far too inexperienced and too young for night duty alone in the Serving Room."

"Certainly, my lord," said May. "But when I was her age, I—"

"How old are you now, May?"

"Thirteen, please m'lord."

"And how old is she?"

"I don't know," May turned to the mouse. "What years have you, Lise?"

"Don't know," said the mouse, shrinking. Did this question mean she might be too young to have a job in the castle? "Please m'lord, please mistress. Maybe eleven years?"

"At eleven you were half a stone more than she is, May, and already able to give Tom Kitchen a hard fight. Can you imagine Lise doing that? And already you're practically Mistress Plyseth's right hand."

" 'Tis only because of her knees and the fall damp, m'lord."

"Nonetheless," said Jim, "we aren't all made alike. I'm giving you an order, May. I want you—you personally—to keep an eye on Lise here. Don't let the others bully her—"

"Got to have some of that in life, m'lord."

"You know what I mean." He turned on Lise. "If you were named for Serving Room night duty, you were supposed to be let sleep during the day. When you tried to sleep, did others keep waking you?"

"I—" Lise glanced at May.

"Tell m'lord!" ordered May.

"Well, yes they did, m'lord—a little," said Lise, glancing uneasily at May.

"What did they do? Throw cold water on you? Put things on your pallet so you'd roll over in them and wake up? Did they try to make you drink extra beer when suppertime came?"

"Well, yes, m'lord—and other things," said Lise, now squirming with embarrassment.

"You hear, May?" said Jim. "No more of that until she's settled in here. Tell them it's my orders. It disturbs my magic-making! You don't want that happening, do you— either of you?"

He glowered at them.

"Oh, no, my lord" they both said, in perfect chorus and perfect sincerity.

"Then that's settled," said Jim. "And, May, teach her how to fight while you're at it. Lise, you take a nap here in the Serving Room for the moment." As he spoke, he walked back toward the High Table, with May Heather, perforce, following.

"Now, May," Jim went on, "who's in charge of setting up the pavilion for the quarantine place outside the gates? I want to talk to him. Now!"

"The carpenter, m'lord," said May, hesitantly. The Master Carpenter was one of the civilian officers of the castle—a somewhat crotchety old man, and miles above May in the hierarchy of the civilian castle staff. "But I doubt not he's been asleep these three hours past."

"Now, my lord," came the voice of Angie, approaching behind him, "don't go waking up Master Carpenter at this hour after one of the hardest days he's had in years. All my guests are gone from the Solar, and it's time we two were getting some rest for tomorrow."

"What's tomorrow?" asked Jim, turning to see her approaching from the direction of the corner next to the tower stairs.

"Tell you when we get upstairs," said Angie. "May, handle it anyway you want, but make sure someone's on duty in the Serving Room—and take that child in there now off to her pallet before she falls over sideways."

Chapter 13

" . . . It wasn't Lise's fault," Jim finished explaining. He was already in bed, watching Angie go through her last few moves before doing the same. "Because she was little and didn't know the ropes, the older servants were having fun— their idea of fun—picking on her. I just had her bring me May because I wanted May to take care of her until she was able to take care of herself. But what was all that about tomorrow? You said it was going to be a full day."

"Oh, that was mainly to start a rumor among the servants that something even more might be expected of them. They're all going to be big days, even with an added five days to be ready."

She crawled into bed.

"So Geronde's reconciled to waiting another five days?"

"I wouldn't say reconciled—but she knows as well as anyone else that if it's not this weekend, it's got to be on another. That means more time for even more neighbors to get here, and two Masses instead of one—a Sunday Mass as well as the wedding one, since the chapel will be in shape and the priest from Malvern here to celebrate it—not many of our neighbors have household priests, and none locally have anything resembling a chapel. . . . I do have something to tell you."

"Good news or bad?" said Jim, preparing himself for the worst.

"Both, I think," said Angie, wriggling around to get herself into her favorite position under the covers and plumping up her pillow. "There's the matter of this idea of all of us going to Tiverton with you. Geronde wasn't happy about an added wait for the wedding—not happy at all. The only thing is—though I don't think that Geronde suspects it, not knowing as much as you and I do about kings and their courts, it might make her wait even longer than she expects. She thinks it's going to be just a few days so you can have your audience with the King—with the rest of us maybe having to show up once, briefly, so His Majesty can get a look at us."

Jim propped himself up on one elbow to stare down into her face.

"Make it longer? Why? What do you mean?"

"Ah, that's better," said Angie, lying happily still at last in her nest. "Well, you've got to understand it was Joan who came up with the idea, then did the real job of talking Geronde into going along with it. She's a very clever woman, Jim—a *very* clever woman!"

Jim snorted. "All right. But what's this idea you were talking about?"

"The idea of you having an audience with the King, of course. Well, as usual, she first had to talk Edward—young Edward—around to it, and she did that before he left. Since you can't let him bring this Verweather fellow here, he's been fretting about how to get Joan into Tiverton with him, without sending old Edward into one of his rages. You know—"

"I know," said Jim. "The famous Plantagenet temperament and all that. It happens I must know a dozen knights that're just as temperamental, or worse, but they're not royal, so nobody makes a big thing of it. But—the idea?"

"I'm getting to it. Before young Edward left, she pointed out to him that the King had never met you, in spite of giving us Malencontri to hold directly in fief from him, and the coat of arms he gave you, and letting us have dear little Robert as your ward—"

"It's all because of those half-witted ballad singers," growled Jim.

"Well, old Edward's a king and used to being at stage center. . . . Anyway—the point is, he actually was impressed with what you did, and since then he's heard other stories about you, Brian and Dafydd. Joan pointed out to young Edward that Tiverton Castle may have the best service in the world and be safe from the plague, but it's still a far cry from the King's Court in the Tower of London, with intrigues, duels, fresh noble visitors with good-looking young daughters and ladies-in-waiting coming and going, and Cumberland talking to him all the time. At Tiverton the King's only got his servants, and nothing to do but eat, sleep, drink and sign the few papers sent to him by Cumberland. In short, he's probably bored to death, and that's one of the reasons he'd be more ready to make it up with young Edward himself."

"We've had jugglers and dancers and what-all in the way of entertainers showing up here for the celebration of the wedding. I suppose we could send some of them to him."

"Much better than that. You remember he was quite the warrior when he was young. There was the sea battle of Sluys—and for that matter, his *chevauché* into Normandy not too long ago, that ended with the victory at Crécy."

"What is this?" demanded Jim. His right elbow was beginning to ache from bearing all the weight of his upper body. "The water torture of deliberately withheld information? What was her bright idea?"

"That instead of just summoning you—which would only be good for an interview or two—and me, because of course it was perfectly reasonable for you to assume your lady-wife would accompany you—young Edward could bring Brian and Dafydd, with Geronde and Danielle, and he could have the whole team there and hear firsthand stories from all the men who were in it."

"Good God! Right now?"

"Right now," said Angie, "or rather, as soon as young Edward gets back and we hear how his father liked the idea—and, of course, there's the side benefit that, since it would be awkward for you to empty Malencontri of gentlemen and ladies, leaving a Countess of Plantagenet blood all alone there—maybe Joan could come, too. She said old Edward knew her very well and always liked her. I believe her—people always like her, and as a girl she had lots of opportunity to cultivate the goodwill of the King."

"But how about Geronde? Don't tell me she was happy with a plan that could put her wedding off indefinitely—a plan Joan just went ahead with on her own without asking her?"

"She wasn't at first," said Angie. "But Joan—I told you she was clever—had her excuse set up ahead of time. She admitted it was a scheme to get her into Tiverton with young Edward, but pointed out to Geronde that everybody won with this, if it worked and the King liked them all. Brian's got a terrific reputation as a winner of tournaments, but he's never been in a real war. The result is that when war captains are talked about, he isn't even mentioned."

"He was just a little too young for Crécy," said Jim, "and he didn't have the connections to get taken on as a squire by any knight of reputation—they were already loaded with squires from noble houses. There's a reason Chandos, Audley and the rest are all about the same age. You can't make a name as a war captain if there's no war going on when you're the right age to shine in them—anyway, how's this going to help Brian?"

"Why," she said, "if the King meets Brian and takes a liking to him—and I don't know how he can fail—it'd give Brian status at court. Then, if he and Geronde ever want a favor from the King, like we got the wardship of Robert, his chances are good. I think Brian knows more about weapons and their use than anyone else the King's seen in a long time—and remember, Chandos himself called Brian one of the best swords of the kingdom. It's a chance for her husband Geronde can't pass up."

"I see."

"I don't need to point out," she went on, "that it wouldn't hurt you either to make a personal friend of the King—and I can't imagine that not happening when he gets to know you."

"Even if it does," said Jim—he realized that he felt deadly tired, more tired than he could ever remember feeling, "if Cumberland can turn him against his own son, his oldest son, the heir to his throne, Cumberland can turn him against any liking he develops for me. But in any case I don't want him to like me too much. I'm only one promotion from full Magickian, and I've decided to become active in their Collegiate and try to push myself up to a position where I can help steer them on a different course than the one they're on—"

"You didn't tell me that!" said Angie.

"I'll tell you about it—just as soon as we have some time to ourselves. There's no choice in magic—or magicks however you want to pronounce it. It was talking in the dark to Merlin in Lyonesse that made me finally see that. If you stand still, you're done for in the long run. You've got to keep going, and know where you're going—but never mind all that now. The point is, I don't want to get tangled up with the Collegiate *and* the King's court, with all its plots and rivalries."

"Just as soon as you can tell me more about that, you'll do it?"

"The first minute, but for now we're in our own small piece of space—this Solar. Let's forget plagues, and Princes, and Kings and magick and this whole impossible, medieval world. I've got to get some sleep!"

He dropped down from his aching elbow and buried his face in his pillow. He heard Angie say something indistinct, something he could not quite make out—but he was already plunging deep, deep into slumber.

He woke with a start. It was daylight, though it seemed to him that only a second before he had heard Angie's last, incomprehensible words.

He looked around and she was nowhere to be seen. The Solar was ablaze with sunlight; he had slept hours beyond his usual waking time. He raised his voice—it was an effort.

"Ho! Servant here!" he managed to get out of his dry throat.

The door opened a crack. Ellen Cinders, the Room Mistress, put her long, sharp-boned face in.

"Can you make tea?" he demanded.

"I can, please you, m'lord!" said Ellen. "My lady showed me how, some years past, in case of your need. Would you wish one now, then, m'lord?"

"I would. The sooner the better."

"Yes, m'lord. Soon as the water boils." She came in, a hawklike, unusually tall, rawboned, middle-aged figure, with a plump, brown-haired girl in her teens following her, someone Jim did not recognize. Another of the new recruits, of course. The coming wedding might have something to do with that. All the upper ranks among the servants would be busy as bees by this time—as Ellen Cinders probably should have been. Angie must have given her a special order to be on hand for Jim's waking. He added a few more pillows to the one behind his head and sat up.

"—All right! Watch now!" Ellen was saying sharply to the girl. "Watch everything I do and how I do it, so you can do it, too—watch, I say!"

"Yes, Mistress!" said the girl hastily. "I've been watching everything. I have, too!"

She had also been stealing quick glances at Jim sitting up in bed. He and Angie had long since fallen into the medieval habit of sleeping naked, and Jim, sitting up as he was now, had his bare upper body showing above the covers. To see a famous Magickian with no clothes on was something for the girl to tell her relatives about when at last she should be given the time and freedom to visit them.

The tea came. It was hot and sweet, the two elements that had finally brought Jim to accept it as at least something of a substitute for the morning coffee he had once been used to. Under Ellen's direction, the girl brought it to him on a small tray, with Ellen watching like the bird of prey she resembled. The girl curtsied rather clumsily, and backed off.

"If you'll excuse me, m'lord," said Ellen, "there's a mort of work for my people to do, and I needs be with them to get it all done right. Maybe I could go now, then? Lettice will do for you in my stead."

"Certainly," said Jim, though he knew it would not work. The door shut behind Ellen. "So your name's Lettice?"

"Aye so, m'lord." Lettice curtsied. She was having lurid, impossible daydreams of having caught the eye of this great Magickian and Knight at his first glance . . . and him being already there in his bed, with his clothes off. . . .

"How long have you been at Malencontri?"

"Three weeks less a day, please m'lord."

"I hadn't seen you before." In the back of her head, her imagination, he was saying . . . *I command you! Come to me now.* . . .

"I been in the fine rooms here, cleaning and such when just us servants are around, please, m'lord." Greatly daring, she added, "Would m'lord want another cup, now?"

Ellen's tea had not been bad—but it was not a patch on Angie's. Lettice's could only be worse. Besides, he was awake now and felt like getting up.

"No," he said. "Wait outside, of course, so you can hear me call."

Pop went the daydreams.

"Yes, m'lord," said Lettice sadly, going out the door.

He rose and dressed. He was surprised to feel so totally rested and full of energy. The combination woke his usual optimism even more strongly than usual. For some reason he felt more than able to deal with anything the day might throw at him.

He started to order his usual breakfast sent up—then caution laid a hand on him.

"Ho! Servant here!" he called. Lettice put her head in the door. "Do you know who's in charge in the Serving Room right now?"

"No, m'lord."

"Never mind, then. You can go."

"Yes, m'lord." She withdrew.

He picked an apple—good ones were hard to find this fall, with all the rain—from the shelf where Angie stored a small supply of eatables that could keep fairly well, and went out the door, eating it.

"Morning, Adam," he said, munching cheerfully, to the man-at-arms, paired with Lettice on door duty at the Solar.

"Morn, m'lord," said Adam, concealing a grin, for Morn was a good four hours past.

Jim paused and swallowed.

"I'm going down to the Serving Room, Adam."

"Yes, m'lord."

He finished the apple and threw the core out an arrow slit as he went by, regretting the move immediately—he was becoming more of a medieval man all the time. The core would end in the moat. They had been at great pains, he and Angie, to teach the castle staff to keep the moat clean—with only partial success. At least Malencontri did not stink quite so badly as other castles.

He was mulling over how to improve this situation, when two more turns of the stairs around the inside of the tower brought him face-to-face with Harimore, resolutely striding up toward him with a determined face.

They met one step apart—which left Jim looking down into the face of the other knight—but that sort of symbolic gap in their social ranks had never seemed to bother Hari-

more in what little contact Jim had had with him. In a sense
Harimore seemed something like Dafydd, too secure in his
knowledge of his earned position in the world to bow very
deeply to anyone else's.

But in this particular situation there was a difference in
the knight's demeanor Jim had never seen before. His face
was pale with determination, mixed with something that
looked to Jim rather like embarrassment.

"My lord," he said. "I have not had the opportunity
heretofore to make my apology to you—a regrettable thing
in a guest. You will remember last Christmas at the Earl's
celebration of that holy time, it happened that we spoke
briefly, and I saw fit—to my shame—to make some personal remarks to you about the way you wore your sword
and such. I was aware at that time of your being a Magickian, but took you for one who merely eked out little knowledge of arms with some equally small knowledge of
magick. I have since learned—not merely from Sir Brian,
but others—that indeed you are a true Magickian, and one
of great skill and accomplishment. It was unthinkable that
I so took the attitude I did."

"Well, it's good of you to tell me all this—" Jim began.

"Pray, hear me out. I honor over all any man who cares
for one art above all others. For a Mage it is understandable
that, if he must carry and use arms, he may not show quite
that care and style with them that another might think he
should. He has plainly given all to his first and chosen art,
but wishes it plain that he is a gentleman and will defend
himself. Consequently, in such a rare gentleman as yourself,
a certain unpolished manner of carrying and using weapons
is entirely permissible, and should be understandable.
Whereas, in my eyes, at least, if a man only plays with two
arts, but expects a name in both, it would not be."

He paused, but before Jim could speak, went on.

"Consequently, I do crave your gentle and gracious forgiveness for my early words, and I will quite understand if

you would rather I left your castle, making such excuses to others as will keep this whole matter privy between the two of us."

Jim winced internally. Harimore's face was looking even more bony than usual, and he was breathing harder than someone in his superb physical shape should, after merely climbing the tower steps. Also, his last words had all the ring of a prepared speech.

He did not want Harimore to leave—particularly if trailing excuses which must clearly ring false to the ears of the other guests—but most of all in Brian's. Brian would be the first to feel that matters were not right, to read Harimore's emotional state more intuitively and correctly—and the first to come and ask Jim what he knew about the sudden departure. Brian's own honor could be at stake here. He was the one who had introduced Harimore to Malencontri—in effect, according to the manners of the day, guaranteeing him to be a gentleman worthy of acceptance.

If Harimore for some reason turned out not to be so, Brian was responsible. Or, if someone else in the castle had offended him, that offense automatically also became the concern of Brian.

"Sir Harimore," said Jim, with all the warmth he could muster, "I can't tell you how warmed I am, by not only your understanding of the state of one who must act both as Magickian and Knight, but the sensitive way in which you have told me of it. Your apology, of course, is as unnecessary as it is gentlemanly to one like myself who has often been offended by the clumsy misunderstanding of my necessary concern with magic. Give me your hand, my dear Sir, and I pray you, do not think of leaving for any reason other than your own desire to be gone!"

"Hah!" said Harimore—that handy single syllable used by the gentlemanly class (and a good share of the gentlewomanly one as well) to express the otherwise not easily expressible. In this case Jim suspected both bafflement and relief. Harimore's hand in Jim's was as hard as a rock, and a sudden realization of what the apology had cost him suddenly occurred to Jim. Harimore had made this offer to leave in spite of knowing it could take him out of sight and sound of Joan of Kent, who, if Dafydd was right, had possibly stolen Harimore's heart away. *This man would boil himself in oil on a point of honor,* Jim told himself.

Their handshake ended, the topic of conversation was now past and sealed, and both men hurried on in their original directions of travel, relieved to have the matter over with.

In Jim's case, his goal was still the Serving Room and whatever was best and available in the way of breakfast. But rounding the corner that would have brought him into it, he literally ran into Angie, coming just as fast from the opposite direction.

"Are you all right?" he asked anxiously, after catching her from falling.

"Fine," gasped Angie. "Battered and bruised, of course. You're like hitting a stone wall nowadays. But never mind that. The Prince is looking for you."

"The Prince!" Jim stared at her. "He can't be! He'd have to have ridden out of Tiverton at three o'clock in the morning!"

"Maybe he did," said Angie.

Chapter 14

"—He's in the Great Hall," said Angie, "getting something to eat."

"Eat," echoed Jim, his mouth beginning to water at the word.

"And he wants to speak to you urgently," she said. "Urgently and privately. You'd better take him up to the Solar.

It'll be cleaned and the bed made up by now."

Jim thought of a High Table already laden with food.

"That fast? Anyway, the Solar tempts him to talk too long," he said firmly. "I'll try and find out what he wants first. Pass the word to the staff—no listening in on pain of Magickal Penalty."

"Don't eat too much yourself," said Angie. "Dinner's in three hours."

He ignored the implications of that, already heading toward the Great Hall. Sure enough, he found young Edward there, stuffing himself on pastries and cold beef, and washing it all down, of course, with wine.

"James!" he said with his mouth full, then swallowed. "They found you speedily. Good!"

"I was on my way here for a bite," said Jim, helping himself to pastries, beef and wine.

"Mph!" said Edward, his mouth too full for more extended conversation.

"Mhmph!" said Jim, nodding his head vigorously while in the same condition.

Finally, Edward gave over eating, took a last swallow of wine, and sat back in his chair.

"Hah!" he said. "No, no, James. I pray you, continue to break your fast."

"I've had all I can hold, Your Grace," said Jim, also sitting back. "You must have been in the saddle a good three or four hours before daybreak to get here this early in the day."

"And so I was. Time was of the essence—strike while the iron is hot, as they say. My father has always been of a less than good humor on waking—though later in the day he becomes merry enough—under ordinary circumstances. There was a chance, though only a slight one, that he might have rethought his invitation. But I was gone before his eyes could be open. Great success, James. All are summoned."

"All?" said Jim. "Summoned?"

"To Tiverton, to audience with your King—but I take you by surprise, James. You know nothing of this." The Prince laughed. "The Countess is a sly one, James, her wits forever at work, and this time she has come up with a ruse that has great possibilities for us all."

"As a matter of fact, Your Grace, I do know about it. At least about the plan for you to speak to the King. So it went well, did it? I was only surprised to hear you say all were invited. You do mean—everyone?"

"I do mean all, even that stiff fellow—though I understand he is a more than ordinary man of his hands, and like Brian a winner of tournaments and such. My father was in somewhat of more than ordinarily . . . cheerful . . . mood last eve when he spoke of whom he would care to see. All gentlemen and ladies presently beneath your roof—this, you see, includes Joan—that is, the Countess. I bear his command to you all to present yourself to him at Tiverton without further delay."

"Remarkable!" Jim said automatically, his mind spinning with the possibilities that immediately presented themselves, now that the trip was to be certain.

"Is it not?" said Edward, with well-fed self-satisfaction. "I can think of no one else who could have accomplished it. He is my father, and in my way I know him better than any other Christian soul—though it was only a matter of talking you all up and then choosing the right moment to ask which of you he wished most to see."

"Not a small thing at all, Your Grace," said Jim, still automatically. "We will be overjoyed, all of us, I'm sure, to obey the King's command." But now his mind was beginning to work to some purpose. "We can come in a body in ten days or so, as soon as the wedding is over."

"Ten days!" Edward suddenly sat rod-stiff upright in his chair. "No, no! Two days! Three at the outside! The King summons you, man! What is this nonsense of some wedding?"

"I assumed Your Grace knew—that the Countess would have mentioned it. The Lady Geronde is to be wed to Sir Brian, and they've both overcome years of troubles since they were playmates as children and first fell in love—just as you and the Countess knew each other as children, and now the moment's come. It'd be cruel to delay them any longer."

Jim had gambled on that last bit about Edward and Joan as children. Angie had not told him that part of their lives had gone exactly as it had gone in the history of the world they had come from—but his graduate studies as a medievalist had made him well acquainted with what the books had to tell him. Not to have it the same here as in the histories of his world would have skewed the present situation in this older England to the point where some fairly large mends would have had to be made—and there was no sign of any such.

"Cruel be—" Edward caught himself. "Ten days is absolutely beyond all question, James—particularly that much of a delay for such a reason. If a wedding they must have, they can have it at Tiverton, with the honor of the King's blessing and presence. Tell them that—I vow they will leap at the chance! Then let us hear no more of it."

"Much as I would like to ease your mind, Your Grace," said Jim cautiously. "The matter of Holy Church enters into the place of the wedding. You recall the Bishop of Bath and Wells from your previous visit I'm sure—"

"The overweening prelate—" Once more the Prince checked himself in the nick of time. "What has he to do with this?"

"Well, you see," said Jim, "the banns were read, as you know is customary, at Malvern Castle, the home of the bride-to-be. But a fire so damaged the chapel there that it was unsafe to hold the ceremony there, to say nothing of a following Mass which was planned. So it was decided to hold it here at Malencontri, instead."

"Joan said something of this. . . ." muttered Edward.

"Unfortunately, though, the chapel here at Malencontri had been mistreated by a previous owner—not only in common ways but with certain unholy activities which made the chapel unclean for any Churchly use—"

The Prince absently crossed himself.

"—and would have been useless as a substitute if that same good Bishop of Bath and Wells had not come to Malencontri and not only cleaned and blessed the chapel but gave the Lady Geronde his permission to reread the banns for a marriage at a place not her home. So now the Church is somewhat concerned with the marriage."

"Hah!"

"You have met the Bishop," Jim went on, "and you'll be as capable as I am to judge of his reaction to the idea of a second removal of the wedding and Mass—let alone a third reading of the banns."

"Only too well, James!" said Edward. "Only too well! And while I, myself, am not adverse to dealing with that Bishop on the matter, there is my father's attitude to Holy Church to be considered, he having some little argument on other points with Her at the moment. . . ."

Edward abruptly got up from his chair, turned and paced along the narrow foot-space on the the dais behind the side of the table.

"Well, James," he said sharply, turning again and pacing back to look down on Jim. "What are we to do?"

Jim got hastily to his feet. In the narrow space behind the chairs it was a little ridiculous, the two of them standing face-to-face to talk. But he could not in manners sit while the Prince stood.

"It is indeed a problem, Your Grace," he said. "What complicates it is the matter of the wedding being put off twice already—otherwise I might suggest we all make our visit to Tiverton before the wedding. But since the banns have been read for the second time, and the wedding date itself is now hard set and less than a week away—"

"James!" said the Prince sharply. "I did not ask you to rehearse for mc the difficulties that seem to make obedience to a royal command a laggard matter, if not impossible. I looked to you to tell me what *will* make it possible. As a councilor, you leave much to be desired."

"Of course," said Jim. "Pray forgive me, Your Grace. It is just the shortness of time between now and the wedding that preys on my mind. A visit to the King, of course, can hardly seem courteous if—counting the time to ride there and back with baggage—it could only make possible a stay for a mere three days and nights—"

"True," said Edward grimly. "A stay of only three days is unthinkably short. Impossible."

"So I thought myself, Your Grace," said Jim. "Only to be considered if there was some powerful reason—or person, such as the Earl of Cumberland—who could convince the King the visit had to be that short."

"Are you mad, James?" said Edward.

His face had hardened at the moment of Jim's mention of Cumberland's name.

"It may be true that Cumberland can, upon occasion, make black seem white to my father," the Prince went on. "But he is not the only one—nor the best at achieving that. You should understand that, James!"

"I crave the gentleness of your forgiveness, Your Grace. Out in the country here as we are—"

"Naturally. You have forgotten who I am and the fact that I am now gaining my father's ear in some respects. The problems of the Bishop, the banns and so forth—if *I* explain them to him, together with other perfectly reasonable reasons which may occur to me between now and when *I* talk to him—plus a promise of a quick return of his guests after the wedding—yes, *I* could arrange the visit for as short a time as that. Even better, when you and the others leave at the end of three days, the Countess could stay to console and amuse him, thus achieving at least one of our ends. My father has always had a strong liking for her."

"Indeed, Your Grace," Jim said, making a real effort to have admiration sound in his voice. "You have solved the problem yourself—and with a solution only possible because of who you are."

"I'm glad you see that, James," said Edward. "Never underestimate one such as myself. The skills of a war captain apply to much of human life. It is our duty and skill to take a shard of a thought and make a full battleplan of it."

"Yes, Your Grace."

"Well, then," said Edward, good humor completely restored to his face and voice. "I must take a small nap now, because of my early start from Tiverton, and meanwhile you can inform the others of my decision that they make a three-day visit before their wedding weekend. Then I will stay the night and start out fresh tomorrow morning to tell my father—or rather, on second thought, I may delay and make the trip with the rest of you tomorrow. He can hardly argue with their coming if they are already within gates where he is now staying."

Cheerfully, the Prince turned, stepped down from the dais and went off in the direction of the tower stairs. Jim watched him around the corner and out of sight, and then raised his voice in the direction of the Serving Room.

"Ho!" he shouted. "Servant here!"

There was no immediate scurry of feet on the stone floor, no appearance of what he had called for. He took a moment to glance once more toward the corner that hid the tower stairs, and listened. But there was no sound in the silence of anyone going up or down. This whole area of the castle seemed to have become deserted.

It was probably the best of signs—meaning everybody was busy as a beaver at something to do to get the castle into protective shape against the plague. But it gave him a sort of ghostly feeling, along with more than a slight touch of unreasonable suspicion. Dammit, when the lord of a castle shouted, things were supposed to happen.

"May I be of service, m'lord?"

They were the right words, but the wrong voice. He jerked his head back to see Angie standing by the dais, grinning up at him. He took a long step down from the stair and confronted her.

"What's up?" he demanded. "I call for a servant and I get you."

"Please, m'lord," she said, still grinning, "but there was no other servant in the Serving Room, so I came. But if I displease m'lord—"

"Come on now, Angie! Stop this! Where's everyone—working on plague preparations, I suppose—but what were you still doing there if there were no servants to direct?"

Angie sobered up.

"Of course they're all working—every one—and the reason I was standing in the Serving Room was to listen to what you and Edward had to say to each other."

"You heard?"

"The whole thing, from the minute you showed up!"

"But after you told me the Prince was here, I thought you were off to oversee—something!"

"True," she said. "I'd been out to look at how the pavilion was going up. Carpenter said he needed more men to handle the heavy work. So I went to the Nursing Room to send out some of the men working there, and then the Prince arrived—and I was heading up to tell you when we met."

"Well, at least I don't have to tell you about what the Prince said. Now the question is getting everyone ready for this trip."

"We'd better divide up the people we talk to—things are complicated enough around here right now without both of us talking to the same people and getting our wires crossed. I'll do the talking to Geronde—that's a full-time job by itself, right now—and you talk to Brian."

"At least I got something to eat," Jim said.

"You *and* the Prince," she said. "The way he was wolfing things down, I thought he'd be full in a matter of minutes, but he fooled me. The capacity of these people is unbelievable—"

"So's ours. We live in fifty-degree temperatures and all kinds of weather. We miss meals and need to make them up—anyway, the point is you stayed and heard everything," Jim said.

"As I told you in the beginning." Her voice softened. "You did a beautiful job of talking to him, Jim. That boy's got a swelled head. He's nowhere near being considered a war captain by any of the real ones. At Poitiers he had Chandos and others holding his hand."

"Sure—but he was only sixteen years old, then. That swelled head is really an insistence on the kind of respect he should have as heir-apparent to the throne—and almost nobody who counts gives him that, what with Cumberland doing his best to destroy his reputation and the King not listening. Anyway, you heard it all; we leave for Tiverton day after tomorrow—that'll put us back on the Thursday before the wedding weekend."

"Geronde is going to love this!" said Angie.

"Come down hard on the advantage of the King getting to know Brian personally."

"That tune's getting a little old. By rights, both she and I should be spending all our time on getting her and the wedding ready—if it wasn't for the plague."

"I know." Jim softened his own voice. "She's waited so many years for this—anyway, if you'll take care of telling her, I'll take care of telling everybody else about this trip. The guests who don't want to go can stay here or leave."

"They'll all want to go."

"I hope. Where is Geronde now? I haven't seen her this morning."

"I was hoping she would have gone to the Solar—it's the

only decent place with room enough to lay out clothes and things."

"And here I thought a wedding in this time, on the steps of the church, was nothing more than a business transaction."

"She'll be leaving right from here for Smythe Castle. It'll take at least three sumpter horses to carry what she'll need for the first three months or so."

"She doesn't have to stay there for three months without a break."

"Tell her that."

"Well," said Jim, "that's not my territory. I'll leave it up to the two of you."

"And Danielle and Joan—we can't shut them out of the process. You know, Jim, you've got to *really* talk to the Countess and get to know her, first chance you get. She's well worth it—and her influence over young Edward's critical. She'll be calming him down tonight, wait and see— but look, I've got to get going up to Geronde. Luck!"

She kissed his cheek, turned and headed toward the tower stairs.

"And to you, too!" he called after her. She waved a hand without turning her head and disappeared around the corner.

Left alone, he mentally debated whether to go to the pavilion or the Nursing Room first—but his thoughts were interrupted by a small voice from the fireplace.

"M'lord?"

He turned to see Hob walking out of the flames there with a hobgoblin-sized sword held crosswise before him in both hands, as if he was about to offer it up for sacrifice. He brought it to Jim and held it out to him.

"Something wrong with it?" Jim asked.

Hob shook his head.

"Not it, m'lord," he said, in the saddest voice Jim had ever heard from him. "Me. The noble lords say I'll never make a fighter with it. No, never in this world."

Chapter 15

"Sir Brian told you you'd never make a fighter with this sword we had made for you?" said Jim, unbelievingly—for Brian knew Hob well from all their journeys together and had seen proof of the little hobgoblin's real personal courage. Surely Brian would have found a kinder way of breaking that news to him.

"Not Sir Brian, m'lord. The other noble lord knight—"

"Just Sir Brian and Sir Harimore, Hob. Neither one is noble. But they're both knights, and that alone is nobleness enough for most people."

"But you're noble, aren't you, m'lord?"

"Just barely," said Jim. "But never mind me. It was Sir Harimore who told you, then?"

"Yes, m'lord. The knight who tossed me his dagger—you remember, m'lord. He said I'd never make a fighter with this sword, never in this world. Sir Brian didn't say anything, but he looked sad and shook his head."

"Well, this doesn't make sense," said Jim, more to himself than to Hob. "What had you been doing to make Sir Harimore say that?"

"Just what they told me to. They called it exercises, and I thought they liked what I was doing. They said I was very quick to learn and clever. But then Sir Brian wanted me to try to hit him with my sword—and I couldn't do that. He didn't have any armor on, just a sword himself."

"And did you?"

"Oh, I couldn't, m'lord! What if I had hit him?"

"Hob," said Jim. "Both Sir Brian and Sir Harimore are very expert swordsmen. You could try to hit either one of them all day long, and if either one had a sword himself, you'd never touch them with yours. His sword would always be in your way. Sir Brian was just trying to show you that."

"Oh!"

"Yes."

"But what if some accident happened, or I slipped, or some thing like that. I couldn't bear to hurt either one of them."

"Could you hurt a deep-earth goblin?"

"Oh, yes. That would be different. Besides, a deep-earth goblin would be trying to kill me. I'd *like* to hit one of them—lots of them!"

"Actually," said Jim, "they don't seem to be very able to do any killing—being small as they are, small enough to ride on rats. Their spears were just very painful."

"But the spears will kill, you know, m'lord, in a little while. That's what they're supposed to do. The goblins just like people to suffer before they die."

"Ah!" said Jim. "I'm glad you told me that. But they're still no threat to a man wearing armor. The ones we saw were just too small."

"They're shape-changers, m'lord. They just made themselves small when you were with the Bishop, so as to ride on the rats. Remember how some of them tried to make themselves like knights? But the fact is that really they're as big as me."

"Are their spears bigger then, too?"

"Yes, m'lord. That's another part of their magic. That shape-changing was part of the magic I told you they took away from us hobs when they drove us out of the Kingdom of Devils and Demons."

"Where're Sir Brian and Sir Harimore now, do you know?" asked Jim.

"Sir Brian's leading Blanchard up and down in the courtyard to see how he walks," said Hob. "Blanchard kicked the wall of his stall very hard, and Sir Brian was concerned he might have lamed himself some, m'lord. Sir Harimore is off riding with the Lady Countess, now, the two of them together."

"He is!" said Jim, thinking that Dafydd's counseling must have been loaded with dynamite to cure Harimore's shyness so quickly and so effectively. "When did Harimore ask her to do that?"

It was a rather foolish question to be addressed to anyone else in the castle since it assumed whoever was asked had been with the two of them at the moment of asking. But Hob, thanks to the network of chimneys he moved about in—every room in the castle necessarily had at least one— and a sort of preternatural hobgoblin sense of where something of importance was being discussed, seemed to know everything.

"Oh, he didn't ask her, m'lord. She asked him."

"Ah!" No sudden dynamite after all, yet. The fact that she had done the asking was much more in the order of their natures.

"How did that happen?" Jim asked.

The way it had happened, it turned out from Hob's information, had been that Joan had shown up to get her horse from the stables in the courtyard and go for a ride—a pleasure for most of the equarian class, plus a good practice for keeping a penned-up horse from becoming restive in this horse-dependent age.

But then, already mounted, she had hesitated, telling Brian and Harimore that it was probably womanish of her, but she couldn't help feeling a little unsafe, going riding in strange woods without an escort. Sir Brian was obviously very occupied at the moment with his magnificent horse— Joan felt she could hardly ask him at this moment—

"Good of you—devastated not to be of service—" Brian had replied in an absent-minded, irritated sort of tone, barely glancing up from his inspection of the walking Blanchard.

"—But if the good Sir Harimore would be indulgent enough . . ." Joan had gone on, smiling at Harimore.

"Honored! Happily!" Harrimore had jerked out in his stiffest fashion. "Stablemaster! My gray gelding!"

So the two rode off together. Definitely no dynamite, but with Joan giving the matter her full attention, reflected Jim, much might yet be done.

Anyway, for Jim the coast was now clear. He headed toward the door from the Great Hall to the courtyard. Brian, happily, was just seeing Blanchard back into his stable stall.

"Better let me talk to Brian about this problem by myself," he told Hob, who was now back in his favorite place under Jim's shirt—how had he managed that while holding the sword? More take-for-granted by Hob's magic, no doubt.

"Better leave us," Jim muttered sotto voce to the little fellow. "Brian wouldn't like anyone listening in."

"No, m'lord."

Hob made himself scarce.

"Brian," said Jim, as his friend came back out of the stables, looking satisfied, "I need to talk to you—in some privy place."

"No one in the Great Hall right now, I think," said Brian. "I could use a small cup of wine—Blanchard had me worried there for a bit. . . ." He continued to explain until they were seated facing each other at the High Table with wine before them. "Well, James, what is it?"

"It's about Hob—Hob and his sword."

Brian winced. He took a swallow of his wine.

"He told you what Harimore said, then?"

"Yes. But you know how brave, almost fearless, Hob can be at times. You didn't say anything yourself after Harimore came out with that?"

"What could I say?" Brian drank again. "I know—what you say about Hob is true. Fearless, yes. I know that, of course."

"Then why didn't you speak up?"

"Mainly, James, because I thought Harry was right."

Brian pushed the wine cup aside. "Hearken to me, James. Hob is too small and light to wear armor and stand up to any of our kind, afoot or on horseback. But in a melee with others no bigger than he is—or better even an armed brawl with creatures more his own size—"

"The goblins are just the size of hobs. They're the same, after all."

"Then," said Brian, "he could be dangerous indeed. But he never will be—"

He took another swallow from his wine cup.

"—Do you understand what I'm trying to tell you, James?"

"No," said Jim.

"Never will be dangerous. It takes more than skill at arms to make a fighter who can even hope to survive. He must be ready to finish off an enemy who is trying to kill him. You and I do not have to be taught that, James. When the knife is at our throat, we do not hesitate to thrust back. Most who go on two legs or four have it naturally. But Hob—he would have such an enemy at his feet and put his own sword away, saying, 'Oh, I'm sorry. Did I hurt you? Let me help you up'—and as he was helping him up, the enemy would put a knife in him and kill him!"

Brian stared at Jim.

"You will do him no favor by sending him out to be killed."

"But he's willing to be killed!" said Jim. "That's the point. He expects to be killed—but only by deep-earth goblins—and only after he's taken as many of them as possible with him. He wanted a sword so he could die with a ring of his dead around him."

Brian still stared at Jim, but now with a different expression.

"This is in the nature of a feud then—betwixt him and them? He did not tell us this."

"He probably doesn't even know the word 'feud.' But

it's that, only maybe greater. Hobgoblins are the same people as the deep-earth goblins—they were the least of the Lesser Devils in the Kingdom of Devils and Demons where Ahriman comes from—you remember Ahriman from the time we found and brought home Geronde's father."

"I remember," growled Brian.

"Trouble started in that kingdom when humans began to block them out by faith and signs of faith: the Greatest and Greater Devils all blamed the Least among them—the goblins—who couldn't even enter human houses now without being invited. And they in response turned on the freaks among them like Hob, who didn't like hurting anything, and laid all the blame on them. They drove out those like Hob and stripped them of all the magic they had as goblins. But thrown into the world, magicless, defenseless, hobs learned new magics of their own. Being harmless, they could enter houses, sit happily in a hearth fire, ride on smoke. But they never forgot what the other goblins had done to them."

"Damned if I would either!" said Brian. "Like being betrayed by your own family!"

"Meanwhile, the Greater Demons were still not appeased. They drove out all the Lesser Devils and the goblins, and those goblins found their own kingdom deep, deep in the earth, and *they* never forgot to hate humans and hobs for everything that had happened to them."

Jim stopped. For a long moment neither he nor Brian said anything. Brian slowly drank his wine, looking at nothing in particular.

"Still," he said at last, "no telling if Hob—our Hob—will really face up to these other goblins when the time comes."

"Well, you've seen him stand up to situations like that champion the Witch Queen of Northgales sent out to kill me, and he would have, too—but Hob spoke up and sent the Queen's champion back into her castle."

"Hah! But Hob knew he had you and I, James, with him!"

"Do you think he was counting that, at that moment? I

don't! And maybe you'll remember other times—"

"Well, maybe. But it's no use your trying those arguments on Harry. He's turned his back on Hob, once and for all. Harry thought Hob was afraid to strike at me while we both held swords, and Harry does not change his mind easily."

"I can believe that," said Jim. "But Brian, it doesn't need Sir Harimore. Couldn't you teach Hob just one thing—how to fight poison-pointed spears with that sword of his?"

"You just cut off the spear point first. Nothing to that."

"But what if the spear-carrier knows what he's doing," said Jim, "and is guarding against the sharp point of his weapon being cut off?"

"Ah, yes. I take your point, James. Perhaps there are some things I could teach Hob."

"Then you'll do it?"

"Well, yes," said Brian. "So it's an honorable death he wants. One couldn't in decency refuse to help anyone to that, man or hob."

"I'll tell him," said Jim, relieved. "Wait, on second thought, no. Could I ask your kindness in telling him that yourself? I don't want to make it seem as if I—"

"Certainly. I understand," said Brian promptly. "Mustn't let these retainers get the idea you're playing favorites. Geronde always says—well, you know the sort of thing Geronde always says. No doubt there's some sense to it, but by Heaven, if I favor one man over another, I'll say so. If the others don't understand it's because that man's better than they are, they'll come to know—or if they don't they can go elsewhere. But I understand—don't want Hob thanking you, do you? No reason why you should have to put up with it. Where are you going?"

"The pavilion—for the quarantine quarters outside the gates," said Jim, stepping off the dais. "I've been trying to get to that for two days now."

"Looks like any other pavilion to me," said Brian, but

Jim was already halfway down the aisle between the two long lower tables, and pretended not to hear him.

Across the courtyard, over the drawbridge, down into the cleared space around the castle. At first glance Jim could tell it would never do where it was, beside the moat, and the immediate question became how was he going to break this news to the Master Carpenter.

Master Carpenter—no one in the castle remembered his name apart from that—was, as everyone knew, cranky. Age and authority had made him almost immune to rank. He would give anyone an outspoken argument.

The Master Carpenter had long since forgotten what his age was: certainly mid-sixties, and possibly he was actually in his eighties or even older. But he was as loyal as the day was long, knew his business like no one else, and would work until he dropped, rebuilding something half a dozen times if necessary to make exactly what was wanted.

Jim found him in the pavilion. It was light and airy within, and would be too light and airy as the temperature of the late fall nights got colder. Right at the moment, the old man was supervising the stretching of a cloth partition down the middle of the large tent, to divide it into male and female quarters.

"Oh, Master Carpenter," said Jim, approaching him, "there you are!" The carpenter slowly revolved to see who was speaking to him. "I've got some news for you."

"Hah!" said the Master Carpenter, recognizing Jim. The common people did not ordinarily use the ejaculation that was in common practice among the gentry—but in the case of the carpenter, it meant "Good news? I *don't* think!"

". . . m'lord," he added, in his usual growl.

Jim had decided from his first glance at the pavilion, as he crossed the drawbridge, that there were times when flat-out lying was completely permissible.

"Yes, I'm sorry to do this to you, Master, but I've just magically received word from the Collegiate of Magickians that any structure like this being built right now must be set up inside the curtain walls of its castle. The order cannot be disobeyed, of course."

"Of course."

"Yes."

"Take it all down here. Set it all up again in the court-yard—if there's enough space for it there."

"Oh, you'll manage. I know you."

"I suppose. What must be, must be."

"Quite right, Master," said Jim, cheerfully.

"Well, we'll get on it right away . . . m'lord."

The trouble with the Master Carpenter, Jim told himself as he went back to the castle, was that you were continually left with the feeling you owed him an apology.

I'm pretty good at talking in most instances, I think, Jim told himself, but uttering repeated apologies seemed to make them only more and more inadequate. If he could only take Brian's attitude: tell the truth and if they can't adjust to it they can go someplace else. But he wasn't Brian.

Everyone born in this primitive century would consider him slightly insane to worry about what he might have said to even an upper servant. The rain fell, luck went against you, you were hung or starved to death—those were matters beyond your control. Everybody had to live with what was.

Angie was not in the Nursing Room, nor in any other parts of the lower castle when he looked. He could simply send servants scurrying around to locate her and tell her to come to him—but he didn't want to do that most of the time—and now was an example. He climbed the tower stairs and found her where he should have looked first—of course—in the Solar, humming to herself, once more laying out travel clothes—women's clothes this time, thank Heaven—on the bed.

"There you are," she said, as he dropped into a chair. "Did you get everyone notified?"

"I'm sorry," he said. "No, I forgot all about it."

She looked at him penetratingly.

"Well, put it out of your mind, then. I've been doing it too, anyway, after all. I told Joan, who had already heard it from the Prince. And it seemed that every time I turned around, I ran into one of those you were going to speak to. So I told them, just to make sure. They all want to go, just as I said they would."

"Good," he said, feeling again the unexpected weariness he had been bothered with lately. He was in no mood to pursue the subject. "Angie, I told Carpenter to move the pavilion quarantine station inside, to the courtyard."

"Jim!" she said, dropping loose on the bed the riding cloak she was holding. "That'll make two centers of contagion inside the castle—I thought the idea was to keep potentially infective people outside! And how'll the servants get back and forth from the kitchen and the stables and everything else out there? They'll all catch it before the rest of us!"

"I've thought of that," he said. "I'll set up a ward around the pavilion no flea can get through. Servants, food and other needs will be able to get through the ward, but nothing living—including anything infective. Also, something like porta-potties for both the men and women's side. Some of them there will also have to train to be nurses to the rest—and some other things. But magic will take care of the details—Carolinus will lend me some more magic if I need it."

"But—"

"I know, I know. But I think it can be handled, and when I looked at that tent outside, not even magic would make it safe for them—or anyone we had to send out to them with food or supplies. They'd starve to death inside the ward, if I put one up for them out there and we couldn't feed and help them regularly. If I didn't, night marauders would kill or even eat them—and some may be neighbors or friends.

We've got to have them inside the castle where we can defend them."

Angie shook her head and went back to the riding cloak.

"I suppose you're right," she said, after a moment.

"I hoped you'd think so," said Jim.

"But I'm glad you feel that way," she said. "Because I've got a comparable surprise to hand you. As I told you, everyone wants to go—including Harimore. But we leave tomorrow morning, not the day after."

Chapter 16

"Tomorrow!"

Jim sat straight up.

"Yes," said Angie gently, dropping the riding cloak to turn and talk to him. "I'm sorry, honey. But Geronde won't give up a day we could use before the wedding."

"And the others—they know about this, and they're going to be ready to go in the morning?"

"Every one of them. The Prince and Joan can't wait to get there, anyway—and the rest, Brian, Harimore, Dafydd and Danielle, are all used to traveling without much baggage on the spur of the moment. Also Dafydd and Danielle's three children will stay here. They're wild about the idea, think of it as a holiday without their father and mother. They're in for a surprise, though—Danielle and I left them in the care of May Heather."

"You don't suppose she'll be too hard on them?" said Jim, remembering what it had been like to be a boy, himself.

"No harder than their father and mother."

"Well . . ."

"Don't worry, Jim. It's just that she's the kind of person who, if she says 'no,' the child she said it to doesn't come back with 'aw . . . please!' "

"That's true," said Jim. May was one of those rare natural commanders who can step in anywhere and take charge, because everything about her signaled the fact that what she said, she meant, with every atom of her mind and body.

I wish I was like that, Jim said to himself wistfully. Chandos was that rare sort of human item . . . and Brian. He woke up suddenly to the fact that Angie was still talking to him.

". . . and I want you to take this chance to really get to know her—"

"May? How can she be going—"

"No, no! Joan—of Kent—of Salisbury. The Prince may be King one of these days, and she might just end up being Queen. This ride to Tiverton's the ideal chance. You've been her host here. You're a Baron, after all, and none of the others going have titles. It's natural you should ride together."

"How about the Prince, himself?"

"He's going to go ahead fifteen to thirty minutes in advance of the rest of us, so he can swear on a Bible he just came to bring the news the rest of us are coming, but not so far in advance that you won't be inside Tiverton by the time he's delivering that message to his father."

"I see."

"Yes. So everything's taken care of. I'm doing all our packing, except for putting it on the sumpter horse. All you'd need for a visit like that—being male—is one suit of clothes for the three days, but I'm giving you two to impress the King. Kings, from what Joan tells me, are very much like banks up in our own time, who only want to lend you money if you've already got lots of it—kings like to give things to people who already have things. There! Now, let's get ready for dinner—it's almost time."

Dinner was less formal than usual. Geronde was not there, and had food sent up to the room she shared with Brian. Everyone else made a short meal of it, having things

they wanted to get done before tomorrow morning. Since
Joan had been traveling with little baggage, in her squire
disguise, Angie was lending her a couple of robes—she and
Angie were much the same size—and they had to be refit-
ted. The Prince had been supposed to bring a suitable dress
from Tiverton but had failed to do so. Also as usual, in his
open-handed improvident way, he was flat broke.

"If I've ever needed fresh clothes—" Joan reported him
to Angie as saying in the privacy of their room.

"As you always do," said Joan.

"—I can pick out any courtier at court my size and say
'I like what you're wearing. I wish I had something just
like that,'—and so, of course, we'd trade clothes."

"But," Joan went on to Angie, "I can hardly say that to
a lady without looking ridiculous."

Jim spent the afternoon telling Master Carpenter how he
wanted the pavilion set up in the courtyard, and Mistress
Plyseth how he preferred the Nursing Room to be handled.
He was listened to, promised everything—and went away
knowing he would get only what they chose to give him of
it. He also had a longer and much more satisfying interview
with John Steward, his chief servant, who promised to keep
everybody working at full speed, and could be trusted to do
so.

Supper was quiet, rather exhausted on everybody's part;
breakfast the following dawn a chaotic affair utilizing the
table dormant—and they were ready to go.

After the early breakfast, the Prince took formal farewell
of Jim and Angie, then galloped off to get his head start on
the rest of them. They finally got on the road themselves.
The day warmed as the sun came out, and Jim found Joan
had chosen to ride with him at the head of the cavalcade.

"I would wish to be sure, Sir James," she said, "that you
know how I appreciate your making this trip at such a busy
time. It is a great kindness for Prince Edward and me."

"There're benefits in it for the rest of us, as well, my

Lady Countess," he said. "We don't get to meet the King every day."

"It is no great thing, meeting kings," she said. "The sweat they stink of is very like that of other men. But pray, Sir James, may I simply address you as James—seeing you are an old friend to Edward, and I have come to love and speak on first names with your wise and beautiful wife? She calls me Joan—as I beg you do, when we are not on our manners—and I call her simply Angela."

"It may take a little practice," said Jim. With the warmth of the sun and this easy beginning to conversation between them, he was beginning to relax. "Angie—Angela—has a high opinion of you, too. She said you were brilliant."

Joan laughed.

"Like a diamond?" she asked.

"No, no," said Jim. "Excuse me, I pray. Angie and I have this odd way of talking between ourselves—it was the way people talk where we come from. She meant your mind—your wits—were brilliant, and she wanted me to take advantage of this trip to talk to you."

Joan sobered suddenly.

"That was thoughtful of her, then, as well. For your ear I should say I found her a remarkable woman in many ways. Most wives never look past my face and body and want their husbands to have nothing to do with me."

"There's no one like Angie!"

Joan smiled.

"I see."

"See?" Jim looked at her, puzzled. "See what?"

"Just so. You are fortunate to have such a wife, James. Few marriages are that happy. The Lord knows mine were not, and I have had two of them—though the first one still touches my heart."

"Two?" said Jim, a little startled. His researches back in his original time had made him somewhat familiar with the story of the Fair Maid of Kent, but now he found himself staring at what looked like a fresh-faced adolescent girl, riding beside him. . . . But then, he reminded himself, in this time people lived early, and died early and suddenly. "Sorry. I didn't mean to pry."

"Pry? Heavens, no! You do not know my story? I thought the whole world knew it. The name of my first husband was Holland, and for me the sun moved from dawn to dusk at his command. He was a soldier—still is. I was twelve when we were married—quite legally, but secretly. But then, the family which had me to ward began to worry that I was growing and acting like a grown woman too fast and made haste to get me safely married off."

Jim shook his head wordlessly. Nothing came to his mind to say to this.

"Holland was in the east at the time, fighting the heathens, and I was still very young. I knew the King would have gone into a rage at my marrying anyone without his permission. I said nothing about the earlier marriage and let myself be married to Salisbury. He is not bad. He puts up with whatever I choose to do—as long as it is not too public—but I do not love him. Under Church law, Holland could recover me, because my marriage to him is legal and obvious—that makes the one to Salisbury illegal. But because I am royal, the ruling for that must come from the Pope—an expensive process. Holland does not have the money, and no chance of getting it short of a capture that will bring him a rich ransom. So now you have it all."

"But there's Edward," Jim found himself saying—not the sort of interjection that would normally have come from him, but the flood of such an open confession from Joan had overwhelmed like a tidal wave his usual sensitivity about other people's affairs.

"Ah, yes," said Joan. "But Edward—my Edward, young Edward—is an entirely different matter. We grew up together at court, and I have loved him all my life. There are the makings of a great King there, and if I can protect him until he becomes one, nothing will stand in his way. I have only my looks and wits to go by, but you would be surprised at what can be worked by them—Angela probably would not."

"Probably," said Jim humbly.

She laughed again, that open, free laugh of hers.

"Do not carry modesty to the edge of foolishness," she said. "Few good men will admit how good they are—few believe they are as good as they are. A great thing, by Saint Peter. But do not let it lead you into overmodesty and error. I think you are good for young Edward; you, and Sir Brian and the archer with the name I cannot pronounce. It reminds a Prince there are those in the world who are not venal, avaricious or selfish. You three are like a breath of fresh air to him. You keep your vows."

All but swept away by Joan's frankness, Jim was on the verge of telling her he had never taken any vows—knightly or otherwise. He checked himself in time—there was nothing to be gained by mentioning the fact; and, in fact, it would surely cause trouble later on. But the impulse had been there. One life-story frankly told begets another.

"What do you plan—" he began, but this time his sense of caution had no trouble stopping him.

"At Tiverton? I must reestablish myself with old Edward. This is what I had been aiming at all along, but had to wait for a moment when Cumberland was out of the way. He is not short of wits, himself, my Lord Earl. He would only have to see me on good terms with old Edward to know what I was there for, and to take measures against me. He is rich and powerful enough to put serious pressure on Salisbury to keep me away from both Edwards. To gain the results I want, I must be with both in person. Letters will not do."

A poignant flash of memory out of his days as a graduate student came back to Jim. In the history of the world he and Angie had been born into, this woman now riding be-

side him had, in her old later life, written to one of her sons
by Edward—a son who by that time had become King
Richard III—begging him to spare the life of his half-
brother, a son of Joan's by Holland, who was under sentence of death. Richard had ignored the letter and gone on
with the beheading.

Was that same thing to take place in this parallel world?
The execution was said to have hastened Joan's death.
Middle-aged, widowed and heartbroken—it was painful to
think of this as the future of the vibrant young woman who
was riding so surely and hopefully into that same future
beside him now.

He shut out the possibility. Here, as at home, there was
no predicting the future.

"Have you any idea what Tiverton's like?" he asked her.
"And what we might expect when we get there?"

"I know nothing of the castle, itself—its stairs and
rooms," she answered cheerfully. "But because the King is
in residence, I can tell you about everything else."

"Everything else is exactly what I want to know," said
Jim. "I'm more concerned with our getting away at the end
of three days than anything else."

"I will help you make that escape," she said. "But to tell
you about the rest, the manners and customs particular to
the court—"

"It's more the layout of the castle, where everyone is, or
will be, that I'm after."

"To be sure. But the manners and customs may also
prove useful, my Lord Baron."

There was an infinitesimal moment in which Jim realized
he had been subtly rebuked for interrupting a Countess.

"Of course!" he said hurriedly. "I didn't think. I should
have realized that what you had to tell me on these court
customs is absolutely necessary to everything, but the layout
of Tiverton may also have everything to do with our getting

away when the time comes. I forgot for the moment you'd be staying."

"Hopefully," she said. "And I'm properly reminded, James, that I, myself, am if anything much more so ignorant of the manners and customs of your homeland. May I make amends by telling you about what you call the 'layout' of Tiverton first, after all?"

"Whichever you prefer," said Jim, as gallantly as he could.

"Well. Then layout it shall be. As I say, I have never seen the castle myself, but I know that it was built this century and is said to have a magnificent gatehouse—but I have talked with several of the Courtnays who owned it. That is the family that built not only Tiverton, but Bickleigh and Powderhame in Devon, all in this same hundred years. However, on the matter of Tiverton, in most ways it is very like your Malencontri. . . ."

"Good," said Jim.

"The King, of course, will have been given the best and most secure and private rooms in the castle for his personal use. In this case, that means, as at Malencontri, probably the top floor of its tower—like your Solar—but more likely divided into a number of smaller rooms than your large one—some not much bigger than the small one you divided off for Robert Falon's nursery. The King's guests will be on the floors just below him—again just as you do at Malencontri; to make room, he will simply dispossess anyone already in a room he wants."

"We don't do that at Malencontri," said Jim. "Of course we might have to ask someone if they wished to vacate a room, and they always do."

"Of course. To someone of older blood or superior rank it is only courtesie. . . ."

Between the layout, and the manners and courtesies, the two of them talked away the rest of the trip, and when they finally rode into Tiverton's interior courtyard, it was plain that the Prince's announcement had found no change of the royal mind. Smiling stablehands helped them off their horses, and smiling servants escorted them to their rooms.

Curiously, Jim could feel Hob—sword and all—shivering under the back of his shirt, but he had no time to find out what was bothering the little hobgoblin now. The Prince was knocking at his door, and walked in without even waiting for an invitation to enter.

"My father will see you right away—cannot wait to see you," he said. "You are commanded to his presence immediately, and never mind the travel stains. Damn it, come *on*, James!"

Chapter 17

Angie was just completing her curtsy to the King when Joan and the Prince entered behind her. Jim stepped forward as Angie moved aside to give him room and essayed the deepest and most respectful bow he had ever made. It was more tricky than he had imagined before he had begun to practice it—for one thing, it was easy to lose your balance on a very deep bow—unless you did it just right.

But he managed correctly this time and came erect again to find himself looking into the King's face, a heavily bearded face with more white than blond hairs in it now, and above the beard a pair of the blue Plantagenet eyes with almost invisible white eyebrows, and white hair that had retreated considerably from its original frontier.

The King did not look in the least untidy in his dark red robe, though his reputation had him often so.

"Ha! My paladin!" he said, his blue eyes staring almost hungrily at Jim. "At last you come to me!"

"I have hoped for this day, Your Majesty," said Jim. *Already I'm talking like a courtier,* he told himself

"Then why did you not come sooner?"

"I did not want to intrude without an invitation, Your Majesty," said Jim, thinking at emergency speed. Courtesie—always courtesie.

"Why did I never get him commanded to me before this?" The King turned his stare on the Prince.

"You were going to once of which I have knowledge, Your Majesty," answered his son. "But I believe the Earl of Cumberland pointed out to you that your time was about to be taken by Parlement, and a later moment might prove better."

"Hum," said the King, pulling at the beard on his chin, "you are probably right, Edward, though I could swear there was another time also I thought of calling him, and there was no great mass of duties to interfere. But somehow . . . however, he is here now, with his three great companions."

"—And high time it is," the King continued, speaking now to Jim. "There has been much I wished to ask you. How I wished I, myself, had been with you there!"

There could be only one place, of course: the Loathly Tower of Jim's first ballad-material adventure when he and Angie had first inadvertently come to this world. Jim was about to say diplomatically that it would hardly have been worth the time of a King, when he realized he had heard an odd, wistful note in the King's last words—and he realized suddenly that the other man was literally hungry for what he could no longer possibly have: the martial life of his younger years, the life he, as all others of the upper classes, had been brought up to love.

"I wish you had, too, Your Majesty," said Jim—it was an out-and-out lie. The already-aging monarch could have done nothing but get in the way. Even a magnificent swordsman like Brian had needed all day to kill the Worm, and what archer in this world but Dafydd could have held off the harpies, bursting without warning out of the low-lying clouds to swoop upon them?

And who but Carolinus, among all Magickians, would have been able to hold back those evil clouds from dropping even lower . . . it had been a dirty, not a glorious, day. A long, long, dirty day, striving to keep from being killed so you could kill the thing you fought with.

That was what the King had been wishing he had been a part of. In any modern world that wish would have seemed ridiculous. But then Jim remembered the very true story of the Thirty at the Oak, when the leader of the fifteen picked French knights had raised his voice desperately in the day's late hours:

"*. . . I must drink, comrades!*"

—and the answering voice from among his companions:

"*Drink your own blood, Beaumanoir!*"—followed by the cackle of laughter from the equally dry throats of those same staggering, exhausted companions.

Particularly, there had been nothing attractive in the fight at the Loathly Tower for Jim. He had gone though it himself only because he was determined to get Angie back, even if he died for it.

But here were these men of the martial class yearning for just such an encounter. He remembered young Sir Giles de Mer, confessing shyly to him, Brian and Dafydd as they sat around a campfire, that he wished to accomplish one great deed before the moment of his death. Barely old enough to grow the luxuriant blond mustache he sported—and his dream had been of a glorious death.

—And this aging shell of a man Jim faced now, so honored and powerful, obviously shared a dream of the same kind, and still clung to it, in the form of that largely fictional part of a ballad that Jim was here now to certify, to make it even more real.

But now the King was speaking to Angie.

"Will you sit, Mistress? You will no doubt be kind enough—" He broke off. "What's that?"

The Prince, who had moved to stand close beside the

King's heavily padded chair, was now whispering in his ear.

"But I never made him a Baron!" said the King, quite out loud. "Oh—you mean he was when he came to England."

He turned back to Angie, who had taken advantage of the invitation to occupy something that was more like a small stool with a scant back—Jim was still standing.

"You will forgive us, my Lady of Riveroak and Malencontri, for miscalling you out of your proper address," he said. "We also rest in the assurance that you will show us the indulgence for which your gentle sex has ever been noted, if we talk about arms and battles as men so often do."

This speech having been rattled off with the speed and assurance of long habit, clearly conveyed the information, which Angie could have no doubt of, that she had been properly apologized to, King-style, for having been called a mere Mistress, instead of a "Lady," as the wives of even minor nobles were entitled to be called. Further, she was notified that her presence here was that of a reference piece—the classic heroine needing rescuing—and that comments from her were not required.

"Certainly, Your Majesty," she answered agreeably.

The King turned back to Jim. "Sir James, one of the duties of a knight is the destruction of anything evil. Why did you think it necessary to write me for permission to attack the Loathly Tower?"

Since Jim never had done so—outside of the verses of the ballad-makers—he was caught unaware by this question. Clearly, he was now to endorse the fiction.

"I'm afraid it was my ignorance of English law, your Grace," he said. "There are strict laws here about the pursuit of any game that properly belongs to Your Majesty—that the beasts may not be hunted out of season to scarcity, so that their numbers dwindle. I did not think these extended to such things as Dark Powers, but I wished to make sure—"

"Indeed," said the King, "such thoughfulness does you credit, Sir James. I would indeed have dealt with the Dark Powers myself, given time. But I am busy, sir, busy! So your petition was welcome, and I had all the more pleasure in writing to give it to you—which you will remember I did without delay."

Jim studied the blue eyes and beard before him. Was the King really believing all this, or was he making himself believe . . . or what? Maybe this was the way history was made.

"I had intended to keep your letter as an example of courtesie," the King was going on, "but it has somehow disappeared. We have so many communications, and even our best of secretaries are a careless lot—not like the staff of this castle. . . . I am much taken with Tiverton. But I do have the rough copy of my answer to you—which I thought you might find interesting. Edward, would you call for—"

But a servant was already at the side of the King's chair, proffering a single strip of parchment.

"—the Earl of Cumberland did indeed promise me outstanding service from them," went on the King, "but I must say they have exceeded my greatest—"

He broke off, passing the paper to Jim, who took it in hand, but found it completely unreadable, by him at least, written as it was in the most elaborate of clerkly styles.

"Remarkable," said Jim, staring with no understanding at all at the letter. "It all comes back to me now. How can I thank Your Majesty for such a kindly letter?"

"You can not. So, you read Latin also, Sir James. That is but another of your virtues, though rare among paladins. We, ourselves have always held that a little Latin and more English are not bad for a fighting man to have. French, of course—though I see no use for Greek, whatsoever. We who are Kings have a need to know such things, and must study them in our youth—though some are better scholars than others—"

He cast a disapproving glance at the Prince, who pressed his lips tightly together but said nothing.

The King extended his hand and Jim gave him back the letter.

"I will have another copy made for you," the King went on, "against the time when the original in your possession may be mislaid or lost. But now, let us talk of the battle itself. I would fain hear the truth of it from your own lips— no false modesty if you please, Sir James."

This again! It seemed to Jim that he must have told the doings of that day a thousand times. Normally he told the truth—and to hell with how it disagreed with ballad versions—leaving his listeners to choose between the two. They all, invariably, twisted his account to fit the ballads, which were much more attractive if Jim had met the Ogre in his human body and armor and performed a sort of St. George-and-the-dragon bit by his conquest.

Here, however, it occurred to him it might be well to adapt the truth at least enough to satisfy what the King might be expecting.

But it was a long story to tell in the details his listeners always required. Halfway through, however, the King was merciful enough to let him sit down to tell the rest—and have in some wine and water to refresh his dry throat, and a stool like the one Angie had been sitting silent in. It was hard and too small, but at the moment it felt like the best of all the chairs he had ever dreamed of having.

Happily, the King did not prolong the session once the creatures of the Dark Powers had all been killed and the Powers themselves had to allow Carolinus to drive them from the Loathly Tower. He took a large drink of wine— unwatered—and said, "Ah, now I know. We shall take a little rest now. You may leave. Edward, you will see they are shown to their rooms?"

"Yes, Your Majesty," said his son.

"That was just in time" said Jim. "Five minutes more in

that excuse for a chair and my back would have been broken."

"No one is allowed to look down on the King," said Angie, "remember? And, what about me? I sat in one longer than you did."

"So you did—and never said a word. He should have sent you off after being introduced to him. I wonder why he kept you around all through the story?"

"It was the picture he wanted. The heroine, the hero, and the King who had caused it to happen, all in the same picture while you told your tale."

"Maybe you're right. That makes sense—the way things are here."

"I particularly asked Joan to warn you, thinking you'd remember it better if it came from her. So I thought she had. Manners are laws around the King—and you talked to her all through the trip. What do you think of her?"

"You were right," he said. "She *is* bright—and she obviously knows more about the Court than I could learn in a lifetime. I like her a lot. Does my opinion finally match with yours on that?"

"Ugh!" cried Angie, leaping up from the bed in the room, where she had stretched out, and flicking something off her wrist.

"What is it?" Jim shot to his feet from the chair, thankfully padded, in which he had been getting the kinks out of his own back.

"A flea!" She stared around. "I was going to step on it, only it got away. I should have been watching. But everything was so spic and span around here—"

Jim instantly threw a ward around her—and on second thought he threw one also around everyone who had come with them from Malencontri, wherever they might be in this castle—cursing himself for not doing it sooner. "Angie, did it bite you? Can you tell if you've been bitten?" he asked, anxiously.

"It didn't have a chance. I saw it just as it landed and knocked it off my hand—but I wish it hadn't gotten away now."

"So do I," said Jim, glaring at the floor. In all of the *Encyclopedie Necromantic* there ought to be some magic that could work as a general insecticide, but there was nothing that would kill anything at all, according to Carolinus. That would be an offensive act by any Magickian, who were committed to only a defensive use of their art.

Hob had slipped out from between Jim's shoulder blades without being felt, with that unconscious magic of his Natural kind. He stood now between Jim and the room's fireplace, with his sword at his side—looking remarkably as if he had worn the weapon from the first minute Jim had met him.

"M'lord, is it all right if I go look for the Tiverton hob, now?"

"What—oh, sure," said Jim.

Hob vanished upward over the small fire.

Jim frowned after him for a second. There had been something pale and strained about Hob's face that Jim had never seen before. He hoped the sword hadn't gone to that small, round head, so that he was about to do something foolish, like challenging the resident hob to single combat to determine which of them was superior to the other.

"Hob, come back here!" he called. Hob reappeared almost instantly.

"Yes, m'lord?"

"You aren't going to—" Jim hesitated "—make an important matter out of having a sword now, are you?"

"No, m'lord," said Hob, with a quiet dignity that was entirely new to him. "But I can best serve you by learning everything there is to know about this castle, and its hob can tell me."

"Oh, I see." Jim felt a touch of embarrassment. "Certainly. Of course. I hope I didn't give you the wrong idea by what I said about your sword."

"By no means, m'lord. It may even prove to be a protection to me and this castle's hob, too. *They* can't touch cold iron, but we hobs can not only touch, but use it."

"I see. Well—good luck, then."

"Thank you, m'lord." Hob zipped out of the room and up the chimney.

They, of course, Jim reflected, would be goblins, but there had been no sign of them on this trip.

"Time for bed," said Angie.

Chapter 18

It was a cloudy morning in Devon, their first whole day in Tiverton, and Jim, with Angie—and thankfully, both of them dressed for the day—was having a peaceful, private breakfast that had been brought up to their room, when there was a loud knocking at the door.

Jim's first impulse was to shout "Go away!" but he remembered that young Edward knocked like that. His next impulse was simply to ignore the call—until he remembered Edward still might just walk in—and further remembered that the doors of guest rooms in castles like this did not have locks—or even latches, for that matter.

The knocking came again, but this time the Prince did not just walk in. His voice came through the three inches of wood.

"James! James! It is I, Edward. I have someone for you to meet, and we must talk!"

Hastily, Jim threw a ward on the doorway and the wall surrounding it. As an afterthought he made it a ward which let him hear what was said on the far side of it, but made sure anything being said or done inside the room could not be heard outside.

Barely in time. He could now hear, faintly but understandably, the voices of the Prince and of the male servant on duty outside the door.

"You said you saw them both go in?"

"Yes, Your Grace."

"And they haven't come out since?"

"No, Your Grace."

"Well, get somebody up here with an axe—or whatever he needs, this door is stuck. I want it open. Now!"

"Yes, Your Grace."

The Prince's voice went on in a somewhat lower volume.

". . . bear with this, Mortimer. Sir James is a Magickian, and the saints only know what he's up to at this moment. But we'll soon have that door down and find out what it is."

"You better let him in," said Angie. "You'll have to see him sooner or later."

But Jim had already begun to calm down himself and come to the same conclusion.

"You're right," he said.

"Then you'd better do it now, before he does something more serious."

"Yes," said Jim and, going to the door, removed the ward. "Ah, Your Grace. I thought I heard your knock. Pray enter, you and this other gentleman."

"Your door sticks!" said the Prince, entering with his companion behind him. "—My lady!"

"Your Grace," said Angie with a smile and a curtsy. The Prince shut the door again behind him.

"I have been looking forward, James, to naming this gentleman to you—the Viscount Sir Mortimer Verweather, currently of the King's wardrobe—"

"Honored to meet you, my lord," said Jim, who had remembered the man at first glance. He was still tall and thin, and his small, fashionable mustache still seemed unrealistically dark against his mouse-brown hair. The long nose on his tanned face seemed to be testing the air of the room for unpleasant odors.

"A great honor to meet you, my lord," he said with all a courtier's smoothness. "I saw you once before, I believe, but you would not remember me."

"The more shame to me that I do not," said Jim with equal elegance. "Perhaps it was at the Duke's—"

"However and whenever—" broke in the Prince impatiently, "I have brought Mortimer to consider you for the gift of a suit of clothes from my father. But the discussion must certainly be boring to your lady. Perhaps she has other things—"

"She has not," said Jim reflexively, meeting him eye to eye, exactly as he had done in a matter of the Prince wishing to talk privately with Jim in the Solar. This might not be Jim's castle, but by the almighty, it was his room, and according to medieval custom it was as much his as his castle. Edward was going to have to learn a magician could not be pushed around.

"You forget, my lord," said Angie quickly. "I had promised to go immediately to meet Geronde—"

"Hah—yes!" said Jim. Angie was right as usual. No point in starting a fight unless necessary. "Well, if you've given your promise, you must keep it, of course. Turns out it's all for the best."

With his back to the Prince he winked at her and spoke as sternly as he could. "Should have reminded me, dammit!"

"Forgive me, my lord," said Angie meekly. "It seemed to have slipped my mind."

"Well, get along."

Angie took her leave.

"Women!" Jim explained to the Prince.

"Ah, yes," said Edward. "Even the best of them, among

which I have no doubt your lady is numbered—but we have more important things to discuss."

"By all means, Your Grace," said Jim. "Would you care to sit?"

"Certainly. Sit, Mortimer."

The two of them took the room's two chairs. Jim sat on the bed.

"But first, James," said Edward. "Have you any way of making our talk here secure against listening ears?"

"I have, Your Grace. But as I mentioned on another occasion, the laws of the Collegiate of Magickians—"

Edward held up a hand.

"My dear James," he said with a winning smile and an abruptly confidential voice, "understand me. This is in nowise a command from me as your Prince, but merely a favor asked by one old friend of another. If you have such a skill, I would be very grateful now if you could use it to protect our conversation of the moment."

"Ah, well—yes," said Jim, trapped by a different convention of the age. "There. It is done, Your Grace. We are secure."

"That quickly?" said Edward, looking startled. "Thought you would have to burn foul magic powders or recite an incatation—incan—"

"Incantation, Your Grace? No. Such are needed only by beginners in the Art. One experienced in the Art is like a ruler who says 'let this be done' and it is accomplished. Say what you will, now. No one will be able to overhear."

Edward looked at Jim with the first expression Jim had ever seen on his face of frank admiration.

"Say you so?" he asked.

"I do indeed," said Jim.

"Good! That is all I desire. Well, James, the matter is this—by the by, I am making great strides upward in my father's estimation. Sometimes I think we could almost be back in the happy days of the *chevauché* into France that ended so well at Crécy. . . . Still, I must face facts. Cumberland will not stay long separated from the King, the fount of all he's gained over the years, and then I shall shortly have my reputation in my father's mind to do all over again. What is needed is a voice other than Cumberland's, when I am no longer with my father to protect myself from my half-uncle's lies and slanders."

He paused and directed a sharp gaze at Jim.

"You understand the need?"

"Yes indeed, Your Grace. Unfortunately, I and those who came with me are only going to be here these three days—"

"Yes, yes, we'll see how things work out. But by clever use of you while you're here, much good may be done. Now, my father thinks well of Mortimer, here. He has managed to let it slip into my father's ear that it was he, rather than Cumberland, who suggested this castle of Tiverton, with its cleanliness and excellent staff, as a safe place for the King of England in this time of plague."

"Ah?" said Jim.

"Yes indeed," replied Edward, "and well indeed he did so; Cumberland would never have given him credit for it. Consequently, my father thinks well of Mortimer—but not enough to have his voice outweigh that of an Earl who is his half-brother. Rank alone is not the problem—witness Chandos, who has chosen in spite of many chances to advance himself, to be no more than a knight, yet Chandos' voice is the single one at court that my father will listen to in counter to Cumberland's."

"He is a peerless knight," said Jim—and meant it.

"Indeed. But above all there is one thing the lack of which will make Mortimer's voice in my father's ears always less than that of Cumberland. It is not that he is French—which is slander. Not but what they are many great men of war in France wearing the swordbelt and golden spurs of knighthood. . . . No, Chandos is a war captain—of all in England the wisest. So is Cumberland, and my father, of course. But poor Mortimer here, through no fault of his own, has never seen a battle, nor has he a name for recontres with other, single knights."

"But a man can be a man for all that," said Jim, giving the customary answer to this sort of personal history.

"Exactly. But the Countess said something—exactly what, I forget—that started an idea in my head. I had watched happily my father's pleasure in accounts of rencontres and other weapon-work, and it occured to me that if Mortimer should fight one of you three paladins, with blunted weapons of course, for the King's amusement, and do well—I do not say win—it might raise him greatly in my father's opinion and make his words much more of a counterweight to Cumberland's foul lies. It should not be you he should fight, of course; too much honor in it, and of course there would be no hope at all of him looking good."

—If you only knew! thought Jim.

"—and the archer, of course, is not a fit opponent for any belted knight. But Sir Brian would be an excellent middling choice."

Edward paused, almost beaming at Jim and obviously waiting for applause.

Hell's bells! thought Jim. Aside from this assumption that a guest should be casually drafted into a mock duel with blunted weapons—only slightly less dangerous to life and limb than sharp ones—the idea was the worst in the world. He had to spike the whole notion, somehow without offending the Prince, and do it right now.

"A charming thought, Your Grace!" he said. "And one which Sir Brian will be overjoyed to hear. Yet if I might mention one point. . . ."

"One point?" Edward's beam was suddenly a frown—almost a scowl.

"Why yes, with your indulgence. I think you ought to know that after such a trial with blunted weapons at Mal-

encontri one day, it was Chandos himself who named Sir
Brian one of the best swords of England."

Edward stared.

"Chandos said that?" he managed after a moment. "He
must have been speaking of you."

"Forgive me, Your Grace, but I assure you he was not. I
had not had sword in hand that day, and it chanced that Sir
Brian and Chandos, with sharpened swords but in play, of
course, were contesting Chandos' entrance to my Great
Hall."

The Prince looked visibly shaken. Inwardly Jim heaved
a sigh of relief. He had been afraid that Edward might have
outgrown his younger hero-worship of Chandos.

"Well, well!" said the Prince, still half-shaken but also
half admiringly. "He did indeed say it to Sir Brian, then!"

"So he did," said Jim, "and in such a voice that all around
heard. So it strikes me there is some danger he might show
so much superiority over Sir Mortimer as to diminish what
credit Sir Mortimer would get from this, and as you say,
Daffyd ap Hywel is not of rank to encounter with a knight,
while certain obligations of my own to the Collegiate of
Magickians. . . ."

"Well, yes of course!" said Edward, rising like a buoyant
ship from the monster wave of a suddenly storm-wracked
sea. "But Mortimer is no village lout with his sword, and
of course you could, you understand, mention to Sir Brian
how much I—and for that matter—he stands to gain from
this exhibition if he . . . well . . . you understand. . . ."

Real anger was kindling in Jim, now.

"I fear, Your Grace," he said stiffly, "I would not know
how to go about doing that."

"Eh?" Edward stiffened, a thundercloud beginning to take
possession of his brow now at this, almost a direct denial.

"Sir Brian, like Chandos, has always most strictly observed his knightly vows, one of which was to always do
his utmost. I don't believe it would accord with his honor

to do anything else, and, to tell you the truth, I don't think it would accord with mine to suggest it to him."

Braced as he was for the roof to fall in, to Jim's utter astonishment the thundercloud vanished. Edward smiled ruefully, and his whole body relaxed.

"Certainly, all my hopes depend upon Sir Mortimer here making a good showing to my father. But that the day should come that I ask a knight to go against his vows, may Heaven forbid! We must trust in Mortimer's good right arm and what skills he has learned from some fine swordsmen, and we all know France has those who are among the best. Come, Mortimer!"

He started to turn toward the door, but Mortimer spoke up.

"By your leave, Your Grace," he said. "A moment more only. I would say just a word to my lord."

Edward turned back.

"I would say two things, my lord," went on Mortimer, but now to Jim. "One is that in spite of the accident of life that caused me to be brought up in France—a land that is dear to my heart but not my own land—and named with a French title—"

Jim suddenly remembered that the French laws of inheritance differed from those of England. In England only the oldest son of a noble family was entitled. In France, as in some other European countries, all the sons were. That explained the hard time Mortimer had gone through, before finding a niche at the English Court, if he was only a second, or even later, son.

"—One is to say that I am wholly English, of mother and father both. It was only circumstance that caused me to be raised in France. The second thing I would say is that while France will ever be dear to my heart, the vows I took there were no less than any knightly vows made here, and I would accept favor from no man in a test of arms!"

"Brian will love you that you feel that way," said Jim, as

forcefully as he could. "He would feel the same way. I'll tell him what you said."

"Thank you, my lord. Your Grace, forgive me for slowing your departure," said Mortimer.

"Forgiveness is unneeded. James, can we just walk out? Or does that enchantment of yours carry dangers for any who might wish to pass through it?"

"It is harmless, Your Grace, and already taken away."

"Then, we will talk further with you later. Nobly said, Mortimer. Come."

They went out.

Jim drew a deep breath. Once more he had had a discussion with Edward without giving in on everything the young man wanted, but also without creating bad feelings between them. But now there was no point in putting off uncomfortable news.

Jim turned to the table, which in addition to the two pitchers, one of wine, one of water, held mazers—instead of ordinary wine cups—since he was a lord.

He filled one of them from the water pitcher. It made a rather odd-appearing scrying glass, but it should work. He gave it the necessary command, and a three-quarters view of Brian's head and shoulders showed up in the still surface of the water.

"Brian," he said to it.

Brian looked around himself confusedly.

"James?" he said, searching the empty air.

"You needn't speak out loud, Brian," said Jim. "I'm just talking to you in your head. Just think the words you'd say to me, if you've got anybody with you who might wonder why you seem to be holding a conversation with nobody. I've just had a visit from the Prince and Sir Mortimer Verweather. It was about you. I'm up in our room. Can you come now?"

"Certainly," thought Brian. "I'm only—tell you later."

He was obviously having trouble producing words without speaking them aloud.

"Fine," said Jim. "I'll let you go, now."

He wiped out the scrying-glass command, emptied the
mazer, and taking another, splashed a little wine into it,
unmixed with water—having had experiences with the
product of local wells in places other than Malencontri, no
matter how well mannered the servants. It was less than ten
minutes before Brian knocked.

"Brian, James!" he called from beyond the door.

"I'm alone!" Jim called back. "Come on in."

Brian came in, carrying in one hand a bulging sack that
gave forth a chorus of whimpers, mixed with occasional
very high-pitched squeals. He paused to one-handedly pour
himself a mazer of wine—also waterless, but in his case for
reasons of taste—and then casually passed the bag to Jim.

"Here, James," he said. "I was down at Tiverton's kennels and they had some rat-terrier pups. You said you
needed some for Malencontri, so I took some. They'd only
have been drowned otherwise."

"Thanks," said Jim, holding the bag at arm's length un-
certainly. It would never do to tell Brian that these were far
too young to have time to grow up before London's plague
reached Malencontri—though, if the plague lasted in Somerset, they might become old enough to be useful in the Nursing Room. It was unthinkable that he should admit that the
pups—probably just born a day or so before—touched his
heart with their crying, jumbled in the sack like unliving
chunks of just about anything. What was he to do with them
the rest of the time he and Angie were here?

He had an inspiration. Hob had a soft heart for everything
living. Hob could take them away up the chimneys and take
care of them.

But for now—he pointed a free finger at the sack and
said "Sleep!" and the noise instantly ceased. For a moment
the thought touched him that he might have overdosed them.

Then reason returned. He had used magic, not medicine. As long as he didn't keep them sleeping too long, it shouldn't do them any harm. He put the sack, still silent, gently down beside his chair.

"Why did you do that, James?" asked Brian, obviously intrigued.

"Magic reasons," Jim said. "We've more important things to talk about."

"So I was thinking when you spoke to me in my head," Brian answered. "James, do you know it is very hard to say words in your head without moving your lips?"

"I do know. But it gets easier the more often you do it. You and I may be doing it more often from now on, and you'll see how easy it gets."

Brian frowned doubtfully and took a drink from his mazer.

"But the important matters, James?"

Jim frowned in his turn. He was wondering how to break the news to Brian.

"The Prince and Sir Mortimer were just here. I promised Mortimer to tell you what he told me—that he was completely English on both sides of his family and had only been brought up in France because of circumstance. But that the knightly vows he took there were no less than a knight would take here, and he desired favors from no man at any time."

"Well, that is only as a knight should—pardon me James while I pour myself a little more wine—but how did he come to tell you it?"

"Actually," said Jim, "it was because the Prince—you know how he is—had suddenly come up with the idea of Mortimer fighting you with blunted weapons for the amusement of the King, and was all set to make it happen without even asking if you'd want to do it."

"But why should I not?"

"It would be only courtesie to ask you, first."

"Well, the lad is still young in many ways. Also being a King's first son may make him a trifle thoughtless, at times. Was this the urgent matter for which you asked me here?"

"I didn't know how you'd take the news."

"It would be only ordinary manners on my part to entertain the King. He is a jolly old soul, if he does stink somewhat, despite his fine clothes. Plied me with some fine Spanish wine this morning and wanted to hear about every small bicker or tournament I have been in—though I lacked time to tell all I could remember. But one cannot blame a man for stinking in some small degree or other, though I, myself have a penchant for the feeling of cleanliness, as you may remember from the morning after our first meeting. I mind my grandfather—but there, enough of that."

Jim was not likely to forget it. He had woken up one morning to find Brian, in the first days they had known each other, naked, bathing in the ice-cold water of a brook with every appearance of enjoyment.

"Well," he said now. "I'm glad you feel that way about it—particularly the business of the Prince not asking you first."

"It is great sport, James. Not to be compared with jousting or a real rencontre with all weapons sharp. I look forward to it now that you've told me."

"I gather," Jim said carefully, "that the Prince was hoping Mortimer might show well in the contest—that way making him a better advocate to the King of the Prince himself, when young Edward's not there to speak for himself."

"Why, and mayhap he will."

"Perhaps. The Prince did say, too, Mortimer had trained with some of the best swordsmen in France. So he may be dangerous to you, after all."

"Tush, James! What matters is not the teacher of swordsmanship, but the swordsman, once taught. And you must remember, this is merely play. It is not as if we were making use of sharpened weapons."

"If you say so," said Jim, holding himself back from mentioning that at the same kind of play at the Earl of Somerset's Christmas party he had seen knights carried off the field with a broken arm or leg, and one with concussion.

"So," said Brian, tossing off his last splash of wine and getting up, "I thank you for telling me all this, James. But, forgive me, I must get back to the kennels. How the Kennel Master there ever won his position, I do not understand! Agreed with everything I had to say, but when I fished for what knowledge he had of his own, he showed none. Most Kennel Masters—Hunt Masters—whatever one calls them, are of a custom to have their head so jammed with iron-clad notions out of ages past that one needs a battle axe to get through to them with any new idea. But this fellow was just the opposite. Seemed to have no notions of his own at all, and nothing else. Agreed with everything I said—'Yes, Sir Brian—,' 'Of course, Sir Brian—,' left me feeling as if he hadn't understood a word I'd said. But I'll get some sense out of him, yet. At any rate I got your terriers for you, and it's been kind of you to sit and listen to me. My thanks, James."

"Don't thank me, Brian." Jim also stood up. "It was good of you to interrupt your talk—and thanks again for these terrier pups."

"They're only a few days old," said Brian cheerfully, going toward the door, "and as I may have mentioned, the Kennel Master had no need of them, being over-burdened with terriers—"

At this moment the door to the room opened just as he reached it, and he almost bowled over Angie, who was coming in. "—My most abject apologies, Lady Angela! Grant me the mercy of your indulgence for such clumsiness!"

"Quite all right, Brian," said Angela. "I wasn't looking either. No harm done."

"May the saints be thanked for that—I am no lightweight—and thank your own gentle self for excusing me so readily."

"Nonsense. On your way, Brian."

"I will make sure to be more careful in the future," said Brian, going out. Angie came the rest of the way in and dropped into the chair Brian had vacated.

"Sometimes Brian overdoes the manners bit—" She broke off abruptly. "Saints above! What's that?"

"Puppies," said Jim, who had just awakened them again.

"Puppies?"

Chapter 19

"Terrier puppies." Jim lifted the noisy bag in front of her. "He knew we needed terriers, and the Kennel Master of this castle evidently had some he didn't want, so Brian took them and just brought them up here."

"Put them down at once! Let the little things out! You don't carry puppies around in a sack as if they were pieces of wood! How could you let them stay in there?"

"I haven't had time—" Jim was starting to say as he carefully lowered the sack, which was already more than a little smelly, down to the floor, opened it and let its prisoners out. Angie fell on her knees beside them.

"They're all still alive—and hungry, too, poor babies!" she said. One of them had found the end of one of her fingers and was trying to suck on it, to a chorus of miniature yelps and whimpers. "It's a miracle they're all alive, joggled around like that. I can't understand Brian. The kindest man I know in this world, treats that horse of his as if it was his only child, and then carries helpless little creatures around like this."

"I think the Kennel Master gave them to him that way.

He didn't have any other way to carry them up here, and I hadn't had time—"

"You should have made time!" The puppies were already beginning to make a mess of the thankfully uncarpeted floor.

"—and they're too young yet to be taken from their mother," she was going on. "They need to be back with her right away if they're going to live, and they'll never grow up in time to be useful in the Nursing Room. Anyway, how did he think we'd take care of them here and get them home?"

"Probably the same way he would. Turn the responsibity over to servants."

"Well, we're going to take care of them! You go out to whoever's on duty at our door and tell him or her you want their mother up here right away. And this castle's carpenter and the Room Mistress—and some warm, fresh milk! And you tell them I do mean *warm*—not boiling and not icy cold, either! We want that immediately. Little ones this age have to eat constantly—and lots of clean, soft cloths. All right away. Immediately, not fifteen minutes from now."

"You known what, Angie?" said Jim. "I think if you gave them the message the way you told it to me you'd do a better job of impressing them with the speed you want."

"You forget the century we're in! They don't know me, but they know who and what you are—and particularly that you're a Magickian. Make magickal noises at them if they don't get everything done fast!"

"All right," Jim said. "Maybe you're right." He went out into the hall.

"Hah!" he said sharply to the guard and servant on duty there. "I want the bitch that whelped these pups Sir Brian just brought me, *warm* milk, the castle carpenter, and the Room Mistress, all here as fast as everyone can run. If you're not here by the time I finish drinking a cup of wine, I'll turn you and every one who should be into beetles.

Armsman, you get the Kennel Master and carpenter. You, woman, the milk and your Room Mistress. Go!"

He glowered at them, but they were already in flight.

He went back inside.

"I heard every word you said," Angie greeted him—Jim had left the door ajar when he stepped into the hall, and now realized that she was telling him something else by the statement. For a moment he remembered the sound-conducting ward he had created when he had wanted to hear what Edward was saying outside the room, which allowed anyone inside to hear those speaking in the corridor. But he had disposed of that earlier.

"Well, you're the one who reminded me about the century we're in," he responded somewhat weakly.

"Did you have to call the woman 'woman,' like that?"

"I don't know her name the way I would at Malencontri. I'd have called her 'man' if she'd been male."

"Oh, I know. Sorry. Do you want to pass me a blanket from the bed? These pups are all trying to cuddle up to me and crawl into my clothes for warmth and hoping to find a teat to suck on. How long before we get those people here?"

"As fast as can be," said Jim. "Everybody, including the Cliffside Dragons, have always taken the beetle threat very seriously."

"It can't be fast enough for me—ah, there's someone," said Angie, for there had been a scratching at the door. "Come!"

"Matilda, Room Mistress, my lady," said a plump woman whose long-nosed face displayed no expression at all on seeing Angie wrapped in a blanket and seated on the floor, covered by squalling, piping pups. "You wished something?"

"Blankets! Lots of them. And soft cloths the size of a handkerchief. Both fast!"

"Immediately, my lady. How many blankets might my lady consider 'lots'?"

"Six—eight. At least eight!" said Angie. "And I want them *now*!"

"Yes, my lady." Matilda, Room Mistress, went out.

"Jim," said Angie. "Come help me count these little devils. I don't want anyone stepping on one that's gotten buried under a blanket—or one getting lost and we find him dead in a corner two days from now."

"I wouldn't worry about one getting lost," said Jim, moving to help her. "They huddle together with no mother around. It's instinct."

Together they counted that there were twelve pups.

"Is that all?" said Angie. "I could have sworn there were fifty—there's the door again. It'll be the Room Mistress back with the blankets—and just in time."

"Come!" both she and Jim shouted at the same time. But it was not Matilda, but the servant who had been on watch at the door, panting and carrying half a pitcher of milk.

"Good," said Angie. "Give it here—give it to me, that is."

The servant handed it to her. Angie tasted it gingerly from the edge of the pitcher.

"Fresh enough," she said. "But not what I'd call 'warm.'" The servant fell on her knees before Jim, clasping her upraised hands together in supplication.

"Oh, of your great mercy, my lady, don't have my lord turn me into a beetle! It was somebody else warmed it and gave it me!"

"He won't," said Angie. "Will you, Jim?"

"Not this time," said Jim.

Another scratch at the door.

"Come!" called Jim. A boy looking about twelve years old—which probably meant he was fifteen; there were a few straggly blond hairs on his upper lip—came in, carrying a friendly looking, full-grown terrier, who began to wriggle in his arms as soon she saw, and undoubtedly smelled, the pups.

"Adam, Kennel Master's apprentice, my lord," he said. "Master's compliments, and where do you want the bitch?"

"Put her down here on the blanket with her pups!" Angie snapped.

"—And tell your Master not to dump pups into a sack like so many rocks to carry them!" Angie went on.

"They'll be dead by the time they get where they're going," Jim said as the boy put the dog down. "Tell him that from me. He's to find some other way of getting them where they're being taken." The pups scrambled to their mother with eager whimperings, and a second later they were all either nursing or fighting for a teat.

"Yes, m'lord. He's still talking to Sir Brian. It's your man-at-arms—just said you wanted the bitch."

"All right," said Jim. "On your way, then!"—For Adam was showing signs of wanting to stay around and find what this was all about.

The Room Mistress showed up with another woman laden with what turned out to be ten blankets.

"Put them in the corner," said Angie. "Where're the soft cloths?" The other woman produced them. They had been stuck into her girdle in the small of her back.

"That's fine," said Angie. "You can go, now." They went.

The pups' little bellies were bulging out. Their mother was lying on her side with them all around and on top of her, using her tongue to clean those closest to her, but looking relieved, as well she might if she had been overloaded with milk and with no pups to take it from her.

Angie put the milk pitcher and cloths on the table.

"That's that, then," she said, unwrapping the blanket from around her. "Now I can get out of this robe."

The scratching at the door was repeated.

"Hold it!" shouted Jim at the door. "Wait!"

Angie hurriedly started to change.

"There!" she said after a minute. "The other robe will really need cleaning." She picked up the cloths. "We won't need these now, after all. I was going to dip their corners into the milk and let the pups suck it up that way until we got the mother. You can let whoever's there in now."

"Come!" shouted Jim, and the Master Carpenter came in.

He looked like a Master Carpenter—old, bent, creaky, and sour-faced—a relief to Jim after all these odd, if however efficient, other Tiverton servants.

"You wanted me, my lord?" he asked Jim.

"Yes," said Angie before Jim could answer. "We want a pen."

"Yes, my lady." The Master Carpenter turned and headed toward the door.

"Wait a minute!" snapped Angie. "You don't even know what size pen, let alone what kind."

"No, my lady. What size and kind of pen would my lady like?" Jim felt a twinge of disappointment. The carpenter was turning out to be a far cry from their own at Malencontri.

"I'll tell you!" said Angie energetically. "I want it four feet square with a solid wood bottom, and an edge high enough so those pups can't climb out, but not so high their mother can't get out easily."

"Their mother, my lady?"

"The—" Angie found the word distasteful, "bitch lying there with them right now. What did you think I meant by 'mother'?"

"Crave pardon, my lady. I wasn't sure."

"Well, now you know. I want a pen to hold the pups but leave the mother free."

"And we want it now!" said Jim.

"Yes, my lord."

"Go and make it, then."

"Yes, my lord." The carpenter turned and shuffled out.

"Thank heaven," said Angie. "That's over—oh, this floor will need some cleaning." She raised her voice. "Servant, here!"

A servant came in from the hall.

"Clean up this mess the pups made of the floor," Angie said. "Has the Room Mistress got soap?"

"Soap, my lady?"

"You must know what soap is!" She got a blank look.

"Something you clean with," Angie continued patiently. "If the Room Mistress hasn't got it, go ask in the castle washroom. They'll know what it is there. Get soap and water and wash the floor."

Angie dropped into a chair and reached for the wine jug to pour a dollop into a mazer. She reached for the water jug, then checked and started to get up before she remembered who she was and where she was.

"Wait!" she called to the servant, just disappearing out the door. "Do you see that roll of blankets on the floor at the foot of the bed? It's got a flask in it. And I always put a little holy water in my wine. Get the flask for me, will you?"

The servant froze.

"What is it?" asked Angie. "What's bothering you!"

"Oh, my lady! I couldn't think of touching anything so precious!" The servant burst into tears. Angie stared at her. But she and Jim were used to encountering strange ideas, customs and beliefs among people of this century.

"Never mind, never mind now!" she said. "It's all right. You go ahead and get that soap and water."

The weeping servant nipped out the door, shutting it behind her.

"Well, well," said Angie, settling back in the chair after watering her wine with the safe water carried in her flask. "What next? Come to think of it, I haven't seen Hob since we got here. Where is he?"

"He went to find this castle's hob," said Jim. "Come to think of it, I'd have expected him back before this."

He got up and went to the fireplace, which had a

seasonal-sized blaze crackling merrily in it, and shouted up
its chimney.

"Hob! Wherever you are, come on back for a minute! I
want to talk to you." The chimney of this fireplace might
or might not connect to other chimneys, but the smoke from
the fire in their room would carry the message to Hob
wherever he was in the castle.

He and Angie sat, comfortably drinking wine for perhaps
five or six minutes. Then Hob stepped out of the fireplace—
but not alone.

He was carrying another hob in his arms like a child.
Even familiar as Jim was with the fact that hobs were
featherweights, he was a little startled to see the small Natural had the strength to carry someone his own size and
kind in this way, which must put all the burden on his arms
and shoulders.

The other hob's eyes were closed. He hung limply, and
his body—noticably paler than Hob's—was a mass of cuts
and bruises.

Hob's face was tragic.

"They were very cruel to him!" he burst out to Jim and
Angie. "As cruel—as cruel as you humans! Always so
cruel—" He broke off suddenly.

"Oh, my lord! I did not mean you and m'lady and those
like you! Pray forgive—"

"That's all right, Hob," said Jim. "You're dead right. We
humans can be cruel—deliberately, or just because we don't
stop or bother to think. You don't need any forgiveness. We
can be just as cruel to each other as to any other living
things. Is this the Tiverton hob?"

"Yes, m'lord. Can you help him? He is like one dead,
except I know he isn't!"

"I think so," Jim said, bending forward to peer intently
at the little creature still being held in Hob's arms. "I ought
to be able to. I just haven't tried it on a Natural before—

these are wounds and contusions, after all, not sicknesses. ... Let's see...."

He tried doing away with the wounds and their effects first. The bruises also vanished at his magic order. But the eyes of the tortured hob stayed closed, and he still hung as limply in Hob's arms as before. Mentally crossing his fingers, Jim ordered all invisible injuries like concussions to disappear.

Nothing happened for a long moment, then the Tiverton hob's eyes fluttered and opened. He looked around himself, wonderingly—and at the sight of Jim, he made a weak, spasmodic effort to climb around Hob and cower behind him.

"It's all right, hob," said Malencontri's hob, still holding the other gently, but tightly, in his arms. "These are real humans. Friends; and one is a mighty Magickian who just healed you all up. Are you all right now?"

"Yes, I think so...." said the Tiverton hob after a short moment. His voice was husky and a little more highly pitched than Hob's. "Could the good Magickian do something so I forget the—"

Jim shook his head.

"That, I'm afraid," he said, "is beyond my powers."

"Anyway, thank you, Mage—let me up, hob!" Malencontri hob, a little reluctantly, set him on his feet, but he seemed to be standing alone quite steadily.

"He is my lord Sir James de Malencontri," Malencontri hob told the Tiverton hob. "And in the chair is the good Lady Angela whom he has to wife. They are both good, kind, real humans."

"Then you must be the Magickian all hobs talk about!"

Malencontri hob cast a guilty look at Jim.

"No, that's probably the Mage Carolinus," Jim said. "I've done nothing but follow his example."

"No, m'lord. All know the Mage, of course. But it is of you I speak, I'm sure. None have been into such adventures as yours!" The Tiverton hob turned around and hugged Hob. "How fortunate I am to have been saved by such a hob and such famous humans as my lord and my lady! When I think of what would have happened—"

He had turned back to face Jim and Angie, his face radiant—but even as he did so, he stumbled and began to fall. Hob caught him before he could touch the floor.

"I'll have to take him back to Malencontri," Hob said, softly. "To where he can be in friendly, safe chimneys and where everybody likes a hob, and he can slowly become all well again. Have I my lord's permission to do that?"

"Certainly," said Jim.

"Oh, Hob," said Angie. "Could you take that dog and her pups too, while you're riding the smoke with this other hob?"

Hob looked at the bitch, covered and surrounded by her puppies, some now sleeping, others fighting with each other—or perhaps playing, they made the same sorts of noises either way.

"I am so sorry, m'lady, but I don't think I can. Tiverton hob or the dogs, but not both. It isn't that they'd weigh too much, but—"

"That's all right. I understand," said Angie. "Get your hob friend there first. We'll handle the dogs."

"Thank you, m'lady. I'll be back as soon as I can leave Tiverton hob safely. If he wakes up in a strange chimney without me there, he may do something foolish."

"Of course. Go ahead," she said.

Hob turned with Tiverton hob in his arms, leaped into the fireplace and vanished upward on the smoke.

"Now I've got to get cleaned up. I wish we had a bathtub here, as we have at home—and hot water."

"You can send for that," said Jim.

"I'm going to. But there's no use asking for a tubful, even if they could heat that much in a hurry. Then I've got to dress for dinner. So do you."

"I'm already dressed for dinner."

"Not if at the last moment we're invited to dine with the King. Put on your cote-hardi." She raised her voice to carry through the door. "*Servant here!*"

The same servant who had been sent for the soap and water came in.

"You haven't cleaned the floor yet," said Angie.

"Forgive me, my lady!" the servant wrung her hands. "Those wicked people in the washroom are still hunting for a soap fit for Your Ladyship."

"Never mind that," said Angie. "I've got my own soap for myself. What I sent you for was soap to clean the floor here. Their ordinary, everyday soap will do."

"I'll fetch it right away, my lady—" The servant whirled about and started to run for the door.

"Wait a minute!" The servant skidded to a stop, almost falling. "There's something I want you to do first. Go to the Serving Room, or whatever you have here to keep the dishes from the kitchen hot until they're served, and have them start heating a pitcher full of water—as fast as they can. Then go to the washroom, get everyday soap, come back to the Serving Room, pick up the pitcher of hot water—and this time I mean *hot*, and also one of cool water and a basin I can wash in. If you need help to carry it all, tell them I said they were to send somebody along with you to help. You've got all that?"

"Oh, yes, my lady. Go to the Serving Room—"

"Never mind repeating it all. I trust you. Go!"

And the servant was on her way with the last word.

"I didn't manage to ask Hob who treated the local hob like that, before they left," said Jim, vexed with himself.

"I wonder if it was these local servants," Angie said. "They're an odd bunch here!" She looked at the closed door.

Buttoned into the tight, form-fitting jacket that was the cote-hardi, Jim remembered too late there was a spot halfway between his wrist and elbow that had been itching, which he had not had time to scratch. He tried now to reach the annoyance through his left sleeve, but the stout, thick wool fabric and the narrow sleeve protected the itch as well as if it had been under armor.

He gave up. He was gradually sliding into the medieval idea that if nothing could be done about something, there was no point in considering it—the equivalent of the supposed cure for a headache in ancient Greece.

"Oh, that reminds me," he said, "I haven't told you about Brian."

Chapter 20

"What about Brian?" Angie had unrolled her bedroll and was busily examining the extra clothes she had rolled into its center.

"He and Sir Mortimer are supposed to fight tomorrow to entertain the King—with blunted weapons," Jim added hastily.

Angie abandoned her clothes suddenly and sat down hard in a chair.

"Why didn't you tell me this before?"

"I haven't had a chance!"

"It's a lot more important than a load of puppies!"

The mother of those puppies looked out at them and licked the air in their direction, to signal that she was really appreciating being a house dog. She liked them both and hoped they would soon be friends again.

"You spoke up about the puppies in the sack before I could get started."

"What if Brian gets hurt and is laid up here for days—maybe weeks? What about the wedding?"

"It's just sport, Angie!"

"You know what kind of *sport* that is. So do I for that matter!"

"Angie, this is ridiculous. Brian's not going to get hurt. He's too wise an old swordsman—even if he is younger than I am."

"How much younger?" asked Angie, suddenly curious.

"Two or three years. I don't remember which."

"He looks older."

"I know. But that's because he started living as an adult years before I did."

"Anyway, even if he is a wise old swordsman, accidents can happen!"

"You don't get to be a wise old swordsman unless you come to know how not to let accidents happen to you."

"You, yourself, ran a spear into him once."

"That was in a melee. We were both on horseback and got crowded into each other; still, the only reason I speared him was because he raised his spear so as not to run me through."

"See there? Just as I said. Accidents happen."

"But Brian's not going to be raising his sword so as not to hit Verweather."

Temporarily stopped, Angie took a deep breath.

"All that's probably so," she said. "But Geronde's not going to be very happy about this, and the fact Brian's a wise old swordsman's not going to keep her from worrying—anyway, I've got to get back to getting dressed."

She returned to the contents of the bedroll. The terrier licked out her tongue at both of them again, and Jim thought about taking off his cote-hardi so he could scratch his itch, then abandoned the idea again. He would forget it as soon as they started moving. "The fight'll be held just after breakfast, almost certainly," he said. "Before the King's too deep in his day's wine."

It was. Tiverton had a small interior courtyard; the buildings around it cut off the wind. With the sun out to warm the air, it was not exactly balmy, but more than bearable for this time of year. Besides, none of the people belonging to this place, in their layers of clothing worn indoors and out, paid any attention to the temperature.

A padded chair had been set up for the King.

"Hah!" said the ruler of England to the Prince and Jim, both of whom were standing beside his dais. "A fine day for a trial of arms—even if in sport." His two bystanders hastened to agree.

The warriors came forth, through doors at opposite ends of the courtyard. It was evident this was not the first time this space had been used for such exercises—and probably the majority of them had been with sharpened weapons, Jim suspected.

Verweather bulked surprisingly large and capable-looking in his armor. Brian was light-footed and businesslike, but looked small compared to his opponent. Jim noticed, with a small twinge of worry, that the scabbard holding Verweather's sword looked half as long again as Brian's— probably a bastard sword, as they were called, halfway in length between the usual one-handed broadsword and a sword designed to be held and used in two hands. If Verweather was adept at taking advantage of that extra stretch of blade, it could even the odds between him and Brian.

"Sir Verweather's sword has considerable extra length," Jim said to the Prince. The two of them had pulled back and to one side of the King's chair, so as not to seem to have an official part in the proceedings.

"Hah! Yes! Longer even than mine," said the Prince. There was little doubt of which gladiator young Edward was backing. Jim gave up the notion of getting any more useful information from him.

The two combatants walked forward until they met, then turned and, side by side, approached the King, halting in front of him without a word.

"Fight well!" said the King, waving one hand without

lifting its elbow from the arm of his chair—the other hand was occupied by his postprandial mazer, half-full of wine. And with that informal command, the two facing him backed away the short distance to the courtyard's center, slung their shields on their left arms, and drew swords with their right hands. They stood for a moment facing each other wordlessly—and then they were at it.

The first action was a flurry of sword blows from both men—so rapid that Jim, who still had not had enough experience, nor profited enough from Brian's teaching to follow the fine points, could not see an advantage on the part of either fighter.

Brian was continually in movement. He could strike faster with his shorter sword than Verweather could with his longer one. On the other hand, Verweather could strike blows that were heavier. But Jim was able to see that Brian was catching nearly all of the force of these on his shield, or using the shield to glance them aside.

Brian was continually in movement. But Jim noted with approval that he contrived to handle his retreats in such a fashion that they moved around in a circular manner, and Verweather was not able to drive him back against the wall at either end of the courtyard. But when he looked at the King and the Prince to see if they had also noticed these pluses, he saw no sign of it in their faces at all.

"Hit him, Sir Brian!" shouted the King, thumping an arm of his chair with his free hand. "Carry it to him, man!"

Even as the King spoke, Brian struck two lightning blows, coming so close together they almost seemed a single blow—one full-arm, and one half-cocked. They stopped and staggered Verweather, but then Brian was back to his circling and dodging again.

"Neville Smythe knows he cannot stand to match him," said the Prince to his father. "Verweather is wearing him down—aptly is he named!"

Jim longed for the presence of Dafydd, with whom he

could compare notes on the fight. But Dafydd, being only an archer, had automatically not been invited. Jim glanced over at where the women stood—as indeed everyone but the King was doing. Angie's face was expressionless. But Geronde's was fierce.

The first furious interchange of blows had slowed down sometime since, and the two fighters were circling each other warily, striking out mainly with the hope of drawing the other off balance, or causing him to expose himself for a moment from behind his shield. There was plenty of strength plainly left in both of them, but both were keeping it as much as possible in reserve for an all-out effort when the opportunity might present itself.

There were occasional quick flurries of exchanged blows, but these were not the supreme effort that would come later, when one or the other showed signs of tiring, or some other indication of vulnerability—usually invisible to the watchers, or at least to Jim.

In short, this bout had reached what Jim had always considered the almost boring middle stage of such encounters. So far neither man seemed to have taken any kind of a serious blow.

But now, abruptly, after what had seemed no more than another minor flurry, as they drew apart to sword's lengths, a small trickle of blood could be seen coming down the side of Brian's face. It became more than a trickle, running down just past the outer edge of his right eye. He ignored it.

"I thought these weapons were supposed to be dulled," said Angie's voice, clear in the tense stillness, otherwise unbroken except by the ring of iron on iron. "Didn't that include the points, too?"

The watching men all glared angrily in her direction, and even Geronde looked sharply up at her. Nobody answered. There was, Jim noted, also a bright scratch on the side of Brian's helmet, stretching down to the trickle of blood on his face. Theoretically, even a blunted point could scratch, if it scraped past lightly but at the right angle.

Or it could be that a blow on Brian's helmet had been heavy enough to cause the scalp beneath the steel to begin bleeding—which did not, Jim told himself, bear thinking of. Still, for a little while he watched Brian's movements closely, for fear he should see some sign of a new slowness or weakness in Brian's actions. But he saw none. And the trickle thinned, stopped.

For the first time when watching such a fight, Jim found himself able to observe with what was almost a trained eye. In many hours of working out with Brian—usually in the forest, safely out of the sight of people in the castle—Jim had actually learned a great deal of what Brian had tried to teach him. But knowing what he should do and having a body and hands that would do it—and as automatically as the fingers of a concert pianist, when he thought of music, would cause it to sound from the instrument before him—were two different things.

But that practice had made Jim familiar with Brian's fighting movements—and very aware of how helpless Jim, himself, would be, faced with an enemy of Verweather's ability. That awareness was what had caused him to accept almost humbly the truth in Sir Harimore's statement at the Earl of Somerset's Christmas party last year, when Harimore had said bluntly that it would be foolish for someone as inept as Jim to try to face him, sword in hand.

Now Jim was only too aware of how right that had been—and probably always would be. Like Brian, Harimore seemed to have been born with a weapon in his hand. And there were many others, even if their skills were nowhere close to that of Brian, Harimore or Sir John Chandos, who could dispose of Jim with ease. From the moment Jim had begun to realize that, he had gone back to trying to learn more from Brian—who never tired of teaching the use of arms—and it was the result of those lessons that had him now watching the actions and conditions of the two fighters before them as intently as the Prince and the King did.

And he saw things, accordingly, he would not have noticed a year before.

The most important of these was the fact, obvious now to Jim, that Brian was continually testing Verweather in what seemed an endless number of ways—even leading the taller man to demonstrate some of the advantage of his extra arm length and longer, weightier sword.

Verweather was clearly aware of this, and was almost certainly holding back for the final moment when they both began to tire, before using some of the more obvious advantages of his longer blade.

That time was approaching. Jim would have lost the fight from exhaustion alone, an hour or more earlier. But, in remarkable shape as these two were, they were flesh and blood—not metal automatons. Their testing strokes were becoming more perfunctory. They were not moving their feet around so much.

With a hollow feeling in his chest, Jim began to realize that it was Brian who was showing signs of tiredness more obviously. His footwork was undeniably slow now, and the point of his sword drooped slightly as he withdrew the weapon after a blow.

What was wrong with him, Jim wondered, almost frantically? He had never seen Brian tire so obviously, not even in his fight with the near-giant Bloody Boots, aboard the pirate vessel, years back. Now he was coming close to missing his latest stroke on Verweather completely. It was reasonless . . . unless that blood earlier had indeed signaled serious damage beneath his helmet, and only Brian's unbreakable will and years of habit with his weapons had hid the damage he had received until now.

The fight had been going on for nearly three hours—but suddenly now its whole pattern changed.

With no warning movement, Verweather suddenly let his shield slide off his arm to the ground. His near-bastard sword had a pommel large enough for both hands to close around, and he gripped it now in that two-fisted fashion and began to rain blows, with the full force of both arms and his shoulder and back muscles, on Brian's head and shield. At the same time he was taking advantage of the greater leverage of his longer blade from the safe extra distance of his longer weapon.

But then, to the astonishment of everyone, including Jim, Brian also dropped his shield. With an overlapping handgrip on the pommel of his shorter sword, he fought back.

Suddenly, he was the old, swift and sure Brian, apparently as fresh as the moment they had started the combat; he neither tried to block the overhand blows, nor dodge them, but stepped inside the circle of Verweather's swing, so that only the relatively light impacts of the upper part of the long blade could strike him—and began to hammer lightning two-handed blows horizontally at the lower body below Verweather's ribs.

The blunted edge of any sword could never have cut through a chain-mail shirt, but no stomach muscles beneath the chain mail could long endure the sort of hammering Verweather's were getting.

Verweather fell, struggling for breath a moment before he dropped into unconsciousness.

"Well struck! Oh, well struck, Sir Brian!" cried the King, now on his feet, age, heavy belly and wine cup alike forgotten, spilled unheeded to the sparse grass of the interior courtyard. "Prettily done, Sir Brian! You saw, my son! That is the sort of fate to risk if you go against a paladin!"

Jim felt a tugging at his arm and turned.

It was the Prince.

"Sir Mortimer seems oddly hurt, Sir James. Can you help with your magick?"

He certainly ought to be able to, Jim thought as he went with the Prince back to the center of the courtyard. There could be nothing wrong with Verweather but wounds, and it was only sickness magic could not touch. But when he got to the fallen man he found other hands had already stripped the knight of his armor and clothing, except his fourteenth-century variation of underwear. That was soaked—more than soaked—with blood.

"He's wounded?" asked Jim unbelievingly, for the blows with which Brian had hit him should not have drawn blood at all—let alone in this quantity.

"Something's broken inside him, my lord and Mage, I think," said a young man with all the clothing, speech and demeanor of a squire. He was kneeling on the other side of Verweather's fallen figure. "I can find no wound on his body, but he is bleeding badly, front and back."

Of course. Understanding jumped to Jim's mind even before the squire had finished. Possibly liver, or kidney hemorrhage. The squire was looking up at him with tears in his eyes. Jim would not have thought Verweather capable of inducing that kind of loyalty—until he remembered how easily tears came to the eyes of everyone—not only women, but men—in this period. Perhaps the squire thought it part of his duty to weep over his knight. But the youngster, as well as everyone else, was now looking at Jim expectantly, and with perfect faith.

"Hm," Jim said. A wound was a wound, inside or out. His magic *ought* to work.

It did. Where Verweather's underwear had been stripped away, they could see the bleeding that had been oozing through the skin, stop abruptly. But the man remained unconscious.

For a moment Jim considered restoring the lost blood to Verweather's body, but he decided that by now that lost fluid could well have picked up all kinds of infectious matter—the shorts, for one, did not look particularly fresh or clean.

"He is mended!" Jim told them in a voice full of an authority he did not completely feel. "But I cannot give him

back the blood he has lost. He must make that up himself."
He knelt and felt for a pulse in the closest lax wrist.

"He must take to his bed for a week and do nothing but
rest. In that time, he is to have no wine or strong liquid.
Only water and perhaps a single mazer of small beer with
his food—though he should eat as well as his appetite will
allow."

"Damn!" said the Prince, in a vexed tone. "A whole week
out of action?"

"That reminds me," said Jim, still being authoritative, "he
is to have no excitement. I'm sorry, Your Grace, but these
rules must be strictly obeyed if he is to live."

"There is no other thing to be done?"

"None."

"Ah well," said the Prince. "It was God's will, clearly—
what are you looking about for, my lord?"

"Sir Brian."

"My—the King has taken him off to his royal chambers
to celebrate. No doubt Sir Brian will have to fight the fight
all over again in words, though he might rather be abed,
himself."

The Prince laughed.

"Ah," said Jim. "Of course. Thank you, Your Grace. I
merely wished to tell him that I must now get to my room
for a couple of hours of solitary meditation, as I am required
to do by magick law after such a working as I have made
on Sir Verweather."

"Oh, of course," said the Prince. "May your med—
meed—"

"*Meditation,* Your Grace. It may be I did not say it
clearly. I beg your forgiveness."

"Meditation. No, no need. May your meditation go well,
and we must not keep you a breath longer."

"Thank you, Your Grace. I bid you all good day. Sirs—
be very gentle now with carrying Sir Verweather to his
bed."

Amid a chorus of assurances, he went.

When he got to his room, Angie was already there. With her were Dafydd and Geronde.

"I was just leaving, James," said Geronde, rising as he entered.

"You don't have to."

"Yes, I do. I've got to go see if I can get Joan to pry Brian loose from the King before the King decides to keep him all day—awake or asleep! I'm much better now after talking to Angela; and Dafydd is just here, no doubt with matters of importance to discuss."

She did not wait for any protests, but was out the door almost before she had finished speaking.

"Had to work some healing magic on Verweather," said Jim, dropping into the chair Geronde had just vacated. "Sit down, Dafydd!" For Angie was sitting on the bed, leaving the other chair free.

"Thank you, James."

"Actually, Jim, I think I ought to leave, too," said Angie, rising.

"No, no," said Jim, hastily. "I just want to tell Dafydd about Brian's fight, since he couldn't be in the courtyard, and about the way Brian won it. I'd like you to be here, too, since you were there and saw what happened, too. In fact I would have liked Geronde here as well, but she was too fast for me, and probably what she aims to do is a lot more important, anyway. Sit down."

"Pray, stay with us," said Dafydd in almost the same breath. "But will you not take the chair?" Angie sat down on the bed again. "Thank you, my lady."

"Lady, nothing," said Angie. "To you, Angela. You know that!"

"Thank you, Angela." Gravely, Dafydd sat down in the chair. "But I must tell you, James, I had a good view of everything that passed in the courtyard—from an arrow slit in a wall behind the English King's throne, looking down.

It was no more than I might have expected from Brian, yet my heart warms at the beauty of it. I have always been drawn to work well done."

"Now that's the thing," said Jim. "I understood more of what was going on today than I ever saw when two men were matched that way. You talk as if you believe Brian had it all planned out before the fight ever started?"

"I believe he knew what he wished to do before swords ever met," said Dafydd. "He is far more learned and skilled in swordwork than I will ever be, and I am not a man to say a thing is, when it only may be. But beyond what he wished to do, I believe he left the fine points of his fight for the fight itself, and how Verweather should prove himself to be, to decide, and trusted himself then to bring it to the end we all saw."

"Angie?" said Jim. "Were you that sure of him, too?"

"Anything but. My heart was in my mouth. Geronde might have been—she knows him better than anyone. But you always worry, with any fight like that."

"Then he did plan the whole combat," said Jim. "I suspected it, but I didn't know enough of swordwork—as you say, Dafydd—to be sure. Now, I'll ask him when we've got time to talk. I've got a lot to learn."

"What man does not?" said Dafydd, diplomatically.

"Now, don't you go fighting duels," said Angie to Jim. "It was hard enough on me watching Brian today."

"No. I can always plead the defensive-only law of the Collegiate of Magickians. But I've run into fighting before this, and there can't be much doubt I'll run into more unexpectedly from time to time. The more I can learn the better."

"What happens when you run into some wise old swordsman unexpectedly, then?"

"Wise old swordsmen usually don't do unexpected things. They're too sure of their own skills. I can beg off, surrender or whatever. It's just the people that jump on me without warning that I have to worry about."

Angie did not look convinced. But she said nothing more—with an effort, Jim suspected—and mainly because Dafydd was there.

There was a scratching at the door.

"Come!" shouted Jim.

The door opened. A man-at-arms stood there—not the one on duty.

"I come charged with a message for you, my lord. The Lady Geronde sends to say that Sir Brian Neville Smythe is now back in their room, but is sleeping and should not be waked until further notice. But His Grace the Prince Edward of Wales may pay you a visit. No answer is requested."

The armsman still stood, however, in case Jim should have some word to send back with him.

"Good. Go," said Jim in the proper abrupt manner of his rank.

"I am away." Dafydd stood up as the door closed behind the messenger.

"You don't need to go just yet," said Angie. "The Prince may not even come at all."

"He will come," said Dafydd, moving toward the door, "and it is as well he does not see you and I, James, too often together. Also I have a wife, and a room of my own I am somewhat overdue in. But I thank you for your kindly thought, Angela."

The door closed behind him.

"He wanted to save me the embarrassment of having to order him out of the room, if the Prince showed up. This rank business is hell, sometimes."

"It certainly is!" said Angie.

Chapter 21

No invitation came from the King for them to have dinner with him.

"He's probably tired out himself, after the day's excitement. More excitement than he's had in days, around here," Jim suggested.

"It's half an hour to an hour before time to go down to the Great Hall, here."

He started to take off the cote-hardi.

"You keep that on," said Angie. "You might as well, now you've got it on. I'd like the Prince and the others to see you've got *some* good clothes."

"My arm itches and I can't get at it through this elephant-blanket material!"

"Ignore it. Be a man."

"I already am one," said Jim, annoyed. But he kept the cote-hardi on.

The restraint was not wasted. The voice of the man-at-arms outside the door came through the wood.

"His Grace the Prince of Wales to see you, my Lord!"

"More fuss and flummery . . ." muttered Jim. He went to the door and opened it.

"Your Grace!" he said. "How good of you to come by!"

"Not coming at an inconvenient time, am I?" Edward strode past into the room. "No, I see you're already dressed for dinner—ah, good eve to you, Lady Angela."

But this time Angie made no excuse to take herself out of the room and leave the two of them alone. She rose briefly from where she sat, smiling, curtsied and sat back down again.

"Will Your Grace take a chair?"

"No, no. I believe not. Think better on my feet, James.

With poor Verweather laid up the way he is—ugly sort of wound that, inside a man—I am somewhat at a loss in my campaign to regain the goodwill of my father. Now, you people had been talking about the fact you might want to stay only three days—leaving the day after tomorrow. But doubtless it would not put you out too much to stay until he's on his feet again?"

"I'm afraid it'll have to be only three days, Your Grace," said Angie. "There is no more time to visit before Lady Geronde's wedding, and perhaps James told you about the Bishop cleansing our Malencontri chapel just for this, and the attention of Holy Church upon the day set for the wedding."

The Prince looked at her briefly and as sourly as manners would allow. Pointedly, he continued to speak to Jim.

"Surely, under these circumstances . . ."

"I crave your pardon, Your Grace," said Jim, "but as my lady's just reminded you, we have no choice. We dare not disappoint Holy Church, no matter what the reason."

"Well, I suppose not. But a brave man deeply wounded, undoubtedly dying if—but of course you will have taken that into consideration, being the one who saved him from bleeding to death. But I must say it is awkward, damned awkward!"

He chewed on his lower lip and turned abruptly to the door.

"Well, if that is the way of it, there it is! I will see you at dinner—that is, unless the Countess prefers to eat in our room. So, give you good eve."

He went out of the door, closing it somewhat sharply behind him.

"Countess, hah!" said Angie. "He'll keep her in the room to work out some new solution for him, never mind what the rest of us want and deserve!"

"She can't be completely free of conscience about all these plots and things."

"She can where he's concerned. She'd turn the world upside down for him if she could, and never mind the people that'd fall off. I haven't had the time to tell you, but that was what Geronde and I were talking about when you came in after the fight. She feels the same way I do—that it was almost surely Joan that came up with the idea of the fight, hoping it would be Brian who was laid up, and we *couldn't* leave until he was fit to ride—some days anyway."

"I thought you liked Joan; even admired her," Jim said.

"I do. She's good-hearted and smart. Too smart for our own good, when it comes to a situation like this. Bet you a golden florin she has some new scheme by dawn tomorrow."

"Well, if she does," said Jim, determinedly, "I'll come up with something to settle our leaving once and for all. Come on, we're close enough to dinner time to go down now, and neither the Prince nor the Fair Maid are going to be able to make trouble for us with everybody else joining us at the High Table."

"Don't be too optimistic," said Angie as they went out the door. But then she put her arm through his and squeezed it. "I know you can get us out if you really want to."

He squeezed her arm back to reassure her.

"I wonder if Brian will be there, after this morning and the session with the King?" said Angie, passing the flask of clean water they had brought with them to Jim just before they entered Tiverton's Great Hall. "Even if he got a little rest, he must still be knocked out."

"He probably is," said Jim. "But he wouldn't miss dinner simply because of being tired, and in this case, he won't mind being congratulated any more than anyone else would. I'll bet you everyone else is already at table."

"The King, too?"

"There you have me, but I doubt it. He had first crack at Brian right after the encounter."

They went in, and there was indeed a crowd already at

table. Among them were five well-dressed men—probably, Jim thought, top functionaries in the King's traveling household—whom Jim had not seen before; obviously gentlemen, and probably some of them also knights. They stood up at the sight of him—a sign they considered him of superior rank. No sign of Brian or Geronde yet.

About the only fault Jim could find with the gathering was that Dafydd was not at the High Table. Sir Harimore was there, once more as stiff as he had been since he had first set eyes on Joan. What appeared to be three squires sat at the top of the lengthwise right-hand table just below the High Table—one of them the one who had been kneeling over the fallen Verweather after the combat.

Jim and Angie were seated. None of the men stood for her, that particular politeness not having become a general custom yet, and the naming of the five to Jim took place— across from Jim there was Sir Mathew Stairbridge, the oldest, in his late thirties or early forties. Beside him in order were Sir Osborne Leeds, Sir William atte Bowe, Sir Tore de Main and Sir John Crait, all of whom addressed Jim as Mage and clearly had known in advance who their table companions were to be. They all also praised the magick skill with which Jim had saved Verweather from sure death.

"All in the day's duty," said Jim.

Wine was poured, appetizers served by the table servants. Jim took up his flask and uncapped it.

"I'm sure none of the gentlemen present will be offended if I water our wine with a particularly magicked water. I am obliged to drink it after an exercise of the high Art to which I am committed. Since my Lady is exposed as well to much of the magick I must work, I always give her some also."

The gentlemen all hastened to assure them that they were not in the least offended. The long-faced senior, Sir Mathew Stairbridge, however, had something more to say.

"Most humbly I crave your pardon and beg you to stop me if my question is impertinent, Mage—"

"Forgive me in my turn if I correct you, sir," said Jim. "I am not a Mage, though somewhat qualified in our Art. That address is for only the highest and best of we Magickians accepted by the Church. With your indulgence I prefer simply to be addressed as Sir James."

"By all means," said Sir Mathew. "I will then venture on my question, hoping you will stop me if I am impertinent. But I have never known, nor even heard before of a magickian who had a wife. Is it that—"

"It is easily explained," said Jim, interrupting for a second time. "I was married before I began my study of the Art."

"Of course! That never occurred to me. It is gentle of Your Magickianship—forgive me—Sir James, that you gave answer to my rude question. But perhaps, if you would be so kind, I might also ask—"

But Jim was spared any further grilling by the arrival of Brian and Geronde, Brian looking somewhat pale but otherwise the same as usual. This time everybody in the room stood, including Jim and Angela. The gentlemen at the High Table all had their mazers in their hand, and Jim hastily picked up his.

"Sir Brian," said Sir Mathew. "It is an honor to us all that such a warrior as yourself should dine with us. With your agreement, sir, may we drink to you and the lightning of your sword forever."

"Sirs, you honor me above my deserts," said Brian with his usual modesty, as he and Geronde mounted to the dais. "It was a mere engagement with blunted weapons; and nothing of which a knight should take more than passing notice."

"Still we would drink to you then for what you are, Sir Brian, not just for today. It is noised about that Sir Chandos has named you as one of the first swordsmen of England, and it would pleasure us to drink to you as a moment to remember and tell of to our children. If you do not object."

"Sir Chandos also honors me—far above my station or deserts." Brian's pale cheeks were faintly stained with pink. "But if it will pleasure you to drink, never let it be said that a Neville-Smythe stood between gentlemen and their wine."

Everyone at the High Table drank, as did, informally, those at the lower tables, who were also standing. Curiously however, Jim noted, none of the latter cheered or otherwise made a sound. At Malencontri there would have been a good deal of normally forbidden freelance cheering from among the lower tables—to be immediately and sternly repressed by the masters and mistresses of the various castle departments. These Tiverton servants were perhaps too well trained in some ways.

Meanwhile, at the High Table, the drinking included Angie, who had picked up her own mazer, and Geronde, who had been passed one by a servant.

They all sat down again. Brian and Geronde took their seats at the far end of the board. Clearly the empty near end had been left free for the Prince and the Fair Maid, who continued not to show up. This seating put Sir Harimore at Brian's left elbow, seated on the long dimension of the table but next to the end, and he did not hesitate to make use of the closeness.

"Sir Brian," he said, "I must congratulate you on a plan of battle excellently planned and beautifully executed."

Jim could not be sure—one of the table candles was now between him and Brian—whether another touch of color came to Brian's cheeks. Praise from a respected fellow-expert always meant more than that from the less qualified.

"Oh", Brian said, "I had no particular plan to speak of. As for the execution, I only took advantage of an opportunity when it occured."

Sir Harimore's eyes met his with a look that Jim interpreted as rather plainly saying, *We two know better, don't we?* But he did not pursue the subject.

"I am sure Sir Brian is correct," said Sir Mathew, frowning. "He fought as a knight should, thinking of nothing but his next sword-blow."

Sir Harimore turned his gaze on the tall knight with keen anticipation.

"Say you so, sir?" he said.

"I do indeed, sir," said Sir Mathew, heavily.

"An interesting division of opinion," said Sir Harimore. "Perhaps you and I, sir, might go further into its discussion after dinner, just the two of us, since it would not be fit to speak opinions simply between the two of us, when all are at table."

"Sir, I look forward to such a pleasant eventuality—"

Jim felt an explosion beginning to kindle in the air of the gathering. Hastily, to divert attention from it, he spoke up with the first thing he could think of that would attract the attention of the others.

"I now have a terrier bitch and a litter of her pups in my room," he informed the table.

It worked gratifyingly,

"In your *chamber*?" echoed Sir Mathew. "May I ask why, Mag—Sir James?"

"Oh, it was a stroke of luck and the kindness of Sir Brian," said Jim. "At present I'm busy putting my castle of Malencontri into preparation against the movement west of the plague now in London." He dived into the details of this preparation, getting all their attention and winding up with the usefulness of terriers as rat killers.

". . . the only drawback to having these dogs under our noses, so to speak," he ended, "is that I begin to think they may have carried some fleas in from the kennels. You have been here at Tiverton longer than I, Sir Mathew. Have you noticed many fleas about?"

So addressed, Sir Mathew had no choice but to answer.

"Oh, one or two, now and then," he said, "Fleas are everywhere, as all know, but the great cleanliness and attention to duty of the staff here has kept Tiverton quite remarkably clean of all vermin."

"Fleas can never be escaped entirely," opined one of the other knights to whom Jim and Angie had been introduced this evening for the first time.

"True," said Jim, and denizens of the kennels having been brought up, the talk among the men turned to hunting. Harimore and Sir Mathew found themselves agreeing strongly on one point connected with this, and both knights smiled agreeably at each other. Angie and Geronde, separated from each other by three male bodies, each eager to have their say in the hunting discussion, a topic where every man had a different opinion, looked at each other in eloquent silence. But when the first of the main dinner dishes began to make their arrival, the matter died as all started taking the first edge off their appetite.

When talk began to revive again, it had broken up into a number of separate conversations between people sitting next to each other. Geronde and Angie, even with a little distance between them, began a discussion on the subject of keeping a castle in a constant state of readiness for the unexpected, and the men between them were listening with not only politeness, but also a tinge of respect, as Angie was the wife of a Magickian, and Geronde the wife-to-be of the day's victor.

At the end of the table, Brian and Sir Harimore had now fallen into a highly professional conversation concerning how to balance the need for stouter harness on a destrier (that would not break on the coming together of their riders in tournament) against the fact that such harness might lessen the agility of the animal just when it was most needed.

Only, from time to time, Jim noticed Harimore casting eager, but disappointed, glances in the direction of the stairs down which the Fair Maid and the Prince would be coming if they decided to join the dinner after all.

But by the end of the dinner neither had appeared. As the gathering began to break up and everyone stood, Geronde and Angie moved closer to each other at last. Geronde whispered to Angie.

"Brian must go to bed again. This dinner was hard on him on top of his strivings of this morning. I'll come to your room as soon as I can after he is full asleep, and I will bring Danielle and the Countess. It is she we must set straight on the matter of our leaving, day after tomorrow."

"You're right," said Angie. "See you then."

Geronde returned to Brian, whom she had left only briefly, and steered him off toward the stairs.

"What's all this confab about with the four of you?" Jim asked Angie as soon as they were well out of the hearing of everyone else and climbing the stairs themselves.

"Oh, just a sort of small war party amongst the lot of us," said Angie. "Nothing you need to worry about—just to get across to Joan the absolute necessity of our getting back to Malencontri as planned. Joan's the one who gives young Edward his ideas. All she has to do is stop doing it, at least as far as it involves keeping us here."

"That sounds kind of serious."

"Don't bother about it, as I said. Just talk. No danger of Geronde going after her with a boar spear."

It was notorious that a boar spear—with its cross-piece to keep the boar from madly hurling himself up the shaft of the spear penetrating him, to savage the man holding it—was Geronde's favorite personal weapon. In fact, Jim recalled, it had been with one such she had threatened him the first time she had met him in his dragon body.

"Hm," Jim said, a sense of foreboding still lingering.

They reached their room, and once in it, Jim stripped off the cote-hardi with a sigh and rolled up his sleeve. About to scratch in relief, he checked and stared at three very obvious flea bites. Angie was the first to speak.

"Jim! I thought you warded us all who came here against fleas!"

"I did!" said Jim stupefied, staring at his arm. Nothing warded against could get through that ward—all the magic he had learned reeled around him. If wards could fail—

"I know you did. I heard you do it."

"That's right!"

"Unless . . ." said Angie, thoughtfully, "you forgot to ward yourself. I don't remember you doing that."

Jim thought wildly back to the moment of his warding. He and Angie had just come back from a first session with the King—

"Maybe you're right," he said unhappily. "I remember warding you first, then everybody else—by God, maybe I did forget myself!"

Suddenly coming out of searching his memory, he magically erased the bites. Aware of a certain tension in Angie, he said cheerfully, "they're only wounds, after all, and getting rid of those is my most-used magick. You were right. I did forget to protect myself. But no harm done."

"I certainly hope so," said Angie, sounding—and looking—anything but reassured. "As I remember it, when a plague-infected flea bites and sucks out blood, it also regurgitates some of the plague virus—and that's how the bite victim gets infected. I'd be a lot happier . . . oh, why didn't I let you scratch when you wanted to, earlier? We'd have found it was bites, then—and maybe even caught the flea in action! That way, when you magicked the bites away, anything he'd regurgitated into the wounds would've gone with the wounds themselves—the magick does that, doesn't it?"

"Absolutely!" said Jim. "All foreign substances, as long as you get them before the body takes them up, one way or another. Anyway, there's no reason for thinking that simply because there's fleas here, any of them are carrying the plague. The plague's in London, the last we heard—remem-

ber? That's a long ways off, and nobody here at Tiverton
has shown any signs of having it. Fleas are everywhere, as
Sir Mathew, or one of the others we met at dinner said. No,
any idea the flea or fleas that bit me were carrying the infection is nonsense!"

Angie looked at least partially convinced.

But Jim's own heart sank a little. He had first noticed
that itching the night before, but had ignored it, as he was
already halfway into sleep. Once an infection had left the
original site and was free in his body, as he had just told
Angie, the part of the magick that cleaned out foreign matter
would not have been able to touch it. A wound would have
become a sickness.

But, then, even if by some wild chance he had been infected, it would still not help to tell Angie about the itching
of the previous night. It would only make permanent her
worry about it. No, telling wouldn't change anything.

Chapter 22

It seemed like no time at all before there came the voice of
the man-at-arms on duty at the door, announcing "The
Countess Joan, the Lady Geronde, the—"

"Yes, yes!" called back Angie. "They're all welcome!"

Three woman came in, including Danielle, led by Joan,
looking not the least uncomfortable or annoyed to find herself one of a company that included an archer's wife.

"Good afternoon, Sir James," they all told him, cheerfully
enough, but he could take a hint as well as the next man.

He cleared his throat.

"Good afternoon, ladies," he said. "Angie, I want to talk
to that Kennel Master who supplied Brian with these puppies—and incidentally, find out what the carpenter's done
with the pen we ordered. So if you all will excuse me. . . ."

Expressions of regret on losing him, and he was out the door.

"I take it," he said, to both the man-at-arms and the waiting on-duty servant, "both the Kennel Master and the carpenter are to be found in the main courtyard?"

"Oh yes, my lord," they answered.

He headed for the stairs. He had no real interest in the Kennel Master, but he was definitely interested in why the pen had not shown up. One ordered at Malencontri would have been there, finished, within a couple of hours of the order being given—and the staff at Malencontri made no pretense of being the well-oiled human machine that those here had the reputation of being.

Then, after finding out what had held up the old man's delivery, perhaps he could find some other male to talk to.

However, his route to the main courtyard necessarily required him to pass through Tiverton's Great Hall, where he found Sir Harimore at the cleaned-up High Table, sitting alone and drinking.

"Sir Harimore!" he said, meaning to pass on with nothing more than an exchange of salutations. But it was not to be.

"Sir James!" said Harimore. "I have been hoping to speak further to you and, if possible, alone. Will you join me in a cup?"

There was no polite way Jim could refuse such an invitation, unless he had a very good or real excuse. He did not.

"Gladly," he said, stepping up onto the dais and taking a seat across from the knight—though there was no real gladness in him at the prospect of more wine just now. "We've had all too little time to talk either at Malencontri or here."

The "cup" to which Harimore referred was of course a mazer, capable of holding at least three ordinary full wine-cups of liquid. Pouring only a little wine into the one before him, he stole a glance at the figure opposite him and noticed that not only was the wine in Harimore's cup unwatered, but he must have been drinking here since lunch. No evidence of drunkenness showed, however, in his erect figure or his voice.

"That is so," Harimore said, "and I have a couple of things I have been wishing very much to speak you on. The first is I had forgotten also to tender you my heartfelt sorrow and apology for addressing you so discourteously in that moment when we rode together back to the Earl of Somerset's last Christmas party."

"I remember no such discourtesy," said Jim hastily. A further apology from this knight could be a prickly matter for them both. He took a swallow from his mazer to hide his face from this perceptive, but ordinarily unemotional, man.

"You are generous," said Harimore. "But it was discourteous. It was churlish. I do not mean to try and lessen my offense, Sir James—"

"Call me James," said Jim. A little bit of informality might ease the present uncomfortable situation.

"Then I must insist on your calling me Harry—as I was saying, I do not mean to lessen the added offense I gave that day by mentioning, with your pardon, that you frequently have an odd way of speaking and, as I said in apologizing at Malencontri, I, unthinking as I was, mistakenly assumed that you were not one born and accustomed to the state you occupied—probably no more than a jumped-up squire."

"You pointed out, that day, quite properly," said Jim, "that I was wearing my sword incorrectly. I have since thanked you many times for that instruction and have amended my bad habit."

"Correct speech and courteous speech, even between equals, is one thing," replied Harimore, "courtesie, something else again, particularly when one is in the presence of a superior."

"But I'm not superior—" said Jim, his command of

fourteenth-century polite upper-class English beginning to break down.

"Pray, James, let me finish. This apologizing is not something I am familiar with. But truth above all. I after learned from Sir Brian not only that you are much more of a Magickian—regardless of the title by which you should be addressed—but of your bravery against the ogre at the Loathly Tower, and on divers other occasions, which he had witnessed—feats of arms I shall probably die without equaling. Therefore, I once more beg the grace of your pardon for my ill manners."

"If pardon be required—which I doubt—" Jim was beginning to appreciate the pain in the other man that had driven him to this unaccustomed apology, and Jim's heart warmed to Sir Harimore in a way it never had before, "—you have pardon freely from me. And now let us forget that moment, and drink as close friends should, Harry."

"James," said Harimore, "you cannot realize what a weight you have lifted from my conscience. I have never been able to do wrong to any man without striving to amend the matter as soon as possible. The duty preys on me 'til done."

They drank together, Jim more heartily than he had ever expected to when Harimore had first spoken to him just now.

"What do you think of the situation in this castle, James?"

"I'm not too happy with it," said Jim, with rare openness. An unusual but very real thing in the male world had taken place: he found himself not only liking, but trusting the man opposite—a mixture of understanding and respect.

"Hah!" said Harimore. "For me it has only been an uneasy feeling. But before I left to visit Brian, I took care to not only have myself shriven, but to buy from a pardoner a pardon for any sins I should commit until I was home again. With those two things out of the way, a knight has only to take care to behave honorably and die an honorable death, if so be the will of God. Therefore what could trouble us? But I am curious to find if you know."

"I'm afraid I don't, any more than you do," said Jim.

"Ah, there you are wrong, James. You know and understand a great deal more than I do about some things. For one, you seem most happily married."

"Well—yes, I guess I am," said Jim.

"Strange," said Harimore in a musing tone, "I know so few in that case. Only you—and Brian, so soon to be—and I suppose you could add that archer . . . what is his name?"

"Dafydd ap Hywel," said Jim, wishing he could tell this newly closer friend that Dafydd was actually a Prince in the Drowned Land.

"I lay it," said Harimore, "to a man having strong, close companions. We none of us know when we may need someone to stand back to back with us against the world—but that is not what I have been wishing to ask you about. It could be fairly said then that you understand women?"

"Good Lord, no!" said Jim, jolted into forgetting fourteenth-century speech completely. "Any man who says he does . . ."

He ran out of words, boggled at the idea.

"On the other hand," he went on, "they don't completely understand us—though they seem to understand more about us than we understand about them. To be fair, it may be that we don't talk to them enough, and they talk at the drop of a hat—I mean, they have no trouble talking. We have to work at it and remember to do it—most of us, that is. Of course there are silent women, too, just as there are men who pour words out. No single rule. But for most of us, a few words may make us a friend for life, or make an enemy who won't rest until he or you is dead and buried. Two sexes with two different sets of problems in two different versions of the world . . . on the other hand, when you really come to love a woman . . . I can't describe it."

He checked himself.

"Forgive me for running on," he said, "but I don't believe even Merlin could explain the difference—" *Not that he ever would,* Jim added to himself.

"But this is the matter I have wished deeply to talk with you on," said Harimore. "You see, I believe I love a woman in the manner you describe—"

Oh, no! thought Jim. *New friendship or not—not this, first crack out of the box!*

But this was the fourteenth century, not the twentieth—or the twenty-first, by this time, back home. Harimore was plowing ahead with his problem, and Jim was obliged to try to help if he could.

"—and my honor will not permit me ever to even tell her about it. She has a husband in the Earl of Salisbury, I understand. Her being with the Prince of Wales, now, then is . . . ?"

"A close cousin and close friend since childhood."

"Hm," said Harimore. "In any case she is married. That is all, and to someone else. I cannot speak my heart to her. In any case, I would not have the words. But that is not my great concern, James. It is that I must see her daily, and it is a torture to me, James. I feel that every word I say to her is wrong. Nor do I know about what a man should talk to a woman. He can hardly talk weapons and weapon-work, only slightly less can he talk of horseflesh and hunting, even if she has shown a preference for those things, and only a coxcomb would seek to amuse her with tales of his combats. Can nothing be done for me? Perhaps . . . magick?"

So that was where Harimore had been heading all this time. *You could have stayed at Malencontri where you wouldn't be daily tortured by being unable to speak, after we'd all gone off to Tiverton here,* thought Jim.

"Magic," he said, "won't give you a golden voice and an endless fund of words, I'm afraid. That's not one of the things it's made to do."

"And you, with your experience with a wife and clearly

being happy, therewith—you have no helpful advice for me?"

"What I could tell you that works for me, might work exactly wrong for you. As I think I may have said earlier, everyone is different, both man and women."

"But surely there is something you can say."

"Treat her like a sister," said Jim, in desperation.

"But would not that in itself be dishonorable? When I know I feel . . ."

"Not at all," said Jim. "It's merely an exercise in manners to make conversation easy between the two of you. You're only *treating* her that way for courtoisie. It is the polite thing to do as a gentleman, since you can do no otherwise— and you may find yourself with more words in her company as you get used to conversation with her."

Harimore brightened visibly.

"You think so?"

"It's a definite possibility." *In fact,* thought Jim, *she may not like being treated like a sister all the time, and go to work to draw you out.*

"It is a noble suggestion, for which I thank you, James. Unfortunately, I never had a sister."

The man's impossible, thought Jim.

"Did you ever have a female cousin, about your own age, when you were young?"

"Oh, yes. I never liked her."

All the better, thought Jim.

"Try it anyway," said Jim. "What've you got to lose? And it's perfectly honorable, a mere politeness."

"Well, perhaps I shall. You should understand, James, of three sons I was the only one who lived beyond the fifth year, and my father was a stern man. We had a holding of some worth, and I have never lacked for funds, but he was first and foremost a knight. He gave himself few pleasures and no more for me than he allowed himself. In short, I was raised like a monk—but a monk-at-arms. I do not resent him for this. What I know today of the marvelous art of weapons I owe to that upbringing, but it has left me without much of the ordinary gentleman's graces."

He look piercingly at Jim.

"What I am endeavoring to say, James, is that my heart fails me—as it has never failed me with weapon in my hand in my life—when I think of doing as you advise. But you do think that the effort will help me if I endeavor to essay it?"

"I do," said Jim.

"My deepest thanks to you. You are a light in my darkness."

"Nothing remarkable in what I said," answered Jim, gruffly. "But now, I must be off on the errand I was about to do when I found you here."

"Of course. And once more my undying gratitude."

Jim escaped to the castle's outer courtyard, in which, as was the case at Malencontri and many castles, were situated the castle's outbuildings. They were generally placed there because they were made of wood, more easily worked and cheaper and faster to build than the stone castles themselves; wood which might pose a danger to the main castle if the work often carried on in them should cause them to catch on fire.

"Carpenter?" he asked the first courtyard denizen he encountered—a raggedly dressed youngster of perhaps twelve.

"The fourth outbuilding to the right, my lord," said the youngster. "Where the planks are piled before."

"Oh, yes," said Jim. He went toward it and found another urchin of about the same size in the front part of the building, but no one else.

"Master Carpenter!" he commanded. "Take me to him, immediately!"

"He is not here, my lord."

"I can see that!" said Jim. "Fetch him to me at once, then!"

"Grant me the indulgence of your grace, my lord. I don't know where he is. He did not say on leaving."

Jim looked at him with suspicion. This boy, like the first one he had spoken to in this courtyard, had a clarity and correctness that made his speech close to the language of the upper classes. Certainly interior servants of any castle practiced to get their words right, but this was seldom encountered in courtyards among staff with broad local accents.

"Takes a nap at this time of day, does he?"

"Oh no, my lord. Never."

"Well, where could he be?"

"Begging your forgiveness, my lord, I do not know."

Jim gave the boy up as a source of information. He strode past him into the workshop proper. Looking around there, amid the comfortable odors of newly sawed wood, he found what must be the pen Angie had wanted. But it looked as if someone not even merely of apprentice level had done the work—more like something an eight- to twelve-year-old might throw together on impulse one summer afternoon.

But it might hold together for the present, anyway.

"Carry this," he told the carpentry's sole visible representative, a lanky young man.

"My lord, I was to stay and watch things—"

Jim broke in. He had no choice but to act the part he had fallen into on landing in this medieval world. Such protest by someone like this boy against someone of Jim's rank was not supposed to be tolerated. The words to use were words he had no choice but to use.

"Sirrah!" he roared. "Do you speak so to a knight, and one who is a guest of the castle? I will have you—"

"Sir, I will do it! Immediately I will do it! Pray avert your anger—see, I take it up right now!"

The lad sounded honestly terrified. Where his speech and answers had rung false before in Jim's ears, there was no doubt at all that he was speaking the truth now with every fiber of his being.

Jim turned and led the way back up to his and Angie's room. The other women were undoubtedly still there in the Solar, but at least he could have the boy carry it in, and then both of them, with apologies, could leave once more.

But when he finally knocked on the door and shouted to Angie that he was coming in for a second, she opened it almost immediately, and he saw the room was empty. Neither of them said anything until the boy had carried in the pen and taken his leave.

"Well, your talk didn't last long," he said to Angie, busy dealing with the puppies' mother, who was expressing some silently expressed unhappiness at losing the blanket she had come to regard as her own. It had plainly been washed and folded, but Angie unfolded it now and let the dog carefully and thoroughly sniff it all over before acknowledging it as the blanket she had once owned. Angie immediately refolded it and laid it down inside the pen, then went to wash her hands in the basin.

"Where's my soap?" she said to herself in a vexed voice. "Ah, here it is."

The mother dog leaped inside the pen, carefully sniffed the blanket again to make sure it was still the same one, then examined around the pen's edges, nosing back the pups that tried to join her. Finally, she began carefully scratching the smooth blanket into the wrinkles proper for herself and her family to lie upon.

She licked the air in Angie's direction in apology for her nosiness with household affairs, lay down and let the pups crowd around her. Taking them one by one gently between her paws, she went to work cleaning each of them with her tongue.

"Well at least the pen didn't fall apart," said Jim. The two of them had been watching, fascinated by the dogs adjusting to their new enclosure.

"Yes," said Angie, "and at least the sides are high enough to keep the pups from roaming all over and dirtying up the floor."

"But what about the women?"

"Oh, none of them except me seemed to mind."

"But I mean," said Jim, "I hadn't thought your talk would have been that short. Why?"

"Oh, that." Angie abandoned the pups and turned to look at him. "In as few words as possible, it was simply a matter of giving my Lady Joan of Kent, etc., an ultimatum, so she could pass it on to the Prince."

"What ultimatum?"

"In short, we told her we all had husbands who would listen to us—"

"Oh?" said Jim, his male ego raising its head suddenly like an alerted wolf.

"—and if necessary those husbands would go to the King in a body to say good-bye to him, since, as he knew, we had only been able to stay the three days. She took it very well. Probably used to being faced with ultimatums."

"And you just went ahead and told her that without telling me, and before you made that promise in my name."

"We had to see if it would work with her, before getting you all stewed up."

"You could have told me."

"Well, maybe I should have," said Angie pacifically. "But you will do it if I ask you?"

"Well, I suppose I could. But how I'm going to suggest something like that to Brian, and especially to Dafydd— who, don't forget, in this place is officially just a common archer, and archers don't tell kings off to their face. For that matter, no more do minor knights like Brian and myself— particularly Brian at the moment, when the King's so tickled with his win over Verweather."

"But the King loves all of you—particularly Brian and yourself, right now!"

"He doesn't love us so much he can let us talk that way to his face. He's the King of England, Angie! And this is the fourteenth century!"

"Jim . . ."

"Don't look at me like that, Angie."

"But you *will* do it if I ask you, won't you?"

"I suppose I could—probably better than anybody. After all I'm a Magickian—well, almost a Magickian—once I'm voted in by the Collegiate. He wouldn't want to offend not only the English Magickians, but those of the whole world by doing anything drastic to me. But what about Brian and Dafydd?"

"They'll agree to do it if you do."

"Fine! Their doom is in my hands now."

"It'll be all right. You see, Joan is on our side now. I told you she was sharp. She understands it'll be better for her and the Prince to keep you alive and well. So she'll talk him into going to the King first and smoothing the path for you."

"And she promised that?"

"Not in so many words, but she promised. She's not a liar, Jim—either directly or by implication."

"And even if she does, you trust young Edward to do it?"

"Don't you?"

Jim hesitated.

"I don't know!" he said. "Sometimes I think he's a man, sometimes I think he's still a kid. He's got guts—he proved that at Crécy, according to Chandos Herald. But that was war. This isn't war. It's his father he's been trying desperately to get back into the good graces of."

"Well, what exactly do you think, then?"

"Well, maybe he will. He jolted me the other day. He looked ready to blow up from pure selfishness when I told him what he was asking for would be against Brian's vows. Calmed down right away, accepted defeat with a good grace, and smiled it off. He wasn't kidding about the smile, either, it was genuine. He said God forbid the day come when he asked a knight to go against his vows. Now, those are words ninety percent of the ordinary knights I've met here wouldn't have answered with."

"Well, good!" said Angie, hugging him. "I'll make you a cup of tea."

"I'd rather have something to drink after hearing about this."

"I'll make some tea," said Angie. "This day's not yet half over—"

The words were prophetic. Even before the kettle had begun to boil, there came a scratching at the door—an almost timid scratching.

"Now what?" Jim said. He raised his voice. *"Come!"*

The Prince came in—hesitating abruptly as he saw Angie.

"Er—James," said the Prince. "Could you step outside for a few words with me?"

"Of course," said Jim. "Honored to do so, Your Grace."

"Good. Oh, good day, my lady."

"Good day, Your Grace."

"He will be back shortly."

"My thanks to you, Your Grace, for your gentleness in telling me."

"Not at all," said the Prince gruffly. He turned and went out through the door again. Jim followed, casting a reassuring glance over his shoulder. Angie raised her two clasped hands over her head and shook them in a boxer's signal of victory.

Chapter 23

The Prince led Jim away from his doorway and the servant and man-at-arms there, whose interest was showing clearly on their faces. It was a dull job, Jim recognized, just standing there either all night or all day. It was not something that he and Angie insisted on at Malencontri, either. It was the staff itself that insisted.

What, leave the door to their lord and lady's room unguarded and unserved? As if he was some ordinary knight instead of being a paladin who had fought beside King Arthur, and a famous Magickian, to boot? Here at Tiverton they would undoubtedly feel the same about their King and any noble guests of his.

After all, servants everywhere knew how things should properly be done in *their* castle.

Still, the Prince led Jim away from even these faithful followers, clear around the curving corridor that followed the shape of the outer wall of the tower, until they two were completely private.

They were alone now in the corridor, close to the stairs. The afternoon sunlight from a single arrow slit fell squarely on the face of the younger man, looking stern with concern in a way Jim had never seen it appear before.

There were no doorways to rooms visible now, either before or behind them; nevertheless, young Edward lowered his voice when he finally spoke.

"This is madness, James!"

"Your Grace?"

"You must know what I mean. This plan of your wives to ask you, Brian and the archer to confront my father and tell him you are leaving, whether or no."

"What other choice do we have, Your Grace? The wedding day set, the chapel readied for a Mass the moment the wedding itself is over—our obligation to Holy Church—"

"Yes, yes, I know all about that!" said the Prince. "But not for God's sake in that hare-brained, arrogant manner you, or they, plan. My father will not even wait to hear your last words, but have you thrown in dungeons, all six of you—there to rot though even Chandos himself, if he was here, should beg mercy for you! The wives and your friends may not see that, but surely you do!"

"Indeed," sighed Jim. "But what other way in honor is there?"

"There must be some! I myself will not be able to do anything for you if you attempt such a rash act. Probably lucky not to be thrown in dungeon myself for bringing you here to insult him. For he will take it as an insult, without doubt! You do not flout the royal will!"

"I know," said Jim.

"It is not of myself I am thinking. True, this could put an end to all my careful plan to regain his good graces. But you must believe me, James, when I say that in this hap it is you and the others that I am concerned with, in that I urged you to come, and what happens to you here is my responsibility. More than that, indeed, I have some small love for you and Brian—the archer as well, even, though nothing but a common man and Welshman to boot, poor fellow."

There were moments when Jim's throat went dry, and his gullet burned to tell people like the Prince that Dafydd was their equal—and more than their equal—in royal heritage. But his promise to Dafydd kept him silent. Young Edward was going on.

"—did you not all rescue me from that mad Magickian who kept me captive and made a simulacrum of me from snow, to put among the French knights and claim that I had changed sides against our honest Englishmen? I would save you all if I could, but if you insist upon running naked upon a swordpoint, what is there I can do!"

"Gladly would I relieve you of that responsibility, Your Grace," Jim said in the best tradition of fourteenth-century politesse. "But I see nothing I can do."

"Come, man!" said the Prince impatiently. "You are a Magickian. Surely there is something!"

"Well . . ." Jim looked out the arrow slit thoughtfully. "With your kind assistance, perhaps . . ."

"Anything! That is to say—whatever is actually possible

for me to perform. Simply tell me what it is."

Jim sighed doubtfully.

"Let me see . . . it would involve you saying a word or two to the King before we come to bid him farewell, for that is all we planned to do, after all, Your Grace. . . ."

"Yes, yes! Say what?"

"Well, it would merely be Your Grace begging him to pay no attention to the rumor."

"Rumor? What rumor? There are no rumors here."

"Yet there may be one. Messengers come and go from the Earl of Cumberland on crown business, papers for the King to sign and that sort of thing. One of them might well have been a man who had served in a household of which the Countess was a part, and had an admiration for her, so that when he was coming or going he had the chance to speak her. She would not have remembered him, of course."

"I should think not!"

"But he might have passed on to her the latest rumor in London."

"Yes . . . and so?"

"A rumor that the Earl of Cumberland might already have heard, also—that here in Tiverton the King had been talking to and entertaining enemies of the Earl. Of course, once the Countess had heard this, she felt it her duty to tell you this—saying what a shame it was she could not recall the messenger's name—it had not occurred to the man to re-mind her of it—and would not even be sure if she could recognize him again."

"But James!" said the Prince, impatiently. "My father has been doing no such thing!"

Jim turned from the light of the arrow slit and looked him solemnly in the eyes.

"But, Your Grace, were you not aware that I myself, Brian and Dafydd ap Hywel, are all enemies of the King— according to the Earl? Indeed, he's already managed once to have articles of treason drawn against us—though they've since been withdrawn—possibly due to the good efforts of Sir John Chandos . . . and there are others who were at that time accused."

For a long second the Prince stared. Then the stare gave way to a look of fierce exultation,

"Like myself, by all the saints—you would say! Though my father would never permit Cumberland, no matter how powerful, to accuse me of any such thing! He would have him in the Tower of London, first—in no such pleasant place as his usual quarters there! But how does this—aha! I see. There is no real love between him and this ambitious half-brother of his. I tell you that frankly, James. But Cumberland is the most useful of all the great lords to him; and at his age, he would avoid trouble if possible. He wishes merely to live his life comfortably and sign papers."

"You will, of course, Your Grace," said Jim, tactfully, "know your father better than any man living."

"And I do. I do!" The Prince clapped a hand on Jim's shoulder. "I knew that Magickian's mind of yours would come up with an answer to this coil! I must tell the Countess; and, all being well, will see my father yet this afternoon, or perhaps early evening."

"And perhaps you'll let me know by tomorrow morning if you've seen him?"

"I will. My word on it. Now, I shall release you to return to your lady. By the way, what possessed you to have a bitch and her whelps in your room?"

"It's something of a long story, Your Grace."

"Ah. Well, then, I have no time for it now. Later, perhaps. Give you good day, James."

He turned, and could be heard a moment later clattering down the stairs.

Jim went back to Angie.

"Well?" said Angie, as he came in.

"Nothing to it," said Jim, throwing himself into a chair.

"James Eckert—"

"I'm just about to tell you," said Jim. "He warned me his father would throw all three—no, all six of us, including you wives—into the dungeons here for such presumption, if we talked to him as you suggested. He'd take it as a personal insult. I sighed and said our honor and promises gave us no choice but to do it . . . and then, when he was fully worked up, I gave him a possible way out."

"Go on," said Angie. "Don't just sit there smirking."

"I never smirk!" said Jim, stung.

Angie said nothing. One argument at a time.

"What I suggested to him was that he go to the King and beg him to pay no attention to the latest rumor from London. Now, you could at last ask me what that rumor was."

"What was the rumor?"

"Something one of those almost-daily crown messengers bringing business matters from the court—papers to be signed, and so forth—stopped to tell Joan: the latest rumor at court was that the King, far off here at Tiverton, was entertaining enemies of the Earl of Cumberland."

"The King's not *afraid* of Cumberland, surely? He can do what he royally well wants?"

"Oh, of course. He could have his head chopped off. Cumberland, like Oxford, can count on a considerable armed strength, but the King has all England to back him up in whatever he wants to do. But the King isn't young any longer, and Cumberland takes a lot of the dull work of running England off his hands—so the King would rather not have any fuss—so it'll be just easier to avoid trouble if we leave—but I haven't told you the best of it yet. Young Edward asked me 'what enemies?' and I reminded him that Brian, Dafydd, and I were all known enemies of Cumberland. He caught on immediately, and even admitted he was, too."

"You were smart."

"Thank you," said Jim smugly. "So I don't think we'll have much disagreement on his part when the three of us request an audience with his father tomorrow morning and beg his permission to get back to Malencontri."

He got up from his chair.

"I think that calls for a drink," he said, going to the table where the wine pitcher and clean mazers sat.

"For once I agree with you," said Angie, joining him. "Just a sort of half-glass now, not a gallon, in my mazer, Jim—"

"M'lord! M'lady!" piped a familiar voice behind them. "We're back!"

They turned to see not only Hob, sword at his side, but also the Tiverton hobgoblin, with a somewhat rusty old dagger in its ancient, cracked leather sheath, which Jim recognized as being off one of the walls of the Great Hall at Malencontri, roped around his waist. His face looked about as fierce as a hob's could.

"He wanted to come back with me," said Hob—their own hob. "I said he shouldn't, but he wanted to, and he was perfectly all right since you mended him, so we both rode the smoke back here to be ready in case you needed us."

"I want to pay them back!" said the Tiverton hob. "I'll cut out their liver and lights!"

"Liver and lights?" said Jim, intrigued. "Do goblins have liver and lights?"

The Tiverton hob looked at Hob.

"Don't they?" he asked. "I just guessed—"

"I don't know. *We* do—" Hob appealed to Jim. "Don't we?"

"I don't know if you don't," said Jim. "I'm a little doubtful about the lights."

The two hobs looked at each other.

"It doesn't matter," said the Tiverton hob, with a startlingly real grimness in his voice. "I'll cut out whatever they have wherever their liver and lights should be if they haven't any!"

"Well, that ends the liver and lights question," Jim said,

"and in any case there's no chance of our encountering any goblins until we're on our way home, tomorrow."

The two hobs stared at him with such shocked expressions that Jim stared back.

"What's the matter?" he asked. "Is there some reason you can't wait for tomorrow to find some goblins?"

"But, my lord!" burst out Hob. "They're all around you! They're all goblins here at Tiverton, except the little old lady they keep to light the fires they fear to light themselves. The only humans are you, m'lady, and those the King brought with him—and m'lord Verweather!"

"All goblins?" said Angie.

"Yes!" said Jim. "What do you mean 'all goblins'? What about the men-at-arms and the servants, and the whole castle staff!"

"But every one of those are *goblins*, m'lord! I told you they could change shape—remember when I explained they'd made themselves small to ride on the back of rats, when they attacked you and the Holy Person Bishop on his way back to where he'd come from? And you saw how some of them tried to make themselves over to look like human men in armor, though they didn't do it very well."

"I remember now," said Jim. "They didn't even look like the real thing—and their armor wasn't armor at all."

"They're shape-changers, m'lord. It's just one of their little magics we hobs can't do anymore. But we can enter buildings, even if they've got holy marks painted on them— and they can't do that—but we hobs can also pass through fire and order the smoke—none of which they can do."

"In fact," said Tiverton hob, "they're main terrified of fire. That's why I thought I could stay safe here in my castle until real humans came back, as long as I stayed behind a fire. But they doused the flames with water and got me anyway."

"And you saw what they did to him, m'lord," put in Hob.

"And that's why I was able to find him here, up in the roof rafters of bat country."

"I crawled away, when they left me after one session—that's what they called them, m'lord," added Tiverton hob, "and hid. Not that that would do me any good if Hob here hadn't come along in time. They'd have found me again, finally. They had my castle to themselves before the King and the few humans with him came! It'd been cleaned out of all souls a month before by order of him who gives the orders to Verweather. So they hurt me and hurt me!"

"Poor Tiv," said Hob, putting an arm around the other hob's shoulders.

Tiverton hob shrugged it off.

"Not no longer! I got a human weapon now, and the next goblin that gets close to me'll feel the point and edge of it in his liver and lights! See how much fun they get from that! In fact, m'lord, that's what I'm going to ask them—'How much fun was that? Want me to do it again?' Just like they kept asking me!"

"Come to Malencontri," said Angie. "Nobody will ever do that to you again."

Both hobs looked shocked—but not in the astonished manner they had done before.

"Oh, m'lady, I couldn't do that," said Tiverton hob. "It's only one hob to one people's place. That's our own made law—"

"That's right," said Hob.

"Besides," went on Tiverton hob, "I've got to stay here and take care of my castle."

"That's right, too, m'lady," said Hob. "A hob can never leave his home unprotected."

"Who's this person who gives orders about goblins to Sir Verweather?" said Jim. "You can't mean King Edward, himself?"

"It's a lady, m'lord—I think. But there's a man comes sometimes," said Tiverton hob. "She makes him come by

magic, then sends him away again, the same way. But he
gives the lady's orders to the goblins."

"Was he a lord?" asked Jim, knowing his own hob used
the term for any human of the gentry class.

"He *sounded* like one," said Tiverton hob cautiously.

"You actually saw and heard him—and the lady, too,
here in Tiverton Castle?"

"I did that, m'lord, twice."

"And they both came here and went away by magic?"

"Yes, m'lord."

"How do you know she did it with magic?"

"There were six goblins sitting on the floor in a room that
had only two chairs in it—but all the goblins sat together
on the floor, cross-legged, shoulder to shoulder in a curve.
Then suddenly the lady and the lord, if that's what he was,
m'lord—a real lord, I mean—were there in the chairs, and
later, they were both just gone. He sounded real mean, even
to the lady. Besides I could smell the magic when they came
and went. I was watching from the fireplace—that was before they caught me."

"You can smell magic?"

"Of course," said both hobs at once.

"Everybody can but humans," added Hob. "It smells like
burned food—burned bread, maybe, m'lord. I think it would
have been the loud man and the Agatha who's always with
him."

The "loud man" or "noisy man" was what Hob had always called the Earl of Cumberland, ever since he had first
seen and heard him.

"Could Agatha not only get goblins to work for her, but
be able to move herself around like that?" said Angie. "And
someone else, too? I thought she barely started to learn
Witchery before she gave it up."

"A little more than 'barely,' I think," said Jim. "But
you're right. Transporting oneself and another is pretty advanced magic for Magickians—and come to think of it, she

once transported herself and a couple of men, I'd guess from the Royal court in London to Lyonesse, to try to lure us into a trap. Which is something I still can't do without help from Carolinus or Kinetete. But I'll bet I know a lot of other magic she never even dreamed of."

"Besides," said Angie thoughtfully, "Agatha's smart—not in Joan's class, of course, but smart enough. She could have kept trying on her own and learning."

"You're probably right," said Jim. "That's just what she must have been doing. It's what every Magickian who amounts to anything does, and it makes him or her different from all others. Then, too, there was that time she spent as a child, being a sort of pet for the old troll of the Earl of Somerset's castle."

"But trolls are just Naturals with some instinctive magic, that's all. One of them couldn't teach her anything."

"But they might have a sensitivity to magic—that troll is over a thousand years old; being around him might have helped to point her in the right direction. Kids pick up more than people ever think from people around them—but never mind that now."

He turned back to the respectfully listening hobs.

"What did the lord want?" he asked.

"To make the King sick," said Tiverton hob.

"Sick?" Jim and Angie stared at Tiverton hob. Angie was the first to pick up on his meaning.

"You don't mean sick with the plague that's now in London?"

Tiverton hob nodded.

"That's it, m'lady," he said. "Those goblins m'lord ran into taking that Holy Person home might have been some of them that was herding rats with lots of fleas down here."

"What makes them so sure rats carry the fleas that make people sick with plague?" Jim asked.

"Maybe the lady told them," said Tiverton hob, "or maybe they just saw fleas being sick into the place where they'd bitten some human to get at human blood."

"*Saw* it?" Jim echoed.

"Yes, m'lord. Haven't you?"

"No. Their bite's so small, and they're gone so fast."

"We hobs can see it—can't we, Hob?" Tiverton turned to Malencontri hob.

"Yes, m'lord," said Hob. "Maybe it's because we're smaller than humans. But the fleas do it every time, whether they've got sickness in them or not."

"I can't believe it," said Jim, turning again to Angie. "Even Cumberland wouldn't try murdering the King—or would he?"

"Maybe Agatha talked him into it. She wouldn't have any qualms about doing it. And you told me once he does want to be King, or Regent."

"Then maybe he would," said Jim. "This is a hell of a mess! Nobody would believe it—least of all the King. Probably not even the Prince. Angie, if this is actually what's going on here, I've got to do something to stop it! Carolinus has been hammering into me that my first and greatest duty is to keep the King alive—but he'd never say why, maybe because I'm not a full-fledged Magickian yet."

"Jim—" Angie began.

"But evidently," he rushed on, "it's the first duty of every Magickian, and I'll be told that, along with other things, if I'm ever voted into the Collegiate as one of them. But all the rest of you had better clear out now without waiting— I mean this minute." He was feeling things that needed to be done pushing him faster than he could think about them. "I'll use magic to make your going invisible and then work it some way as if you're still here, when I ask the King for permission to leave tomorrow."

"I won't go without you!" said Angie. "Dafydd won't either, or Brian, of course, and that means Danielle and Geronde will be staying, too. Yes, Geronde definitely. On second thought, Danielle will absolutely go, so there'll be her at least to take care of her children if Dafydd doesn't make it back from here, but everybody else will stay." Then she paused in her turn for breath.

"Can you be sure that's what's going on?" she asked.

"You're right. I need some evidence. Tiverton hob!"

"Yes, m'lord?"

"How can you be sure they're trying to make the King sick, you hobs?" said Angie

"I watched from behind the fireplace fire one eve and saw the lady give m'lord Verweather his orders," answered Tiverton hob.

"When was this?"

"A fortnight ago—no, maybe three weeks agone."

"But that's not going to help you much," said Angie. "The word of a hob, particularly one with a grudge against the goblins—how can we be sure the staff here's *all* goblins?"

"If I just knew even one of them was, it'd be a start," said Jim. "I could try to counter whatever magic makes a goblin . . . turn it—or him—into his real shape. But then if I could, I'd have alerted all of them. . . ."

He thought a moment. Then he suddenly snapped his fingers.

"We can use our own full-length mirror in the Solar—the one I silvered the back of for you. Hang on a minute. I'll get it here!"

Chapter 24

Angie looked carefully at the full-length mirror Jim had just transported from the Solar back at Malencontri. It was really a rather beautiful mirror—as well as being the only one like it in England.

True, its images were a little wavery, since the glass was

fourteenth-century window glass—rare enough in its own right. It was some of the glass Jim had gotten for the rare luxury of having real glazed windows in their towertop residence. But the Malencontri carpenter had made for it as beautiful a frame as was within his power: no figures of course, but some excellent ornate carving on the edges.

"I hope nothing happens to it here," she said. "I didn't have time to suggest it, you acted so fast, but couldn't you just have made a copy, now you've got the first one?"

"I could not," said Jim. "Magic doesn't understand silvering—mainly because I don't either. I'd have to make another from scratch—and you remember how long it took me to get the silver to stick to the glass, last time."

"You're right," said Angie. "I forgot. I'm not really worried about it."

"All right. Now a touch of magic to make it invisible. Good. And a touch more to make it reveal things."

"But you haven't made it invisible—" Angie began.

"Yes, I have. Not to us. But it'll be invisible to any goblin or anyone else magically trying to pass his or herself off as something different. Now we call in the servant or the man-at-arms. Maybe the hobs better be invisible, too."

"Tiv and I can be up the chimney," said Hob, "and still see and hear everything."

"Fine," said Jim. "A pinch of magic saved is a pinch of magic earned. Angie do you want to be the one to call the servant, or the guard?"

"*Servant, here!*" Angie raised her voice. The servant came in.

"Over here, by me," Angie said to her. "Stand right there—that's right. Now look at this pen here. Now, I want that cleaned four times a day and *always* when I'm expecting guests. You understand?"

Lured into perfect range of the mirror, the servant was suddenly reflected no longer as a woman, but exactly like a hob, except for a light coat of buff-colored hair.

"Oh yes, m'lady," said the individual projecting this image.

"Good," said Angie, in a perfectly controlled voice, "you can go now." The door closed behind the servant. "Jim!"

"Yes, I saw," said Jim.

The two hobs were back in the room. Jim was beginning to be able to tell them apart. Tiverton hob was slightly shorter than Malencontri hob, and a little more burly—if that word could legitimately be used to describe any hob.

Jim had been standing in a trancelike state looking at the two hobs, his mind whirring away and getting nowhere like an electric motor out of control. Suddenly he came out of it, knelt down and began sculpting empty air with this open hands.

"What are you doing?" Angie said.

"Making a model of Tiverton." Jim stood up from his work. What he had created was a shape of mist that resembled a castle—but only in that it had a surrounding wall and a tower attached to a broader, lower section. "Now we'll cause a green light to show for each one in the castle who's a goblin—my God!"

Pinpricks of green lights were showing all through the model, in uncountable numbers.

"How many are there?" he asked.

The two hobs looked at each other. "I don't know, m'lord," said Hob.

"More than two hundred," said Tiverton hob.

"They don't need that many to run a castle the size of Tiverton, do they, Angie?" said Jim, dazed.

"Seventy would do it," Angie said out of her experience as Chatelaine of Malencontri. "Jim, if they ever find out we know about them—"

"You don't have to spell it out—" Jim broke off. "Sorry, Angie. Didn't mean to bark at you. We'll just have to make sure they don't find out."

"How will you do that, m'lord?" asked Tiverton hob, plainly interested. Jim stared at him.

"By just giving no sign we ever knew any different," said Jim. "And if you and Malencontri hob stay in the chimneys and out of their sight, they'll have no way of finding out **that anything unusual has been going on.**"

"Oh, but they will know that soon anyway, m'lord," said Hob.

"Yes," Tiverton hob chimed in before Jim could respond, "I understand what you mean, Hob."

"Well, *I* don't!" Angie said. "Jim, what are they talking about?"

"I think," Jim said slowly, "the hobs are saying that that goblin who was being a servant will have smelled that magic was at work in the room a moment ago." He shook his head. "I should have remembered that Hob said the goblins can smell magic."

"But you work magic all the time," Angie said. "So smelling magic around you shouldn't make them suspect anything."

"What do you think about that, you hobs?" Jim asked. "You both know more about them than we do. Will they be suspicious?"

"Maybe not right away, m'lord," Hob said, after exchanging a look with Tiverton hob, who simply nodded. "But later that goblin is going to remember how m'lady had her stand right in front of the magic she smelled and get suspicious you magicked her, for some reason."

"But what of it, if she doesn't know we could see her true shape in it?"

"But she'll tell the other goblins," Hob said, "and one of them is going to guess you might have magically seen through their shape-changing. Very suspicious, goblins are."

"A goblin would guess that? That's pretty good guessing," Angie said.

Tiverton hob nodded, and looked at Malencontri hob,

who continued to answer for the two of them.

"Goblins are always worried," Hob said. "Especially when there's magic involved. In the Kingdom of Devils and Demons they always had to be afraid because the higher demons might be after them at any time."

Paranoid goblins, Jim thought to himself. *I suppose it might be a survival trait for them.*

"It probably doesn't matter how much they really know about what we've learned about them," Jim said out loud. "Fear alone may drive them to act against us all."

"Yes." Hob nodded. "They probably wouldn't know *how* the magic the servant-goblin smelled could tell you what they really are, but that's the purpose for it they fear most."

"Wait a minute, Hob—my hob—some of those that attacked us on our trip with the Bishop tried to turn themselves into imitation knights, but they managed only very clumsy imitations. The servants here look exactly like humans!"

"They have to practice, m'lord," said Tiverton hob, "and that's what they did. I watched them from the fireplaces. There must have been no cross on this castle door—or whoever was here didn't have that much faith in a cross. So they came in—making themselves almost as small as insects so they wouldn't be noticed—and spent some time studying and practicing, each on a different human, until they could look and act just like that human. Then they made themselves big, killed all the humans in the castle, and probably ate them."

"That explains why that one servant would do anything I told her," said Angie, "except touch my flask of boiled Malencontri water after I said it held holy water!"

"Hmm, yes," Jim said. "Tiverton hob, you think they might take only a short time to figure out that we might know from the report of the one that was made to stand in front of a mirror?"

"Don't know, m'lord. Probably pretty quickly. They're

not too wise about lots of things, but very quick about magic and suspicions. It could take them only a few minutes, or—"

"Then we can't waste time!" said Jim. "We've got to move right away! We've got to get out of here—all us humans. You hobs, too!"

Angie looked alarmed. The two hobs looked very interested.

"What are you going to do?" Angie asked.

"Fort up, to start with!" said Jim. "We're in the top story here under the tower floor. First get all humans in the castle collected here, where we can defend the stairs. Then move us all to the King's rooms around the hall. Ward the whole top floor, and the King's quarters, so we can do a nose count—tell you the rest later—where's that water pitcher?"

"Right by your elbow,"

"Oh, good!" Jim stared into it. "Edward—Prince—to here!" And the Prince appeared in their room, looking about him. He opened his mouth to speak, but Jim was already moving on, unheeding.

"Joan? Joan—there you are." She appeared, looking startled. Jim's voice had risen in the room.

"Now, the King's own knights—to me, here. Silence! I'll explain everything in a minute!"

"What is this?" cried the Prince, in an outraged voice.

"Emergency!" said Jim. "Pray patience for a moment, Your Grace. Brian? Is Geronde with you?"

A tinny voice came from the pitcher, not understandable out in the room.

"I don't care how she's dressed. Here, now! You're dressed enough, Geronde. Both you and Brian here, now? Good. Dafydd, you alone? Where's Danielle? Oh, sorry Danielle—it's getting so crowded here I didn't see you. Danielle, Dafydd, here are your bows, and all the arrows you two can carry!"

Jim and Angie's room had become jammed with people.

Jim took a moment to expand the room, adding the corridor to its space while keeping it walled off, with the castle servants remaining outside. People were demanding answers.

"I said I'd tell you all in time and I will. No, Geronde," he said, "you, Angie, Dafyyd and Brian—close over by me and His Grace and Joan, here. Stand close so you all can hear me over this noise. Silence, please—all! First I've got to talk to my Lord Prince and Lady Joan. Then Angie, Brian, Dafydd, Geronde, Danielle."

He threw an extra ward around them.

"Silence all!" he said again. At that magical command the people in the room were unable to speak. At that point Jim became aware that the terrier bitch was barking excitedly, her barking interspersed with growls at the people standing closest to her pen full of puppies. "Silence," he roared, "you can't bark anymore, as of now!"

Jim had forgotten for a moment that magic did not work on animals. But the little terrier had apparently been trained to the order of "Silence!" She stopped barking, but began to whine, looking at Jim.

"Don't whine either!" he told her. "You can make noise later, after I'm through talking." Surprisingly, she obeyed that order, too.

"Hob," Jim went on immediately, "can you talk to her—explain everything's going to be all right?—Oh, that's right—you hobs can both talk again."

"I can tell the dog, m'lord," said Tiverton hob eagerly.

"M'lord ordered me to do it!" Hob snapped at his fellow hobgoblin. "There, she understands, m'lord."

"All right, Hob. But now you and Tiverton hob be quiet unless I ask you something." Jim looked about the room, then turned back to the Prince and Joan, making sure he had brought the model of the castle close where they could see it.

"I wanted to talk to you first, Your Grace and Lady Joan, because you'll be quickest to understand what we're up against. See this? It's a sort of picture of this castle, which I made with magic. All the green lights show where goblins are inside this castle. They are magically disguised as the servants of this castle." The people listening looked stunned, and there could be no doubt that Jim would have been inundated with questions if they had been able to speak.

"Yes," Jim went on quickly, "they're shape-changers, and they've made themselves look like humans as part of a plot to infect the King with plague and kill him that way. I don't know just why. I'll find out and then I'll get us all out of here."

He paused for a moment. The belligerent look on the face of the Prince was being replaced by a look of dangerous determination. Taking a chance, Jim removed the command that had imposed silence on the group immediately about him. He was rewarded by a wary silence.

"Meanwhile," he went on, "we've got to deal with the goblin man-at-arms on watch outside, as well as guard the staircase. I've put a ward around this whole floor, but I want to take some goblins prisoner, so I'll open the stairway soon. We ought to be able to defend that against an army. Your Grace, if you'd take over the fighting men of the King's personal service, we can feel secure—just one thing, though. Brian, Dafydd and I have been fighting together against enemies for some years, now. I would wish you to leave them to me to command."

The Prince frowned, but before he could respond, Joan spoke quickly.

"Amazing, Sir James!" she cried, understanding immediately as Jim had expected her to. "If anyone but a Magickian like yourself had told us all this we could not have believed it." She paused to take a deep breath.

"Thank Heaven you are with us, James," she went on in a calmer tone. "You know how to confront these demons and goblins! I think your plan to keep Sir Brian and the archer under your own magickal command an excellent idea, is it not, Your Grace?"

"I'm not so—a war captain like myself—" the Prince broke off and coughed. "Yes, possibly. Thank all the saints you are with us this day, James!"

"Good," said Jim. "We're making progress. Now let's take a look at who all I managed to rescue." He plunged into the mass of other people, still talking, freeing them from their silence. "You'd know better than I, Your Grace, how many souls the King brought with him when he came here. Where are the King's knights? Ah, Sir Mathew, and the rest. Good!"

Sir Mathew, who was only dressed in his hose, shirt and shoes, looked at him grimly.

"Sir, I honor your magickianship, but may I ask—oh, good day, Your Grace."

"Mathew," said the Prince sharply, "may I suggest you use a more polite tone of voice toward the gentleman who has just saved your life and that of everyone else here."

He had raised his voice enough to be heard by all the gathering in the now extended room. Jim felt grateful, but only for a moment. His mind was spinning with other things to be done immediately.

"Hark to me all here!" continued the Prince, raising his voice.

There was an instant attention from all in the room.

"—from this moment on, all gentlemen present here—except our three paladins—are about to engage with a horde of goblins. You knew them as Tiverton's servants and men-at-arms, but in fact they are a damned horde of devils, shape-changers, out to murder our beloved King. We must prevent that or die in the attempt!"

"Alas, Your Grace," said Sir Mathew. "I am a naked man at the moment, completely without my weapons."

Jim, who had forgotten this necessary element, interrupted his other urgent thoughts to silently order that the men find themselves clothed, armed, and armored. There was a satisfied rumble of male voices from around the room and a certain amount of clanking as they checked the accouterments they were now wearing.

"Now, Brian and Dafydd—" began Jim, turning to the group of friends. He found himself almost stumbling over something soft. "Look out, child!" he said, and then saw he was talking not to a youngster, but to a tiny, worn-looking woman hardly more than three feet tall and in servant clothes.

"Crave your gentle pardon, Mage," she said in a high, shrill voice. "I be the only one of the Tiverton servants still here. They kept me to light the fires for them, and they were main mean about it! Never a kind word, find my own food as best I could, and working night or day, whenever they wished a fire made for the King and you other high folk. And never the silver shilling they promised me, too, for helping them."

"Beg pardon, my lord," piped up Malencontri hob, "it's that they can't stand fire, as I said."

"I remember," said Jim, a little shortly. He focused on the small servant. "What's your name?"

"I be Mêg, if it please Your Mageship."

"Well, Meg, I'm glad you're with us. Maybe you can help by answering some questions about the goblins. Do you know how long it'll take them to know all of us humans are safe up here, now?"

"They knows already, please Your Mageship. And not all of ye's safe. That one younger squire to Sir Mathew be dead as a doornail in 'is bed, stuck full with they mean little spears so 'ee looked like a porcupine. Cried pitiful, 'ee did, from the pain 'o the spear poison—but 'ee died quick because he was so full stuck. I seen it happen just before I was all at once 'ere. Didn't know why they did it when I watched. Know now."

"Walter Thorncraft!" cried Mathew's voice. "The poor

lad! The poor lad! I'll kill a few of the devils in his name. William, why weren't you there to help your fellow squire?"

"Beg your forgiveness, my lord, but I didn't know. I was on my way to the privy, and suddenly I found myself here!"

"If they know, then we have to move fast," said Jim. "Brian and Dafydd, take care of the sentry on the roof! Your Grace, will you pick a knight to keep watch on the stairs. The goblins can't get past the ward I've put on this whole floor, but they ought to be watched—"

"Mathew!" snapped the Prince. "The stairs. Send your wisest knight with the command in his keeping!"

"I'll go myself, my lord!" There was a stir in the closely packed crowd, as Sir Mathew pushed himself hastily through it. His voice floated back. "Beg pardon, Your Grace, but I can't find the door."

"I left the room sealed when I took the space of the corridor," said Jim. "Door! There's one now, Sir Mathew!"

"Thank you, Mage!" There was the noise of a door opening, slamming.

"—and Angie, Your Grace, Lady Joan—" Jim continued, throwing up another ward of silence around the four of them. "Your Grace, we've all got to move into the King's quarters. The King will have to be told what's going on and maybe you—"

"Perhaps I would be best to do that," said Joan, quickly again. "He will listen to me for a moment, at least."

"And in that moment you will know how to keep him listening," said the Prince, obviously relieved. "She is right, James. He will bite my head off before I have three words out and refuse to listen to more. But we must all go before we bring this ragtag crowd to fill his rooms. But Lady Angela, perhaps you should go with my lady Countess—"

"My duty is to stay here, your Grace," said Angie sharply, "with Sir James!"

The signals from her were unmistakable to Jim. He had planned on going himself, and taking Angie, so they could both measure the King's reaction to Joan's and the Prince's persuasion. But she was right; he had to stay here to keep things under control—as might be expected, she would not leave if he was here

"Of course," he said, thinking quickly. "I would have only sent her if she was needed to tell me of what happened, in case the two of you found you had to stay with the King for more time than we expect."

"A wise decision, my lord," said Joan, coming down strongly on Angie's side. That sealed the matter. Jim magic-ed Joan and the Prince on their way.

"How goes it, James?" said Brian's voice in Jim's ear. Jim and Angie turned to see his two friends had returned from the Tower roof.

"The sentry disposed of?" said Jim, firmly holding down a slight touch of squeamishness at the thought of what must have taken place over his head. The sentry would never have stood a chance.

"Disposed of indeed," said Brian cheerfully. "Looked completely like an actual man-at-arms, even to clothes and spear—real spear and clothes. Turned back to looking like a hob swamped in cloth when he was dead, though."

"Don't let either of our hobs hear you say that!" said Jim. "In their eyes the goblins look very different from them. They'd be insulted and hurt if they heard you say so."

"I will guard my tongue if you wish, James. But outside the sentry being hairy instead of smooth, I'm damned if I see much difference."

"The difference's inside them. But no goblin would, or could, have taken you for a ride on the smoke to cheer you up—though you almost didn't remember it—when you were a homesick boy. Besides, if the two different kinds were different beasts, only one of which you were hunting, you'd pick up the differences at first sighting, and recognize them immediately thereafter."

"But I have remembered it, James—after your hob reminded me of it. I remember it very clearly now. But you are also right that if the goblins were warrantable prey and the hobs not, I would know the differences very quickly. The hobs are good little Naturals, and I will guard my tongue. By the way, Dafydd and I debated throwing the corpse over the side of the tower to the ground, but did not for that it might alert the other goblins to the change of guardianship up here—"

"Hola!" cried a distant voice—the voice of Sir Mathew. "Spear-armed goblins on the stairs! We are attacked!"

"Take charge of the men at the stairs over Sir Mathew— say I said so—will you, Brian?" said Jim, for the other knights were jostling each other to be first out the door. "Tell them I commanded you to. Dafydd, you might as well stay here. There'll be too many to waste your arrows, this early—save them for an emergency."

"Indeed," said Dafydd in his usual composed fashion. He had not said a word so far while Brian talked. "But I think I must look more closely at these goblins. I am not a man eager to the fighting, but it is wise to know your enemy on advance if possible."

He turned and went off after Brian, who had joined the eager crowd-jam at the door.

"I think I've got to sit down for a moment," Jim said in an undertone to Angie, and sank into a nearby chair.

"Are you all right?" she said, looking at him closely. She put a cool palm on his forehead. "You feel feverish."

"Who wouldn't, having to handle this mess? Besides magic's an energy force; and I've been doing enough magic to do the usual Magickian of the Collegiate for a month. I feel a little hot. I probably got warmed up by the bleed-off of energy I was directing."

"If you think that's it," said Angie. "Still, it might not be a bad idea for you to slow down on everything you're do-ing, including using your magic. The Prince and Joan are

handling the King, and Brian can command the knights at
the stairs better than you can, possibly."

"No doubt about it," said Jim, glumly. "I'll never know
a fraction of what he knows in that department. If it wasn't
for this crazy business of top rank always ending up in
military command—whether he's the best man for it or
not—I'm sorry, Angie, but I think I better go take a quick
look, anyway, at the situation on the stairs. Dafydd was
right, you know, about needing to know your enemy; I only
saw them in a sudden flurry before, that one time with the
bishop, and not a second to stand back and measure them
up."

He got up from the chair somewhat heavily.

"I'm going with you," said Angie strongly.

Chapter 25

When the two of them approached the stairs, the knights
there looked relieved to see Jim, disturbed to see Angie.

"Brace yourself," muttered Jim under his breath. "I'm
going to have to bark at you. Try to sound meek." He raised
his voice.

"My lady!" he snapped. "Watch if you must, but stand
back and do not bother us with talk!"

"Yes," replied Angie with beautifully tuned meekness
and cast-down eyes, "as you command, my lord."

She stopped, accordingly. They were about five steps
from the knights.

"My lord," said Brian formally, meeting him. "We are
glad to see you. For some reason the goblins hang back,
though they are many in number—" Jim glanced down the
stairs. The goblins were there, and this time in their real
shapes; now they were full hob-sized, rather than the
smaller size Jim had seen them at when he had been at-

tacked before, with the Bishop. They filled the stairs, almost spilling off each step as far down as Jim could see. Their spears were correspondingly longer than they had been before, and looked strangely dangerous in the afternoon light from the arrow slits in the side of this tower, which made their jeweled tips glint in deadly fashion at every movement. The glitter of goblin eyes was if anything almost as bright and threatening as the spearpoints.

"They aren't hanging back," Jim said. "They're right up against the ward I put around this whole floor to stop anyone coming up from below. That's whats stopping them. The question is whether to remove the ward and attack, or leave it in place for now. Attacking might make them more cautious. The party of them that attacked us when I was escorting the Bishop of Bath and Wells seemed to think at first that our armor was simply another use of magic, and they tried to imitate it—by shape-changing to look like they were wearing it—they didn't manage to look very convincing, though."

He had been thinking out loud for the benefit of the knights standing about and looking impatient. They had not welcomed the arrival of their armor and weapons only to stand here at the stairs and wait.

"Yes!" he said. "We attack!"

Cheers from the knights and a general crowding down the stairs.

"Hold!" snapped Jim. "Advance all together in line, and only two to a step, remember! They could push any of you who're teetering on the edge over it with sheer numbers. Sir Brian, marshal your gentlemen!"

Brian took over surely and efficiently. Jim stood back to watch—until it suddenly occurred to him that by the standards of the day he and Brian should have made up the first two.

But the knights were on the very edge of quarreling among themselves for place. Hopefully, thought Jim, they would think of his standing back as an indulgence to those who wanted a first try at the enemy.

Then he suddenly remembered that, just as he had forgotten to ward himself, when he had warded all the rest of the Malencontri party against possibly plague-carrying fleas—he had now forgotten to armor himself. Almost blushing, he was about to do so now, when he realized that no one else here thought that, as commander, he did not have a duty to take care of himself in this case, and not indulge his (undoubtedly) ferocious desire to be on the stairs meeting the enemy with the rest of them.

When Brian was ready, Jim wiped out the blocking ward, and the knights, with Brian and Sir Mathew leading, started down the stairs.

The goblins surged forward, found the invisible barrier gone, and rolled up the stairs, like a black and poisonous wave, sprinkled liberally with the reflections of bright stars that were their spearpoints.

And so they met.

But this time was not as it had been at their battle against the Bishop's group. On that occasion Jim had been the only knight present, and even he had not been wearing full armor. This time the goblins were meeting not only fully dressed knights, but knights carrying shields and who knew how to use them for defense. The diamond points of the spears stuck in the wooden shields but did not penetrate them, and the razor edges of the broadswords cut through their narrow bodies as if they had been stalks of wheat.

Jim even noticed Brian—he had taken the outside edge of the step he was on—using his shield, bristling as it already was with stuck spears, as a sort of broom to sweep the goblins facing him off the stairs to a lethal drop to the stone floor below.

So the knights cleared goblins from the steps before them without any being crippled by the magic poison of the spears. But those steps were immediately being filled from what seemed an endless horde below. It could only be a matter of time, Jim saw, before even these iron men should begin to tire—and the goblins were nothing if not brave. Those in the forefront came on to their deaths like the most legendary of human heroes.

Jim was already beginning to work his brain as fast as it could be worked in his present, somewhat groggy shape, when there was an unexpected addition to the conflict. He had been dimly hearing, somewhere in the distance behind him, barking—a vague irritation for the moment. He assumed without thought that someone back in the room had aroused the mother terrier—possibly someone handling one of her pups without permission.

But it was nothing so trivial. The barking abruptly grew louder as it approached, and before he could turn, the little terrier bitch was past him and hurling herself down the stairs toward the fighting knights. A terrier, of a breed famous for fearing nothing, regardless of size or armament, and who is also currently a mother, does not lie idle when enemies close to her pups are clearly attacking. She pushed her head between one of Brian's legs and that of Sir Mathew, and began snarling and barking at the goblins.

And they—all of them—suddenly recoiled in panic, piling up on each other and pushing the more unfortunate of their number over the side to their deaths below.

The knights stopped. Jim, with Angie now standing beside him, stayed where he was, staring, as the terrier, left alone, barked and growled a triumphant warning to the retreating foe.

The two hobs came pelting from the room to join Jim and Angie.

"Forgive me, m'lord," gasped Malencontri hob, slipping into familiarity under the excitement of the moment, "I forgot to tell you. Goblins have a deathly fear of *all* dogs!"

"They do? Why?" said Angie.

"Because—m'lady, you remember—magic doesn't work

on animals, and they can smell it from a distance if the
wind's right. Their magic-poisoned spearpoints are just ordinary points to dogs, and a real angry dog doesn't even
feel any hurt when it's fighting. So they learned to avoid
any place where a dog was, because a dog'll kill them if it
thinks they're on its ground. It's the same way with houses
having cats—"

"Cats?" said Angie. "But goblins are much bigger than
cats!"

"Doesn't make any difference, m'lady," broke in Tiverton
hob triumphantly, finally getting a word in edgewise. "Cats
hate goblins. Cats chase them and try to kill them, if they
can, and goblins run. Cats is all claws and teeth. They climb
up on goblins and tear at them, and cats aren't killed easy!"

"I was just going to tell them that," said Hob, glaring at
Tiverton hob.

"Well, you didn't. I did."

"Peace, you two," Angie told them.

"Yes, my lady," they both said.

"My lord is busy thinking and mustn't be disturbed by
your squabbling."

"Crave your gentle pardon, my lord." A soft two-voiced
chorus.

"Granted," answered Jim absently.

Meanwhile, the knights had come back up the stairs.

"Well, my lord?" said Brian, taking off his helm and revealing hair soaked flat with sweat. "I judged it wisest not
to follow the goblins too far. What are your commands?"

"Er," said Jim, hating equally his woozy head and this
business of Brian, who was a far better judge of military
matters than Jim himself, "I'd be glad of your counsel, Sir
Brian."

"Then I would suggest, my lord, that once more you put
your magic shield in place. The goblins seem numberless,
and while we might drive them completely without the castle, we would need the help of the dog to do it—and who

knows how far she will willingly go from her pups without worrying those she chases might somehow sneak around behind her and harm them."

"That is good counsel," said Jim. The knights, who had found the fighting with the goblins become somewhat monotonous—less like real battle than the cutting of grain in the harvest season, when everybody from lord to serf turned out to the fields, getting in the winter's needs before bad weather robbed them of it—clearly agreed. They preferred an enemy who could hit back—not quite as hard as they could, of course.

The terrier was still barking and snarling at the goblins now baffled by the ward once more. Angie scooped her up in her arms to carry her back.

"I can take her," said Jim, low-voiced to Angie.

"That's all right," said Angie. "She's light."

With a few last barks, the small dog dismissed goblins completely from her mind and turned her head to try to lick Angie's conveniently reachable face.

Angie dodged.

"She's just trying to tell you how much she thinks of you," said Jim.

"Think where that tongue has been—especially with her pups," answered Angie tartly. She held the terrier, now in a tight grip, out to Jim. "Here, do you want to let her lick you?"

"No, no. You're probably right."

"You're darn right I'm right."

They went back into the crowded room, together with the knights, and dumped the terrier in her pen. Dafydd—who had watched without a word, and an assortment of other people from the room, who had come out after all to see the fighting—had returned with them.

"M'lord—" said the familiar voice of Hob. Jim turned to see both hobs pressing closely on his heels.

"Not now," said Jim, turning back. He had caught sight

of the Prince and Joan, just entering the room, undoubtedly returned from seeing the King—whose quarters, after all, were just at the end of this top corridor. But such a quick return suggested they had won the King's approval to move everyone into his quarters right away. Fast work. Jim was eager to hear the details. The King's rooms were all connected by inner doorways rather than openings on the corridor, making them a much better defensive position than this one overcrowded space—until he could get his brain, at present strangely dull, to work seriously to a better and longer-term goal.

He waded through the crowd to Joan and the Prince, and threw a privacy ward around them all, including Angie, who was close beside him.

"How do you feel now?" she asked in a low voice, seeing him glancing at her.

"Fine," he said. He had no time to worry about his health, now. But he did make the ward's circle around them generous, to give himself breathing space.

"You're back!" he said to Joan and the Prince. "That was good."

"Not good at at all, Sir James," said Joan. "The King will not even consider any movement of those here to his quarters. I'm afraid I—"

"The fault is mine, entirely!" The Prince broke in. "I should have given her more time to soften him up to the plan. He has always loved and been indulgent toward her. But I spoke too soon—rash! rash! Rashness is a great fault in military matters, too, as you can guess, James. The Countess was doing beautifully when I dropped the whole story in his lap, and it has always been his way to correct me, and disagree on principle with anything I said. He wound up losing his temper—wouldn't believe the fleas in this house were sick with the London plague, absolutely dismissed the idea that the staff were goblins in disguise— and wound up swearing there was no such thing as a goblin anyway; and if there was he, as an anointed King, would have nothing to fear from them!"

"Oh, great!" muttered Jim, seeing his immediate plans crumble into dust. The goblins might run from the terrier once, out of tradition, when surprised by her, but it was inconceivable that in their numbers they would let her stop them long, even if it meant burying her in attackers while the rest of them went around her.

"Great, James?" The Prince was staring at him.

"I think the matter requires only a little rethinking," said Jim desperately, though his thoughts at the moment were being no help to him, at all. He was used to starting to talk before he knew how to get himself out of pinches, and had always found a glib answer of some kind at least put off the problem until a more practical excuse or solution could occur to him.

The trick was not working now, however, he realized in panic, as he found himself absolutely without an idea.

"M'lord!" said the urgent voice of Hob behind him, and he suddenly realized that both hobs were also inside the privacy ward, having apparently closely followed him across the room.

Any excuse for a moment in which to think. He turned sharply, saw both hobs and said, equally sharply, "Hob, what are you two doing here? I'm having a very important private talk with Prince Edward and my Lady Joan. I'll open the ward I've set up around us for privacy and you two get out of it—"

"But m'lord, begging your pardon!" cried Hob. "We could get a goblin and bring him to show the King there are such—and they're here!"

"Nonsense! Now, you go—"

"Pardon me, my lord," said Angie, in a meek but dangerous voice, "in this present peril, might it not be wise to at least listen to Hob?"

"Indeed," said Joan, "I can see no harm in that."

"Oh!" Jim's mind was still failing to produce even a temporary answer to their situation. "Well? How? Who's we?"

"Me and Tiverton hob, m'lord—and the little dog."

"You two and the dog?" Jim stared.

"Yes, we could, my lord!" said Tiverton hob. "No one knows this castle as I do."

"How does that help?" Jim said.

"And you know we hobs can talk to animals," Hob went on heedlessly.

"Yes, yes."

"So I'd make the dog understand what we were going to do, and promise her that m'lady'll keep her pups safe here until we're back. Then, Tiv and I will take the dog on the smoke through all the chimneys of the castle, until we can find just one goblin—or maybe only a few—in a room with a fireplace."

Hob paused to look for signs of understanding or approval from Jim.

"Go on," said Jim.

"Then we grab the goblin—and if there's more than one goblin in that room, the rest of them won't dare do anything with the dog there—I'll have to tell her to growl only, and not attack them. Then one of us carries the goblin—that'll be me—and the other the dog, and we carry them away up the chimney where the rest can't follow—"

"I want to carry the goblin," said Tiverton hob, fiercely. "It's my castle!"

"Well, I suppose you've got the right—anyway, m'lord, we bring the goblin back to you, you put magic around him so he can't get away, the little dog goes back to her pups and you take the warded goblin up to show the King."

"Is this possible?" the Prince asked Jim.

"I don't see why not," said Jim slowly. Actually, it did sound like at least a possible idea.

"But how will these two get up and down chimneys—particularly carrying a goblin and a dog?"

"Oh, they travel on the smoke. Malencontri hob's been from the Holy Land to England here, and then back to me, on onc waft of smoke. He's even carried me on the smoke."

"Everyone knows that," said Tiverton hob.

The Prince ignored the remark.

"Well, I'll take your word for it," he said to Jim. "Then once we have the goblin you can lock him up with magic so the Countess and I can take him to show to my father?"

"Absolutely, Your Grace."

"And this time," said Joan to the Prince, "let me do the talking until I ask you to speak."

"If you wish it that way," answered the Prince, a little stiffly in spite of himself.

"I want you to use your forceful voice for a military appraisal of the situation, now that we've seen their numbers on the stairs—" said Joan.

Jim realized that the two of them must have gone to the stairs after they got back, no doubt having been told that there had been a battle, by someone still out in the hallway.

"—Your father will listen to you on that," Joan was going on, "only let me tell him about the fact that Cumberland *may* have sent his King here to die from the plague. Your father, Your Grace, won't find it easy to accept that."

"No, by Heaven! So it shall be as you say, sweeting— Countess. You have had him always in the palm of your hand."

"Not always," said Joan, somewhat dryly. "Otherwise I would not have married Salisbury. I would have confronted him with my marriage to Holland. But I was only twelve then—come to think of it, I do a much better job speaking to him nowadays."

"That was all to blame on me—but come," said the Prince, as if suddenly remembering the other ears listening to his apologies. "So you guarantee this hobish expedition, James?"

"I guarantee nothing," growled Jim. He was not feeling

in shape to be particularly polite at the moment. "I've said I think it'll work, and I'll stand by to do whatever magic's necessary if it does, Your Grace!"

"Your word is well by me, James," said the Prince, in as close to an appeasing tone as he probably could manage. "I am much indebted to you in many ways."

"I do not count it so, Your Grace," said Jim, making an equal effort to recover his politeness.

"Nonetheless," said the Prince, "I shall not forget."

"That alone is recompense, Your Grace. Hobs, you better get busy, then!"

"Come Tiv," said Hob, "I've got to talk to the little dog first—I'll let you talk to her, too, if you want, after I'm done."

He turned and led Tiverton hob out through the crowd— neither of them bumping their noses on an unyielding, invisible surface, as Jim hastily removed the ward he had set up about them all.

"Come sweeti—Countess," said the Prince, "let you and I walk out in the corridor in the direction of the stairs, for a breath of air."

And they two walked off, Jim turned to Angie. She looked him squarely in the eye.

"I'm going to clear off everyone on and around the bed," she said. "And *you are going to lie down! I mean that!*"

Chapter 26

"I mean that!" Angie repeated. "You're looking more and more like death warmed over, every minute. You lie down. *Now!*"

"Well . . ." said Jim, thinking how ridiculous he would look in the midst of this crowd, lying on the bed when most of them could not even find a place to sit down. Then he remembered that people of this time were used to being on their feet for long periods. And it also occured to him how good it would be to stretch out for a moment. . . . "Until the hobs get back with a goblin, anyway," he answered.

Indeed, once he was lying down on the too-short bed (What posessed these medieval people to build beds for three-quarters-size humans?) he began to believe that he might actually need some rest.

Once horizontal, with all the crowd around him casting curious glances in his direction, but warned off from asking questions by Angie, who was standing by the bed with a grim look on her face that effectively announced that this was Magickian–knight business and none of theirs—Jim's head had begun to swim.

He was exhausted, his body told him. How the hell had he gotten this way? He had slept well enough last night. . . . He closed his eyes—and opened them, it seemed only a second later, to find Angie gently rubbing his forehead, reluctantly bringing him back awake.

He stared.

Beside his bed, facing him, was a goblin, his arms pinioned behind him, and flanked by a triumphant-looking Hob and Tiverton hob. The goblin's eyes glittered malevolently. There seemed to be no cowards among these enemies, at least.

The Prince and the Countess stood like giants behind the three small Naturals, and the rest of the crowd in the room had somehow compressed itself to put a respectful distance between them and the gathering at the bed.

Reflexively, Jim threw a privacy ward around the little group by his bed. He was surprised at the amount of mental effort it took—perhaps it was because he had been lying down. He sat up on the bed and found that equally effortful. Manners said he should be standing if the Prince was standing, but his legs seemed to have lost their strength.

"You got him!" Jim croaked at the hobs.

"I—" began Hob.

"We—" began Tiverton hob in the same second. They glared at each other for a moment, then Malencontri hob went on alone.

"I must report to my lord," he said, "that the prisoner was secured as expected."

"There were five in the one room we could find that had the least in," said Tiverton hob eagerly.

"—The little dog growled at them and they didn't dare move a muscle," broke in Hob, once more. "I chose this one, the biggest, carried him off and we went back up the chimney—"

"I carried the prisoner—" Tiverton hob broke in.

"Yes," said Hob, "asking him all the way if this was fun and should you do it again! What were you doing to him?"

"Never mind," said Tiverton hob. "I may have pinched him a little from time to time because of the way I had to carry him."

"And you had the dog?" Jim asked Hob. It was an effort even to speak. But he wanted an end to this chitchat.

"I did!" said Hob. "See her, back in her box, now?"

Jim looked in the right direction. Because of the crowd's retreat, he could see a corner of the pen; the terrier was there, fussily and rather roughly tongue-washing all her pups over again.

"Enough of this!" broke in the Prince. "We have the goblin. Make him magically caged and helpless at once, James, and send us back up to my father without further delay!"

"Your Grace—" began Angie, in a tone of voice that eerily evoked in Jim's long-familiar mind an image of a cougar crouching, ready to make its spring.

"Come, my lady," said Jim hastily. "His Grace is right. There's no time to waste in more talk."

With an effort that felt tremendous, he created an impenetrable ward around the goblin, disintegrating his bonds in the process. With an even greater effort, he transported goblin, ward, Countess and Prince once more to the King's suite of rooms.

Head swimming, he fell back on the bed into what seemed to be a bottomless hole of lightless sleep.

He woke again—or *was* he awake? He seemed to be two versions of himself: one lying utterly unconscious on a bed, the other—bodiless, impalpable and invisible—standing over it, its lower legs seeming to be buried up to the knees in the bed. To his astonishment the crowd was still pulled back respectfully, and besides Angie, not only Kinetete, but Carolinus was at his bedside.

"Carolinus!" he shouted soundlessly. "Can you move all these human people, including the King, back to Malencontri? I don't seem . . . somehow I don't seem to have the strength—"

Carolinus, in Jim's vision, seemed to move without moving, to look down at him.

"Sleep!" commanded Carolinus.

But he—that astral part of himself—stayed stubbornly awake and standing upright.

"He's not responding to the sleep command!" said Kinetete, sharply. "What in the name of—"

"You couldn't do it yourself, in any case, Jim!" said Carolinus, speaking directly to Jim's astral self as if he could see it perfectly clearly. "You don't have enough magic left in you to tickle a mouse!"

"What is it?" Kinetete asked her fellow Mage. "I've never seen a command fail like that. Shall I try?"

"No, no," said Carolinus irritably. "It wouldn't do a bit of good!" The irritation went out of his voice. "Actually, Kin, I'm not surprised you haven't. I've only seen one case before—and that not nearly as bad as this. He's simply drained himself of all possible human energy—spent more magick in the last hour or so than a self-respecting C-class Magickian would use in a month. He's achieved a complete separation between the spirit and the body, while still living.

Take a look there, above the bed—that's his spirit talking to us."

"Saints forbid!" said Kinetete. "I see him—the other him, now. James, how could you do such a thing?"

"Don't bother the boy!" said Carolinus. "There's nothing he can do to help himself now. You and I have to do it for him. That and complete rest. First step, get him back to Malencontri—"

"And everybody else!" cried Jim, from his astral body. "I tell you they're all in danger of being killed here by plague—and the King, as well! All of them—the only safe place for them's Malencontri!"

"Hah!" said both Mages in the same instant. "The King?"

"That's what I said!"

"How—?" said Kinetete, looking at Carolinus.

"I don't know. And he's in no shape to tell us!"

"Get the hobs in!" cried Jim, noiselessly, frantically.

"Very well. Hobs here!" said Carolinus.

"Have them tell you," said Jim—and gave up, exhausted. The room started slowly to rotate around him.

The two hobs appeared.

"Sir James is sleeping?" asked Malencontri hob, a little anxiously, looking at the still figure on the bed.

"That's right," said Carolinus. "But I can talk to him. He wants you to tell me everything you just did. Do so!"

"Oh yes, Mage Carolinus," said Hob, making the elaborate stage bow the traveling actor had taught him, when Hob had had dreams of becoming Jim's squire.

"Another Mage?" said Tiverton hob, open-mouthed with awe. He tried to copy Hob's bow and failed utterly.

"Sir James is *not* a Mage," said Carolinus. "However, beside me here is Mage Kinetete, who is."

"Two—" managed Tiverton hob again, once more trying the bow and falling flat on his face.

"Get up! Get up!" said Kinetete, testily. "It's not necessary to bow to Mages when you meet them, Tiv. Carolinus may like it—"

"Not necessarily," said Carolinus. "Now, with Sir James unable to tell me, you two have to. What have you been up to?"

"We captured a goblin for His Grace and the Countess to take to show the King," said Hob. "The King didn't believe there were goblins."

"The place is swarming with them," said Kinetete.

"Yes," said Tiverton hob, suddenly bold at the unhesitating way Hob spoke up. "They were part of a plan to kill the King with sickness. Plague sickness!"

"How do you know that?" Carolinus turned to him.

"Because I used to watch Sir Verweather talking to the chief goblin," said Tiverton hob, proud at being center stage. He added smugly, "The goblins were having a lot of work pretending to be humans—they'd changed shape to look like castle servants, but they'd each had only two days to study how each human was going to be talked and acted. Some of them were pretty good at being servants and men-at-arms, but none of them really knew how to be special people like sirs and ladies, or blacksmiths or stable masters, and they couldn't understand why the King didn't catch the plague, when they kept putting all the plague-sick fleas in his rooms."

"You saw this? You heard them?"

"Oh, yes, Mage."

"That is odd," said Kinetete.

"The King was Destined, of course. But Edward III must be much more strongly Destined than I've ever given him credit for. Nonethless, Kin, we've got to get him and these others out of here right away if he's swarmed over with plague fleas. Tiv, think of the room where you saw the goblin talking to . . . to . . ."

"Verweather," said Kinetete. "Tiv, just imagine the room as you know it—ah, that's better!

All at once the hobs, the Mages, Angie, and even the bed Jim was in, were in what must be one of the guest bedrooms lower in the tower—a room in which there were now at least a dozen goblins, who spun about to face them.

"Still!" said Carolinus absentmindedly. "No. There're too many of you to ignore."

He flipped the back of his hand at them. "Got to the— go to the kitchen!"

The goblins vanished.

"All right, Tiv," said Carolinus, "now when did you see them together last?"

"The night my Lord James and the other with him, came—just two nights agone, my Mage."

"Just Mage, hob. Very well." Carolinus brought down his skinny, extended finger sharply, twice, like a conductor giving the beat to his musicians—and suddenly the room had other occupants.

They were Sir Mortimor Verweather and a single goblin. They seemed entirely unaware of those standing and watching. But Tiverton hob shrank back behind Kinetete.

"It's 'im!" he hissed at Hob. "The one who was cruelest of all to me!"

"Don't worry." Hob drew his sword. "I'll kill him before he can get to you ever again."

"No! It's I wants to kill him!" said Tiverton hob, pulling his own weapon from its cracked leather sheath.

"That's not very hoblike of you, Tiv," said Hob, looking quite stern and reproving. "If I kill him, it's just me defending you. But if you kill him, it's revenge. My lord never uses his magic except in defense—nor the Mages don't either!"

Jim, watching and listening in his astral body, blinked. How had Hob come by that bit of knowledge? The only possibility was that he had overheard Jim telling Angie about the Magickian rules, before the time Jim had ordered him never to listen in on private conversations between his lord and lady.

"Put those weapons up!" Carolinus was saying irritably. "Neither of those two can see or hear us. For them it's the day before two nights past—look at the arrow slits!"

Those with him—except Kinetete—all looked. There was sunlight beyond the window.

"—Why are they here?" the goblin was asking. It was the first time Jim had heard one of them speak when not in human form. This one had a dry, thin, sharp and high-pitched voice that matched well with the glitter of his eyes.

"Because the Prince invited him, as you just heard him tell his father!" said Verweather. "Don't worry. They are no more hungry to stay here than you are to see them go. I'll raise my voice with the King on that matter, when I speak privily to him."

"And if your man–king falls ill with the sickness so that all can see, while they're here? Why is it he has not become sick before now? Best from the beginning as I said that we simply slay them all. That's always best."

"Are you mad?" Verweather said. "Malencontri—the Knight Dragon—is likewise a Magickian, and a close friend of Mage Carolinus, who is wise, old and powerful beyond our knowing. Carolinus would see the death of Dragon and read all our plans!"

"Then why did you let him and those with him come here?"

"Do you think I can stop the winter storm? I have some influence with the King, secretly, in Lord Cumberland's name, but I cannot check the Prince. Like his father, he dares anything and will do as he wishes first and deal with the consequences afterward. The King still loves him, but will not say so—to him least of all—moreover the boy is his first son, heir to the kingdom. Do not come between the lion and his cub, Master Goblin—or if you do, you do it without me!"

"Perhaps we do not need you, at that," said the goblin in his thin voice. "We have our own fighting goblins, in numbers too great for them to oppose. We have the rats and the plague lice, more than they can count. We will take back the world from those cringing hobgoblins and take their place, with humans for our slaves in their castles and houses—"

Tiverton hob made a fierce inarticulate sound in his throat, and started forward, drawing his little knife.

"Peace! *Still!*" said Carolinus. "Did I not say these are only shadows from three days agone? Your weapon can't touch them. Now, *unstill*, Tiv, and step back. I think we've heard enough, anyway—" Verweather and the goblin blinked out "—we'll get back to the others."

"I think—" began Jim, as they found themselves back in the crowded room.

"Think nothing!" snapped Carolinus. "You've done too much of that, and using magick with every thought. Kin and I will take care of everything. Your job is to rest—the only cure for magick shock—for the next few days! *Accounting Office!*"

"I am here," said the usual invisible voice some four feet or so off the ground.

"How did he manage to overdraw his account to that extent? He's still my apprentice and under limitations!"

"The how of it is beyond my explanation. I am only designed to keep records of magick energy passing through me. He seems to have accessed extra raw energy from the continuum, itself. It would be the only other way that those touched by magick could gain what I had not given them— and none has ever gained so before. I give only what they have earned for some great accomplishment. But he has made none such since I last paid him. I gave only what he had in his account."

"Get out!" said Carolinus.

"I go, Mage . . ." and that was the last Jim heard. Room, people, light and life itself seemed to go from him. All came to an end.

Chapter 27

Jim drifted slowly back up to consciousness, his whole body feeling numb. He was in a different place, a strange place—no, it was not a strange place. It was the Nursing Room they had set up in Malencontri. He was in a sort of extra-long, extra-wide bed on the dais they had built there, with curtains set up and drawn all around him.

Then he forgot all about where he was. Incredible pains suddenly seemed to grow into his awareness, lancing though him from both his armpits and his groin. They grew until they were beyond bearing; and in spite of himself, a hoarse grunt from the unbearable agony came from his throat. Then another. And another.

The curtains parted and Angie was with him, looking pale and tense and carrying something. She dropped it on the bed beside his legs and put her arms around him—but only for a second.

"Thank God!" she said. "You're awake! Here—" She picked up from the bed what she had been carrying and put one end of it between his lips. It was a sort of pipe with a ridiculously small bowl and a long, four-sided stem. She also produced a small black ball of something and put it in the tiny bowl.

"Light!" she cried, angrily, and May Heather burst through the curtains, holding a splinter of wood, glowing at the end with small flames. She gave it to Angie and backed out.

"Here, dear," said Angie. There were tears in her eyes. She held the end of the pipe to his mouth; the mouthpiece was smooth and cool on his lips. She put the glowing end of the splinter to whatever was in the bowl. The acrid odor of the burning stick was in his nose, along with another, strange smell.

"Inhale now," she said. "Inhale deep, sweetheart. Smoke it, now. It'll help the pain."

"What is it?" managed Jim thickly around the end of the mouthpiece. "I don't smoke. You know that."

"Opium. Carolinus got it for you from a Magickian in China. Smoke it. It'll help."

He coughed on the smoke—but he tried. After a moment or two, the coughing stopped. The odor in his mouth and nose was all of the strange kind he had smelled, overwhelming the wood smoke.

"Opium?" he tried to say, but with the pipe in his mouth and the pain, all he could do was mumble the word.

"Don't talk. Smoke," she said. "Just keep smoking. It'll help, you'll see."

That's right, said a crazy, unconnected part of his brain, *opium had been used as a painkiller in the East at least as early as the fourteenth century.*

But against the incredible pain it seemed relief did not come swiftly. Finally, though, at last, he began to be able to tell a difference. The pain did lessen, but more than that, it seemed to move off a little way from him, as if it was a voice sounding lower because it had pulled away.

A hand from his own body somehow managed to reach up and draw the mouthpiece of the pipe temporarily from between his lips.

"It's working," he told Angie. But Angie seemed to have gone off a small distance, too, along with the bed and the curtains. Still, he could see she was smiling at him. Her face came toward him. He felt her arms around him again, and her warm tears on his neck.

"You are my life!" he heard her saying, but further and further off, as if she was withdrawing from him. There were colors around him, drifting and changing. They were friendly, however, soothing, and the pain was undeniably distant now. He heard her say something again, but could not quite understand, almost as if it was in some language he did not know. But he knew her love flowed around him; he felt it like the touch of her arms. It was his own mind that was going away—going away peacefully into relief and happiness. Angie . . .

. . . He must have dropped the pipe, but he could see it nowhere on the bed. Things were close again, but he was still at peace, and while the pain was back, it was nowhere as bad . . . in any case, he was at still at peace.

"Angie!" he called.

She was instantly there, through the curtains.

"I'm much better," he told her.

"Oh, my dear," she said, and her eyes overflowed again. "You've got the plague—and I joked! I joked about the itching of your flea bites!"

She put her head down on his chest, burying her face against it. Clumsily he stroked her hair.

"Of course," he said gruffly, "Naturally. Who wouldn't? I'd have joked at you."

She did not answer. She just lay there. After a little while she said, "I'm so sorry."

"Nonsense!" he said, helpless for want of the right words to stop this. "Ridiculous. Stop it at once!"

He felt her starting to shake against his chest, and was filled with sudden despair. He could not stand this—then he realized she was laughing.

She hugged him and sat up, wiping her eyes.

The opium took him away again, just as he became hazily aware that Carolinus had appeared; he barely caught a fragment of the Mage's first words, "—not supposed to work that way . . ."

He woke to the unspeakable pain. Again—Angie with the pipe. Again, the pain went, and there was an interlude in which he may have dreamed, a dream shot with color. The only thing he remembered clearly was an image of Geronde with the scar on her face gone.

Again, a sensible—more or less—period in which the pain was gone, and he talked with Angie.

"You shouldn't be here with me," he told her. "You'll catch it from me—just from being close and my breath. Catch the pneumonal form of plague."

"Too late now," said Angie serenely.

"But just to be safe, you go back up to the Solar and stay there—"

"I can't."

"Why not?"

"The King's settled in there, now," she said.

"The King's here? What's he doing here?"

"Carolinus and Kinetete took every human out of Tiverton to here, just as you asked—from the King down to Verweather in his bed."

"Bed?" Jim's mind was working slowly, but for once the slowness did not bother him. He waited benignly for it to produce, like a loaf of bread being baked. "But why the King in our Solar?"

"The King always gets the best there is any place he visits," she said. "You know that. He's got all the top floor, except for little Robert and his nurse in their small room. I begged him to let them stay, and he did."

Jim pondered this. There was something more important to ask. His slow mind found it.

"Angie, can you remember which had the best chance of surviving the plague: the pneumonal or the flea-bitten?"

Her face changed. In a dreamy way, he was sorry he had asked.

"The kind you've got!" she said. "With these terrible swellings, the buboes in your armpits and groin."

"No," he said. "Do you really remember that for sure? Really, sure?"

"Oh, Jim!"

"It's all right. I need to know, and it won't bother me to hear."

"I'm—almost sure. The ones with the buboes had a better chance of living, and they got well quicker, even though they went through torments first."

"Don't worry, then. I'll live."

Her arms were holding him tightly again.

"Of course you will! Of course you will!!"

Things went away again. He slept and woke to pain, smoke, surcease, in regular rotation . . . sleep came and went for some indeterminable time.

Finally there came a time when he woke to find himself less dreamy, more quick-minded than he had been for some time, and the pain was less—though he had not had the pipe again yet.

This time it was Carolinus, not Angie, who was standing beside his bed.

"I hope I haven't become addicted," said Jim. "I mean—go on needing to have to have the pipe from now on." But he had little hope, actually.

"You shouldn't," said Carolinus, surprisingly. "The Magickian who found it for me said that those who took it for pain only, and had no other desire for it, would not thereafter go on needing it once the pain was gone."

"Who was the Magickian?" Even as he said it, Jim remembered that Carolinus did not like to be asked about his connections. But evidently this time was different.

"Son Won Phon," said Carolinus.

Jim's mind was not so clogged with drug now, but it was still not up to his usual speed. He pondered this answer, too, for a moment.

"But he did it, knowing it was for me?"

"Why so surprised?" said Carolinus, with a touch of his

old testiness, that had been remarkably absent all through their talk so far. "I told you he was a man of principle!"

"Anyway, thank him," said Jim. "Tell him for me? I would have lived anyway—I've got things to do—but it would have been hell until I did!"

"I will," said Carolinus gently—for him. "You wanted to live, clearly."

"You're damn right!" said Jim, surprising himself by the words that came out of his mouth. Unexpected as they were, though, he told himself, they were the truth. He knew it in his bones. He had reasons for wanting to live: Angie, Robert . . . and the once-misty shape of his goal in this world with magic.

This world that he had not known clearly until he had had those talks with Merlin, in the blackness of the tree in Lyonesse, where the ancient seer had magically caused himself to be imprisoned, and was striving to see all of time from beginning to end. And little Robert Falon, who must grow up in this century uncrippled by the fact that those who were his ward-parents were from a far future time.

"On another matter," Carolinus was saying, "the King has been asking after you every day since he got here. We had quite a talk, earlier today. Neither I, Kinetete, young Edward, Hell or Heaven, will make him admit to being convinced Cumberland was behind the goblin matter—but that's beside the point. He thinks very highly of you, so he wants you to move back into the Solar as soon as you're able. He'll take rooms on the floor below, but four of them, and they must have inside connecting doors from room to room and proper furnishings."

"Malencontri can do that," said Jim.

"No doubt. But if necessary I can do it. You're not the only one who's been sick, and you've lost some people— though it was far from being as bad as it might have been if you hadn't taken precaution. The plague reached here, but wasn't as successful as usual because of what you'd done—I had my work cut out getting the people here from Tiverton, through all the wards you set up. You seem to have warded everything but the kitchen cat!"

"Do I have a kitchen cat?"

"Of course you do. Didn't your hob ever tell you? Cats and hobs are natural friends."

"No, he didn't," said Jim. "The things I don't know!"

"If you think you are telling me something new, you are sadly mistaken!"

"But the goblins? What abut the goblins?"

"Your hob has been in touch with them. Tiverton hob wouldn't leave his castle, but since all of you from here got back, your own hob has bravely gone into regular contact with them. They were so shocked at his effrontery the first time he showed up, they didn't kill him without asking what he was there for. He told them he was an ambassador from all hobs, who were now armed like himself, and we humans. He laid it on thick, as you would certainly put it. He's also been giving them daily bulletins on your recovery—he never had any doubt at all you'd recover—and it's made them very uneasy. If you can survive the plague, maybe many other dangerous humans can."

"They believe that?"

"Why not?" Carolinus bristled. "It could be true. "There are us Magickians—and not a few men and women—who have a reason to live, as you were just saying."

"Maybe I should show myself to them—" Jim made an effort to sit up in bed, but could not manage it.

"Later, when you're stronger."

"Well, then, you make me stronger."

Carolinus stared at him, then turned and literally stamped away several steps toward the foot of the bed, checked himself, turned about and stamped back to glare down at Jim.

"How can I make you stronger?" he snapped. "Even if I could you'd have to pay for it later, and then's just when you'd be wanting strength again! Where do you think is the only place strength like that is going to have to come from? From you! You'll have to pay it back to yourself later by more rest—and that's when you'll be wanting it more, not less!"

"Mage Carolinus—my Master-in-Magick—" Jim was beginning to lose his temper as well "—I've seen you do things you said were impossible before. Is this really impossible? For you?"

"Yes!" shouted Carolinus. Angie came bursting in through the curtains, the opium pipe hanging down, forgotten in one hand.

"You promised you wouldn't excite him!" she cried to Carolinus.

"He's the one who's exciting *me!*" roared Carolinus. "By—no, I won't swear over this—James Eckert, you are an Apprentice! You do not argue with me when I say something cannot be done. I mean what I say—no more, no less—"

"Magickal energy can't be turned into physical energy?" Jim interrupted.

Carolinus checked himself with his mouth still open to roar again. Slowly his mouth closed.

"Jim," he said after a long moment, in a perfectly ordinary, reasonable voice, "you will either be the wonder or the terror of all time—and I shudder to think which! You aren't entitled to it, you don't deserve it, but I'm going to tell you squarely. What you suggest is a possibility neither I, nor any other Magickian I know of, has ever considered—the next thing you'll do is ask me to help you go to the gates of Hell so you can demand a cool cup of water!"

"Forgive me for putting it the way I did," said Jim, genuinely sorry. "But I had to ask."

"Yes, you did! And the worst of it is, you've opened up a question that now has to be answered, sometime!"

"Maybe Merlin—" said Jim.

Carolinus snorted.

"Anything is possible with Merlin," he answered. "But much good it'll do us. I could knock on his tree for a thousand years and he still wouldn't answer me! Would he answer to you?"

"He told me never to bother him again, last time. But he thinks well of you. He said as much the first time we talked. And as I say, he talked to me twice and sent me a message once—the last one saying not to bother him again. Don't you think it's worth your trying?"

"I do not! To him I'm just a lad Magickian, only a few years—never mind that. You and Angie are somethings from somewhere beyond this world. You're interesting. I'm not. He's been approached by dozens like me, and he's sat there thinking for a thousand years—not that he was ever one to do or tell anything but what he wanted to!"

"But—"

"And he looks at all time from its beginning to its end. Do you know how small that makes the situation we're in here and now? Too small to waste a single thought on! But to us, with a man who, in spite of his human faults, has been a good King to England and is needed a few more years yet—let me show you what we're up against."

"I don't like this at all!" snapped Angie. "Jim's not up to this kind of effort, yet—"

"It's all right, Angie. I'm over the plague. I can hardly even feel the pain now!"

"That's because you're in overdrive!" she said.

"Let me show you," Carolinus repeated. "Solar!"

Jim, Angie and Carolinus were suddenly in the Solar—Jim still in his bed. There was no sign of the King, who had evidently already vacated it for its true owners. Signs of careless royal occupancy were everywhere.

"Will you look at this place?" said Angie. *"Servant, here!"*

The door opened and a female servant popped her head in.

"M'lady!" There was astonishment and joy in her voice. She popped the rest of the way in and curtsied. "Terrible sorry, m'lady, but he never wanted to be disturbed—"

"Well, clean it up! Get the Room Mistress. Tell her to get a crew in here to help—tell her I told you to tell her so. If we're still here when the crew comes, they can clean around us."

"At once, m'lady." Exit servant.

Meanwhile Carolinus had pushed Jim's bed—which was floating in midair at about the same height above the floor as the dais in the Nursing Room had put it—over to one of the Solar windows, which he opened to the crisp outside air. Accustomed now to the hothouse temperature of the Nursing Room, Jim unthinkingly pulled his bedcovers up around his neck.

"Good idea," said Carolinus, watching him. "But don't let them down there see you. Take a look outside and see what we're up against."

Jim looked. He saw goblins. Starting at about the halfway point in the cleared space around the castle, the ground was thick with them. They were carrying spears. But none seemed inclined to stray any closer to the castle.

"How did they know we came here?" he asked Carolinus.

"Where would you look first," said Carolinus, "when your quarry had just vanished?"

"The castle where the Knight Dragon Magickian lives— of course," answered Jim. "Yes, I see what you mean. How many of them are there, just outside?"

"Several hundreds all around the castle, and more in the woods behind them. No telling how many more scattered though Somerset. Of course, the local predators are having a fine old feast off them."

Jim felt a slight queasiness

"You say they're being eaten?"

"Certainly—they're easy prey. Solid meat—no bones or tough hide to speak of. Just as hobs would be if all the animals hadn't learned long ago that hobs are their friends."

"But *eating* them!"

"If that upsets you, those dragon friends you have at Cliffside Eyrie have been taking them, too. They've got to eat also, you know. Why should a goblin be so shocking when a lamb or calf isn't?"

"But . . . *my* dragons?"

"I don't know how much you can call them yours. Your dragon self has been accepted into their community, that's all," growled Carolinus. "I don't think any of them would be too happy with your talking about them as if they were servants of your castle and lands."

"I didn't mean it that way," said Jim. "But what about those spears? Pretty discouraging weapons."

"Only because of the poison of the magick in their tips, and—"

"I remember," said Jim, "magic doesn't work on animals."

"That's right," said Carolinus. "Only on those who use magick—humans, Naturals and spirits of all kinds."

"And, as I just said, not animals!" Jim glared at him.

"One must never pass up the opportunity to teach Apprentices," said Carolinus, serenely. "On more important subjects, what do you think of the situation, now?"

"We've got to get rid of them. Drive them back underground where they belong."

"And how would you go about doing that?"

"I don't know," said Jim. "Carolinus, I still hurt like hell, and I'm getting kind of exhausted. I don't think I'm up to making plans now. Don't you have anything in mind?"

"If you mean can I snap my fingers and transport them all to deep earth, I can't. There're too many of them. But Jim—" the tone of his voice changed "—forgive me. I should give you another day or two to recover."

"That's all right. I'm glad to know—and, Carolinus, thank you for getting me the opium. It worked like a charm, though I'd hate to live with it—it'd be like living in a bad dream."

"Don't thank me."

"Of course. I meant, and convey my thanks to Son Won Phon when you get the chance."

"I shall."

"And now," said Angie, suddenly appearing and with a hard note in her voice, "it's time for Jim to get some rest."

"Of course," said Carolinus—and was no longer there.

"I think he flicks in and out like that deliberately," said Jim.

"Now that he's gone, though, do you want the pipe for just a bit?" Angie asked, pushing his still-floating bed back deeper into the room, where it gradually sank to the floor. "You can stay where you are until the Solar's cleaned up, but then I'll move you back to our own bed. Still, there's going to be quite a fuss and bother around you until it's done. Should we just shift you over now?"

"Yes. No! Dammit! I'll have to call Carolinus back. Chandos!"

"Chandos?"

"If anyone might know how to handle that army outside, it'd be him. I'm out of magick, and Carolinus would undoubtedly say I shouldn't try to use it if I had it. But he could bring Chandos here in a twinkling—"

"I already tried to," said Carolinus, appearing again. "This is *not* my usual practice. He can't come. He's fighting a single-handed battle to keep Cumberland from taking over everything while the King's gone. But he said he had no ideas for us. There's too big a force facing us, and he knows nothing of goblins."

"Were you listening in on us just now?" Jim looked at him sharply.

"Certainly not. I just have myself alerted to your needing me. Clearly, the present need is ended."

He vanished once more.

"Give me the blasted pipe, Angie!" said Jim.

Chapter 28

The opium blurred the bustle around Jim that was the returning of the Solar to the state in which he and Angie were
used to it, but he was beginning to hate the stuff. It put an
end to any sharp thinking he might have done, and he re-
sented that. His mind had kept him alive and solved all his
problems for him, as well as making life interesting, and he
did not like being separated from it.

On the other hand, what was left of his buboes were still
hurting enough to make him want it. The pipe moved that
hurt a long, long way from him. Furthermore, he was beginning to realize for the first time how exhausted he really
was—as if he had put in a huge day's work under normal
conditions. Sleep beckoned, and he went with it.

He woke up in the middle of the night in his accustomed
bed, with the comforting presence of Angie slumbering beside him. He put an arm over her. She stirred, but did not
wake. This was one of the great things about being married
a while, he thought, this warm, accustomed, semi-awake
togetherness. He was hardly hurting at all, and his mind was
almost his, again—he went back to sleep.

He woke a second time, fully awake this time, clear-
headed and still almost without pain. It was still dark outside
the Solar windows, and from the sound of it, a little rain
was hissing against the very expensive but very welcomed
window glass.

He wondered how the goblins were dealing with the rain.
Huddling under trees? They could not be used to the falling
water, but they had not seemed to have anything in the
nature of tents or other shelters set up. There was one way
in which hobs were better off than those who had kicked

them out of their original kingdom: hobs were always warm and dry—

He sat up suddenly, his mind clicking. Disturbed by the change of weight on the bed and the removal of his arm, Angie started to wake up.

"Nothing . . ." he said to her softly. "Nothing . . . go back to sleep."

She did, and he sat upright there, his back to the head-board, thinking, thinking. . . .

Of course! Those who could afford it always carried the fourteenth-century version of tents, if they expected to be spending nights in the open. The poorer classes were not so fortunate, usually. He had been forgetting the very large difference between the technology of this age and the prac-tically primitive goblins, whose only evidence of anything beyond the Stone Age was their magic and their spears.

Unless they had some way of using magic to shelter themselves. Setting up wards or something like that—but no other Natural he had ever heard of had that as part of his or her instinctive, built-in magical abilities. Carolinus could probably tell him. Could he wake Carolinus, wherever the Mage was now, and ask him?

No.

But Hob could be called at any hour, and he might know—almost certainly would know.

Jim eased himself out of the bed—gently, so as not to wake Angie—and went to the welcome heat of the fire, crouching down before it so he could look up the chimney beyond the flames.

"Hob!" he whispered to the chimney.

Hob's face appeared a second later, upside down, peering out below the top edge of the fireplace opening.

"M'lord!" he said, in a normally loud voice.

"Shhh!" said Jim, casting a glance at the bed. But Angie had not stirred. Hob came all the way down from the chim-ney and stood upright, staring at Jim. It occurred to Jim that this was the first time the little Natural had seen his lord unclothed. Both Jim and Angie had adopted the medieval habit of "going to their naked bed"—or, in more modern word-fashion, going naked to bed. Not that this should make any difference. Hob had plainly never worn clothes in his life, and neither Jim, Angie nor anyone else had ever paid any attention to the fact. The period, in effect, paid little attention to many of the later days' privacies.

"Is m'lord cold?" whispered Hob. "Would he like me to wrap some warm smoke around him? I won't let it get in his eyes."

"Yes," said Jim, suddenly conscious of gooseflesh and the nighttime temperature of the Solar outside the bedcovers. Smoke curled out from the fire and enveloped him up to the neck, its further end reaching back to the fire. It was indeed warm and pleasant. His gooseflesh subsided.

"Hob," he said, "do the goblins have any magical ways of protecting themselves from the kind of rain we've got outside, tonight?"

"No, m'lord. They only have magic for making things like their spearpoints out of diamonds or Great Silver."

Great Silver was something beings like the Gnarlies could perceive in ordinary silver, and which they greatly prized. It had a jewel-like appearance. It was not surprising that the goblins, also now a race living in Deep Earth, could also perceive and isolate and work with it for their spearpoints.

"Then they're getting very wet right now."

"Yes, m'lord, very wet," said Hob happily. "Of course, they're not *afraid* of water, the way they are of fire."

"And of course you hobs are right at home with fire."

"Oh, yes m'lord. Fire is kind to a hob, and as m'lord knows, smoke is even kinder."

"So what kind of magic can they do, compared to hob magic?"

"Almost no magic, m'lord. As you know, we can pass through our friend fire and ride our friend smoke and all sorts of things they can't do. Oh, yes, we can even ride the smoke anywhere, even clear around the world—did m'lord know the world is round?"

"I did."

"Of course. Forgive my being so stupid. Of course, a great Magickian like m'lord would know!"

"Fairly great," said Jim. "But that wasn't what I asked. I want to know what you can do that goblins can't."

"Very sorry, m'lord. Well, we can do just about anything. Live with the fire, make friends with some humans, be very brave—Oh, and we can ask the smoke to do anything we want—like wrapping around you, just now. Smoke would wrap thick, top to bottom around the whole castle if I asked it. Would my lord like it to do something like that for him?"

"You mentioned hobs being brave. Goblins aren't brave?"

"Oh, no, m'lord. Goblins are never brave. They're just fierce."

"I see," said Jim. "That's different?"

"Isn't it, m'lord?"

"Well, maybe it is. Give me an example of the difference, though."

"Why, we hobs aren't scared to death of a cross marked on a building, the way goblins are. We can go right in— through a chimney usually, of course, but it doesn't have to be a chimney. We all like each other!"

"I remember now," Jim said thoughtfully, "You told me about that. But goblins don't like each other?"

"They hate each other, like they hate everybody else— just as they used to hate even the Great Demons, back when we all were in the Kingdom of Devils and Demons. But they hated us who became hobs most, and that's why they cast us out. They said we were freaks and not fit to be there, but it was really because all the other devils and demons were blaming them for not being able to get past any kind of holy mark anywhere in the world; and they were cast out of the Kingdom, too, after we were gone and there were still things to blame on someone. . . . M'lord doesn't mind that I was born a goblin?"

The last words came out a little tremulously.

"Never!" said Jim. "Where I come from, it's what a person is, not what he or she was. That's the only thing that matters."

"It must be a lovely place you come from, m'lord," said Hob wistfully.

"Well, it has its faults," said Jim, feeling a twinge of guilt. "So you hobs evidently adapted to what you are up here?"

"We always were what we were, but what we were helped us to adapted. . . ." His voice faltered. "Forgive my ignorance, m'lord. But what's 'adapted'?"

" 'Adapt' is when you change yourself to make it possible for you to do things you couldn't."

"Oh."

"Yes."

"So we adapt—" Hob hesitated, glancing at Jim, "—ed?"

"In this case you'd say 'adapt*ed*.' "

"Well, all I can say, m'lord, is that I'm awfully glad we adapted. It's much nicer being a hob than a goblin. When I want to, I can even touch cold iron, like the sword you had made for me, instead of getting terribly burned the way I would have if I'd stayed a goblin."

"It really burns them to touch or be touched by it, then?"

"Oh, yes. It can burn them bad enough to kill them."

"Is that so?" said Jim, suddenly very interested. "And Tiverton hob said they don't like fire."

"It burns them right up—as if they were straw—but only one at a time. I mean, m'lord, they can't catch fire from each other."

"Damn!" said Jim, his abrupt dream evaporating of setting fire to the whole goblin swarm around Malencontri with a single torch touching off just one of their beseigers.

Just as well, he told himself. No creatures, not even goblins, should be burned to death. "What?" he asked, for Hob had started to talk again.

"I just asked, m'lord, begging your pardon, but is he really a king—the man who was staying in the Solar here until today?"

"He is," said Jim. "You sound disappointed."

"Well, m'lord . . ." Hob writhed, a sure sign of embarrassment, "I thought he'd be bigger."

"Bigger."

"Double your size—I mean no offense, m'lord!"

"None taken," said Jim. "Why bigger?"

"I don't know. I just thought so. It seemed to stand to reason. If you saw Hill now, you'd see how much bigger than other Gnarlies he's become since he became King in Gnarlyland. He doesn't like the goblins, either."

"I know. Just as much as the rest of us do."

"Then why doesn't the King send for an army of knights to come here and chase them away? They'd be safe in their armor, and their horses wouldn't hardly even feel the magic poison in the speartips."

Jim's mind suddenly lit up.

"Hob," he said, "you're a genius!"

"I know, my lord. You told me so once before. Forgive my ignorance, though, but I'm still not quite sure what it is—being a genius."

"Tell you later when we've more time to talk," Jim told him. "Right now, though . . . Hob, this smoke of yours is very comfortable, and all that. But I've got to do some thinking, now, and I do my thinking best in bed. So I'll say goodnight for what's left of it, and go back to my pillow and covers. You remember the rule about not listening in here?"

"Oh yes, m'lord. I never ever listen to you and m'lady anymore."

"Of course you don't. I shouldn't even mention it. Just habit, I suppose."

"Goodnight, m'lord. Do you want the smoke to keep you wrapped until you're in bed?"

"If it would be so kind."

"But smoke isn't kind, m'lord. Or unkind either. It just does what it's asked to do."

"I see," said Jim, his thoughts already galloping away from the present conversation. It was idiotic of him not to think before of what had just occurred to him—but for now it was only the grand outline of an idea. He would have to work out the details before he mentioned it to anyone. He got up and started back to bed. "Goodnight, Hob."

"Goodnight, m'lord—though it's really morn, now."

"Oh?" said Jim vaguely, and got cautiously back into bed. He made it safely without disturbing the slumbering Angie, and snuggled down himself under the covers.

"Jim!" said Angie, suddenly awake. "Do you smell smoke?"

"No," said Jim.

He lay thinking while the first light fought its way through the heavy clouds beyond the windows. The rain had stopped, he thought, but there was every indication that it would be a gloomy day. Angie had returned immediately to sleep—a knack of hers—after being reassured about the smoke smell.

He was feeling almost perfect, he thought. The excitement in him was overriding the pain of what was left from where his buboes had been—more a stiffness from the healing parts than pain.

Angie slept. Jim lay awake, his mind spinning with plans, counterplans, scrapped plans that he had thought might work—until, worn out, his relentless brain gave up at last and sleep took him without warning.

He woke to broad daylight and a suspicion that the day must be half over.

"Want some tea?" Angie said. "I've kept the water hot on the hob. How do you feel?"

He looked around, found her standing by the fireplace, and became aware of the singing of the kettle on its hob—the long metal arm that allowed anything hanging on it to be swung about so it would hang over the flames, but be easily reachable.

"Fine," he said, springing out of bed—or rather, trying to spring out of bed. He not only did not spring very well, but he wobbled on his feet with uncertain balance, once he was out.

"You've been in bed for a while," said Angie. "You haven't got your land legs back. Take a little time."

"No time to take time," said Jim, collapsing heavily into one of the chairs at the dining table. "Where're my clothes?"

"Oh, we burned them all," she said.

"Burned all my clothes?"

Angie gurgled—something between a giggle and a chuckle.

"No, of course not. They're already back in the wardrobe where they belong. The servant brought them all in just a little while ago—" Jim made an effort to get to his feet "—except for what I thought you might want to wear today. Those're all laid out on my side of the bed. Here, I'll get them for you."

"Why didn't you say so, then, instead of giving me this business about burning all my clothes?"

"I'm sorry," said Angie, carrying the clothes from her side of the bed to his, where he could reach them easily, "but after days of caring for you night and day, and sweating out your chances of living, I had to blow off a little steam, some way." She kissed his forehead. "Forgive me?"

"I suppose so," he growled. But then he stopped putting on the shorts he had picked up first, and looked up at her from his chair. "It must have been really rough for you. I know how I'd feel if—and I haven't even said thanks!"

"Yes, you did. You did it by living. You just didn't know it." She came and sat down on his lap. He kissed her.

"I love you," he said.

"I love you," she said.

"Now what?" said Carolinus, suddenly appearing. "Ah— pardon me."

He disappeared again.

Chapter 29

Carolinus is certainly taking his time before coming back. If he'd waited a second, he'd have seen for himself it was nothing more than an innocent kiss," Jim said, some half hour or so later.

"He's certainly showing more delicacy than anyone else in this antique world," said Angie. "Anyone our rank from Brian on down would have said something like 'Hah! at it are you? Well I'll leave you to it!' And any servant would have apologized all over the place, but only the same way she would if she came in when we were having an argument."

"You're right." Jim looked toward the fireplace. "The tea. I could use another cup. How long—"

"A minute," she said. "The water is boiling now. I'll pour. . . ." She did so. "There! Three minutes more and we can both have another cup. . . . It's so nice that the servants are now trained to bring us everything we like up here. What a relief to be back!"

She bore the steaming pot to the table, two metal cups with wooden handles dangling from her little finger, and the sugar jar with spoon in it in her other hand.

"Here you go," she said, setting all of this on the table before Jim. "The milk's in it now, but sugar it yourself, since you change about all the time."

Jim took a cup, pouring from the teakettle, and helping himself to sugar.

"I need strength," he announced. "Lots to do today. Are we past the noon dinner time yet?"

"Not for about half an hour."

"Good. The time will be the same in London. I want to talk to Chandos; no time to eat something, first—woops, I forgot. Chandos can't come. And I'm out of magic, too. If Carolinus doesn't show up in two minutes, he'll have forgotten us and I'll have to call him again."

"He'll be glad to see how good you're looking now," said Angie. "He loves you, Jim, as if you were family—as if you were his own son."

"Hah!" said Jim. "He's interested in me, but that's a far cry from loving anyone. Anyway, we don't have any family here—except for little Robert, who can't really be called family because he's only our ward."

"Robert *is* my child as far as I'm concerned!" said Angie. "Yours, too—you just don't realize it yet. The fact he's got a different last name makes no difference at all. And you're wrong, too, about Carolinus. He was here every one of the twelve days while you were down in the Nursing Room, to see how you were, and did everything that his *magick* could do to make things easier for you. That opium pipe didn't come easy, you know. He does love you, Jim. He probably didn't start out that way, but he does now. Don't you know he's got the softest heart in the world?"

"Great-great-grandson's more like it," said Jim.

But he was remembering the continual parade coming to Carolinus for attention. Wood nymphs, sprites, other woodland Naturals and animals from meadow mice to the ox-sized boar he had talked into letting itself be magicked into looking like a destrier as a steed for the Unknown Knight at the tournament during the Earl of Somerset's last annual Christmas party.

"—I suppose you're right," his conscience prodded him

into saying. Something else she had said registered on him. "As a matter of fact, I have a sort of a bit of memory about hearing his voice saying something like '—not supposed to work that way—' What do you think he was talking about?"

"You weren't following the usual pattern of someone with the buboes form of plague."

"I wasn't?"

"No," said Angie. "That was something any one of us in the Nursing Room would have known by a few days after you got here, but Carolinus spotted it right away. The bubonic form you had usually has buboes visible by the third day at the latest—you didn't have them full-sized until the fifth day after we got here."

"Five days!" Jim shook his head.

"Carolinus blamed it on your having been hit by two things at once: the plague and this rare magicians-only sickness. He said you were affected as much by your burning up an unreasonable amount of your magic—in fact, every scrap of magic you had in too short a time—and on top of that somehow pulling more out of the ether."

"Was that it?" said Jim, deeply interested in this business of extra magic from someplace else.

"Yes," she said. "And the double dose of making magic out of nothing on top of the fact you were already sick and ignoring that was calculated to throw you into something like a severe state of shock."

"He didn't say any more about where the extra magic had come from?"

"He didn't seem to know. Nor did Kinetete. They seemed to be guessing that, unconsciously or otherwise, you did what no other magician on top of the earth here has ever been known to do. Because you needed more magic and didn't have any left you started drawing on the raw, unknown magic energy that's all around us in this world, like the weather. You remember you guessed there was something like that after you got back from Lyonesse this last time? Because people like Morgan le Fay and Merlin didn't have an Accounting Office to meter out their earned magic to them?"

"I certainly do—and so Carolinus knew about raw energy all the time and never said anything to me about it, damn his eyes!"

"I think he said you would've been told about it. Along with a lot of other things, once you got voted in as a plain Class C magician."

Angie sat down in the chair across the table from Jim.

"It's not a short story," she said. "I meant to tell you in bits and pieces, if you asked, but now that I've dived into the whole thing . . . are you sure you want me to tell you everything now? You're not really back in full health, yet."

"Yes, I am!" said Jim. "A little wobbly, but what's that? Pain's just about gone. Tell me everything—take your time. But come to think of it, you're worn out from taking care of me. Here, drink first—"

"All right, if I'm not gearing you up too much. That's half your trouble. You go into overdrive, and when there's no energy left you just keep going on, on plain will power."

"I'm not excited. I won't get excited."

"Hah!" said Angie, "—on both counts. But you'll pester me to death now if I don't tell you. But I'll be watching you, and if you start overdriving on me—"

"I won't. I'm sitting still, just listening. See?"

"Well, Carolinus tried to figure out what was happening to you. For the first two days he was in and out all the time. But he couldn't tell what was shock and what was plague. Neither he nor Kinetete could figure you out—you were unconscious nearly all that time—"

"I don't remember anything except the bit about Carolinus saying it wasn't supposed to work that way."

"Yes," went on Angie. "Anyway, he and Kinetete talked you over and talked it over without getting anywhere. The two best magickian minds in the world, probably, baffled.

They even called in the only other A triple-plus magickian. You know him: a small fussy man, middle-aged or a little older looking, called Something Barron—two r's—or Barron Something. Carolinus and Kin just called him Barron."

"That goop!"

"He may be a goop, but he knows his magick," said Angie. "He was the one who suggested the shock and the plague could be working against each other as much as they were working together against you. He also said we shouldn't forget to lance your buboes to keep the pus there from going in and poisoning you. But I—we all in the Nursing Room—I mean we ordinary non-magicians—already knew that . . . as if we'd forget to do it for you! I told him as much. Kin and Carolinus both backed me up. He stuck his nose in the air and vanished."

"You didn't need him any more, anyway. He hadn't said anything useful. Why do you say he 'knew his magick'?"

"Because he did. Both Carolinus and Kinetete were really struck by his suggestion the two things were fighting each other. Carolinus said that was probably the reason you were having an easier time than the other sick ones with buboes—"

"Easier?" exploded Jim. "Angie, if only you knew what that pain was like—"

"Yes, dear. I didn't mean to make light of it. But I was nursing you and nursing some of the other sick ones, too, and in spite of the fact they didn't make as much noise about it as a modern person might, I could tell how the others were suffering—and they *were* having that part of the sickness, anyway, harder than you were. Believe me."

With most of his pain gone now, and still alive to boot—most plague victims, he knew, died in a few days—Jim felt a twinge of shame.

"And I was the only one with an opium pipe, too," he said.

"Yes, my love. But you mustn't feel bad about that. Carolinus just couldn't get any more and none of the staff who had sickened begrudged your having it. They all believe God had sent the sickness to them for their sins, and they were all sure they must be much worse sinners than you were. Besides, you were the lord."

"Of course," said Jim bitterly. "It's always that—"

Carolinus chose this moment to appear again. He cleared his throat.

"Intruded, didn't I?" he said. "My apologies. I'd become used to finding you sick and in bed, Jim."

"Of course," said Jim. "No apologies required. But what did you mean, saying 'What now?' just before you thought—just before you disappeared again?"

"You were going to call me."

"How'd you know?"

"I knew. That's sufficient for you to understand. I was busy at the moment and—well, why were you about to call me?"

"Hob reminded me of something. Goblins can't stand the touch of cold iron—"

"Teach your grandmother to suck eggs! What of it?"

"He asked me why the King didn't send for a force of knights in armor to defeat these goblins and get rid of them. In full armor they would be almost covered by cold iron, and maybe armor would stop the goblin spears, while the horses, being animals and immune to magic—"

Carolinus held up a hand.

"He's already tried that."

"Already?" said Jim. "Then a royal force's coming?"

"Not at all!" snapped Carolinus. "As I say, I've been very busy—"

Jim saw his opportunity to hold up a hand in turn. "I know. You've been spending a lot of time seeing me through this bout of plague. Thank you."

"Merely one of many concerns. As I was about to say— it's been done. Kinetete took a letter from the Collegiate to the King and he dictated a letter to Cumberland in London, telling him what had happened and asking him to send a force in armor to drive off the goblins—also hinting at the falsity of Cumberland's suggestion of Tiverton as a safe place against plague—"

"Oh, yes!" said Jim. "Come to think of it, did I ever get a chance to tell you—Verweather—"

"James," said Carolinus, "I do not mean to be severe, but sometimes you worry me with this endless string of interruptions you seem to think you have a right to make. Don't you remember I already knew that? Once and for all, you will wait until I have said my last word on what I am telling you. Is that understood?"

"I might point out, Mage Carolinus," said Jim, becoming heated in his turn, "that you started interrupting me—"

"A Master-in-Magick may do so to his apprentice. But not the apprentice to the Master. Of course. Now, as I was saying, since I was so busy and no one can get in or out of your castle right now except a qualified magickian, Kin took the letter to Cumberland, who, as the King's Chamberlain, was the one to act on it."

Carolinus paused.

"And?" Jim prompted.

"And of course Cumberland promised to get together an armored force—as soon as man and God could make it possible."

"Good. Then relief's on its way!" said Jim.

"You are a babe in politics, Jim. No such force will appear here until too late to do any good. It will turn out to take longer to put it together than Cumberland's best will can seem to make it. That was obvious to Kin, immediately."

Carolinus paused again—clearly, Jim thought, daring Jim to try interrupting.

"And so?" Jim said, after an uncomfortable moment of silence. "What happened then?"

"She pointed out to Cumberland that the Collegiate of Magickians, and of course all England, were concerned with preserving the King's life. He has been a good King, except for the extra taxes Cumberland pushed him into—"

"What reason did he give for doing that?" asked Jim, forgetting, sidetracked and intrigued in spite of himself. Carolinus glared at him.

"Jim, this is your last warning!" he said. "Just to begin with, you can do without explanations, if you interrupt again."

"Fine. Fine—I won't," said Jim hastily.

"Well, then, if you must be told: Cumberland told the King the treasury was low and the crown needed funds.— Where was I? Kin knew of course Cumberland would see no help came in time. Forcefully—and that wom—Mage can be forceful if she wishes to—she hinted that the Collegiate might make sure this eruption of the goblins could be traced to Cumberland's faults. Possibly, no more than that would be needed. Even the other magnates—the great lords that do not personally favor the King—do not want to see the King dead until young Edward is really ready for the throne. Especially when they know that, mainly because of Cumberland's own efforts to blacken the heir's reputation, there would be no strong, experienced hand to replace him—"

Pause.

"That produced no change of heart in Cumberland. He only grinned at Kin and repeated his worthless promise. Kin thinks he relies too much on what little Agatha Falon has of witchery. In any case, he cannot have any idea what the world's Magickians can do to him if we act as a united group."

"What, for instance?" ventured Jim.

"None of your apprentice business!" Carolinus snapped. "You can make up your own mind about such things *if* and when you ever get voted in—which is far from certain. Kin, for one, thinks she may vote against you."

"But I thought she liked me!"

"She does. Heaven itself knows why. But her voting's no business of yours either."

"Would you vote for me?"

"A fine matter it would look if I voted against the very apprentice I was proposing for membership!"

"Well, anyway, that's beside the point right now," said Jim. "If Cumberland's not going to help, how's the King—to say nothing of the rest of us—going to escape the goblins? Wait a second. You could just magically take him somewhere else. Somewhere safe."

"I can't take him anywhere unless he personally asks me to. I've told you he's Destined—because he *is* a king. Will he ask me?"

Jim hesitated.

"I don't think so," he said, at last. "I don't think he'd ask anybody for anything."

"Neither do I," said Carolinus, "and I know him better than you do. Order, but not ask. He lives to be a king, and he'd die rather than ask help of an inferior—inferior, meaning anyone in England or elsewhere in the world."

Jim nodded slowly.

"Besides," went on Carolinus, "what about the rest of you? Don't tell me to take the castle and everyone in it to safety. I don't have that much magick, and the Collegiate isn't going to help me out in something like that."

Jim nodded again, unhappily.

"Well," said Carolinus, "haven't you any ideas, yourself, lad? You usually have more than are good for you!"

"Hah!" said Jim. "But as a matter of fact, I do have an idea or two. However, how much magic are you going to be willing to lend me to spend on what I suggest?"

"Whatever's necessary—to save the King. I can draw on

the resources of every Magickian in the Collegiate, if I deem it necessary."

"That's good," said Jim. "Because this may cost more than the most you can imagine. By the way, wouldn't you like to sit down?"

"I would not. I'm not like all those who want to rest every moment they can. Besides I think better on my feet."

"Let me suggest you sit down, anyway—as a favor to me. This may take some time to explain, and I can explain better if I can talk to you on a level."

"You could stand up yourself!"

Jim took hold of the edge of the table before him and pulled himself wobble-leggedly to his feet.

"Sit! Sit!" said Carolinus. "Forgive me, my lad. Of course I'll sit down!"

He did, taking the end chair of the small table, so that the three of them sat as close together as conspirators.

"All right," said Jim, "let's look at the situation. If nobody's going to come to our rescue, we're going to have to drive off the goblins with what we can pull together ourselves."

"Five knights and one squire among the King's men—plus you and Dafydd and Brian, and maybe your men-at-arms—what few you've probably got left? Have you gone mad, Jim?"

"There's also Hob and maybe Tiverton hob. But I was forgetting the plague for a moment. How could I do that? Angie, how many people of the castle have we lost?"

"Twenty-three," said Angie. "Ten women—all servants, no mistresses; but thirteen men—nine of them ordinary men-at-arms, no masters, but Master Carpenter is in the Nursing Room, very close to dying. Buboes like you had, Jim, and he's an old, old man!"

"Carolinus! Lend me just a handful of magick!" Jim started to his feet with hardly a wobble, "just enough to get me down to the Nursing Room and back!—Where's the opium and opium pipe, Angie?"

"Right here. I'll get it!" she said, jumping to her feet and darting off toward the wardrobe.

"We'll all go down," said Carolinus. "You've got the opium things? Here we are, then."

And there they were, standing beside one of the beds below the dais, looking down at the carpenter. Age had long ago shrunken him from the size he must have been when he was younger, but now, lying in his sickbed, he looked even smaller and more ancient. He was not making a sound, and his eyes were closed, but his chest stirred with shallow breaths.

"Light here!" shouted Jim. "Angie, you've got opium in the pipe? Give it to me. Now, where's that light?"

But May Heather was already running toward him with a lighted splinter of wood, as if she had read his mind the moment the three of them suddenly appeared. Jim put the mouthpiece between the carpenter's tightly pressed lips.

"Light it, May!" Jim got the pipe started himself, then looked down at the old man in the bed.

"Open your lips and take the mouthpiece into your mouth, you stubborn old man!" snapped Jim.

The carpenter's eyes flew open at the sound of Jim's raised voice, and his mouth gaped. Jim put the mouthpiece into the opening.

"Now inhale!" he ordered. "Breathe in. That's right—"

The carpenter's chest heaved. He burst into the same kind of explosion of coughing as Jim had, on his first breath from the pipe. Jim held the mouthpiece firmly between the chapped and withered lips.

"Keep breathing in," he ordered. "It'll help the pain!"

The carpenter turned his head to one side to let the mouthpiece slide out from between his lips.

"Give it to one of the younger ones," he managed to whisper. "One with some life and use, still . . ."

"No!" Jim pushed the pipe end back between the lips. "You, Master! You're to get well. You're the only one who knows everything! Hear me! You're to keep breathing in on that pipe until you're all right again. The castle needs you! That's an order!"

"Yes, m'lord. Always rush, rush, rush . . ."

His whisper died, but he continued to suck on the pipe.

"Watch him, May," said Jim. "Don't let him stop smoking or pass the pipe to anyone else!"

"Yes, m'lord."

Carolinus, Jim and Angie were once more back in the Solar, standing around the table. They sat down.

"Now, what was the gain in that?" said Carolinus. "You could have given the pipe to a man-at-arms, or at least someone able-bodied."

"Would you have?"

"I might have!" But Carolinus avoided Jim's direct stare. "Now what was this nonsense about counting on hobs?"

"If we're going to be fighting goblins and we can get the word out, we might get hobs from all over. Dozens of them—maybe hundreds."

"But they're just as vulnerable to those magick-poisoned spears as we are—and none of them will have ever touched a weapon in their life before, and where do you plan to get weapons small enough for them to wield?"

"They bring them with them when they come—whatever they want to fight with. As for being vulnerable to the spears—not if we armor them."

Carolinus stared.

"How in the name of the First Magick do you plan to do that?"

"I'll tell you," said Jim. "But Carolinus, let me finish before you start asking questions, please. This is going to sound a little complicated."

Chapter 30

"I would hardly," said Carolinus, grimly, "be an A-triple-plus Magickian if I could not sit still and listen."

"I never doubted that for a minute," said Jim. "All right, in a nutshell: without help from London, we're going to have to put together an army with what's available. As I just said, the hobs could be one source."

"Rather like sending sheep to fight wolves, wouldn't that be," said Carolinus, entirely forgetting his promise of a few seconds before. "Will hobs actually fight the goblins?"

"Yes," said Jim. "Don't forget they have the same goblin heritage. Our Hob, who's the most gentle creature in this world, and I believe would aid even a goblin who was helpless and in trouble, immediately begged me to get him a sword to fight with, and the hob of Tiverton, who was captured and tortured by the goblins in that castle, can't wait to take on the whole goblin breed. Oh, they'll fight all right. In fact, we'll have to teach them to wait for the order to attack."

"Well, well—hobs then. But who else?"

"There're our neighbors, if we can get messages to them asking if they want to volunteer. Don't forget they've all seen the plague, now here in Somerset, and death in battle is a much kinder death than the one plague puts you through. They'd have their own armor and weapons, of course, and they're not likely to hesitate once they hear the goblins were the ones who brought the plague here. Then there're the dragons."

"Dragons! Jim, I *know* dragons—better than you do, for all they've accepted you into their eyrie in your dragon form. Dragons have their good qualities, but they're not going to put their lives on the line for mere friendship. They're as hard-headed and practical-minded as your wolf friend, Aargh!"

"They won't have to. I think they might jump at the chance to be in on the excitement, if there's no danger to them—particularly the young dragons of this Dragon Patrol Secoh's organized. They can also overfly the goblins for us and bring back information."

"Well, maybe," said Carolinus. "Come to think of it, Secoh's the one dragon who might fight for you. He considers himself one with you, Brian, Dafydd and Aargh, and Secoh'll do anything to prove he's still a Companion."

"Then," said Jim, "there're our common men, who, just like the knights, would prefer a clean death in battle to dying of the plague, and they like a fight as much as the knights. If a safe way can be made to get them past the goblins and into the castle here, they could make up perhaps the largest contingent of our force."

"Hmm, yes. But getting them in—how would you do that?"

"I'm not sure yet. There're several possibilities . . . and then, of course there's the Earl of Somerset. He's got knights and we're in his shire, after all."

"Hmm . . ." said Carolinus. "It's true, he could give you more of a real force than anyone else. . . ." He left the rest of his sentence unspoken. But then he added, "You're going to ask him?"

"Actually, I was going to ask you to do that."

"Me?"

"He thinks more of you than of any other man alive," put in Angie. "His lady wife told me so last Christmas."

"Oh? Well . . ."

"You've got the rank, which I haven't," said Jim carefully. "He'd take your word for something, where he wouldn't take mine."

"There's one objection to my giving him my word about

'something,' " said Carolinus acidly. "I've got to know that something is true, myself. Show me your hobs ready to fight, your commoners also ready, your knights agreeing to pitch in. If I see those things are facts, I can tell him about them. Not otherwise."

"Of course," said Jim. "I hadn't thought otherwise for a moment. But there's something direct you can do before that. Getting all these forces together and armed is going to take a lot of magick, and I haven't a scrap right now— which reminds me, if you could just lend me a small amount for the equivalent of pocket money, just for the present to get things started—"

"Oh, very well. I'm far too generous and indulgent with you, Jim. I should know better. Next thing you'll be asking me for that large amount of magick you just now mentioned needing, to put the whole thing together."

"I will," said Jim. "But as you've mentioned a number of times, the most important thing is to save the life of the King. How he's missed catching the plague at Tiverton, and even here at Malencontri, so far, beats me."

"Hah!" said Carolinus, suddenly thoughtful. "He's both anointed and Destined, of course—but no telling how long that may protect him from sickness. Jim, if you really can put this patchwork army together with any hope of driving the goblins back to Deep Earth, and so making the King safe—you can count on not only anything I can do or give you, but the full resources of the whole Collegiate as well. Dammit! We should have had you as a full member before this."

"I appreciate the compliment," said Jim. "I want to be a member of the Collegiate, if they want me."

"Quite right and proper attitude!" said Carolinus. "But— have you thought of this? What if the King catches the plague before you have your battle and win it?"

"I think I can protect against that, too—with magic," said Jim. "But since you're going to hold back the large amount of magic I'm going to need to put together the army, can I hold back on explaining what can be done first? I'm still going to need to borrow a certain amount of regular working magic to get started."

"Fair enough," said Carolinus. "You have it, then."

Jim looked closely at him.

"Well, don't you have to call the Accounting Office and tell them I'm to have it? Kinetete did just that when I borrowed from her the time I had to go to Lyonesse."

"Kin," said Carolinus dryly, "has her magick, I have mine. The Accounting Office has already noted that transaction between us. You are supplied."

"Oh, sorry," said Jim. "I should have realized."

"You should have indeed," said Carolinus. "I must be going then. Good luck, lad. And by the by, if and when I do take you into the whole Collegiate in session to propose you for membership, will you be very sure to pronounce the word 'magick' properly? There're enough questions about your difference from the usual apprentice without worrying the members about your strange dialect and accent."

"You have my word."

"I'll count on it—and I'll talk to Somerset as soon as it looks like your army is a possibility." Carolinus disappeared.

"What's this about protecting the King from the plague?" said Angie. "If you have that magic, and you'd used it, you could have saved the lives and sufferings of our own people here in the Nursing Room!"

"I don't have it—not the necessary full magic of it worked out. The idea for it just came to me when Carolinus asked me how I'd save the King before the goblins were routed. It came in a flash—but I only have the fringe of it so far. The back of my head's still got to produce the details—that's why I couldn't tell Carolinus. I don't want that fringe to tear off in my hand, so to speak, leaving me with nothing."

"So that's it. That habit of yours—in thinking."

"Right," said Jim. "As I told you once, it's always worked that way for me, even when I was a child. A good excuse never popped into my head until the last second."

"All right," said Angie. "But tell me the minute you have it. If we can just save the poor people downstairs who are infected but still living, I want to know!"

"I'll tell you—if and when. I can't control these inspirations. But I'll tell you the moment I do."

"I know you will," said Angie. "Well, come on, now. Time we were at the High Table for dinner with the rest. I'm all ready. How about you?"

Medieval dinners were usually expected to be at the noon hour. This one turned out as usual, with a fair amount of wine drunk, some arguments—all carefully held to a polite level—and by Jim and Angie's modern standards, about twice the modern amount of food eaten, per person.

Jim and Angie excused themselves early.

"Sometimes I wonder why they aren't all as fat as pigs," Angie remarked, back up in the Solar. "What was the rush to get away?"

"They aren't fat for the reason you and I aren't," said Jim. "They burn it off climbing stairs, riding horses—all the physical life they—we—all live here. Actually, I wanted to get away so as to start on that mixed army I told Carolinus about."

"Of course," said Angie thoughtfully, "it also helps that every so often they have to miss meals, too—and sometimes for days." She looked up. "So what's first?"

"The hobs," said Jim. He directed his voice towards the fireplace. "Hob!"

"The real problem will be getting them to hold and fight together," said Angie.

"What'll hold them together will be they'll all want to

kill goblins. If I can just convince each different contingent that they all need each other. Now, if I only had half a hundred archers with unlimited arrow supply—" he raised his voice. "Man-at-arms, here!"

"M'lord?" The familiar, high-pitched voice sounded once more.

"Ah, there you are, Hob—enter!" The man-at-arms on duty was opening their door. "Enter! You'll be Tim Tyler?"

"Yes, m'lord."

"I thought so. You're new here. You don't have to scratch for entrance when I call you. Take a message as fast as you can to Sir Brian, Master Archer Dafydd, and my squire. Ask them to come as soon as they're free to do so. Understand?"

"Yes, m'lord. Sir Brian and Master—"

"No need to repeat the message to show you've got it. We're in a hurry here. Just get that message to them. Send other men you meet on the same errand if that'll get them to me faster."

"Yes, m'lord." The door closed behind the man-at-arms.

"Now, Hob," said Jim, "we're going to put together an army to fight the goblins out there."

"Oh, thank you, m'lord!"

"This is for everybody. I'll need help. Particularly I'll need as many fighting hobs as I can get. They've each got to find and bring their own weapons, though. How many other hobs can you reach and ask in the next day—in not more than two days—by riding the smoke to them and asking?"

"Oh, m'lord!" said Hob happily. "I don't have to go. They're already here, a lot of them, and more coming in all the time. But I can send a message on the smoke just as well, to all hobs I know, telling them to pass it on to other hobs they know. They'll be so grateful, m'lord!"

"Grateful!" said Angie. "This isn't a picnic. You Naturals will be poisoned just as much as we humans by those spears of the goblins."

"Maybe not, m'lady. Goblin magic may not work on hob-goblins. But even if it does, it's worth it. Should I send the smoke message right away, m'lord?"

"Yes," said Jim. Hob vanished back into the fireplace.

Angie muttered something about lambs to the slaughter.

"Lambs? What about lambs?" asked Jim.

"Nothing," said Angie. "But except for Hob, none of them have ever seen a human battle."

"Well, you saw how Hob felt about it. All of the rest of us will be taking the same chances. Now, how about getting the invitation to our neighbors? I don't suppose we have message pigeons to many of them."

"But I have for Malvern Castle," said Angie. "And Geronde's here. She could use one of our Malvern homing pigeons to send an order to her castle to send messages to the neighbors. Shall I ask her to do that?"

"Good! Yes," said Jim.

"I'll do that, then! She'll be all for it. I can get her to send a message to her steward. Geronde's got pigeons for at least another dozen families in the shire, and each can send messages—whether by pigeon or a human messenger—to people they know."

"Couldn't be better," said Jim.

"Then I'll go find Geronde right now."

She went.

Jim absent-mindedly poured himself a splash of wine and sat down to think about the fringe of his idea. It was beginning to take shape, when there was a hearty knock on the door. Brian walked in immediately, followed by Dafydd. Relatives and close friends generally entered with no more announcement than that, oblivious to the state of dress or the current activities of the occupants.

"You came quick," said Jim. "That's good. We're going to fight the goblins!"

"Hah!" said Brian, his face lighting up. Dafydd allowed himself a pleased smile.

"Sit," said Jim. "Have some wine—"

This time it was a scratching at the door.

"Squire Theoluf to see you as commanded, m'lord," called the voice of Tim Tyler, back on duty at the door's other side.

"Enter!" said Jim.

Theoluf came in, wearing his helm to signal he was on duty, and took it off immediately, holding it in his hand.

"Theoluf," said Jim. "How many armsmen have we, well enough to fight?"

"Twelve, m'lord."

"How many archers?"

"Three, m'lord."

"Only three?"

"I regret, m'lord, the plague—"

"Never mind. I should have expected something like that. You can go, but I may call you back at any moment. You can go."

"Yes, m'lord. I will return swiftly if needed."

He left. Jim looked at Dafydd.

"Dafydd, we could really use about a hundred archers, with more shafts than they can shoot in three days, to stand in the battle. Any chance of getting them—any chance at all?"

"Of getting archers in that quantity, now, James?" said Dafydd in his usual deliberate, calm voice. "Not in a two-month, not even if you had the wealth of Croesus."

"Just as well," said Brian. "At this range, with besiegers, it would be like shooting ducks in a pond on a village green. You want to leave some of the sport for the rest of us—no offense to you or the rest of your skill, Dafydd! Who is Croesus?"

"A rich King of Lydia, many centuries ago," said Jim, hastily before Dafydd could give a fuller and more leisurely explanation. "Well, that's that, then. We'll have to do without—"

"But—" said Dafydd, "if you only wanted to harass our enemies, I notice you have many of your tenants and serfs sheltering here in the castle at present. Even with the plague, there must be near thirty still on-site and well enough for duty—"

Brian crossed himself. Common people as they might have been, those who would die would still have souls.

"They cannot be called archers, of course," Dafydd was going on. "But there will be none of them among the men who have not had a bow in their hands since they were ten—only, of course, for shooting such as rabbits for their cooking pot—or even an occasional deer, illegal as that is for common folk. If you only wish them for harassing the goblins, and give them bows and shafts, they might help. As Brian says, it would be like a shoot into the village duck pond—short range, slow-moving targets—and aim is hardly needed. If no other thing, they could shoot high into the air, all together, as archers are used to doing in battles nowadays, and hope that a number fall with effect on the massed enemy below."

"It is well thought of," said Brian with unusual seriousness. "Archers have been used to good effect in our wars, lately, and while these lads of the fields and forest fringe are no more archers than I am—"

"You are accurate, Brian, however," said Dafydd, "which speaks well of one who makes only occasional sporting use of the bow. You give yourself too little credit."

"Hah! Well—" said Brian, looking embarrassed, "at duck-pond range, as I say. . . . But does that fill our need for bowmen, James?"

"Well, yes," said Jim, "except that I'd been counting on those same men to make footmen with spears when the proper moment in the fight came."

"There is no reason they cannot do both," said Dafydd. "Put down their bows and take up the spears."

"They will have to be taught to charge together in ranks,

though," said Brian. "I can take care of that if you wish. But, James, this is all beside the point. What you will really need for such a number of those without, weak and unorganized as they are, we'll need knights and armsmen ahorse, armed and armored as best they can be. Aside from annoying the enemy, all else we have spoken of will only tickle and distract a force that large. The point of a battle is to kill or rout your foes, not bother them."

"We're getting pigeon messages off to the neighbors for help of that kind."

"God send it does," said Brian. "Here we are but the King's five knights and one squire, besides ourselves and Sir Harimore, who is a good man, but only one to add to our little number—I do not say that we could not make good effect still upon even those numbers outside, but rout them? You cannot stop with a few spades the ocean tide from coming in."

"Carolinus has promised to speak to the Earl of Somerset for help. If his castle has not been hit hard by the plague, he could bring possibly even a dozen equipped knights."

"That would be a help, James," said Brian, but still doubtfully.

"And you forgot to count the Prince among us. I had thought of him for our war captain—"

"The Prince? Are you serious, James?" exploded Brian. Even Dafydd came as close to looking astonished as Jim had ever seen him.

"He is still little more than a boy, in many ways," went on Brian. "Yes, yes, I know he did well at Poitiers, and proved his right to the knighthood his father gave him the moment he was ashore. But he had Chandos and half a dozen other seasoned captains by his side to guide him! But of course, you are speaking of his commanding in name only."

"Well, yes and no," said Jim. "I had hoped to help bring him back into that same father's good graces, something that would make him stand out. I've had a quiet word that the King might want that as well as young Edward; he could not easily choose to bring to the throne a son as weak and useless as the lies of Cumberland have been continually painting young Edward."

"But surely, James," said Brian, "if nothing else you will take the actual command in keeping for yourself?"

"Better yet—if you will forgive me," said Dafydd, "if you will make Brian the real commander—under your own privy authority, of course."

"Indeed! But mayhap even better would be to make the three of us the leaders in secret, holding the reins on the Prince!" said Brian. "For I swear to you that otherwise he will find a way to lose the battle at his first chance, on some inexperienced choice!"

"You're right, of course!" said Jim. "I didn't want to suggest it myself, but if the two of you think so . . . if you do—"

The two other men nodded vigorously.

"Well, then," Jim went on, "that gives me courage to mention there's one other possible source of armed help for us. I hadn't yet mentioned the hobs."

Brian stared at him. Dafydd's gaze took on a marked seriousness.

Chapter 31

"James!" said Brian. "Did you say 'armed force'?"

"Yes," said Jim.

"James, I am not given to unreasonable objections, you know that. Surely, all that lives will fight when it comes to a matter of keeping its life. But even if hobs are in such manner willing to fight the goblins, they are not fighters by nature. To my best knowing they have never been known to fight—anything. But even if I am wrong about these matters, they have no knowledge of battle, or the use of weapons. What weapons could they use?"

"I told Hob when he invited them to each bring their own."

"Broken kitchen knives and lost eating knives, no doubt!" snorted Brian. "James, what under all that is reasonable possessed you to have Hob invite them?"

"Hob and Tiverton hob were champing at the bit to fight, themselves."

"Your hob—now that is possibly understandable. He has been with you when swords were out, and in divers other adventures. I will not say he has no courage. But as for Tiverton hob . . . I can think of no excuse for such attitude, unless he picked up from your hob."

"He was caught by the goblins when they invaded Tiverton, Brian, and cruelly tortured by them."

"Ah. That at least is possibly more of a reason even than that of your Malencontri hob. But as you said, James, I got to know Hob when I was a very young boy, left alone among strangers for no notion of how long, and I know him for possibly the gentlest creature in Christendom. . . . Well, well, probably only a handful will show up. I cannot imagine my hob of Castle Smythe attacking the enemy, broken knife in hand."

"How many will come is something I don't know," said Jim. "But if they do, they're ways they could be useful. They can ride on the smoke, as you both know, and could maybe be useful spying out the goblins—perhaps even get close enough to the goblin leaders—"

"Do they have leaders, James?" asked Dafydd.

"I don't know," confessed Jim. "But if they have, maybe our hobs can get close enough to overhear their planning— oh, come to think of it, I forgot to mention that I haven't had a chance to ask Secoh this, but I'm all but positive the young dragons of the Dragon Patrol—"

"You mean the ones who fly over Smythe days, and even on nights from time to time?" asked Brian.

"Those are the ones. We can't let them get into the fighting, even if we wanted them to. Have you ever had to face a mother dragon who thinks you've been putting her sixty-year-old son or daughter in peril?"

"No," said Brian. "But I take your point."

"And so do I," said Dafydd. "I have seen my wife, Danielle, when one of our sons has been let wander into a part of the forest where there might have been bears—or even trolls. I tell her that boys will adventure, that it is part of growing up to manhood, but at such times I hardly recognize the gentle lady I married."

Jim said nothing to that, though "gentle" was the last word he, himself, would have chosen to describe Danielle. She was as good a forester as any man in her father's outlaw band—not counting Dafydd, of course. But Dafydd had seemed to have a remarkable way of winning arguments with her, normally.

"In any case," said Brian briskly, "if you plan to use your tenants and serfs—and even some of your castle people— as both archers and footmen, Dafydd and I should waste no time in training them as best we can to advance in order, and simple matters like that. We could be worse off, even if the plague keeps neighbors from helping. Poor Ver-weather is out of it—"

Jim started to point out that Verweather had been working for their enemies all along, but decided that silence was a fine course just now.

"—but all told," Brian was going on, "we have two squires, your Theoluf and the one of the King's party, also eight belted knights—five of the King's, you and I, James, and Harimore—"

The ear-splitting sound of the alarm gong on the tower roof, right above their heads, interrupted him. They all pelted out of the Solar; Brian first, Dafydd close behind him and Jim making a plainly distant third, even at his best speed. The man-at-arms on duty overhead was shouting something, but in the narrow staircase the tremendous clamor of the gong made his words incomprehensible.

They burst out on to the top of the tower and heard him clearly for the first time.

"—*Aux armes*—to arms!" he was shouting to the whole castle. "Escaliers on the curtain wall and tower sides!"

Dafydd, nearest to the circular wall of embrasures about the tower, ran to it to look out and down, just as Brian and then Jim reached his side and looked down for themselves through the same opening of the embrasure.

"Here's one," said Dafydd, with his usual calmness— Brian had already seized one of the long, thick poles lying around the circumference of the tower below the embrasures, against just this sort of eventuality. Dafydd and Brian helped him to get it up and slide it out through the opening, pointed downward at the rough ladder that was leaning against the side of the tower. The ladder's top was just below the embrasure itself, its lower end now sunk deep in the mud of the moat by the weight of the goblins that were clinging to it, carrying their glinting, pointed spears held balanced—unbelievably—between the teeth of their wide mouths.

The towertop was suddenly swarming with people. Men and women servants came running up with buckets of oil to pour into the enormous caldron above the sand-filled heating bed ready to light beneath it. Others, male servants, seized poles and began sliding them out through the low bottom ledge of embrasures as Brian, Jim and Dafydd had done, to push at the tops of the ladders resting against the wall.

Theoluf was already on the curtain wall, below them on the castle's other side.

"Spread out! Spread out!" he was shouting to the men-at-arms coming up the stone stairstep to the wall. "Take the servants between you. Four or more to a ladder. Let them push—you be ready to fight any who come in over the wall! Spread out! Spread out—"

The top of the ladder that Jim and the two others were pushing was starting to lean out, its middle curving in toward the tower like a monstrous bow.

"Much lighter, these goblins," grunted Brian, "than escaliers wearing full armor—there they go!"

The ladder suddenly broke, and with sharp screams, the goblins upon it fell with its two parts into the moat.

"Hah!" said Brian, looking around, "where else now?"

Dragging their pole, they made a circle of the towertop, but all the scaling ladders were already being pried away from the wall by others.

They laid their pole down in an empty space at the foot of the embrasure where Dafydd had found it. Jim ran to the nearest chimney sticking up through the tower roof.

"Hob!" he called down it.

"I'm here, m'lord," said Hob, popping up like a spring-activated toy out of a nearby chimney. "I've been watching from here so as not to get in the way."

"I want to catch a goblin and ask him some questions."

"Let one up over the wall, then, m'lord," said Hob, hopping out on to the roof. "I'll capture one."

Jim turned to the nearest pole-party prying with their pole through the embrasure before them.

"Let one up!" Jim told them. "Brian, Dafydd, we'd better stand by on either side, in case more than one gets up."

They moved into position, Brian on the far side of the pole-party, his sword drawn and raised. Dafydd was beside Jim, the long knife that served him equally well as a sword in his hand. Hob flattened himself against the wall on Brian's side.

A goblin, spear balanced between his jaws, came through the embrasure, his dark eyes glinting fiercely. Hob struck down, half-severing the spear about a foot behind its point.

The goblin, suddenly unbalanced by the weight of the blow, staggered sideways. Hob brought down the flat of his sword on the round, furry head; and the goblin dropped.

"Well, damme!" said Brian, in a tone of surprised admiration. "Not at all badly done!"

The goblin began to stir. Hob raised his sword again.

"No," said Jim, shaking his head. *"Still!"* he ordered the goblin, who ceased moving but went on coming to. His eyes, now aware, fastened balefully on Hob.

"Stand!" ordered Jim.

The goblin got to his feet, but then ceased moving.

"All right," said Jim, moving to confront him. "Who told you about making and using scaling ladders to storm the castle? You didn't know about them or you would have used them before this. *Answer me!* You can't move still, but now you can talk."

The goblin turned his hate-filled eyes from Hob to Jim, but not a sound came from his mouth.

"Do you want me to take him on the smoke into a chimney and question him there, m'lord? There're good fires in all the fireplaces, below."

The goblin made a single, short half-strangled grunt, and began to speak.

"The female!" he said in his high, sharp voice.

"He means a human woman, m'lord," Hob said. "These goblins are very ignorant."

The goblin directed another brief hate-glance at Hob, but said nothing more.

"All right," said Jim. *"Back into the moat with you!"*

The goblin disappeared.

"M'lord!" protested Hob.

"Yes, James," said Brian. "Why in the names of the Seven Foolish Sinners did you let it go?"

"He'll carry back word," said Jim, "which will finally reach Agatha Falon—it has to be her behind this—Cumberland couldn't deal with the goblins in Deep Earth himself. She'll learn I know she's here, and she knows that, even without Carolinus' help, I'm stronger in magic than she is. It may slow her down in helping the goblins. The more time we can gain, the more help may arrive from neighbors or our own Earl here in Somerset. Besides, it's just good sense to scare her—"

"James!" broke in an angry voice. "Why didn't you call me before, instead of going ahead as if I was not even here?"

The Prince was upon them.

"There you are, Your Grace," said Jim, with a gesture about the towertop. "We had not time to." Most of the pole-parties were standing idle, looking at the Prince, Jim and the rest. The defense against the goblins' attempt to scale the walls of the tower had obviously been successful.

"—You and I must talk, Your Grace," Jim went on quickly, looking back at the still-angry face of the Prince. "I think the Solar is the best place for that."

Instantly the two of them were in the Solar.

"Never move me around with your magick without permission from me!" shouted the Prince. "Who do think you—"

"*Still!*" ordered Jim. The Prince froze as he was, suddenly silent, with the outraged look also frozen on his face.

"Edward," said Jim, "I am going to have to speak to you like the magician I am and with the powers I have. It's true that normally only the highest among us have the right to speak plainly so even to all men and women, Kings and Emperors, addressing all alike and speaking to all by their given names. But that freedom is required to be taken, if necessary, by the senior magician present, even if he is still only a lowly apprentice—providing his magic can be of first use in the present duty of we magicians."

He paused a moment to let his words sink in on the mind behind the motionless face before him.

"Our present duty at this time—which supersedes all

other things, even the rank of the heir to the throne—is to keep your father alive. You may move and talk now."

The Prince stared at him, his scowl fading into an astonished look.

"But . . . surely," he said, after a long moment, in an almost reasonable voice, "if my father was safe from those masquerading goblins at Tiverton, he must be safe here."

"The situation has changed, Edward—" The Prince's face jumped into angry lines again for only a second, before smoothing out again. Jim was going on. "—At Tiverton the plan of his foes was that he should die of plague, so that no one could question his death. Now, they hope he will die while *visiting* Malencontri, by the spears of the goblins. That way, also, leaves your father's enemies free of suspicion, for the goblins themselves can retreat to Deep Earth, where no one lacking magic can reach them. This matter is beyond your commanding."

"But I am the only experienced war captain here!"

"Edward, we are facing attack by an enemy you don't know, in a situation beyond your experience. This conflict will involve the use of magic on both sides. You have no magic, nor do you understand it. Nor do you have at your elbow a hobgoblin who, like all hobs, was ages ago a goblin himself and knows how goblins think and in what ways they're vulnerable."

The Prince's face showed bewilderment almost to the point of piteousness.

"Surely what I know and what I can do can be put to use?" he said. "My father!"

It was almost a cry for understanding.

"It can," said Jim. "Brace yourself, Edward, because I'm going to be brutally frank. You proved your manhood and knighthood at the chevauché that led to success at Poitiers. You had Chandos and others there to advise you. It's going to help us all if you do take command of the battle here— but in name only. Here, as at Poitiers, you will be guided in all things by what I, Brian and Dafydd ap Hywel will tell you when the experience needed is in our area!"

Rage flared up on the Prince's face again.

"A country knight and a common archer?" he cried.

"Exactly that—they will command equally with me, and you will listen to those two as I, myself, will listen to them, and as I will listen to you, or to anyone else who might know better than I. Besides, you know perfectly well that Brian is no ordinary country knight. What you do not know is that Dafydd is no ordinary archer, and while I've promised never to tell anyone of this, I believe this is a time when you must be told that he actually has a rank that would cause you to address him as your equal."

Blank silence from the Prince.

"Is this—how can such be true?" he said at last, staring.

"I'll say no more about it," said Jim. "The important matter right now is that your father must be preserved on any terms, and it'll take all of us working well together to make that certain. Our enemy is primitive, but massively outnumbers us—"

They were interrupted by a scratching at the door.

"Not now!" shouted Jim.

"Forgive me, m'lord!" a male voice called back. "This is Theoluf. It is a matter of immediate importance!"

"Come!" Jim called back.

Theoluf came in, his scarred face wearing a serious expression. "Sir Verweather needs to see you as soon as may be, my lord! It seems that he is near to death. He is preparing for it and has just made confession to Lady Geronde's priest. It was the priest who brought his wish to me."

He turned to the Prince.

"He even more greatly also wishes to see you, Your Grace, and the Countess Joan, also Sir Brian and—after that, if may be—the King your father."

"To see me?" said the Prince.

"Yes, Your Grace."

"See us separately, of course."

"No, Your Grace. He feels his death is hard upon him and begs you will all come together. My lady Countess is already waiting to go when Your Grace and my lord are ready, as is Sir Brian."

"Wait outside," said Jim. "We will be with you shortly."

He turned to the Prince, after Theoluf had gone.

"I'll go, of course," he said, "and immediately. Whether you do is up to you, of course."

"I will go," said the Prince. "He is a knight and in my father's service at present. But why should he be dying? Can he have caught the plague sometime back and kept it secret? The blows he took from Sir Brian were a severe drubbing, but surely not enough to kill a man in a mail shirt."

"I don't know," said Jim. "It's unusual, but not impossible, that he had a weakness inside him, and the drubbing broke something that otherwise should leave him not so badly hurt. But not even magic could answer that for me. Certainly, he could not have suffered from plague secretly, here at Malencontri—but possibly some other illness."

He headed toward the door.

"One moment," said the Prince, and the sudden seriousness in his voice made Jim stop and turn, even if the words would not have.

"The Countess has at times accused me of acting as a lad when I should be thinking as a man. Remembering that and with your recent words still hot in my memory, for the first time I would wish to tell you privily that I have a great love for my father, in spite of the ear he has lent to Cumberland's ill-sayings against me—and you are right. His life comes before all. But I must also admit a justice in that, without resentment, I let myself at Poitiers be guided there by knights older and wiser than I. A man is nothing if he does not know enough when to be humble about his prowess. I see and accept I must be equally guided here by you and your two companions. But I remain Prince of Wales, my father's heir, otherwise in all else. That is understood?"

"Absolutely!" said Jim.

"Then let us to Verweather, as quickly as possible, and as he wishes. I would have no belted knight fail to have me beside his deathbed if he wanted me there!"

They stepped into the corridor outside the Solar.

"Theoluf," said Jim to his waiting squire, "refresh my memory. Which room is Sir Verweather in?"

"Third floor down, fourth over, my lord."

"And my Lady Countess? Sir Brian? Where are they now?"

"Outside that door, waiting now, m'lord."

Jim did the necessary magic to gather them all outside Verweather's room, then reached out to open the door.

"Your Grace, my lady," said Jim to the Prince and Joan, gesturing them forward, "Sir Brian and I wait."

Lying in the bed, Verweather indeed looked like a dying man. His face was gray and sunken, and he was much thinner than any of the four had seen him before. He did not even seem to see Jim and Brian standing behind the Prince and Joan, as they moved close to him.

"Forgive me, Your Grace," he said in a whisper of a voice, "—if forgiveness for such sin is possible—that I lied to you and sought to use you as an unthinking ally in the death of your father. I have given my word never to reveal the name of him who was behind this plan, and would not sin further by naming him to you now. But you will have no difficulty in guessing his name. May God keep the King to a long and happy life—and equally keep you and my lady beside you, whom I know is dear to you, as you are to her."

He closed his eyes like a man exhausted.

"If you cannot forgive," he spoke again after a second, "I will understand. It is only right that it be so."

"I forgive you," said the Prince. "I have made errors

enough in my own life, God knows. Also, in all the ways I knew, other than this you have just told me, you were a true and valiant knight."

"I also forgive, if that will comfort you," said Joan.

Verweather's eyes opened.

"I thank you, Your Grace, my lady. I am indeed comforted by these words."

"That is well, then," said the Prince. "But you also wished to see Sir James and Sir Brian. They are here for you now."

He and Joan stepped aside, and Jim, with Brian, moved forward to take their place. Verweather's eyes, which had closed again with the end of his last words, opened once more.

"My Lord Sir James . . ." he husked, "forgive me that I brought treason into your house."

"I forgive you," said Jim.

"I thank you as best a dying man can who is no longer able to make amends. Sir Brian?"

"I am here," said Brian.

"Forgive me my sins and trespasses against you in my attempt to play you a foul trick unworthy of a knight during what was supposed to be a friendly bout, and—" He stopped, seeming to have run short of breath. Then he went on.

"—by using a sword not only capable of being used two-handed, but unfairly sharpened as well. It was my aim not only to harm you badly but to kill you if I could. Forgive these things as well as my bitter thoughts after I had lost and my secret cursing of you in God's name, in the fashion of one who is no good knight, and if you can indeed find it in your heart to so forgive me, I beg you to pray for me, that the fire I go to may eventually redeem my soul."

"That will I, on my word and oath," said Brian, "and as far as these you call your sins and trespasses against me, there are none. Faith, it is not the first time I have fought a man using a two-handed sword, and as for your cursing otherwise, I too have felt on some past times a resentment I should not have felt, against he who had defeated me. To my knowing you have always been a good man of your hands—and aside from this you mention, a worthy knight."

"I thank you for those kind words," said Verweather. "And now, if I might speak another small word to His Grace."

Brian stepped back. The Prince took his place.

"Your Grace," said Verweather, his voice now almost inaudible. "The one I most need to confess all to is His Majesty, the King, your father, for my sin against him was heaviest. Can it be made possible now? For I feel my time growing very short."

"I can go now, and if I may speak to him, ask if he will grant you audience."

"I ask no more than that."

"James," said the Prince, "it is close to the dinner hour, and His Majesty ordinarily dines alone in his rooms. Perhaps you could use your magick to move me directly to his presence, and go with me to bring both of us back with the same dispatch?"

"Of course I can move us," said Jim.

"And let me do the talking, James."

"Certainly, Your Grace."

Jim moved them both to one of the madeover rooms of the King's apartment. The King himself was there, alone, sitting in a chair with a tall glass flagon of red wine on a table beside him. He looked with annoyed startlement, a little owlishly, at their sudden appearance—but most annoyedly at the Prince.

Damn! thought Jim. *Can he be drunk this early?*

"Your Majesty," said the Prince in urgent tones, "forgive us of your great leniency for coming upon you by magick so swiftly and unexpectedly—"

But the owl-like look was suddenly gone from the King's gaze. He sat up in his chair.

"We were attacked earlier," he said. "I watched from the arrow slit here and saw them driven off. Do they assault again? Am I needed?"

"No, Your Majesty," said the Prince. "It is only a matter of a knight taken with you when you moved from London to Castle Tiverton. He is close to death and has been shriven. But he feels he has sinned most heavily against your royal self and deeply wishes to make confession of that sin to you from his own lips while life remains."

"Verweather?" said the King, with an acuteness Jim had not expected. The Prince nodded. "Why does he die? Can no one tell me that—Sir James?"

His eyes shifted to Jim. Jim, standing and listening, had not expected to be called upon to speak. He straightened up and did his best to return the royal gaze.

"There is no telling, Your Majesty," he said. "A possibility is that the hammering he took at the end of his bout with Sir Brian broke some part inside of him already weakened somehow in times past. He has lost much blood and never regained it. That is all I can tell Your Majesty, even with the help of magic."

"Verweather . . ." said the King. "Edward, if he is dying, I must go to him, of course. He became as one of my own knights when I took him with me to Tiverton on Cumberland's suggestion, and to my knowledge he has always served me well. Where is he?"

"One floor down," said the Prince. "My lady the Countess and Sir Brian are now with him, for he had minor sins to confess to them. Their presence comforts him, in this last hour, but they, James, and I can leave when you get there. He can be carried in his bed up to you here, of course, if he will last so long."

"No. No—" The King's fingers drummed on the table beside the now-forgotten wine flagon. "If this sin of his is something of real importance, I do not want myself to be seen going to speak him privily. I must go in alone to him.

But even that could be spoken off and arouse rumor, particularly if those now with him depart as I enter, so that is it noted I see him alone. Any servants must be out of his room, of course!"

"They are already out, Your Majesty."

"Good. But getting there unseen is still a problem—James, are there no privy passages in the walls of this castle of yours?"

"None that would be of use now, Your Majesty. Only one secretly kept so that those too valuable to be captured or killed could escape the castle completely. But, if you would agree, I could take you to him swiftly and secretly by magic."

"Of course. The very answer! You must come with me—and you as well, Edward. If what he has to say touches the throne, you will need to know. Nor may those there now with him leave until after I am gone again."

He stood up with remarkable lightness.

"Lead on, Sir James!"

The three of them were abruptly back beside Verweather's bed. Joan, who had been smoothing the covers, stepped quickly back out of the way, and the King moved to the edge of the bed to look down at the dying man. Jim and the Prince discreetly stayed back.

"Your King is here, Verweather," said the older Edward. "Sorry I am to see you in this sad plight. You wished to tell me something before you go to God?"

"Would that I could go to Him!" said Verweather. "But I know that my path beyond the grave leads elsewhere, for my sins, and it is the greatest of those sins, one against your royal self, I must confess to you before I go."

"What is it, man?"

"The worst sin possible. High treason. I was to see that you died of plague at Tiverton—where it would seem only bad chance that it should happen. I was in league with the goblins masquerading as humans to do so, and I was to try to involve your royal son, unknowing, in the plot."

The King's face stiffened.

"Who put you up to this?"

"I have vowed never to tell his name. That much of my knighthood I hope to save. But as I said to your royal son, you will have no trouble guessing his name."

The King cast a sudden, almost furtive, glance at Joan, Jim, and Brian.

"As you stand now before God, you must tell me! I will bend down, and you may whisper his name in my ear," he said.

He bent down and turned his right ear to put it directly over Verweather's mouth. The others saw the knight's dry, bloodless lips move. After a second's hesitation, the King straightened up sharply. His face was pale, set and hard.

"I do not believe it!" he exploded. "You are lying!"

"As I stand now before God and had hoped for some small . . . and had hoped for some small understanding from you, my King, of how a strange and penniless knight like myself from a foreign court, but English . . ." Verweather's voice was now becoming very labored and weak, ". . . the name of the man I just gave you was the truth. Can you find no such understanding, no shred of forgiveness, in you for me?"

But the King had calmed down.

"If it were not for the fact all this must remain secret," he said, "you would yet be condemned—dying, dead or not—to the punishment reserved for regicides. I am no priest to absolve you—if absolution is possible for such a crime. You have offended against the Throne—the Throne! Furthermore, you have offended not merely it and me. I rule England by God's will, and therefore you have offended Him. But I held you to be a trusty knight in my service and thought well of you until you told me this, and you died sword in hand as I would wish a knight in my service to die—of honorable wounds, though the bout was only a match for my amusement—and insofar as that goes I am responsible for your death. So go in peace, then, as far as I, myself, am concerned. More than that I cannot give you."

"I thank Your . . ."

Verweather did not finish. His eyes closed and stayed closed. All those there but Jim crossed themselves—and he belatedly imitated them.

And that is why Angie and I can never be really like these people in their rigid rules, he thought grimly. *I would have found something more of kindness than that to give the poor devil!*

Chapter 32

Jim woke up suddenly, confusedly thinking he had only lain down for a small nap before dinner. But he was completely undressed, under the covers, and Angie was making tea as only she in this castle—probably the only one on this whole world—could make it.

"It's ready!" she said, seeing him sit up against the cold head of the bed. "Do you feel all right? You'd better get it down and get going. You're going to have your hands full today."

"Yes. Fine. Is it really morning?" he said. "I'm perfectly well—I think. Who would have thought I'd heal up that fast?"

"Don't be too sure," she said, bringing the sugared and milked tea to him. It tasted sweeter than usual. "You were out like a light last night," she went on, "snoring nearly all night long, and when I'd roll you over on your side to stop the noise, you wouldn't even wake up; the next thing I knew you were back on your back, snoring again to split the walls. Yesterday was almost too much for you. Drink it while it's hot. I'll have another one for you."

"Good," said Jim, greedily drinking the hot, sweet liquid. "I'll need another one. Did I go to dinner last night?"

"No. We had dinner sent up. You hardly ate anything, but got your clothes off, crawled into bed and dropped off. You've slept right through till now; and I've been trying to wake you for five minutes."

He looked at the nearest window. Bright morning sunlight—late fall was being kind. He emptied his teacup.

"Here!" said Angie, handing him another.

"Why did you say I'd be surprised?" he asked, drinking this one more leisurely.

"Because there're plenty of things for you to see today that'll start getting you all geared up again. Listen to me now." She sat down on the edge of the bed next to him.

"I'm listening," he said between sips. This second cup was not the nectar of life that the first had been, but there was no lack of taste in it to appreciate.

"I'm going to talk to you very seriously," Angie said, sitting.

"As I said, I'm listening."

"Physically, on your best day, you're no Brian—or no Dafydd."

"I know that," he said, nettled. "You don't have to tell me."

"Then don't try to act like one."

"I don't."

"You do. You just do it without thinking about it. Not only that, but you're just up from a sickbed. But yesterday you overdid yourself—badly. You could have knocked yourself right back into the state of shock—or whatever it was—when you got us all out of Tiverton alive."

"I thought Carolinus brought us all back here."

"Yes, but that was only after you'd made it possible. Anyway, Carolinus agrees with me. Another day like yesterday and you could knock yourself back into the coma you landed in before, from too much magic done too quickly."

"Carolinus!" Jim said, putting the second empty cup down on his bedside table. "I think I know more about myself than he does!"

"You don't know more about what magic can do than he does. Jim, I'm talking to you seriously. I watched you yesterday. You were out on your feet and didn't know it."

Jim opened his mouth to argue, then remembered his wooziness standing in the King's quarters, standing silent while the Prince persuaded his father to see the dying Verweather, and then listening to Brian and the King speak with the knight. He closed his mouth again.

"Maybe I was," he said. "But I've had a good night's sleep now, and I'm completely free of coma and plague, both. What makes you think whatever I'm supposed to be surprised at will gear me up again?"

"I know you."

"What is it that's worrying you so much, anyway?"

"What are all the things that could set you off again, you mean. That's why I want your promise—a real promise—you'll hold yourself down when you go out and see everybody. Don't try to leave here without promising me that! Carolinus warded the Solar so you can't get out, anyhow—before you give me that promise—and I mean it."

"Hell!" cried Jim. He felt he could break most imposed wards, but Carolinus' ward would be . . .

Tentatively he reached out to feel it and try how strong it was. Yep! It was complete, close around the room—ceiling, floor, walls and door: a massively heavy-feeling ward.

"Well, damn his nerve!"

"Damn him all you want," said Angie. "The ward stays there until I get that promise—your word, your unbreakable word, as knights here call it. As for Carolinus, he's your Master-in-Magick, after all."

"Well," grumped Jim, "you've got my blasted word, then. Let me get up up, wash, shave and dress."

Angie stood up from the bed.

"The Solar is all yours," she said. "And I'm going outside with you. If you start to wobble today, I'll blow the whistle on you—I warn you, Jim—" He looked at her, and to his surprise saw tears in her eyes. "Don't you realize what it would mean to me to lose you?"

He growled inarticulately at her, avoiding her gaze, threw off the covers, got out of bed and headed toward their sneakily modernized bathroom with the unheard-of flush toilet—fed by a cistern on the tower roof—a shower and a marble Roman tub, likewise supplied with water from the cistern.

When he came back out and was dressing, he found a breakfast on the table.

"I don't have time to eat that," he said. "Thank you anyway, but with this late start I want to get going."

"You might as well take time to eat it," said Angie. "I've sent for Brian and Dafydd, and it'll take them a little time to be found and told to come here. Besides, you need food. You've eaten almost nothing for days."

"So that's why these teas have been tasting sweeter than usual. You've been sneaking more sugar into them! Hah!"

"I wouldn't call it sneaking. I've been *putting* more sugar in to get more calories into you, and hah! Right back at you!"

"What're Brian and Dafydd coming for?"

"To keep you from being pestered. I planned to get some of the healthy men-at-arms we've got left to escort you, too. But most of our neighbor bully knights would just walk right through them. So I got you Brian and Dafydd."

"A few of the neighbors have got here already, then—with the goblins all around us? How'd they do that?"

"Show you when we get up to the roof," she said. "Now eat, before Brian and Dafyd show up."

He ate. Actually, he found he was hungry. But he had been ready to stuff the food down, anyway, if she was determined not to tell him anything until he could see it for himself. It was no good asking.

The usual hearty knock on the door, followed by Brian, immediately walking in without hesitation, followed by Dafydd. Jim hastily swallowed the last of the hard-boiled eggs.

"Well, James!" said Brian. "Better?"

"We hope so. But don't let him be bothered—I'll be with you, too, though," said Angie. "If I say take him down, it means we want him back here right away, no matter what he wants to do."

"Did Carolinus say so?" said Brian sharply, for he did not approve of wives ordering their husbands about, and only put up with Angie seeming to do this from time to time, because Jim seemed to put up with it. Other countries, other ways of course, and both Jim and Angie were not really English, poor people. Besides, he loved them both.

"He did," said Angie. "We had quite a talk about it. He said too much of anything could put him back in bed again."

"Heaven forefend," said Brian, crossed himself, and took hold of Jim's arm.

"I can get out of a chair by myself!" said Jim, as sharply as Brian had queried Angie.

"Do so, then," said Brian, unperturbed.

Jim got to his feet.

"It's good to see you both," he said, looking at Brian and Dafydd with affection. Brian abruptly kissed him on both cheeks. Dafydd gave him one of his usual smiles, more warmly than Jim remembered him ever doing before.

"Let's go then," he said. They went.

He had expected almost anything. The towertop was full of neighbors—not just the handful Jim had expected, but twenty or more of them—gazing out at the goblin horde, arguing or making sage suggestions which were nearly al-

ways met with argument. Sir Hubert White, Malencontri's
loud-voiced, opinionated, closest neighbor, who, indeed,
shared a boundary with Malencontri's lands—as bad luck
would have to have it—was the first to spot Jim up there
with the rest of them.

"Sir James!" he shouted, and started toward Jim, first of
the armed and armored horde.

"Not him," said Angie in a low voice to Brian and Dafydd, and they both moved forward between Jim and Sir
Hubert.

"Not now, Hubert," said Brian, "of your courtesy, he
must not be spoken with yet, by command of Mage Carolinus."

The words were polite, but Brian's tone left no doubt
about the finality of the message. Sir Hubert stopped, necessarily, but there was a sudden clamor of voices behind
him.

"Let them come," muttered Jim, in a low voice. "I asked
them for help, after all."

"I suppose you have to," Angie said, equally low-voiced.
Brian and Dafydd stood aside.

"Over here, gentlemen!" said Jim, raising his voice, and
reminding himself to speak as much in fourteenth-century
style as possible. Speak formally, with no modern words
that would be half-understood, misunderstood or not understood at all. He tried to remember how politicians he had
heard made their points in their speeches.

They came forward, the older ones, the family heads,
jostling out their sons and squires, so they could be as close
toward the front row as possible. The front row itself con-
sisted of the larger, richer, landowners—which had the bo-
nus side effect of elbowing Sir Hubert toward the back,
where he could not try to lead the conversation.

"Quiet, if you please, gentlemen," said Jim. They did not
become quiet—only toned down their comments and asides
to each other, so as to hear what Jim had to say. Deliber-

ately, he lowered his voice, to force them into a silence general enough so that they would all be able to hear him. They were a rough crowd, a potentially dangerous, individually minded crowd, if they got out of hand. He had to establish a superiority over them at the outset, to keep each of them from constant argument with him.

"Gentlemen!" Jim said again. "I am happy to tell you that in this hap we have a war captain of name and repute to lead us. None other than the Prince of Wales. You will all know of his memorable deeds both as that and in person, fighting against the enemy in the chevauché to the battle of Poitiers. He, with our Lord King, who has ruled battles memorably in his own time, will speak through me to you. There must be no discussion of the orders I carry, therefore."

He paused. To his astonishment they cheered. Time to wind things up quickly while they felt this good.

"Meanwhile, there is much we yet do not know. We are greatly outnumbered, and the enemy uses *magic*—poisoned spears. . . ." He gave them a short account of the Bishop's party rolling in agony on the ground after being speared.

"But magic is also a strength of mine, as you all know, and the Mage Carolinus is aiding us."

They cheered again.

"Right now, the Mage is discovering whether our Earl of Somerset—provided God has spared his household so that it has not been hit too hard by the plague—is able to send a force of his own fighting men to our aid. There is great hope. But also great work to be done, with or without aid from the Earl."

They cheered once more, a full-throated cheer. Did they never get tired of cheering, Jim asked himself? Then he remembered who and what they were. Outnumbered enormously as they were, they still hoped to have the glory of conquest all to themselves.

"That is all for now," he wound up. "I will speak to you

all again as soon as more is known and planned."

They roared in approval like a pack of hungry lions—he had been wrong about calling what they did cheering. He stepped back, and Brian and Dafydd, without prompting in any way, stepped before him, to signal his talk was over, and he was no longer open to questions or suggestions.

They would be either all for him, or all against him, thought Jim, unless he kept himself firmly established in command. Just to make sure the effect of his talk would not be spoiled, he moved to the defense wall around the edge of the roof, and looked down at his castle and particularly his courtyard. The knights gave him, Angie, Brian and Dafydd respectful and generous room to look, and even talk, privately.

"Good," said Angie in an undertone. "Let's go downstairs, while the effect lasts."

But Jim, staring at the roofs and courtyard below him, blinked. He had meant the move to the wall just to break off contact with the neighbors. But what he saw he could not believe.

"That's why I told you in the Solar to brace yourself," said Angie at his elbow. "Not the neighbors. This."

"But there aren't that many hobs in England!" said Jim.

"Apparently there are—and more still coming. You're not looking at a tenth of them," she answered. "The castle's full of them—helping in everything that's being done. Helping and trying to cheer up the sick ones. Some hobs have gone off to get more opium and pipes for all the plague victims. Others have already left on other errands. Some of them have been taking Nursing Room patients brave enough to go for small rides on the smoke—anything to give them heart."

"But—where did they all come from so quickly?"

"Don't underestimate the smoke," said Angie.

"I've got to talk to Hob—our hob," said Jim, turning towards the nearest chimney poking through the tower roof.

Then he remembered the crowd around where he was, and checked the move. "You're right. The Solar. Let's go!"

They went back downstairs, unquestioned and unimpeded. The neighbors were already starting to argue among themselves. But as the four of them closed the door behind them and sat down around the table, Jim reflexively threw a ward around the Solar to let them hear any outside talk clearly, but prevent anyone outside from hearing any word of theirs. Just then the alarm gong above them began to sound again—but with a strange, measured beat that Jim had never heard from it before.

Thud, pause, *thud, thud,* said the gong, continuing to repeat itself. Jim was half-way to his feet, when Brian's words stopped him.

"A dragon coming in to the roof," said Brian briefly.

"A dragon?" said Jim, starting to rise again.

"Sit down, now, Jim!" said Angie. "It's all arranged. The neighbors have already learned to move back to stand with their backs against the embrassures, to clear a landing space."

Jim switched his hearing to make it sensitive enough to pick up the larger noises from the roof, and sure enough, within seconds there was the typical heavy thud and wing-scrape noise of a dragon landing.

"It will doubtless be Secoh, James," said Dafydd calmly. "Full-grown as he is, he is still smaller than most among the young Cliffside recruits to his Dragon Patrol."

"What's going on?" cried Jim. "And how could all these people have gotten here so quickly? You'd think I'd been asleep two nights—not one."

"Three nights, dear Jim," said Angie softly, laying a hand on his arm. "I was hoping for a quiet moment to tell you about it, before this—I knew you'd be upset—but it didn't come in time. You slept like a log for three nights and two days; Carolinus told me not to worry, that you'd thrown off the plague, but not all of the effects of the magic overstrain

that may have saved your life, in a way—if Barron was
right about it. 'Let him sleep,' said Carolinus, 'as long as
he can. It's the best thing to get him back in shape.' "

There were noises from the stairs, scrapings against walls,
grunts, a half-stifled woman's scream, and what Jim, at
least, recognized as dragon curses, followed at last by a
shuffling of heavy feet down the corridor toward them.
When these halted, a heavy scraping of great and sharp
claws at the door, in what was clearly a too-powerful version of the normal polite scratching that asked for admit-
tance.

"Come!" shouted Angie, and the door opened to admit
Secoh, who squeezed in through its opening—that had, happily, been widened to get the Roman bath into the Solar.

"How are you, m'lord?" asked Secoh, squatting on what
any other animal might have considered his haunches at one
corner of the table, which now seemed decidedly crowded.

"Fine, thanks," said Jim. Abruptly remembering his duty
as host, he raised his voice.

"Servant here!" he shouted. One of the women of the
castle staff opened the door and took a gingerly step inside.
Jim was known to be a sort of blood-brother with this latest
visitor—but dragons were still dragons, and once upon a
time had pounced upon stray humans for their lunch, as they
might have on any other animal.

"Mazers and three pitchers of wine here—and two gallons of wine in the special bucket you'll find in the Serving
Room."

"Two *gallons*, my lord?" The servant blanched.

"Certainly. Two gallons for our dragon guest. Get help if
you need, to carry it all at once!"

"Yes, m'lord. Immediately." The staff member curtsied
and went out, partially reassured. She was not one of the
staff who dated back to when Secoh had been in the habit
of making excuses to visit the Great Hall in hopes of what
Jim had just ordered for him. Secoh had finally, gently, had

it made clear to him that such visits should be restricted to times when there was some important reason for a visit. The small marsh-dragon had never intruded unnecessarily again. But his eyes glistened kindly on the servant, following Jim's mention of the bucket of wine. Jim, however, barely noticed this.

"Three nights, two days!" Jim was repeating, shaking his head.

"Be at peace, James," said Brian. "All has gone well while you slept."

Jim looked at him, about to ask if, and how, the Prince might have been sticking his nose into what was going on, with commands that could only tangle matters up, but then he remembered why he had come back to the Solar.

"Hob!" he shouted in the direction of the large Solar fireplace. "Malencontri Hob!"

"Yes, m'lord?" said Hob, appearing out of the fireplace and standing in front of it.

"Come over here and join us."

Hob summoned a small puff of smoke and rode it, sitting cross-legged, to the opposite corner of the table from Secoh—and, as it happened, also at Jim's elbow—ending up level with the heads of everyone there, except Secoh's.

"I'm so glad to see you up, m'lord—and m'lady, and Sir Brian and Master Dafydd . . .and this dragon." Hob knew perfectly well who Secoh was. Secoh said nothing.

"Since I've been dead to the world for three nights—" Jim was beginning.

"Dead, m'lord?" cried Hob.

Brian looked a little shaken at Jim's choice of words, Secoh unmistakably alarmed, Dafydd unperturbed.

"Just in a manner of speaking!" said Jim. "Actually, I was only asleep. But as I started to say—since I was out of things, I'll have to know what's been happening, and I'd appreciate all of you telling me. To begin with, Hob, how did all the other hobs get here so fast?"

"Oh, I sent out messages on the smoke to all my friends, m'lord. A bit of the smoke can carry a simple message like that. I said, 'Come fight goblins. Bring your own weapon. Tell everyone.' "

"And they came? But how did all these others know to come?"

"Oh, each of my friends sent messages to all their friends—except the ones I'd sent messages to—and those sent messages to *their* friends . . . and so it went, very fast. Everybody wanted a chance."

"But how did the neighbors get here? And come to think of it, how about their horses? I suppose a couple of hobs could carry a man in armor and fully armed on the smoke. But what about their horses, all equipped?"

"I can tell you, m'lord," said Secoh eagerly. "Even one of our young members of the Dragon Patrol can carry fifteen or sixteen hobs. There's nothing much of weight to them, you know. In fact, it isn't even so much their weight, anyhow, as the fact that we can't have them riding on our wings, and such. Not decent. Of course an enormous number of hobs are needed to carry a george's big fighting horse back to Malencontri."

"As a matter of fact," said Hob, cutting in sharply, "as few as fifteen hobs—with the smoke to help—can carry a gentleman's destrier right over the heads of the goblins—out of spear-throw. Of course at least one horsewise hob must talk to the destrier first and explain, so the horse doesn't get scared at being up in the air. But lots of our hobs are very wise that way."

He looked smugly at Secoh, having trumped the dragon with his use of the correct terms for man and horse.

"But how—" Jim turned to Angie. "Do we have pigeons to carry messages to that many neighbors?"

"M'lady and I went on the smoke to each of them first, and each telling us of other neighbors we could ask—"

"Let the Lady Angela answer me, Hob."

"Yes, m'lord. Beg your forgiveness, m'lord."

"Forgiven. But let the person I ask do the talking, or else we'll end up with everyone trying to talk at once—you were going to say, Angie?"

"Oh," said Angie, "we went and I talked to each of them. They were all, even those who had lost a lot of people to the plague, wild to come. Many of the dead were family members, and they're all sure it was the goblins that brought the plague to them. They want revenge."

Revenge, as Jim was quite aware, was almost a duty in this time.

"Are there full armies of goblins around the castles of each of them, then?" Most of the castles mentioned were little more than fortified residences, and Jim had a vision of hundreds of thousands of goblins swarming over all Somerset.

"No," said Angie. "But they'd all seen one or more goblins moving past their places. In fact, we've got more coming."

Jim blessed the moment he had thought to announce that the Prince would be their war captain, with him just carrying out the Prince's orders. An implied lie in a good cause. They would never argue with the Prince—nor was the Prince likely to tolerate argument if they did. Jim need not either.

"All right, then. I'll ask Secoh first, Hob, since he probably has less to tell. Secoh, what's your patrol doing now?"

"Watching, m'lord. Malencontri, of course, is under watch from dawn to next dawn. The other members are sweeping Somerset all the time, to find out what's going on. M'lord, if you don't mind, when fighting starts could our patrol members be part of it—"

"You don't mean to say their mothers would let those sixty-year-old youngsters actually fight?"

"Oh, no, m'lord!" Secoh looked uncomfortable. "They wouldn't stand it for a breath's moment! But I mean, if they could all be busy carrying orders swiftly—we're much faster above the ground than hobs, you know—"

"If the smoke is covering a distance, it goes faster and faster until no one could keep up!" said Hob.

"Hob!" said Jim.

"Sorry, m'lord."

"Well, message carrying, or dropping supplies to our fighters, perhaps, Secoh. We'll see."

"Thank you, m'lord."

"That's it as far as what you have to tell me, then?"

"Yes, m'lord. Except that our young dragons are fearless—"

"That's what I'm afraid of," said Jim. He had himself experienced, when in his dragon body, the sudden explosion of excitement and rage that would carry any dragon into combat regardless of any other rule or reasoning. Once it had earned him a knight's lance clear through the body of Gorbash, the dragon he had found himself in on arriving in this world.

"Now that's the last I want to hear from either of you," he said, "until I ask you a direct question. Hob, I'm now speaking to you. What are your hobs busy at, besides bringing in armored men and their mounts and what Angie's been telling me about some of them trying to help the sick ones and do other things here at Malencontri?"

"Oh, m'lord, hobs *like* helping at anything! It makes them feel good. As for what else—we go close above the goblins around us here, especially at night, because since they won't touch fire, it's too dark for them to see us, and so we can even overhear what they're planning to do. That mean lady who's always with the loud man—"

That would be Agatha Falon, Jim knew. Little Robert's rapacious, older half-sister, and the "loud man" had always been Hob's name for the Earl of Comberland.

"Cumberland himself hasn't shown up?" he asked.

"No, m'lord. And they don't seem to know about him. But some of the things the mean lady suggests may have come from him—like the scaling ladders. They'd never have known of those on their own."

"The hobs really have been a help around the place," said Angie. "Did I tell you each sick one here has his or her own bedside hob to bring anything wanted right away? They even offered to take the invalids for rides on the smoke to cheer them up. A few of the men did take them up on it—more out of bravado than anything else, I think. But they went; and they came back all excited and all pumped up. They loved having gone and talked about it so much some of other sick men and women tried it, too. I think maybe it helped their chances of getting better. And you know, as I told you, Jim, some hobs are off trying to get opium and pipes for all those suffering so much."

"Thank you, m'lady. Can I tell the hobs doing it that you said it helped them get better?"

"Yes."

"They'll be so proud and happy!"

"Right," said Jim. "Hob, you yourself better stay close to me here to tell me whatever your people learn of the goblins' plans. That's all for you, then, now. No, wait, how can they get pipes and opium? Carolinus had to get me mine from someone he knew on the other side of the world."

"I know, m'lord. But some hobs live with families whose grandfathers or even farther back had gone on Crusade, and picked up using opium that way. Some of those families have people still using the pipes—secretly, of course—because they've a special chain of friends reaching down and east from across the world, so they can get opium yet. . . ."

"I see," said Jim. "Not an important question, actually, but things are happening so fast here, I thought I'd ask while I had it in mind. Well, now, that deals with the hobs for the moment. Now—the matters that concern Sir Brian and Master Archer Dafydd."

It was only as the last of these words escaped from his mouth that he looked at the two he had just mentioned and saw Brian looking definitely and sternly displeased.

Chapter 33

Jim had not known Brian for some years now without learning to interpret Brian's very rare but unmistakable annoyed-to-angry expression.

"I'm sorry, Sir Brian," he said, "perhaps we should've had our separate talks privily, but I thought it important that all of us here should know what the rest of us knew, since all are to be in command positions."

"Not at all, James," said Brian. "But you know, if talk is not privy, then why not hold it openly . . ." there was a small pause in this speech as his eye roamed over Hob and Secoh ". . . if privy, I might ask why we do not include Sir Harimore?"

"Sir Harimore," said Jim, earnestly and as appealingly as he could, "has no special, already-existing command of his own. Later on, perhaps it'll be different. For now, I was just thinking of him being under your command, with the other knights among our neighbors, and those of the Earl of Somerset—if we get them—also under yours."

"It would pain me," Brian looked grimly at Jim, "to tell Sir Harimore so. I regard him as my equal."

"Then maybe," said Jim, "I should be the one to put that suggestion to him?"

"No, James," said Brian, unfolding his arms, his voice and expression softening. "It will come best from me. He is a gentleman I respect, though no close friend."

"Well, thanks, Brian. I'd actually rather not, myself. He knows how little I actually understand of arms."

Both Brian and Dafydd tactfully ignored those last words.

"Very good," said Brian. "Now, then, may I ask why Prince Edward is not among us, since he is to be our war captain?"

"He holds rank and duty above us all. In fact, you and I and Master Archer Hywel have a special and privy responsibility to him, which I must explain to you only among ourselves—perhaps if you and he will linger after our other friends here have left. . . ."

Hob and Secoh, for a Natural and a dragon, were remarkably quick to pick up Jim's hint. In fact, both had looked very alarmed just now (Secoh's alarm visible only to Jim's dragon-wise eyes) at what seemed to be the beginning of a quarrel between Jim and Brian. Such a thing had never been known before.

Hob was first to speak, but Secoh was not far behind him.

"If m'lords will excuse me . . ." said Hob.

"Those young dragons," growled Secoh. "Likely to get up to anything if I don't watch them all the time. If m'lords will forgive me, I should leave now, too."

Hastily he poured the last of his bucket of wine down his throat and rose from his squatting position.

"Go with God," said Brian genially, perhaps, Jim thought, somewhat regretting now his earlier sternness. The Natural and the dragon both hesitated for a second—and then, apparently deciding there had been no harm in what Brian had said—left. Hob disappeared up the fireplace chimney, Secoh out the door. He could be heard a moment later swearing at the narrowness of the staircase to the surface as he squeezed his way up to the tower roof.

"Good creatures," said Brian, looking at the door where they had seen the last of Secoh. He went on more briskly. "Now, James, what's this about young Edward and us—and what about the King, though if he desires to be in the fight, Lord forbid, at his age and in his . . . state."

"I only mentioned the King as someone who might advise, Brian," said Jim. "As for the Prince, I had a little talk with him—no point in going into details; in a nutshell, I pointed out to him that while it was not only good but necessary for him to be war captain here and now, that his previous experience at command involved men like Chandos at his elbow, and that the same sort of service from us would be needed here. In short it was agreed that he would command essentially in name only—you will not mention that agreement to him at any time, of course. It might pain him to have it known—in name he would command, but he understands we three would actually run things."

"Ah," said Brian.

"I am relieved to hear it," said Dafydd. "I believe he knows little of archers, let alone the art of bow-use itself."

"I'd guess not," said Jim. "While we're on that subject, Dafydd, how many archers have we?"

"Not counting my dear wife and myself, seven living, but four of those sick of plague, three fit to fight—all good Welsh bowmmen, however, the ones you got not long since from the border areas."

"Three!" burst out Brian, completely ignoring the reference to the homeland of the archers.

"It does you credit, Brian," said Dafydd, "to recognize the value, as few English knights do, of trained archers in a situation such as this. But as I was intending to say, since it seems dragons can carry the weight of an armed man, and two hobs do the same, surely one dragon could carry me and some hobs swiftly to archers I know of at various distances, who might wish to be part of our battle since they might have lost comrades to the plague fostered by these goblins while serving in the English east. One or even two hobs could carry each archer back here while the dragon and I went on."

"Good," said Jim. "But I think just a couple of hobs for you, too, would be better. The smoke keeps gaining speed the farther it goes. The dragon, particularly a young one, would tire."

"Very good." Dafydd was on his feet. "I will leave at once, since time is short."

"Hob!" called Jim, directing his voice at the fireplace.

Hob popped out in seconds. "Master Archer Dafydd needs a number of hobs—he'll explain."

"Yes, m'lord. If you'll approach the fireplace, m'lord Dafydd. . . ."

"I am no lord, Hob, as I've explained to you before—"

Dafydd, who had been approaching the fireplace as he spoke, was whisked up the chimney while Hob was still inviting him, and for the first time in his experience, Jim glimpsed a look of startlement on the archer's face.

"Now," Jim said, turning to Brian, "about the handling of the neighbors and the footmen—"

"If you don't mind," said Angie, "I think I'll leave the two of you to it. I'm not really needed here now, and I *am* needed in a dozen places about the castle, starting with the Nursing Room."

"Let me know if the hobs really got opium pipes after all—" Jim called after her, as the door to the Solar shut behind her. He turned back to Brian, who was pouring himself some more wine and judiciously adding three drops of water to it. "Oh, by the way, Brian, how is Geronde? I've hardly seen her since I became ill."

"She avoided the plague, thank God," said Brian, drinking. "You know, James, she may be quite right about my getting used to mixing water with my wine. This isn't half bad. No, she wanted to help in the Nursing Room—that was before we started spilling over with hobs. I told her not to. She argued, of course, but gave in finally—for a change. But she's used to being busy, and this business of standing around waiting so long has worn her down. Wish I could do something for her."

"You two didn't get married while I was ill, then?"

"James, how in the names of the patience of all the saints put together could we be married with all this going on?"

"I thought maybe, after Carolinus brought us all back here and while I was still out with the plague—"

"—And the neighbors all struck by the plague, too, and

not able to get here, and this army of goblins surrounding your castle, James?"

"No," said Jim. "Of course. I understand. She must be very disappointed after this long, long list of delays. Is she very unhappy about it?"

"When Geronde gets unhappy, she gets angry—very angry—and runs around wanting to work her head off. Also she worries about everything unimportant. For one thing, she asked me yesterday if I thought the people at our wedding—whenever we have the good luck to have it—are not going to be watching the scar put upon her by that damnable Sir Hugh de Bois—how does a bastard like that go on living—even among such hedge-sweepings as we found him with in Lyonesse? Next time *I* get to be the one to fight him."

"There was no choice. I had to be the one, that time," said Jim mildly. "And you remember that was some time back."

"Oh, I know, I know. Just blowing off my ancient anger about that, James, but all the same—" There was a nasty cracking sound and the King's special glass drinking vessel, left behind when the King volunteered to give up Jim and Angie's special room for the now-new three-room suite one floor down, was crushed in Brian's fist.

"Now what, damn it all!" barked Brian, thoroughly out of temper.

"Nothing. Are you cut?" Jim got hastily to his feet.

"No, no—scratched a bit. Pay me no heed!" said Brian testily, bleeding from half a dozen cuts on his hand. "Just if you have a tablecloth or something to wrap—" Jim had just discreetly healed the small wounds. "Ah, well. Thank you, James—unnecessary, though."

"Pour another glass," said Jim diplomatically, cleaning up the table and floor. "Now, back to making a fighting force of the neighbors."

"Oh, they'll do all right, if I can get them to charge in

line and keep their lance-tips down. Otherwise, what can you expect? The squires know nothing of fighting, and what little their elders knew was an occasional bicker years ago—most of which they've forgotten. But they'll all fight hard. Somerset men always do, once they get into it. Luckily, they all know me and are not like to argue with what I tell them."

"And the footmen?" asked Jim. "I mean the spearmen on foot, which was how we were going to use my serfs and tenants."

"I do not know," said Brian. "Will they advance in a body when ordered to do so?"

"What?" said Jim, spilling his wine. "Why not?"

"How indeed, James, should I know? They are your people. Common folk, of course, but usually common folk are not without courage. I can hardly think of a reason why they might hold back, but I have an uneasy feeling. Of course, the like of all such as the goblins are known to all common folk as having fearsome magic of their own—and that thought can be daunting to many. But I should think for men who know the ground here and are doubtless poachers to a man, at the pinch they should be able—"

"We'll have to hope so.—Oh, Hob!" Hob had just reappeared, alone. "About the serfs and tenants still at home—"

"Yes, m'lord?" said Hob. "Master Archer and I were talking about them. We'll need them. Tiverton hob is on his way with thirty other hobs, to bring in those tenants and serfs still hanging back. A ride on the smoke should make them think of the magic on our side."

"Good. Never mind that, for now, then," Jim said. "But why haven't they left before this, I wonder?"

"They fear the goblins' evil magics too much to leave."

"But don't the people know how dangerous it is for them, sitting in their mud-and-branch huts? The goblins could break through and eat them any time. Hob, didn't you give me the idea goblins eat anything—even each other?"

"Oh, no, forgive me, m'lord. The tenants and all just think of the goblins as having terrible magic no one's ever heard of, but they know there's only one thing that can foil it. They all painted crosses on their doors."

"And they think that's keeping them safe?"

"Why, of course it is, m'lord."

"Damned strange if it didn't!" said Brian. Jim gave up pursuing the matter of cross protection.

He mentally chewed his fingernails. There ought to be a way to use his magick to gather them all here, if the hob pickup didn't work.

He thought, but his mind came up with nothing, and a quick mental scan of the enormous volume of the *Encyclopedie Necromantic*, which Carolinus had made him swallow some years ago, did not help.

He chewed his lips—literally this time.

"Er—Carolinus?" he called diffidently. "I hate to bother you—"

"What for?" demanded Carolinus, suddenly sitting in a chair opposite. "I've only got a few more nymphs and crickets to see, who've been waiting all that time I was away."

"My outside people are afraid to leave their homes, and we need the men for foot soldiers and spearmen—along with what castle staff's up to it. For me to transport myself to each tenant or serf one by one would be very expensive of magick and right now I haven't got the time. Hob's trying to get them carried in by other hobs—but will they let themselves be taken? I can't seem to think of an alternate way. If just this one time you could tell me how—"

"I never tell. You have to find your own way to do things like this, you know that," said Carolinus. "I suppose you could trust the hobs to bring them in. Luckily, you've got hobs beyond counting—almost. All of England's best of hobdom—almost. But it'd take time to have them do it, and they'd have to come down on the ground where the goblins can get at them. . . . All right, this once I'll do it for you—

there, it's done. Serfs and tenants are now overflowing your courtyard, which was full to start with, and let this be a lesson to you."

"I don't know how to thank you, Mage. It was just that time's so tight and we'll need all the magick we can get—"

"You can't thank me. I must say this is a sorry performance in an apprentice about to be proposed for membership in the Collegiate of Magickians."

"I know—"

"Mage," said Brian unexpectedly. "Always wanted to ask you this. If painted crosses will keep goblins out of huts, why don't we paint one on the castle's great doors, and sit here until the goblins perish in the winter rains and snows?"

Chapter 34

Carolinus stared at Brian.

"There is a small Magickianlike bump in you, Brian," he said. "But I would hate to be the one to have you for my apprentice."

"I am a gentleman of arms," said Brian, a little stiffly. "I have no desire to be a Magickian. If you will forgive me, Mage, you still have not answered my question."

Jim had noticed that. He himself was staring at Brian. Why hadn't it occurred to him to think about protecting Malencontri with a painted cross?

The answer came quickly enough out of the sort of instinct he seemed to be developing these days where magick was concerned. Something in him was sure it wouldn't work for the castle, but he did not have the slightest understanding why it shouldn't. It was lucky Brian hadn't asked him that instead of Carolinus. Why had he waited?

The reason for that came quickly enough to his mind, too. He knew why Brian had chosen Carolinus to ask. The knight had reacted against Carolinus' sharp criticism of his close friend. He had retaliated by asking Carolinus what might possibly be a stickler of a question—even an embarrassing one, if Carolinus did not know—and, after all, Carolinus did not know everything. It was a bold challenge to one of this world's best—if not the best of all—Magickians. . . .

Brian was the soul of courtoise, but he was utterly without fear or hesitation. Jim held his breath waiting to see what Carolinus' answer would be now.

"Brian," said Carolinus, "let's see if I can explain this in ordinary terms. Suppose you are sent under a flag of truce as an envoy with a message to a powerful enemy in position directly across from you. Before you go, you will of course leave behind all your weapons—am I right?"

"You are, **Mage**."

"Very well. You go forth then with your message and return unharmed, because the flag you carry protects you from any assault. Is *that* not so?"

"It is."

"Now, think of Malencontri as you trying to carry a message to the enemy under such a flag. But then let's suppose that halfway to them you drop it. Would the enemy consider that you started out with it and still respect you as protected by it?"

"No, Mage," said Brian, sounding genuinely puzzled. "They'd fear my dropping it might be a trick on my part, so my side could attack while we're talking."

"All right, then. Now think of magick. We humans and also the Naturals—every kind that's been discovered so far—are vulnerable to magick. That's because we—and they—use magick ourselves, to our own benefit; we humans knowing what we do, and the Naturals using it instinctively when they need it. But animals, trees, weather, disease and a host of other things are untouchable by the magick of either humans or Naturals. They are all *innocent* of magick.

Therefore for them, magick does not exist, and those who use it cannot use it against them—but they have to believe it doesn't exist. That's what we humans call Faith. Now do you see what I'm aiming at?"

"No—yes, Mage," said Brian. "You're saying a cross on a door keeps away goblins from those inside—but only as long as one there is not a Magickian."

"A user of magick would be a better description," said Carolinus.

"But Malencontri is not—a castle cannot be a user of magick."

"James is, and since he owns it and it's his home, a cross won't bar its door to the goblins, even if he were temporarily absent. Both we here now and the goblins use magick. There can be no flag of truce between us. We can use magick to watch each other—just as the troll can use his magick light on us and we can use magick on him—if," Carolinus said with a somewhat baleful side glance at Jim, "we know how to do so. You understand now, Brian?"

"Yes, Mage."

"Think of it then in these terms, and hold it in your memory so. We use magick. Those who do not are the innocents. They do not use it, and therefore it cannot touch them. But we have traded our innocence for power, and now that power can be used against us."

With that Carolinus disappeared. His last words stayed in Jim's mind as if printed there. He had no doubt that Brian, with the usual necessity-trained medieval memory, would be holding them even more securely.

"Well, James," Brian said. "I swear there were more words used there to explain a simple thing than I've heard since my grandfather died. Nonetheless, I think I am the wiser for it, as I have been for some things my grandfather said. Do you agree with the Mage?"

"Certainly," said Jim. "He knows much more than I do.

I'm glad it was him you asked instead of me. I couldn't have answered you so well."

"Say you so?" Brian looked at him curiously, as if astounded to find there was anything about magick Jim did not know. "Merely it occurred to me when he was here. At any rate, now we have those to work with who may turn into some sort of footmen—to get back to our planning . . . Shall you go down with me to look them over?"

"I'd like to," Jim said, "but come to think of it, I should have looked up the Prince before this and told him what we've decided so far, so he doesn't feel completely managed by you, Dafydd and me. How we'll feed and keep all these extra people is going to be a problem for Angie and the staff, though. I'd better see them, too."

"Very well," said Brian. "I'll tell you what I think of your field-and-forest people after I've looked them over." Abandoning his new half-full glass of wine, he went out the door. Jim thought of Angie and magickally moved himself to her.

He found himself standing beside her on the dais that had held his bed when he had been a patient in the Nursing Room. She was apparently in argument with May Heather, who was clearly in one of her stubborn moods.

"—but the hobs are quite right!" Angie was saying to May. "They can't catch the plague from the sick ones, but you can—it's a miracle you haven't before this—Oh, Jim! I should be used to you appearing without warning like this, but I never do.—May, Mistress Plyseth needs you back in the Serving Room! Her arthritis is really bothering her."

"If God chose for her to have 'ritis, m'lady, she just has to live with it, like we all have to do with things. Someone's needed in charge here. I say no word against hobs. They are all good-hearted little lads, but someone must be in charge, or something could go terrible wrong!"

Time was too tight to waste on this kind of argument. Jim broke in.

"Never mind that now," he said. "We're going to be getting all our outside people into the castle—the men we're going to use as foot soldiers against the goblins. They'll all need to be fed and found a place to sleep."

"The courtyard!" said Angie. "It was overflowing with horses and people before, but I don't know where else we can put so many. How many are there now?"

"You'd know better than I do," said Jim. "You keep the books of the field-and-forest workers—and then there're their families. Two hundred, maybe?"

"Two hundred!" cried May. "How can we care for them, too—and the moat already choked with chewed bones and sh—all, m'lord? We're in order to eat the last of the castle's food by mid-next month. What will we do for the coming winter after that?"

"I don't know yet," said Jim. "Anyway, the goblin trouble has to be settled one way or another long before then. But right now, those who come in will need to be cared for. May, this is an order. You're needed to see them fed and bedded—some way—leave the Nursing Room to the hobs. I've got all sorts of things to do—see the Prince first, and smooth any ruffled feathers—and you've got your own hands full. But you can at least just check on how these latest arrivals are cared for so you can let me know!"

"I'll do that," said Angie decisively.

"No, no, m'lady! I'll do that a'course. I can do that. Beg pardon m'lord."

"Well," said Jim—embarrassed at his lost temper, but forbidden by custom from showing that. "I've got to go then. Goodbye." He was no Carolinus to appear and vanish without any hello or farewell, he told himself. He moved without thinking magickally to wherever the Prince might be.

Unfortunately, he realized a second later, he theoretically should have moved himself to just outside the door of any room the Prince was in, so he could then scratch on it in polite fashion and wait to be told to come in.

It turned out, however, that the Prince was in his own room, with Joan. Perfectly decorous, though, the two of them, completely dressed and sitting in a couple of the small stiff-backed chairs talking to each other.

"Forgive me, Your Grace, my lady," Jim said hastily. "I meant to land outside your door. But we're all so busy getting ready to face the goblins I forgot to ask for entrance, first."

The two looked at him with only mild surprise. He had forgotten how little people of this period were upset by the sudden appearance of visitors, when they were engaged in any of the ordinary activities of life—including those that in Jim's modern day would be considered very private indeed. Besides, he was their host, and as owner of the castle was entitled to walk into any room in it, whenever he felt like it.

"May I be of use?" Joan asked now, swiftly getting up.

"Absolutely, if you would. Angie was on the ground floor a second ago. You can probably find her there. Ask the servants to help you locate her."

Joan went swiftly out of the room.

"Wine, James?" said the Prince in a somewhat dispirited tone, waving a hand at the chair Joan had just vacated.

"Thank you, Your Grace," said Jim. He did not want wine, but it was the polite accompaniment of talk. He seated himself. "I came to report to you how preparations for an assault on the goblins are progressing."

Already pouring wine, the Prince hesitated—but only for a second. His face immediately showed signs of cheering up.

"That is good news!"

"I beg your forgiveness for not coming sooner—"

"Nay, nay," said the Prince, waving his own wineglass back and forth in a negative manner. "I admit I was not best pleased after our last talk, in which you told me, in no flowery fashion, that I would, in effect, do only what you advised me to do—I would be war captain in name only. But I have since had several long talks with my Lady Joan, and am of more sensible mind now. Finally."

"I did not mean—"

"Of course you did. You meant to bring me to my senses, and as I may have mentioned, Joan has said similar things to me in the past. Who indeed am I to command three paladins, great warriors like yourself, Sir Brian and that noble Day—Daf—"

"Dafydd," said Jim gently. This was one more case of the Prince changing utterly and suddenly from what he had seemed to be before, revealing himself, at least in part, as a totally different and much more likable person—possibly one of the reasons Joan loved him.

"Also, by the way," Jim added, "it may well be, as you come to know Dafydd better, you may find him worthy of the sort of respect I spoke of. But he wishes that knowledge about him to remain unknown to man and woman alike. Brian and I are the only ones who know this. I have never spoken of it otherwise to anyone but you."

"Nor will I," said the Prince energetically. "My word on it—my word as a knight, which is more than the word of a Prince. You and he may rest easy. He is ruler of some foreign land, I presume?"

"Forgive me," said Jim. "I'm not free to say more."

"Of course—of course," said the Prince firmly, but starting to look melancholy again. "For a moment I thought you were accepting me with Brian and—but you are quite right, absolutely right to speak me as you just have. I will be glad to be named war captain, but fully willing to be guided by those who really know. As I said, Joan—but she was completely right, too. I am not the best of companions most of the time, but I promise you, as I promised her, that from this day forward, I will grow as a man and a knight, who, secure in his proficiency of arms, shows always courtoise to all others as well."

"That's said as a knight who is a Prince would say!" said Jim, more deeply touched than he had ever expected to be by this younger man. Edward was a strange mixture of autocrat and high ideals, with an even stranger—for a man of his period—conscience thrown in.

"I thank you for saying so, James. Will you tell me as soon as plans are made in the future, then?"

"My word on that," said Jim. "But would you not rather be one of us as we sit down to the planning of battle with the goblins?"

"Hah!" said the Prince, his eyes all but blazing now.

"I will get word to you when. We will almost surely meet in the Solar. You must not be surprised, though, if some others are brought in briefly by my magick."

"Surprised I may be, James, but object I will not."

"Good," said Jim. "Then, if you will forgive me, I must be about other necessary matters."

"Do not feel you must stand on manners with me, James, I beg you. You know your needs far better than I. Farewell until our next meeting."

"Farewell," said Jim, and shifted himself to the Solar.

Angie was already back there, he discovered, working at her desk.

"I thought you'd still be busy downstairs," he said to her. "You aren't doing castle accounts at a time like this, surely? Did Joan find you?"

"Yes—there was nothing more for her to help with, though, by that time. On the accounts, no. Just trying to check out with my own figures May's statement we had less than a month and a half of food to last until the first of the spring forest-gatherings. Where've you been?"

"Seeing the Prince. You know, I think he can be included in our battle-planning sessions, with Brian and Dafydd and whoever. I'm still surprised you got back up here so fast. I thought you'd be running around with May, getting the cottagers settled."

"Oh, May can more than take care of herself. It's funny. She's still technically just Plyseth's apprentice, but the other castle staff all take orders from her. Of course, I don't think she'd wait two seconds before taking a swing at the biggest man-at-arms we've got, if he argued with a command of hers. She's a tough little devil. You and I'll have to watch out. She's likely to be ordering us around next."

"No fear," said Jim. "You're the image of what she wants to be. She worships you and thinks she could never be half the lady you are."

"Well, I hope so," said Angie. "And I hope it lasts—for everybody's sake. Did you see Carolinus? He popped in here, but said he wanted to talk to you face-to-face, then popped right out again. He said he'd be back—"

"And he is," said the snappish voice of Carolinus, appearing before them. "There you are, James! Are you aware magick leaves a trail when you transport yourself with it? I've been chasing you all over Malencontri."

"Sorry," said Jim. "I didn't realize. But I've been wanting to see you myself—"

"Of course you have. Unfortunately, it's bad news I have to tell you. I spoke to our Somerset Earl about sending knights and men-at-arms to help you here—"

"You don't mean he said no?" exploded Jim. "This is his shire! Malencontri may be in direct feif to the King, but most of our neighbors are in feif to him. It's his shire. He has a duty to defend it—and the King himself is in danger here in this castle!"

"If you will let me finish!" said Carolinus.

"Go ahead," said Jim, calming down but still fuming inside.

"I saw him two days past about help for you. He's an old friend. I believe him. He says, speaking for himself only, he'd give his right arm to be in this, and believed the same could be said for his knights and fighting men—"

"Then—" began Jim.

"But he also had to take time to measure the temper of his common people. It seems by a fortunate chance the plague has missed his estates and castle entirely. His people think they've been specially chosen by God to survive, and that it would be flying in His face to send anyone He has so saved to where they might die—and, he said, they may well be right. Certainly they are grateful to be spared, and the wrath of God is not lightly to be risked."

"—With that, he crossed himself," added Carolinus.

Jim opened his mouth and then closed it again. He could not think of what to say.

"In any case," said Carolinus, "he's sorry. But you know how those things are. A lord or even an Earl can have his own way almost all the time—but when his people all get an idea into their heads, there's nothing to be done about it. You must have run into situations like that."

Jim had. He cooled down all the way, and found himself left with a hollow feeling inside.

"I was counting on those armed horsemen of his, most of them veterans, to turn our mob of neighbors into an orderly force."

"Well, there it is," said Carolinus, in a much kinder voice than usual. "No point in fussing over it—spilled milk, and all that. I'm still with you, and I've spoken to the Collegiate. There were a few objections, but I dealt with them. Each member will contribute as necessary to save the King—but only for that purpose. I can give you all the magickal help you need."

"Thank heaven for that!" said Jim.

"Kinetete will be happy to give a hand, too."

"Even better!" said Jim, cheering up. "Probably the sooner we get our war council together, the better. Meanwhile, the hobs should be bringing in more archers for Dafydd."

"Good," said Carolinus. "I'll go tell Kin how things sit, now."

He disappeared.

Chapter 35

"They'll be coming along any minute now," said Angie. It was about ten A.M. of the next day—a bright morning. "By the way, have you looked outside yet, this morning?"

"No," answered Jim.

"I thought not. I was waiting for some reaction from you. Take a look."

Jim got up from his chair, went to the nearest window and looked at as much of the castle as he could see through it—mainly rooftops of lower buildings and the courtyard.

"What are the hobs all doing sitting on the roofs?" he asked. "Did someone chase them up there?"

"Look again. Those aren't the hobs we had already. As many others again as we had yesterday came in during the night. They're perching everywhere there's space and they won't be in people's ways."

"Hell's bells!" said Jim deeply.

"Why any kind of bells at all?"

"Because," he said, almost grinding his teeth, "between you and me I don't know what we're going to do with them. It'd be slaughter for any we just send out against the enemy."

"How do you know? They've got goblin instincts, presumably. Maybe they'd be more effective than you think."

"Hah!" said Jim bitterly.

"Do you want me to stick around here?" Angie asked, skillfully changing the subject.

"I'm afraid not, Angie," he said. "This is still the Middle Ages—even if it's the High Middle Ages. Joan of Arc is still more than a century away. Women not expected at command discussions."

"Only that long? But, anyway, I'm just as happy not to

be here. Still a thousand things to do. I just thought you might want me for some reason."

"Not this time. This time you're officially desired not to attend—not that I would presume to dictate to my Chatelaine."

"My lord, you know your lightest wish is my command."

"Hmph!" said Jim.

"Who'll be here?"

"Brian, Dafydd, the Prince—"

"You're going to risk having the Prince sitting in on this? He'll want to take charge and mess up everything else," said Angie.

"Maybe. I hope not. But he has to be brought into things anyway, and if he really understands his role in them, the sooner the better. I had a talk with him—"

"M'lord!" It was a shout from beyond the door—the voice of the man-at-arms on duty there. "A wolf to see you!"

Jim and Angie stared at one another. Only one wolf could be at their door here in the castle, and he hated to come inside any man-made structure.

"Aargh?" called Jim.

"Who else?" growled a harsh voice, easily penetrating the door. "There's no other wolves in the territory I keep. Are you going to let me in, or don't you have any more use for this sword-bearing human beside me here?"

"Open the door!" shouted Jim.

It opened and Aargh stalked in—impressive as usual, ears and tail up, the size of a small pony and looking even bigger as he started to fur out for winter.

"What're you doing here?" asked Angie. "You don't like the indoors."

"What sensible creature would? Someone has to keep an eye out for you. Those young dragons Secoh's got flying around have been told by their mothers not to get within treetop distance when goblins are below them. They're no use. The goblins spent the night building long ladders again—but this time wide enough to take two goblins abreast and twice as stout—also more of them, so they'll touch each other all around the wall. They'll start another try to use them at twilight, planning to get even one or two goblins in over the wall at any cost. If they do, they'll let others over, and next thing you'll have ten goblins for every human you've got in this stone trap."

"How did you find this out?" asked Jim.

"I visited them early, just before dawn, to pick one up for a bite to eat, and found the half-made ladders lying flat on the ground in the middle of them, with goblins standing over them to hide them from the young dragons. I'd had a full night—needed a little something before taking a nap."

"Why didn't you tell us this earlier?" Angie stared at him.

"There was the eating, my nap, then I had to think about coming in here," said Aargh, but his voice was less harsh. For some reason, Jim had noticed, wolves all seemed to have more of a spot of affection for women than they ever showed most men. "I thought of leaving a message, but none of your humans on the gate could probably get it to you straight—and when I try to talk to them, they all panic. Now I've told you, and I'm on my way out of here!"

He turned. "Open up!" he snarled at the door.

"Thanks, Aargh," said Jim, and shouted at the door himself. "Open up!"

"Thanks is one of your human words—" Aargh growled, but the door was now opening and he left without finishing his sentence.

He was barely gone before the voice of the guard was heard again through the now reclosed door, proudly rolling out a litany of names.

"His Grace the Prince of Wales, Sir Brian and Dafydd ap Hywel are here, m'lord."

"Well, let them in!" called Angie, always quicker off the

mark than Jim. She reached the door just as it opened, and the visitors began to come in.

"Good morn, Your Grace, gentlemen," she said, walking past them in the opposite direction. "An honor to have you here, but I'm just on my way out."

Then she was gone, they were in, and the door closed with barely a sound.

There was the usual business of greetings, seatings and wine-pourings. "Well, gentlemen," Jim began, "you come in good time. I've just had some important information. Our gathering to plan has now become a more urgent matter of discussing how to deal with the enemy immediately."

He passed on the message that Aargh had just given him.

"You mean that great beast we passed in the corridor coming here?" said the Prince. "What a trophy!"

"He is a friend of mine," said Jim frostily.

"A friend to us all, Your Grace!" said Brian, with an even greater level of coldness in his voice, "and fought with us at the affair of the Loathly Tower."

"Indeed," said Dafydd.

"Oh, *that* wolf!" said the Prince. "I mind me now, in fact, that he and I had at least one talk together. Of course. How could I forget such a magnificent specimen?"

"Perfectly natural, under the circumstances, Your Grace," said Jim, who had only just remembered that fact himself.

"Well, well," said the Prince, "yet one should never forget his friends, even if they are mere animals. But—back to the matters at hand."

"As far as another attack goes," said Brian, "the goblins will be aware that the heart of our command is here in the tower, and so while they will certainly essay the curtain wall, the stronger effort is likely to come here—to take or kill those of us who lead the defense quickly and first. But we may better defend another attack here. This time we can certainly fill the towertop to overflowing with good men and stout spears. Some oil near to boiling would not go amiss."

"We have yet only a few archers, but they could help, provided we do not have to hoard our arrows, however," said Dafydd. "Shooting down from above is an advantage—if we are well supplied with arrows?"

"We have some hundreds in the storeroom," Jim told him.

"And, as I was about to say, there may be one or two men among the cottagers just brought in who can pull a warbow, if you have these in spare, also," went on Dafydd, in his unvaryingly unruffled tone.

"I'm sure we have warbows in store, and I must have thirty or more foresters," said Jim. "The bow is an old companion to all of them."

"Yes, but how many might truthfully be called archers?" said Dafydd. "And how many can pull a warbow more than twice or thrice, let alone for some hours, without being shoulderlame for the day? A fighting archer has built his strength with the bow from early childhood. Occasional shots at specific targets may be well within the doing by your foresters. But how many of them can fire steadily in massed volleys at an onrushing enemy? An occasional deer is a large target for a true archer. Still, this ladder-climbing will make killing goblins easier than a duckpond-shoot. I will have to look your foresters over again."

"Good—" Jim was beginning, but the Prince broke in eagerly.

"Far better to make a sally—armored knights all, as many as we may have—win to these heavy ladders and burn them as they lie!"

"Forgive me for not mentioning it sooner," Jim said, "but I was just told by Carolinus that the Earl of Somerset can't send any men—nor come himself, though he said he'd cut off his arm to be here with us. The plague has spared his castle entirely, and his common people believe this is only by the grace of God. They feel lives have been spared by

Divine Will, and it would be flying in the face of the Lord to send those so saved to die elsewhere."

The announcement produced long faces on both Brian and the Prince. The two crossed themselves.

"If it is the will of God, we must do without them. Let me see, there are my father's five knights, and ourselves, of course. . . ."

"We mustn't forget my neighbor knights, now here in the castle," said Jim.

"Say you so!" cried the Prince. "How many?"

"I don't know. Around twenty, maybe," said Jim. "Those who escaped the plague so far. I haven't had time to count them yet."

Jim was about to go on, but Brian got words out before him.

"Had we a full army with many knights behind us, as was your case in the chevauché that led to Poitiers, it might be both fast and wise to make such a lightning stroke as you suggest, Your Grace," he said. "I would enjoy it, of all things. But of knights and squires here now, wearing heavy armor, we have but this handful. To risk them on the attempt you mention, when more ladders can be built by our numerous enemy, would be like buying a jack of wine which is swiftly drunk, leaving us dry, with no hope of more."

Jim managed to get his words in then, mentally crossing his fingers for not mentioning the magick bargained from Carolinus.

"I might mention also, Your Grace, that the small spears of the goblins are pointed with a special magic metal known as Great Silver. These points can and will find the joints and other weak points in the heaviest armor, and the magic poison on the goblin spears is extremely painful."

"Hah!" said the Prince. "True knights laugh at pinpricks."

"I assure Your Grace no knight will laugh at being struck by the goblin spear-magic. I have seen, and even felt its effect, myself, when I and some of my armsmen joined to escort the Bishop of Bath and Wells safely back to the seat of his see, at Wells."

Jim gave a brief but graphic description of the reaction of those who had been pierced by the spears.

"If not removed by equal magic," said Jim, "the poison of those spears will kill. Luckily I was there and able to deny it in their wounds, so they all, including the good Bishop himself, survived."

"I see I was wrong," said the Prince, with one of his sudden and unexpected dives into honesty and humbleness. "I withdraw my suggestion, which clearly betrayed my lack of proper knowledge."

This unexpected admission threw everybody else there into a moment of unusual silence.

"It is only by sheer chance that I know it myself, Your Grace," said Jim finally. "The suggestion, otherwise, had much merit. I doubt if there is another knight or man in England, outside of those here, who also have the knowledge."

He had exaggerated more than a little by saying that what the Prince had put forth had merit. But that could do no harm. Jim hurried on to other points.

"The real question, gentlemen, is not how we may defeat an enemy who outnumbers us almost beyond conceiving but how we can make them go away for good with what small strength we have here. As I mentioned but a moment ago, the Earl of Somerset is unable to send us aid, and so our numbers are smaller than we had hoped."

"Somerset!" For a moment a frown clouded the face of the Prince.

Suddenly anxious to keep the Earl out of royal trouble, which could later cause him to become an enemy of Malencontri, Jim frantically began to cast about in his mind for something to say in the Earl's defense.

Before he could speak, the Prince's frown cleared.

"I confess I expected better of him. For he has always been cited to me as a courageous gentleman of much grace and merit, who had done noteworthy acts at the Battle of Sluys. Still, when the life of a King is at stake ... but you spoke on his reasons before, I remember. Doubtless his reasons for not coming will prove well."

"In fact, Your Grace," said Jim, "it is beyond his control. For his people, miraculously spared the plague, believe this a special grace of God, against which it would be impious to send those so spared to die elsewhere."

"It would be ill indeed to flout a gift that our Lord has given," the Prince said. "I repent me of my words, and I confess I have no movements to offer beyond my ill-thought one of the sally."

"I believe, Your Grace," said Dafydd quietly, and with such courtly smoothness that the Prince looked at him closely, "that with some archers and enough stout spearmen, we need not concern ourselves with a second attempt at escalade by the goblins. Though, this time—and I do not wish to appear to disagree with what Sir Brian said about a tower attack—my thought is that they will probably crowd the curtain walls more than the tower, which will call for as many hands there as are able to defend."

"Right," said Jim, slipping into American dialect for a second time. "It's still a question of how to drive them off. I'll ask you all, does anyone have a plan by which we could go out to meet them directly with what force we have—and get rid of them?"

"I do not—nor do I think it wise at the moment," said Brian. "Though, if we have no other choice, we must simply meet the matter manfully."

"I do not see it yet, either," said the Prince. "Though I would much desire to do it."

"I have some little experience of armed warfare," said Dafydd in his quiet voice. "But on the basis of what I see,

I would say we have no hope of doing so. Is there no way magick can even the odds, James?"

"Maybe—but if so, I haven't found it yet," said Jim. "I suggest we talk to someone who knows the goblins well— my hobgoblin here at Malencontri, since like all hobs, he is of the same breed as the goblins. I've got some questions for him, and I'd hope the rest of you will ask whatever comes to your minds. No one objects to my calling him?"

No one objected.

"Hob!" called Jim, in the direction of the chimney. There was a slightly longer pause than usual, in which the Prince nearly spoke, but changed his mind. Hob dropped out of the chimney and walked cheerfully unheeding through the flames of the fireplace, to bow to them all. This he did superbly, in the best courtier's style—his supple body built for bowing.

"You wanted me, m'lord?"

"That's why I called," said Jim. "We wanted to ask—by the way, how many hobs have we in Malencontri now?"

"I am not sure, m'lord. Over two tens of hundreds?"

"Two *thousand!?*" exploded Jim. "Angie—I mean my lady—said half of them came in last night?"

"Oh, no—begging your pardon, m'lord—they've been coming in steadily since the beginning. But there really were a lot came last night—that's true. More will be coming."

"There's no room here now!" said Jim. He had completely forgotten his three fellow humans for the moment, and they, on their part, seemed so stunned by the thought of two thousand hobs, when in the normal household a single one was rarely glimpsed, that they said nothing.

"There's no room for them now!" Jim repeated. "Can't you tell them we've got all the hobs we can use? Can't you stop them coming?"

"I'm afraid not, m'lord. The word's out."

Jim struggled against saying, *But we don't want them!* and got himself under control without speaking aloud.

"Well," he managed finally, "we brought you here to ask you some questions about goblins, and maybe with two thousand like you outside and more coming, you'd better stay in case we have more questions later. To begin with, how would we best scare the goblins into going home?"

"By killing them all?" said Hob hopefully.

"I don't think we've got enough strength for that," said Jim. "There're too many of them. How likely are goblins to risk the cost of all-out attack with everyone they've got?"

"Very likely, m'lord. As likely as we hobs would be."

The Prince stared, but said nothing.

"Well," said Jim, "we'd hope to somehow make it so hard for them they'd want to leave. Is there anyone else who could help us? I know the young dragons would be forbidden to get mixed up in anything where they might get hurt."

"That's right, m'lord. They're all very unhappy they can't fight the goblins, too. They keep telling us so."

"You've been talking to them?"

"They fly over and talk to us if they see one of us in the smoke up in the air. I mean they fly over us and call us to come higher, because they're not allowed as close to the ground as we travel. So we go up and comfort them, as a hob should."

"They listen to you?" Jim's mind fastened on that bit of information, storing it away, though he had no idea at the moment of how it could be useful. "And they are comforted, then?"

"Oh, yes, m'lord. They know we're much older and wiser than they are, so they believe what we tell them."

Now Edward stared at Hob as if he had never seen him until this moment.

"How old are young dragons?" he asked, after a few seconds.

"Sixty to eighty of our years," said Jim.

"How old is Hob here, then?"

Hob looked uncomfortable.

"That's a question about a privy matter I've never asked him," said Jim. "Courtoisie, you know."

"Courtoisie? To a hobgoblin?"

"Yes," said Jim, allowing some of the frostiness he had used in talking of Aargh as a friend, "and to dragons as well, Your Grace. Also to any animal or Natural who deserves it. All these know Magickians as friends, and this is one reason for it. We learn more from them and they from us, that way!"

"Ah . . ." said the Prince, sinking back into his chair, nodding slightly, but still looking baffled. "I should not ask, either, then?"

"No," said Jim.

"But he looks so—never mind," said the Prince, back to staring at Hob.

"Have you heard anything else that might help us from the young dragons, then?" Jim asked Hob.

"Just that the dragon fathers are starting to talk about wanting to help you fight the goblins. The mothers don't like the idea, m'lord, but Secoh's been talking so much about how *he's* going to fight them with us that it's starting to get them angry. They know Secoh fought with you at the Loathly Tower, so they respect him for that. But they don't like staying home if he's going to be boasting about being a goblin-slayer, while all the rest of them just sat there in the eyrie until it was all over."

"I thought the mature dragons had been taking and eating goblins."

"They have, m'lord—that's why what Secoh's saying is making them so angry. They know they could fight goblins as well as he could." Hob's voice became diffident. "I think, m'lord, if you went to them and asked them nicely to help, that'd be all the excuse they need for the mother dragons."

"Hah!" said Brian. "Three or four dozen dragons could be a help!"

"One or two dozen at the most, Brian," said Jim, turning

away from Hob. "There're still a lot of father dragons that won't come, because the mother dragons of their young ones will fight too hard to keep them home, or they're too old, or some other reason. The eyrie doesn't have that many dragons in it."

"Possibly," said Dafydd, "they could be useful without actually fighting, James. If you can keep Secoh out of danger, too, there would be no trouble after."

"There's that," said Jim. He spoke over his shoulder. "Hob, you sit tight for a bit while the rest of us talk among ourselves."

"Yes, m'lord." Hob sat down cross-legged on the floor with his back to the fireplace.

"I didn't mean to get into matters with Hob that deeply," Jim said, "without asking how well we're ready with the other parts of our force. Time's getting short. I just learned today the castle's got food for all the people now in it only for another month and a half. And in that time bad weather's almost sure to be on us."

"There are far too many hobs," said the Prince. "They grow more numerous every day. Cutting their number would surely make for a great saving in food."

"Hobs don't eat," volunteered Hob from the floor.

"Don't eat?" said the Prince, staring at the small figure again.

"No. We don't need to. Though we like tasting—" He stumbled and hesitated, realizing what he was about to admit.

"Hob," said Jim, "speak only when you're spoken to. He's right, Your Grace. They do not need to eat. But on to other matters: I take it that the half-dozen knights and that squire can be counted on to take the center of the vanguard if we do attack, along with the four of us here, while our neighbor knights form the flanks."

"Hah!" said the Prince, his eyes lighting up. "You need not even ask. My father's knights fret to be at swordwork—

but I must correct you, James. There are five such knights, and along with the squire, by duty they must charge around me when I take the field. So your answer is yes."

"There is also Sir Harimore!" said Brian sharply.

"Harimore?" said the Prince. "But is he not outlawed? I thought he was in France these several years."

"Certainly not, Edward!" said Carolinus, appearing suddenly. "You're thinking of Sir Harimore Wilts—respected family, north country—but young Wilts lost more than the estate was worth, including taxes. Writs were issued, he fled to France. The man here in this castle at the moment is Sir Harimore Kilinsworth, third cousin of Wilts, perfectly respectable, also a good estate, but loves weapons-use, not dice, and goes around winning tournaments like Brian, here."

"I did not remark him," said the Prince.

"He sat at table with you on at least one occasion when you joined the rest of us for dinner at Tiverton, and you've also seen him at meals here since, Your Grace," said Brian, with something very close to an edge in his voice. "He does not speak easily with anyone, even those to whom he has been named, and, least of all, volunteers conversation with his superiors."

"Ah? Like that, is he?"

"He is also a gentleman of all weapons, without match."

"Not even yourself?"

"I—" began Brian, but Carolinus broke in brusquely.

"Enough of this all this chatter. You will be glad of Harimore riding with you, Edward. There is new trouble on the way. Agatha Falon is back with the goblins, and with her is the Warlock of the West."

"Warlock of the West?" Jim blinked.

"Yes, Jim. A failed Magickian, half crazy, but with a touch of great talent. He may—I say may, only—be able to frustrate even some of the magick I promised you, Jim."

Chapter 36

"Now I remember your mentioning him!" said Jim. "When is he likely to show up here?"

"Go to your window and look out." Carolinus pointed at one that looked forward over the great gate of the castle and the front curtain wall on either side of it.

Jim got up and looked. The other men got to their feet and came to look out windows on either side. Hob started to rise, but a frown from Jim on his way to the window made the hobgoblin sink back to the floor again.

"You see the blue pennon with a sort of child's scribble in white on it?" said Carolinus. "He makes no secret of his presence, for he lives to be recognized and applauded. Actually he has no right to the title of Warlock, which he gave himself, and actual Warlocks are anyway almost nonexistent nowadays. Nine of ten parts pure charlatan, but unfortunately one part true Magickian—though unacknowledged by the Collegiate. One tenth is not enough, even if he would work his magick by our rules—which he has refused to do. He is vastly ignorant of all but a sliver of true magick, and he fills in with stage tricks."

"Can he ward himself, Mage?" asked Brian, who had picked up a few of the names for magick abilities over his long friendship with Jim.

"Anyone who can wipe the mother's milk from their lips long enough to lisp out the simplest spell can throw a ward around himself."

"Ah," said Brian. "No use trying to cut him out, then—"

"Sir Brian," said the Prince, "I will remind you that you yourself explained the necessity of not risking our scant number of seasoned knights."

"I was thinking more of what might be done by an archer catching sight of him. . . ."

"It is a long shot," commented Dafydd, "and could be somewhat difficult for any but one expert with the bow—and the portion of the target in which a broadhead arrow could kill would probably be open for the smallest of moments only after a long watch. But if it is the general wish I try it, I will do so."

"It wouldn't hurt him—remember what Carolinus just said about wards. Besides, you're too valuable otherwise to spend your time waiting for a shot to open up," said Jim.

"Quite right. Waste of time!" said Carolinus. "In any case, you have no time. His presence here means the goblins are ready to try a full attack to take the castle or die in the attempt."

"Would they indeed try to the death, hobgoblin?" asked the Prince, looking back at the small figure on the floor before the fireplace. "Are such beings really capable of such bravery? Evil creatures are always proven to be cowardly."

"Oh, yes, Your Grace. We—they, the goblins—are always brave—I should say 'fierce,' rather, as I once told m'lord, to the death!"

"Hmph!" The Prince went back to looking out the window. After a second, he turned back to Carolinus. "Do you really think they will assault us with all their force, now?"

"A triple-A-plus Magickian does not *think*, Edward!" snapped Carolinus. "We leave that to ordinary mortals. However, I will indulge you this once. I know because I know the Warlock always acts the same way. He shows up at the last minute, shows off some of his eye-catching fake magick, and then gets away again, before he could get hurt himself. You will see this for yourself, within three hours."

"Mage," said Dafydd, "may I ask a question?"

"You may essay it," said Carolinus, looking blackly at him.

"Why are the goblins so fiercely determined to take this

castle and kill the King? What profit to them in doing so?"

"That remains to be seen," said Carolinus.

"Er . . ." said Hob, from his place on the floor. They all turned and looked at him.

"As I think I told m'lord," he said diffidently, "the goblins want to kill off us hobs and take our place in human households. Someone's made them think it can be done if they first kill the King of a country."

"We haven't got much time for talking, then," said Jim. "Gentlemen, if you'll all come back here and sit down, I'll tell you right now what I want to suggest we do."

They all came back and sat—except Carolinus, who came but continued to stand, but back a little and frowning at them all, as if he had weighed their possibilities of success and found these wanting.

"Your Grace, gentlemen," said Jim. "War experts since time immemorial have maintained that the best defense is attack, after all."

He was not quite sure about such proclamations about attack, but none of his audience were in a position to dispute the phrase; he wanted to get their attention from the start.

"Hah!" said Brian happily. "I suppose if we must, then we must."

"Beyond doubt," said the Prince.

There was even something like a squeak of approval from Hob.

"Pray," said Jim, deliberately using the common fourteenth-century word, "let me continue to finish what I would say. Clearly, from what the Mage tells us, there is no time left for other choices. Attack is therefore surely not only our only, but our best, choice. Remember, we are too few to meet them in anything like ordinary fashion. Therefore our aim must be not to defeat them—which is not practical—but to convince them that if they remain we can slaughter them to the last goblin."

The frown on Carolinus' face lightened.

"The Mage's told us," said Jim, into the swing of things now and abandoning fourteenth-century language, "that they've got a trickster on their side. We will use our wits and available help to meet that advantage and overmatch it. The Mage has kindly offered to assist us in the magical area. I must not say more about it than that—the rules of the Collegiate are strict."

Carolinus' frown, which had threatened to return, vanished.

"So I plan to make use of his aid. I also plan to *appear*, at least, to have the help of the dragons, who have been taking and feasting off the goblins since they appeared here. The magic poison of the goblins can kill human beings, but since they're animals, it won't work on dragons."

"Indeed!" said the Prince. "Odd, that!"

"Your Grace—"

"No, no, continue, James. I will not speak again until you are done."

"I'm deeply grateful to Your Grace," said Jim. "So we will try to assault them all at the same time with archers, footmen, horsemen, and dragons—also some magic, which must be carefully tailored by the Mage, and what I can do to assist all forces as the opportunity occurs. We'll be doing this as the chance comes, with things that'll convince the goblins that our combined strengths are doing them far more damage than is actually the case."

He paused, but only for a second, to let his last words sink in.

"I conceive there aren't any other real alternatives to what I've suggested. Our attack, however, is going to have to come in just the right order, with all forces coordinated, to work best. Accordingly, I propose I stay here with the Mage to make that possible, since only the Mage and I can use magic to move swiftly from one force to the other. We will also go right now, he and I, to ask help of the Cliffside Dragons. If . . ." Jim glanced at Carolinus.

"I suppose so," said Carolinus, plainly not thrilled with the suggestion.

". . . and that way we can deal with them, while staying in touch with what the rest of you are doing. Your Grace, please you to ready and order the King's knights, ready to join in with our gentlemanly neighbors who have come to fight with us, under Sir Brian, who will have the direction of all our horsemen in keeping—I suggest this, Your Grace, since this is no ordinary battle, and conceiving you would rather be free to engage in the melee, than standing back with the burden of command, when your royal father's life may depend on our winning. Really good men of their weapons are scarce among us."

Once more he paused. This was the most touchy point he had to mention. Would the Prince insist on his right to command, which Jim now was openly usurping? Or yield it to Brian without objections?

"Damme, yes!" cried the Prince. "I have been well-taught in arms since I was a boy—and is that skill to be wasted when the matter is so dire? Never. Let Sir Brian lead as you advise!"

A most unusual statement from a Prince in this age.

"Very well," said Jim. That hump was over. "Then we must lose no time. Dafydd, will you pick and marshal your bowmen in the courtyard?—No one but fighting men to be there from now on until further command. I will so order all in the castle. I will announce it as my order."

He turned to Brian.

"Brian, you marshal the neighbors, the King's armed men and any else also horsed, in the courtyard, to be followed by the footmen. Your Grace, could I beg you to explain all this briefly to the King, bearing in mind we have so little time? The Mage or I will come to tell you when to move out to the attack. I think that is all—and now we two should be hastening to the eyrie of the dragons."

There was a scraping of chairs on the floor as they all

got up—broken abruptly by a cry from before the fireplace.

"But, M'lord! What of our hobs? What are we to do?"

Jim winced internally, turning to face the little hobgoblin.

"I'm sorry, Hob," he said, as gently as he could. "But while your hobs are here in great numbers, they just have reaping hooks and other ordinary tools for weapons—most of them—and no armor. They don't fit into the present plan of attack. If the chance comes up—"

"But m'lord!" cried Hob. "They came here to *fight!*"

There was a sudden extraordinary silence in the room, a stillness among those at the table. Expressions there had varied from irritation to outrage at Hob's first utterance, but now suddenly they changed. If there was one thing the folk of the Middle Ages valued above all else, it was courage— even in such soft, shy little creatures as these hobgoblins. There was no man there but doubted that the hobs going forth would result in a slaughter that would be remembered for many a year. Yet it was true—they had come to fight, and rightfully were now pleading for the chance to do so. That was an action worthy of men, let alone small creatures who hid in chimneys.

"I'm sorry," said Jim again. It always seemed to fall to him to be the axeman. "It's just not workable right at the moment. But I give you my word—I swear to you—if there's an opportunity, you and your hobs will find yourself in the thick of the battle!"

That opportunity would not come, he knew. If the real fighting forces could not do it, there would be no use sending two thousand hobs out to be gleefully massacred by their worst enemies. Their reaping hooks were the closest of close-up weapons, while the spears of the goblins were of longer reach. The hobs would be pierced fatally—for if goblins did not know where a fatal strike on their own kind would be, who would?—before the hobs could get within arms' reach of their ancient foes. But still, Jim felt like Scrooge before he had a change of heart, and he was sure

Hob was reading the falseness in his promise.

Hob said nothing, but looked down at the floor.

"Mage!" said Jim, turning to Carolinus. "Shall we go?"

The other men had begun to file out of the room—the Prince first.

"Certainly," said Carolinus. "Why not?"

They went.

I'm sorry, said Jim to himself for a third time, just before they made themselves visible in the lowest, central spot of the enormous meeting-cave of the eyrie, with its usual quota of dragons sitting around its upward-sloping sides and arguing with each other at the tops of their enormous voices. Jim prudently became visible in his own dragon-body— recognizable to the dragons as who he was. Carolinus was naturally instantly recognizable.

There was a highly unusual, sudden, complete silence. All the dragons stared.

"Dragons of the Cliffside Eyrie!" shouted Jim in his own powerful dragon voice. "We come to you for help!"

The eyes of every dragon there sharpened. Jim could almost hear each of them thinking, automatically: *If he thinks for a moment that the gold and jewels in my poor little impoverished hoard—*

"Help to save our lives!" Jim went on.

"Urg!" said Carolinus, deep in his throat—but so deep that no one but Jim heard him over Jim's own strong voice, and the now vocal exclamations of the dragons. Clearly, the "our" had stuck in Jim's Master's throat. A Mage needed no one's help to save his life.

But the dragons were now ahum—make that aroar—with a new interest. Not a loan after all, just a plain call for help, then. Dragons had never seen any reason for adventuring their own skins, human style, for duty or glory, unless one of them had lost his dragon temper, in which case reason went out the window.

But being asked about giving help was always interesting. Might they be paid for giving it?

"You have already been aware," bellowed Jim, "that many goblins are in the area."

They had, of course. Several of those present ran long red tongues around the thin lips of their crocodilelike mouths.

"They threaten Malencontri, my family and my people there," said Jim, "as well as some of my neigbors. We will fight, of course, but we are too few to withstand such a host. If they succeed, they will possibly rob the castle—"

A few growls among the crowd. The word "rob," like the word "help," provoked an automatic reaction from them.

"And in this plight," Jim roared on—the central cavern was filling up as dragons out in the passages heard the noise and came hurrying so as not to miss out on anything—"I thought of my trusty friends, the valiant dragons of Cliffside. If I could come up with something in which they could help, without putting any of them in peril—for I would not want harm to come to one of my friends—"

The thunderous humming of dragon sotto-voce comment became definitely friendly. Now, this was really interesting. No risk, and . . . what?

"We plan an immediate attack, as soon as we get back to Malencontri. We hope they will be taken aback at first by such a small force daring to come out against them. If those of you who are interested in helping would leave right behind us, you could encircle them, high up, just as we engage. Then, when I call to you with my dragon-voice, as I speak now, if you would swoop down as I know you have been doing to pick up a goblin for a snack—which has helped, for goblins are a legitimate prey for you. Hobs, by the way are not, but of course I know all of you like hobs and would not knowingly hurt them—but in the excitement of the battle there is always a danger of a mistake. You'll be able to tell the hobs from the goblins because the goblins do not have gray hair all over their body, nor do the eyes of hobs glitter, nor do they carry goblin-style spears."

Jim found now that even his dragon lungs had to pause for a breath. "—But if even one hob is taken by mistake, I personally—" and Jim shifted his dragon-voice to challenge volume "—will myself call that dragon to account—"

"AND I—" thundered Carolinus, suddenly and magically shooting up to Sea Devil height—a head-to-foot measurement that Jim had at one time estimated to be thirty feet, "—WILL LIKEWISE CALL THAT DRAGON TO ACCOUNT!"

For a second time the dragons present were uncharacteristically silent. Neither did any of them move.

Jim went on, quickly dropping his roar to a more conciliatory tone. He did not want to scare the dragons off; already they had been threatened by not only their own george-dragon, known to have single-handedly slain an ogre in fair fight, but also by the legendary, all-powerful Mage Carolinus.

"But then," went on Jim in his friendliest way, "there should be no danger to any hob, anyway, since I do not need you to actually go to earth level. I would like you to break out of your stoops well above throwing range of the goblin spears."

That should be more than enough—I hope, he told himself, for the goblins to believe that they were suddenly also under attack by the mighty, goblin-eating dragons of up-earth.

He went on talking.

"All together, the goblins must conclude that we knew you were coming to our aid, and that was what had given us the courage to sally in attack against their superior forces—we must have known you would come to help."

Dragon heads nodded. Of course, the whole world knew they were not only the most fearsome, but the bravest of all living beings—naturally.

Carolinus had discreetly shrunk back down to his normal size while Jim had gone on talking. Now, Jim looked directly at Gorbash; who, while bitterly opposed to Jim sharing and controlling his body at the time of the Loathly Tower fight, had since grown in social stature and influence among his peers, since some of the glory of killing the ogre had inevitably remained with him.

He had found he had more to gain by pretending he and Jim had been in a willing partnership than to admit Jim had simply taken contol of him, in his desperate search for Angie. In any case, Gorbash was equal to the occasion now.

"I, at least, if no one else here!" he roared. "I will confront those goblins together with the george-dragon, as we confronted the ogre!" And he rolled forward several steps in the awkward stumping gait of any dragon proceeding over a solid surface on his hind legs.

The others were thinking happy thoughts. *Glory! A place in legend! A story to tell countless younger generations of heroic deeds against the terrible goblins!*—and with no real danger to themselves. To a dragon, those about Gorbash stumped forward, roaring that they were with Jim, also.

"Thank you, dragons of Cliffside. Your kindness and neighborliness will never be forgotten. And now," Jim turned to Carolinus, "we must waste no more time, but go. Shall we, Mage?"

"Whatever you wish!" said Carolinus grimly, refusing to play the part of the one who had been behind this visit from the start.

The two of them vanished and reappeared in the Solar. The single figure of Hob, still sitting cross-legged and looking down at the floor before him, remained in the room. Jim went to him and gave him a hand up onto his feet.

"Hob," he said, "don't look so disappointed. I didn't have time to explain things to you—and then all the others were here."

Happily, Jim now found that his mind had had time to

come up with something that might help to mend his decision about the hobs, something that was only half a lie. If
it should happen to turn out that the dragons would really
turn the tide against the goblins, scaring the interlopers back
into Deep Earth to save their lives, then he could throw the
hobs in at the last minute. They could not come to much
harm if the enemy were already fleeing, and it would be
some recompense for their coming here in their numbers
with their almost useless reaping hooks, discarded knives,
and other odds and ends of cutlery.

"You see," Jim said, "it's known in military terms as
throwing in your ready reserve. I couldn't mention it in
front of the others without seeming to doubt what they can
do with their small numbers. I meant what I said. If the
opportunity is there, I'll let you know, and you can take the
other hobs in."

"In where?" asked Angie's voice, and Jim turned to see
she had just walked into the Solar. "Oh, Carolinus," she
went on, "you're still here, after all. I was afraid you'd
already left us."

"I'm waiting for my orders." There was more than a
touch of sarcasm in Carolinus' voice.

"Carolinus! Forgive me!" said Jim. "Have I been sounding that commanding? Forgive me. I never forget for a second you're my Master-in-Magick and I'd be helpless
without you—"

"No need to make a great matter of it!" said Carolinus,
in a different tone of voice entirely. "I get too used to being
listened to rather than told. Pay no attention. I'm with you
to the end of this—just as we all were at the Loathly
Tower."

"Still—" Jim was about to apologize further when Hob
broke in, excitedly.

"Forgive me, m'lord, but may I go now to tell the other
hobs what you said?"

"Go ahead," he told the little fellow with sinking heart.

Of course the others had to hear this wild promise of his. "But come right back and stay with me. I need you for information on the goblins."

"I'll be back before another spark goes out in the fire! Thank you again, m'lord. Oh, the hobs will be so happy to know they're a real ready reserve!"

He disappeared up the chimney. Jim winced.

"Quite an explanation, that of yours," said Carolinus.

"Will the two of you please tell me what you're talking about?" said Angie.

Chapter 37

". . . I was just explaining to Hob why I was holding the hobs back from the battle until there was a good time to come in," said Jim to Angie.

"When's that? You're going to use them, after all?"

Jim sat down in one of the chairs as if suddenly very weary, looking, as Hob had looked, at the floor directly in front of him. Angie studied him for a long moment.

"Carolinus," she said, "forgive me for doing something very impolite and disrespectful. I'm going to ask you to leave us here alone together for a bit, then I'll call you and ask you to come back."

"No need to ask," said Carolinus, "and nothing impolite or disrespectful about it. When you've lived as long as I have, you understand requests like that better than those who haven't. No need to ask. Just call, I'll be right back."

He disappeared, just as Hob erupted from the fireplace.

"M'lord!" he cried excitedly. "Let me tell you how happy the hobs were to hear they were a ready reserve—"

"Now you, Hob," said Angie decisively. "M'lord and I wish to be alone. Off you go, and we'll call you back in a little while. I don't have to tell you not to listen."

"Oh no, of course, m'lady, and I'll make sure no other hob does—" And in his turn, Hob vanished, up the chimney. Angie turned back to Jim, who had buried his face in his hands.

She went to him, putting one arm around his shoulders and stroking the hair of his bent head.

"What is it?" she said.

"I don't know," he said indistinctly through his hands. "I'm just out of gas. Empty inside. Maybe it's from the plague or overdoing with my magic—"

He dropped his hands suddenly, put his arms around her, pulling her roughly to him, burying his face in the warm softness that was the front of her body.

"Angie!"

She bent down, whispering in his ear as she continued to stroke his head.

"Jim, sweetheart," she whispered. "My Jim. Tell me."

"I've lost it, somehow," he said muffledly. "What I always had. Optimism, maybe."

They were pressed together into one person, and as part of that one person she read the answer through their contact without having to make him say it aloud.

"You think we're all going to lose to the goblins, no matter what you do?" she asked.

He did not answer for several seconds. "Yes," finally.

She waited. After a second he went on.

"We can't win. We can put on a brave show, but in the end they'll win because there're just too many of them. They're as unequiped as savages, with just their spears, but they want to win—they know they can win. There're just too many of them."

"How can you be sure?"

"I just am. I even enlisted the dragons, flattering them like a politician. Carolinus is going to back me with magic from everyone in the Collegiate—but it won't help. There's something missing on our side—missing in me. I've always been able to pull a rabbit out of my hat to turn the tide at the last minute, but the hat's empty now. . . . I'm just going through the motions because the people here are going to be happier to go down fighting against whatever odds under someone they trust. They trust me, and they're wrong to do it. I could always pull a little more out of myself, play harder, a few minutes longer, fight on anyway when I was out of strength. But not anymore."

"Jim," she said, "this is Angie. I know you, my Jim. You can't lose what you think you've lost. It's in there, a part of you. If it'd gone, you'd be gone. But you're still here, and so is it—this thing you think you've lost. Believe me, I know. You just go ahead and trust it to be there when you want it. It'll be there. Because you've been sick, you tire easier than you think, and so you think something's missing—but it's not. I tell you it's not!"

He pulled his face back from her and looked up at her face looking down at him.

"I wish I could believe that . . . that you're not just saying it—"

"Jim!" she said strongly. "I don't just say things to you. You know that! Have I ever?"

"No," he said slowly, "no, you never have."

He sighed deeply and his fierce grip around her relaxed.

"All right," he said, "I'll trust you. You're the only one I would trust about this. I'll just plow ahead and hope."

"Don't hope. Be sure. Go looking."

"All right!" His arms fell away. "God, but I love you, Angie. Love makes the impossible possible."

"Of course," she said. "Everyone knows that. So get busy."

He stood up, shaking himself like a dog.

"Where's Carolinus?" His voice strengthened. "And Hob?"

"Just call them."

"Carolinus! Hob!"

Carolinus was there instantly. Hob was a few seconds behind him, but came tumbling out of the fireplace in his rush, and had to do a complete forward roll to come up onto his feet.

"M'lord!" he cried. "Wait'll I tell you—" He broke off, seeing Carolinus standing there. "Forgive me, were you and the Mage talking—"

"No," said Jim. "But it's only polite to let him get a word out first."

"Terribly sorry, Mage, m'lord—"

"Nonsense!" snapped Carolinus in his normal acerbic fashion. "Jim, always take the smallest ones first. Matters are always bigger to them—any Magickian worth his salt should know that."

"I know it now," said Jim. He turned full on Hob. "What is it, then?"

"The hobs, m'lord. I told them all about being your ready reserve, and they're all so proud and happy. They all trust you, m'lord, and we've all waited so many centuries for this chance to strike back. There isn't one out there who wouldn't give his life and everything to pay the goblins back! And now they're sure you'll get them into the fight, one way or another."

"Then I better get busy thinking just how," said Jim, and suddenly he was sure he could do it. Of course it was always possible to throw them in later, just making sure first that they didn't get in the way of the men out there who could really fight. And of course they had earned the right to be in this—he had forgotten all that in his personal misery, the misery that had gone now.

"You're thinking how to use us!" said Hob joyously. "Can I tell them that, too—that you're thinking of us, m'lord, now?"

"I suppose so," said Jim, and at once Hob was gone once more up the chimney.

Angie had exorcised his feeling of failure, as if it had

been evil magic—but of course it couldn't have been that, because Carolinus would have instantly recognized it for what it was, and told him so.

It was just something he had done to himself, temporarily. What was it the English would be calling it some hundreds of years from now? A "blue funk."

Anyway, it was gone now. His old confidence was back.

"And there you are, Carolinus!" he said. "I wish I could set up a trigger to remind me what I'd like to do," he added. "Then I could get busy at something else meanwhile and not waste time, knowing I'll remember when it's due."

"For an apprentice, you—" Carolinus broke off. "Don't concern yourself, Jim. You'll be finding your own way to it."

"I suppose." To his own surprise, Jim found himself feeling not only confident again, but cheerful. *Bless Angie!* he told himself, and turning to her, said aloud, "Hob will be back in no time—"

"He will be," she said.

There was a moment's wait, then Hob shot from the fireplace, landing running forward towards Jim.

"M'lord!" he cried joyously. "I told them you were thinking how to use them. Now they're all taking turns resharpening their reaping hooks on anything they can get. It won't be over before we get there, really, will it?"

"Not if I can help it," said Jim grimly, thinking of a totally different meaning to the word "over" than Hob had in mind. "Stand by, now—for questions."

"Yes, m'lord."

Jim glanced around for Angie, to let her know by their own private code that he was back in operating condition again, but he failed to see her.

"M'lady left just now, m'lord," volunteered Hob.

"Oh, that's all right, then," said Jim, out of his regained clear-headedness. "Forgive me, Carolinus." He turned back to the Mage. "I didn't mean to ask you to come here to just

stand around. But I'm going to need to call up Brian for
the mounted men and Dafydd for the archers and footmen
while you're here, so we'll both know how ready they are.
Then I'll talk to you about necessary magick I may have to
ask you for. I wanted you to hear what they had to tell me,
too."

"Very well—if it won't take all day!"

Brian, Dafydd, he formed the messages in his mind.
*Come as soon as you can. Just think of me, and you'll be
up here in the Solar with me..*

"It'll just take a few moments," Jim said.

"You'll have to learn to speed it up," said Carolinus. "It
shouldn't."

"I mean," said Jim, "it'll take Brian and Dafydd a few
minutes to get here."

"You mean you didn't import them? Shameful!" said
Carolinus. "And here I've already put you up for membership! Teach yourself how to do that, at once!"

"The second I've got a spare minute!" said Jim desperately. "Meanwhile . . . Hob, you said once the goblins didn't
like fire?"

"Yes, m'lord. They're deathly afraid of it. That's why
they can't get into houses by going down chimneys like us.
Of course, they can't get in any way at all if there's a cross
or any other great symbol on its door, with humans inside
faithful to it."

There was no criticism of Jim intended by Hob. Nonetheless, Jim felt a slight note of disapproval in the very
words themselves, where he was concerned—he pushed it
away firmly. *I'm not Hugh De Bois,* he told himself—unfortunately, that very name brought back to mind his long-
enduring failed promise to himself to get rid of the scar on
Geronde's face where Sir Hugh had slashed her.

Roughly, he ordered himself to concentrate on matters at
hand.

"Fire would frighten goblins, then?" he demanded of Hob.

"Yes, m'lord—you could arrange a great forest fire that would creep out to the open space where so many of them are now and destroy them."

"Not practical," he said, looking at Carolinus.

"Burning living things is not allowed!" said Carolinus emphatically. "That's offense, not defense!"

"I wasn't going to consider fire that way, Carolinus," he said quickly. "I've too many practical uses for what you can lend me."

"Lend! Hah!" said Carolinus.

Jim pushed the implications of that last statement firmly from him, also.

"You remember we saw the dragons, just now," he said. "I'd like to make sure they not only threaten the goblins— just by their stooping to earth like falcons to kill—but also actually, magickally arrange for their wings to *seem* to be on fire as they do. That ought to panic the goblins."

"Oh! Yes, m'lord!" said Hob gleefully. He added wistfully. "But if you could just really set them on fire—"

"You heard the Mage," said Jim.

"They burn like torches!"

"They do?" said Jim, wincing inside. But causing his enemies to be burned alive was not in his sort of battle plan— even against goblins. A bloodthirsty hob was a new and difficult individual to adjust to. "No, we'll do it the way I just said. Now, since magic can't touch animals, we're sure the magic poison in the goblin spears can't poison the horses?"

"Certainly not!" Carolinus snapped before Hob could answer. "I explained all about the innocents to you! Magick is strictly a matter for humans and Naturals. They alone can make it, use it, be touched by human magick, but never touch any non-magick-using creature—and well is it so. Trees," he added pointedly, "are innocents."

"Quite right!" said Jim humbly—and became aware that Angie was once more standing at his elbow, but with her was the Countess Joan.

"Go ahead, James," Joan told him. "I can wait until your more important matters are done. Edward is down with the other knights, God keep him, in the first rank, and can hardly wait to sally. Someone in your castle here made him a royal banner, and the lone squire from the King's party is carrying it—a knight's duty, ordinarily, but the desire was to have all the best fighters free to fight."

"Quite right," said Jim, who had never known that before—it made sense, though, with Edward a Prince. "Good of you to wait. If you wouldn't mind stepping out for a bit, I'll send a servant or armsman to get you when we're done."

"Certainly, James." She left. Angie stayed, watching him like a personal guard.

"Good," said Jim. "Thank you, my lady. Carolinus, about that false fire for the dragons—we can talk about that in a moment. What I'm more interested in, right now, is whether you can supply other magick to ward the lower parts of both the horses and their riders. Even without poison, being stuck full of those goblin spears could drive the horses crazy—and of course the legs of the men riding them are vulnerable to the poison. If only those parts could be protected, too—oh, there you are, Daffyd."

"I am here. I wait," said Dafydd.

"I suppose I can protect that much more, too, if it's absolutely necessary," said Carolinus wearily. "I'll fight the matter of all this use of extra magick with the Collegiate, afterward."

"We'll all really appreciate it, Mage," said Jim. "Hello, Brian. Carolinus just told us his magick can possibly protect the legs and bellies of the horses and the legs of the horsemen from the goblin poison—an extra kindness."

"Hah! Thank you, Mage," said Brian. "Very grateful— James, we are ahorse in the courtyard, a damned crowded place now with all of them mounted and the footmen with spears most too long to drag. . . ."

"Good for the carpenter and blacksmith," said Jim with relief, since he had not had time to check on whether the heavy spears that had been ordered had been made, and had been planning for magickal help to produce them in time. Now that much more magick could be available for other uses. "Brian, Dafydd," he went on, "this is why I wanted you here, to know if all the fighting men are ready to move."

"We are ready now," said Brian. "The Prince rides first, by his own wish."

"God be with him!" answered Carolinus. There were "amens" from around the room. "There would have been no hope of holding him back, and destiny is not protecting *him*, yet."

"No," said Jim. "And his natural inclination to be with the fighting men . . . but I wanted to ask about your archers, Dafydd."

"They have been ready for some time," said Dafydd, "and are becoming restive. Their line will be ragged. However, I believe they will fight well. They will follow your horsemen, of course. I have found eight passable men of the bow among your forest people—that gives us fifteen archers, split in two groups, as I presume you plan to put one group on each wing, to harass the goblins who try to flow around the charge of the horsemen. Danielle, my wife, is kept back from being one of them only by the presence of our children. But she is so good as an archer that she can be as effective from the battlements as those bowmen on the ground."

"Sounds good," said Jim. "I—"

Angie was just coming back into the room, Jim saw, with Joan, who was looking fresh and even more like royalty and the Fair Maid of Kent than she had before. *Does that woman ever turn a hair?* wondered Jim. However, first things first.

"Very good!" Jim said, still answering Dafydd. "That's

to be the order of attack, then. The horsemen can if needed
fall back around the ends of the spearmen while the archers
hold up the goblins temporarily, and the spearmen will hold
their ground while the horsemen regroup for the next sally,
and the archers, having been useful with their arrows, can
then run back to the castle for more. Dafydd, what do battle-
experienced archers usually do if the enemy start coming
around the ends of the ground fighters?"

"What you just suggested, James. If no more chance remains, they are to run for the castle. The small gate in your
great one should be ready to open. They are too valuable
to lose and in no place to fight where they are, unarmored
and unweaponed except for knives. They can still be very
useful shooting from the battlements. Also they are light on
their feet to run, unencumbered."

"All right, that's settled then. I can let you both go. I'll
be talking to you in your head, Brian, if necessary. I don't
think I'll need to be in touch with you, will I, Dafydd?"

"No need," said Dafydd. "God be with you, James, up
here."

"And God be with you, indeed, James," said Brian. "You
and the Mage are the head of our fighting body." He was
already turning with Dafydd to leave.

"A moment longer, if you would be so good, Brian, Master Dafydd," said the voice of Joan. Jim turned to her. Angie
was still beside her, and he was now sure that they must
have had some arrangement for Joan to be heard before
everybody left. Brian and Dafydd stopped and turned
around.

"If you will forgive me, Sir James," Joan went on in an
unusually formal voice. "Time presses upon me after all,
and I did wish to see you all together. But what you've just
been talking about touches on one of the two matters I came
to speak to you on—the other I can tell James after you
have left. . . . But, to the first—of course I have no experience of battles, and all I know from what I have read ap-

proves the order of battle you have just settled upon, as a tried and trusty method. But may I suggest this is not the usual sort of enemy, where the knights are in strength to break through the opposing lines so that the spearmen can move up and hold what they have won. Therefore, could I propose a difference to the order you've planned?"

Bold words by a woman in the fourteenth century at a moment like this, thought Jim. But you had to admire her guts.

About to politely say "no" without further thought, however, Jim saw Angie signaling him to listen. Time was very short, but Joan should take very little of it, Jim thought. Brian's eyebrows were drawn tight together in disapproval, and Jim could imagine him saying sternly, "No offense, but what does she think she knows of the war game?"

But Jim's earlier loss of heart had given way to an almost reckless confidence.

"Tell us then, my lady," he said.

"I might just suggest, Sir James, and gentlemen, that since our fighting men are so small in number, would it not be better that the spearmen advance first? There was some evidence that among the ancients this was occasionally a fruitful way of proceeding—the horsemen to come from behind and around the ends of the spearmen, to begin to slay while the spears hold the enemy temporarily trapped."

"A bold and interesting suggestion, my lady," said Brian severely. "But what are the goblins going to be doing when they see, over the heads of the spearmen, our horsed warriors moving to take them on the flank? They will hardly ignore what is in plain sight, but turn to face them."

"In that case, Sir Brian, the spearmen move forward, themselves taking the turning goblins now in the flank. The goblins have only one poisoned spear apiece, and only one pair of eyes, likewise."

"A very pretty move in theory, my lady," Brian said, "but in practice, I have been told by such as Chandos that he

had never seen any fancy maneuvers produce anything but
confusion. The spearmen would have to make up their
minds to charge instead of hold in a eye-wink, without
thought. If we had a month to train them, or a miracle to
divert the goblins' attention while our footmen, each man
for himself, make up their minds what to do—"

"Er, Brian," said Jim, who saw this discussion getting out
of hand, "it happens I have something—not a miracle, but
a great flock of full-grown dragons with flaming wings diving on the goblins at the same time as the move my lady
has proposed. Hob, you're the expert on goblins. Do you
think the flaming dragons would hold the goblins' attention
for perhaps long enough for the horsemen to get around the
line of footmen and attack them?"

Brian happened to be standing closest to Jim, so only he
picked up the mutter under his friend's breath.

"Books, ancients, women who never held a sword or
bow, hobs—what a war council!"

But meanwhile Hob was answering, after a second of
thought.

"M'lord, I think it must. They know the dragons eat them,
they hate and fear fire. Once one of them sees a flaming
dragon diving towards him, that one is sure to cry out, and
others will then look up—they will be thrown into confusion. Meanwhile, the noble knights and other people on
horses can go attack a disordered enemy. If the spearmen
then move forward, forewarned of the dragon attack, the
goblins will not know who to fight first."

There was a long moment of silence.

"What do you think, gentlemen?" asked Jim.

After that there was unanimous approval—the experienced fighting men, practical-minded at bottom, Jim
thought, were more than a little dazzled and gratified at the
thought of dragons stooping to aid them with fire. Carolinus
observed a nonvoting silence. Brian was now emphatically
approving.

"God send we may throw them into panic," he said, "scatter them like chaff, and send them back to their Deep Earth! But if this is to be the course, I must go to the mounted men without further talk and warn them both of it and that the dragons will be on our side. You will warn us of the dragons coming in ample time, will you not, James?"

"Count on it, Brian."

"I, too, must go alert the footmen and archers to this plan, James," said Dafydd. "To save time, perhaps you might magickally return Brian and me to the places from which you called us?"

"I think I can do that—this short distance in a place I know well." Jim glanced at Carolinus, as usual hoping for some sign of approval or nonapproval, but as usual Carolinus' face gave no sign. Jim went on to Dafydd and Brian: "Tell everyone to be ready to sally, spearmen first. I've just got a matter of necessary magick to talk over with the Mage, briefly, then I'll speak to you in your heads, as I did to get you here, and you can give the word to attack."

"Good!" said Brian, very strongly indeed, as Jim sent them both on their ways. They vanished.

"My lord," said Joan, "with that dismissed, mayhap you have part of a moment for the other matter I came to speak you on." She glanced at Carolinus and then at Hob. "I would that none besides yourself and your lady wife—who already knows—should hear this. . . ."

"Speak freely," said Carolinus commandingly. "Neither I nor Hob will hear you until you ask us back into your conversation. My word and magick upon it!"

"Thank you, Mage," said Joan gratefully. But Carolinus only raised his eyebrows in the manner of someone who did not catch the last words someone else had said. "Well, I am grateful and will thank you again when this is all said. James, I have something to tell you about your Prince."

"Yes?" Jim was suddenly alert. From the beginning there had been a fear in him that the Prince would find some way—undoubtedly well-intentioned, but disastrous to the plans that all others understood. . . .

"I have known him since we were children at court together—as you know," said Joan. "Believe me when I tell you something about him."

"I'd be glad to hear it," said Jim, cautious of signing blank promisory notes, even in conversation.

"He has always been the same at bottom. Quick to fly into a temper, like all of we Plantagnets, and ready to try any rash and dangerous action on a moment's notice. But also he has been generous to a fault, even to those who have injured or tried to injure him—leaving himself open to further injuries from them. He worships all about chivalry. He would have given up his expectation of a throne to be in Lyonesse with you when, as stories say, in that final battle Arthur himself appeared only for an hour or so to win the fight."

"Yes," said Jim, with a voice deeper in his throat than he had intended. "I've seen some of these traits in him."

"I am not sure I know what you mean by 'traits,' but I am encouraged that you will listen to what further I have to say with an understanding ear. He cannot say this himself, so I must say it for him: he believes himself deeply in your debt, not only in that you rescued him from the rogue Magickian in France, but for saving his father from Tiverton and many other things, and he has pledged himself to obey you and your friends without question in all things."

She stopped talking. Jim did not know quite what to say.

"And now," she spoke into his silence, "having said that, I will go.—Mage and Hob, thank you for your courtesy. There is no reason to magickally stop your ears further."

She turned toward the door.

"My lady," said Jim, finding his tongue, "I don't have the words to thank you and him—"

"None are necessary," she said. "I leave you here. May God be ever with you, Angela."

The door closed behind her.

Chapter 38

"That was fast," said Jim, staring at the door that had just closed behind the Fair Maid. "Said what she came to say and that was that."

"She knows you're busy," said Angie.

"Still, I appreciate it. It's good news when you hear the Prince will obey his advisors. He could wreck things. Strange young character."

"Not so strange if you were in his shoes," said Angie, "having to play the royal one moment and ask favors of his inferiors the next. I think he's done a brave job of it—but you're busy."

And Angie turned and started toward the door.

"No. Don't you leave!" said Jim. "I may need you to help me remember—I want you here."

Angie came back and sat down in one of the chairs, looking up at him. Jim suddenly realized that, in spite of the effort involved, he had been, like Carolinus, on his feet. Planning a battle evidently was something nobody did in anything less than a crisis mode. Gratefully, he sat down again and returned his attention to Carolinus.

"Where were we?" he asked. "Oh, yes, you'd just agreed to ward the legs of the horses for those on horseback. Now, about the flaming dragons—I'll have to bedragon myself for a moment, fly up and tell them when to go into their act, and about the flames, if that's really to happen. So, how about that, Carolinus? Is it possible to give them all the illusion of flaming wings—I'd better be able to demonstrate on myself that it wouldn't burn them or do their wings any damage—that reminds me, I've got to brief Secoh about this. I'll call him in—I wonder where he is—"

Secoh materialized in the Solar, facing them and looking startled.

"Well, thanks, Carolinus," said Jim. "It's good of you to bring him in. I was wondering how to specify his location."

"Exactly the reason I brought him instead. All right. He's here—speak to him, but by the way, Jim, you'll need to watch yourself on that with the Collegiate. A good number of them think that these little magick coups you've pulled off from time to time have gone to your head. . . ."

"Little!" said Jim, remembering his struggle, with body as well as mind, to acquire the magic staff with which he had been able to safely lead a few people—who were anything but close friends of each other—in a human wall to hold back a tremendous magic force. It had been the only way to drive one of the greatest of Great Demons, Ahriman, back into the Kingdom of Demons and Devils.

"Well, possibly for an apprentice, something more than little. But never mind that. Of course, the illusion of flaming wings can be possible, for you if you're in dragon form and them when necesary. Illusions are not magickally expensive. Just tell them to say 'HAH!' and they'll light up. If they want to turn it off, say it again. If they want to light up a second time, say it once more. Each time it's said, it'll change back to what it was just before. You can use the same word yourself to demonstrate its use to them."

Secoh made an embarrassed, semistrangled sound in his throat. Jim and Carolinus both looked at him,

"Er, Mage," he said, shifting uncomfortably on his back feet, upright, "we dragons don't much say 'hah'—indeed, it's very seldom. In fact, we never say it."

"Try it now," said Carolinus.

"Well . . . hah . . ."

"Louder, marsh-dragon!" snapped Carolinus. "Roar it out!"

"HAH!" exploded Secoh in desperate earnestness, deafening them all in the confines of the Solar. The deafness went away immediately, however, Jim noticed. Carolinus' doing, of course.

"Demonstrate to your dragon friends," said Carolinus. "I chose it just because you don't use it ordinarily. You now understand?"

"Yes, Mage," said Secoh, humbly.

"Then off with you to wait for the adult dragons—"

"They're on wing already, Mage, but staying just out of sight of Malencontri."

Thank whatever dragon gods there be, Jim said to himself, for the caution and wisdom of full-grown dragons. Secoh's youngsters would have been unable to resist the temptation to edge in to see what how the battle was going—and so be seen ahead of time.

"All the better," Carolinus was saying to Secoh. "Go let them practice saying 'HAH!' and tell them Jim will be along to explain the harmless fire from their wings to frighten the goblins." Secoh winked out.

"There you are, Jim," said Carolinus. "I hope that pleases you."

"It does indeed. But now we come to the hard part."

"Hard part?" Carolinus frowned.

"Yes," said Jim. "I realize the toughness of this demand, but it's critically important."

"Well, I told you I had a drawing power now on all the Magickians of the Collegiate—but we can't work miracles, you know—you ought to know."

"I do," said Jim. "I do! This doesn't require a miracle, but it could take a large amount of magick. In a few words, could you make complete, individual wards around each of our footmen, the spearmen and archers alike?"

Carolinus glared.

"How many of them are there?" he said.

"Just a minute. I'll find out."

"You don't have that information at the tips of your fingers?"

Jim ignored the question. Mentally, he spoke to Dafydd in Dafydd's mind only.

"Dafydd, don't let me interrupt whatever you're doing. I'm finishing up my talk with Carolinus. As soon as it's done, we can attack—as we decided, the spearmen and archers go first, then the mounted men. But I need to know how many of both I'm talking about with the Mage. Can you think the answer?"

"Fourteen of what may by courtesy be called archers, and two hundred and nine spearmen," thought back Dafydd promptly, as if he had been answering mental calls for years, instead of for the first time, as now.

"Two hundred and twenty-three, altogether!" said Jim aloud, as shocked by the number as he fully expected Carolinus to be.

"Two hundred and nine!" echoed Carolinus.

"Oh—and fourteen archers," said Jim unhappily. "Two hundred twenty-three, all told."

"Full wards? Two hundred and twenty-three adult humans?" said Carolinus. "Impossible! Totally impossible, Jim!"

"This is war, you know," said Jim.

"I don't care if it's a country dance! Two hundred and twenty-three living bodies—"

"That's the point," said Jim. "To keep them alive against the goblin magic on the goblin spears."

"Why don't you just ask me to disarm all the goblins, magickally? Do you seriously ask me to go back to face the Collegiate and confess I spent the open draws on their magick to that extent?"

"Could you actually disarm them, if you had the magick available?"

"Certainly not!" said Carolinus. "For eighteen reasons. The first being that it would need the complete magickal resources of everyone in the Collegiate—resources painfully built up over centuries. Second, it would be a direct

violation of subsection one of the *Encyclopedie Necromantic*—"

"What subsection one?" demanded Jim. "There's nothing
like that in my copy."

Carolinus glared at him.

"The subsection one that forbids us to use all our magick
except to defend the Collegiate itself. These are things you
aren't supposed to be privy to until you're a member of the
Collegiate yourself. The flat answer is no!"

"But you might be able to individually ward completely
our two hundred and twenty-three footmen."

"Nonsense!"

Jim was thinking. He decided to talk to Dafydd again,
mentally.

"Dafydd?"

"Yes, James?"

"How did you get so many spearmen, Dafydd?"

"There was less than no difficulty. In fact, I had almost
to fight some of the older men and lads below the age of
fifteen, who were bound to be in the line, but I told them
the big spears were too heavy—not to carry, but to use
well—and that some were needed to defend the walls here
if those in the field all fell. It is settled now, though there
was one bad moment when Tom Kitchen swore he was
fifteen and May Heather swore he was not—the two are
betrothed, I understand."

"Good. Well, hang on a little longer. I'm still talking
available magick with Carolinus. We may be able to protect
the footmen to some extent magickally. Call you back in a
bit. Tell Brian it won't be long."

"I will do that." There was almost a chuckle—a rare thing
from Dafydd. "He is having some difficulty as his horsemen
grow restive and eager to sally."

"Well, Jim," Carolinus sounded as if he was chewing on
ground glass as he spoke, "I regret to refuse you on this
wish of yours, but—"

"Not at all," said Jim. "I understand. The death of my men and neighbors, the taking of this castle and the slaughter of all of us inside it—including the King—cannot be compared in importance with maintaining the highest possible level of the Collegiate members' hoards of magickal energy."

Carolinus glared at him, but said nothing for a long second. Jim, judging he had hit the other harder than at any time so far, was wisely quiet. He knew, as well as the rest of the world, that Carolinus had a very real conscience, best left to work by itself. He also knew Carolinus had been not only one of the founders of the Collegiate, but the leader of those who had.

"They will probably throw me out of the Collegiate," grumbled Carolinus.

Now it was Jim's turn to say it.

"Nonsense!" he said it loudly. "Practically the founding father of the organization? If any Magickian suggested it, the rest would arise and destroy him."

"You do not understand yet, Jim," said Carolinus, a little sadly. "Men must die from time to time. Friends—dear friends, even—must be left to be killed, castles must fall, if necessary. The goal is the future, as well as we can see it, and all that has been built towards it cannot be destroyed for one situation, one battle. . . ."

Jim still said nothing, though this was also new to him.

"On the other hand . . ." said Carolinus, "the death of this present King before his time . . ."

"So," pounced Jim, "there is a reason, then, to ward these footmen? Weighed down by great twelve-foot spears meant to stop everything up to charging horses, they'll be standing targets for the goblins' magic spearpoints. Goblins can use all the magic they want, evidently, but we have to be misers with ours?"

"I said you didn't understand," said Carolinus testily. He hesitated for an additional moment. "Perhaps I could ward all these men of yours, but for only a very short time—say a quarter of an hour."

"You know," said Jim, "that no battle was ever decided in fifteen minutes."

"I'm not sure that's true—how long a battle do you expect?"

Jim tried to remember how long the battle had been in Lyonesse when Arthur had reappeared—a white-bearded man by this time, but still an unbelievable warrior—and once more led his unaging, loyal knights to victory over the mercenary army that the Earl of Cumberland had managed to introduce into a land where ordinary humans were not supposed to go.

The Lyonesse knights, outnumbered even with Arthur leading them, had fought until they were weary.

"Six hours," Jim said, playing safe in his estimate.

"Impossible." But this time Carolinus said the word calmly and almost sadly. "Complete wards for six hours for your men simply cannot be done."

"Well . . ." said Jim, "if we were lucky—maybe just five."

"Still impossible. I could give you a full hour, but that would be the limit."

"One hour—fighting an enemy that outnumbers us the way the goblins do? An enemy facing only a handful of neighbors and the people of one estate and castle! There's no way we could possibly win in one hour. Look—maybe I can pull a rabbit out of my hat. Give us four and a half hours, and we'll try to do it in less, so you can take back what's left over! Otherwise, it means we're going to lose some good people, when we're still struggling with the goblins and the wards are suddenly gone, but—"

The argument degenerated into a sordid bargaining session. Carolinus held what Jim badly needed, but with the lives of those he knew and loved up for grabs, Jim was no more ready to lose this fight than any other he had ever been in.

Chapter 39

It was finally settled that the footmen would be completely warded for an hour and a half; the horsemen and their mounts would have their wards for three and a half; the dragons would have their harmless wing fires for the duration of the battle, not to exceed five hours, and up to two hundred dragons would be so equipped.

"—Moreover," wound up Carolinus, "you'd better go warn them right now what to expect, if they're already in the air, set to go. They're animals, after all, and an animal's instinct, suddenly faced with something it's never met before, is to turn and put distance between itself and whatever it's seeing. I remember, shortly after I qualified for my Magickian's robe, I ran into a large bear from downwind, where he couldn't catch my scent before he saw me. I'd known him well, talked to him before, but he'd never seen me in my robe. He took off like a loosed arrow."

"You're right," said Jim. "We all through, here?"

"As far as I'm concerned," said Carolinus. "Don't waste time changing to your dragon-shape and flying out to them. Make yourself invisible and I'll send you to them. Then you can change into dragon and appear flaming before their eyes."

"Thanks," said Jim, and other words popped out of him as he vanished, before he could stop them: "If you're sure you can spare the magick."

"Jim," said Carolinus, in mildly reproving tones, "you know this is barely a drop in the bucket compared to what you were asking for."

Jim's invisible ears burned.

"You're right," he said, out of his nothingness, "I'm sorry, my tongue ran away with me."

"Interesting metaphor, that," commented Carolinus, and Jim found himself some three hundred feet above thick forest, with the huge-bodied, mature male dragons. How the young dragons must have pleaded—in vain—to be among them! Here together, the fathers of Cliffside Eyrie looked like all the dragons in the world, filling the sky, moving around each other and him in tight circles. They were all demanding of each other and Secoh, in voices that could be heard half a mile away, when Jim-dragon was going to show up.

His sudden appearance in their midst abruptly silenced the enormous voices. The dragons took one look at his flaming wings and headed for the horizon in all directions. Carolinus had been right about animals and instinct.

"It's me—Jim-dragon!" he roared in his own enormous dragon voice. "With the flaming wings you're going to wear! Come back here!"

His voice easily carried to the furthest of them. Cautiously, one by one, they began to return until they were back, circling again. They were unusually silent. Not even Secoh, who had flown back closest to Jim, said a word.

"Dragons of Cliffside!" roared Jim. "You see me now in this fearsome form with the flaming wings you yourself will wear and use to terrify the goblins. However, the fire you see is purely magickal. Far from being burned by it yourselves, you will not even feel it."

Mutters of sub-subtoned pleasure at this reassurance came from his audience.

"But I have come to ask you all to pull out of your dives when you stoop upon them. Pull out at least a good double dragon's-length above their heads. Who, better than I, knows our natural dragonly urge to close with an enemy once our blood is up? But the fact is you will terrify more goblins if you stop just out of reach of them than you will if you come right to ground and start killing individuals. Besides, that will be the wise thing to do, as mature dragons like yourselves will at once recognize. Can I count on you all to do that?"

A rising, murmurous roar, a sound only dragons could achieve, came from them all. They were not all sure it *was* that wise. . . .

"I've just come from Mage Carolinus," Jim went on hastily. "And it was his suggestion this is the best way for dragons to begin attacking a large number of goblins, all with spears." It was a lie, of course, but one in a good cause, he told himself.

The murmur changed to a general roar of assent. These dragons, Jim knew, were delighted that they did not actually have to fight. In fact, they had no intention of doing so, no matter what Jim wanted. Why risk yourself for neither gold nor gratification? But they were happy at seeming to be talked into doing just what they, themselves, wanted.

"Thank you, my cousins of Cliffside!" said Jim. "I know what it will cost you to hold yourselves back, but it's the only way to win. And our ground fighters are badly outnumbered, they desperately need your help—" Having taken Carolinus' name in vain, Jim had now done the same with all his human defenders, of whom not merely the human knights, but all of them, would have hated him from this day forward if he suggested they needed dragons to save them from anything.

"Now—I'll tell you when I want you to come to our aid. I'll send a magickal signal to Secoh when I'm ready for you to go into your act—I say 'act' in the sense of making a *diversion!*" he added hastily. A large martial-sounding word had worked with the hobs.

It worked again, here. The dragons roared final agreement. Carolinus yanked him back to visibility, wearing his human body again, and in the Solar.

"Well done," said Carolinus.

"Thanks. So you saw and heard what I said to them just now?" said Jim. "I wish I could do that."

"For the last time," Carolinus breathed out an exasperated breath, "stop wishing. You'll find your own ways of doing such things. How can I get it through your head that we all work at our art differently? You already do things I can't do—"

"I do?" Jim looked at him, astonished.

"—and don't ask me what they are. I've no intention of telling you. All right, what now?"

"Now," said Jim, "we actually do attack. Angie, Hob, you stay with me, here. You, too, Carolinus—if you don't mind. Forgive me—I don't mean to sound demanding, But I might need you once the fighting starts."

"No doubt."

Jim threw a mental question to Dafydd: "Are your footmen ready to attack?"

"All ready," was Dafydd's answer.

"They'll be protected by magick for a short while—after that they're on their own. Start moving them out. If they haven't been told yet, tell them now. They'll lead the attack, but the horsemen will be right behind them, ready to ride around them and stop the goblins' rush."

"I've already told them, James," thought Dafydd, "They took it well. They are eager to the fight as the mounted men—and proud indeed to go first!"

"Good. Now I've got to warn Brian about that," Jim said, and switched his mental connection to his other friend. "Brian, are your horsemen ready to attack?"

"Ready, and champing at their bits. Not happy about the common men going first, of course—but the Prince told them and no one murmured."

"Excellent. Give them my apologies, Brian, and tell them I've been talking to Carolinus. We're going to have help from the Cliffside Dragons, flying on wings that're aflame."

"Sensible idea, that. Will they really fight?"

"I've asked them not to. Just to stoop almost to the goblins, then rise again. They agreed. They're just there to frighten the goblins and disorganize them."

"Good! Our men will want to win the day if it's to be won at all!"

"I'm glad they feel like that. By the way, you know the Prince is to give the command to attack. I want him to do that, but after that don't let him get carried away. You're to be the actual commander in the field. Once you're in the battle, you tell him what orders to give—otherwise, he can simply fight his own fight."

"I will not be easy in my mind doing that James. Aside from his rank, he was at Poitiers, and I was not."

"Do it anyway," said Jim, "or call me in your head, and I'll explain it to him in his—but I don't want to do that unless I have to. I've got to go now,"

"Rest easy James. If must be, I can deal with him out here. Anon."

"Take care—" Jim stopped himself from adding the words "—of yourself." He had not wanted to mention to Dafydd or Brian that the witchery of Agatha Falon or the magic of the Warlock of the West—if he was still there— might somehow cause an unhappy turn for the human side. The less distractions they had, the better.

If Falon and her Warlock were active, it would be for only a short time, anyway, until Carolinus put a stop to whatever damage they could do. Hastily, Jim withdrew from Brian's mind and contacted the Prince mentally.

"Your Grace, this is James, speaking to you. Carolinus and I have decided that the best use can be made of our magick and the small force at our command if your horsemen follow the footmen at first, taking care not to override or trample them in their eagerness to get to the goblins."

"Is this really the necessary way, James?" came back in clear, sharp thought from young Edward. A Plantagnet quickness, there.

"It is, Your Grace," Jim said, and without waiting for an

answer, he continued, "—God speed you. If ready to take the horsemen out after the spearmen, you perhaps would wish to alert them so, now."

"Then I will so command. None of your horsed gentlemen will disobey my order. I shall also myself ride behind the footmen, but first of all others. I would like to see the simple country knight who would dare ride before me."

"Thank you, Your Grace. I've warned Brian you might do so. Also, there will be dragons helping us, too—he can tell you something more of them."

"Dragons? Very well. I will not delay you longer, James. I take it you may speak to me like this during the engagement with this rabble of Naturals?"

"Yes, Your Grace."

"Good. Go then."

Jim broke the connection.

"You make rather free with my name, I notice, Jim," said Carolinus dryly.

"Forgive me, Mage, but I'd make free with anything that will help us now."

Jim went to one of the windows to look down at the courtyard. Already the spearmen and archers were massing in orderly fashion by the great gates, now opening. The Prince could be seen on the horse he had ridden into Malencontri originally, giving his order to the horsemen—no sign of resentment from them so far, but it was hard to tell from this angle and distance. RHIP—"Rank Has Its Privileges"—was one of the dearest-held rules of armies since time immemorial.

He became aware of Angie at the window on his left, Carolinus at the one on his right. The Prince finished speaking and turned his horse's head about, ready to lead. The great gates, cranked out by the men on duty there, were now open, and the footmen, led by Dafydd—on a horse today, so he could both be seen and better heard by those he commanded—were already going through.

The fleet-footed archers could now be seen running to the right and left, once they were beyond the drawbridge, to cover the emergence of the spearmen. Surprisingly, the thickly surrounding horde of goblins retreated almost entirely into the surrounding woods.

The sun was shining brightly, but the earlier morning's breeze had fallen, now failing to flap or ruffle any article of the footmen's clothing. Behind them, the Prince had positioned his horse ready to follow.

Jim felt a strange urge to be down there with them. He pushed it back. Had the feeling been just conscience? Or a primitive urge that had grown in him, after the several years now that he and Angie had spent in this violent age, to join in the fight?

In any case, it was out of the question. His place was up here, where he could see not only all of Malencontri's defenders once they closed in battle with the goblins, but all of the cleared ground in front of the castle that would be the battlefield.

"They're wearing helmets still," said Angie suddenly. She was speaking of the helmets Malencontri had been able to issue to the spearmen. They would be little use against the goblins; but wearing them made the footmen feel rather as if they were accoutered like real warriors. They had always produced that effect before on the castle staff, when they had been needed to look like men-at-arms on the curtain wall, to the eyes of enemies threatening the castle.

"Maybe," said Jim, turning to Carolinus, "I'm wrong, maybe I ought to have told them all more detail about the magick you're going to use to help them. But it seems to me that the fewer any one of them out there—except the dragons, who had to be told—knows of the magick involved here, the better."

"Jim," said Carolinus, "there are moments when I no longer despair of your hopes of becoming a Magickian of worth."

The chatter of the hobs on the roofs suddenly rose to a clamor.

"And here come the goblins!" said Angie.

The footmen had emerged from the gates and begun to spread out. With that, suddenly the goblins surged forward, a wave of bodies alight with glittering eyes and glinting spears. The spearmen were spreading out to form a single line across the space some thirty yards beyond the moat.

Suddenly impatient with the closed window before him and the feeling of separateness from what was happening beyond it, Jim threw open the glass. The keen, cold air of the slight breeze cooled his face, and sounds from outside the castle wall came more sharply to his ears.

The spearmen's line was complete; their last man had joined its right end. Dafydd, mounted on his horse before them, called a command, the words of which Jim could not quite make out. The spearmen gave a roar and charged the oncoming goblins. The horsemen poured out behind then, the Prince and his flag-bearer riding two horse-lengths in front. The great gates were now closing. They could not be quickly opened again in case of a need for a sudden, rapid retreat.

The smaller gate set into the left-hand great gate could be opened in a flash, but that was only capable of letting in one person at a time—or two together, in a pinch. In the courtyard, however, men were standing by it, ready to rescue those they could, if the need arose.

Out in the open area, the Prince raised his sword and shouted. The riders broke into a gallop forward, which almost immediately had to be reined back to a trot to stay behind the spearmen.

The goblins, meanwhile, checked for a moment by this new spectacle, began anew to boil forward to meet the spearmen—some of them meeting the attack head-on while others sought to come around the ends of their line. The archers, each equipped with an extra quiver of arrows, had halted, calmly stuck half a dozen of their shafts into the ground before them, and then begun to take them up one by one, to fire into the lead goblins.

Perhaps surprised at this unfamiliar weapon in the hands of opponents who could kill from beyond the reach of even their thrown spears, the goblins stopped again for a brief interval. But seeing how few these long-distance slayers were, they flooded on again. The horsemen, at a command from the Prince, had split themselves into two groups, each coming around an end of the footmen to meet the goblins.

To Jim's eyes watching from above, everything being done by the human fighters, with the exception of the archery, was being performed both clumsily and in an undisciplined manner. Then he realized that he had been expecting to see an orderliness of attack all but unheard-of in any fourteenth-century battle. Particularly was this true in the case of the horsed gentry, who were used to going, individually and directly, straight toward the enemy, and to hell with anything and anyone in their way.

For a short time, the attack of these horsemen, coming on top of the effect of the arrows, checked for a third time the forward moment of the goblins trying to go around the end of the line of footmen, even as the central part of the line, with its longer, heavier spears, was pushing back the light-bodied multitude of goblins in front of them. For that brief period, they—and the trampling, biting and kicking horses—seemed to be making a battle of it that had a promise of success.

But then the archers, their two quivers apiece emptied, began, one by one, to turn and run back to the small door in the great gate, where other, filled, quivers were waiting to be handed to them. Taking advantage of what they must have thought of as the first signs of retreat, the goblins forged forward again, trying to get around both horsemen and spear-line.

With a jerk, Jim came out of something very like a trance.

He had been as caught up in what was happening before him as if he indeed had been down there with the castle's small army.

"Secoh!" he called mentally, commandingly. "Get the dragons there! Now! Tell them to dive on the goblins who seek to surround our men!"

"We're coming, m'lord!" Secoh's mind called back.

Chapter 40

The dragons came. It was fairly early in the afternoon, but already the sun of these English latitudes was a red ball approaching the tops of the trees to the west. Jim knew it would seem to hang there for hours before finally slipping from sight. Through the daylight, the magic fire on the great spreading dragon wings seemed to burn somewhat palely, but it was more than plainly visible in the light of the declining northern day.

Meanwhile, the dragons had encircled the field, and were beginning to dive on the goblins.

High voices shrilling in panic and warnings, the goblins scattered at the first dives, forgetting all about the enemies on the ground before them. Clearly, each had in mind one thought only—*Not me! Let the one stooping closest pick anyone but me!*

With this change in battle fortunes, the footmen and horsemen plainly appeared to draw fresh strength—though the horses themselves seemed somewhat of the goblins' minds, but under the urging of their riders, they pushed forward against the disorganized goblins, and for the first time hope woke in Jim that they actually might win, and the goblins might be driven back to Deep Earth.

But the panic of the goblins did not last. It was unbelievable, Jim thought, that they should be able to adapt to changes in the fortunes of the day this quickly, without an obvious leader and organization. They must simply all think more alike than humans would in a similar situation. Already they were starting to notice that the dragons dived, but did not come all the way down with their fiery wings, to set a ring of goblins ablaze. . . .

If it was true, they clearly seemed to reason, that they had no real intention of coming to earth and spreading fire like a plague, then the dragons above them could be ignored.

The goblins closed again, drove forward, and began to push both the horsemen and the spearmen back, apparently reckless of the number of their own killed to gain the ground. It was either extreme bravery on their part, or—thought Jim, remembering the scarred, cut-up figure of Tiverton hob, limp in Hob's arms after some days of being tortured by goblins—an extreme callousness even to the sufferings or death of their own kind.

They fight like animals in a pack, Jim thought—forgetting everything except tearing into whoever was opposing them.

Then Secoh, his own wings flaming, scrapped the day's plans. He had been diving with the Cliffside Dragons and also pulling out short of the ground. But now, instead of pulling out of his dive, he went down right to earth in the midst of the goblins, killing the goblin that was his objective, but also staying down there, striking right and left with his fiery wings—setting no fires, but killing several more goblins each time he struck out with both powerful wings.

The goblins around him scattered again—but not far. They began to throw their spears at him from a distance. Already two of those spears had found lodging between the horny scales that helped to protect his back. Secoh, untouched by the magic in the spears, was clearly now in a dragon rage—that instinctive response to danger of his race, which as a mere marsh-dragon he had once believed he had lost, but found again when he had joined the old, stroke-crippled Smrgol in fighting the huge rogue dragon, Bryagh.

"Secoh!" thought Jim, furiously. "Get back out of there! They'll end up killing you. Do what the other dragons are doing!"

"M'lord!" came back Secoh's thought, triumphantly. "They did not fight at the Loathly Tower. I did! I'm different!"

"Different enough to get killed—and I need you to pass on my orders to them. They'll all get carried away and want to come down, too—and all get killed faster than you will! Get up in the air again, Secoh! That's an order!"

Dragons had no experience with orders given or taken. Jim held his breath against Secoh ignoring him. But Secoh had been too close to him and other humans too long.

Heavily, he took to the air and rose towards the heights, shaking himself like a monstrous cat as he went, until the embedded spears finally fell from him one by one. Jim breathed out in relief. Dragons had a remarkable resistance to infection. Secoh's spear wounds should heal cleanly enough.

But the space among the goblins where Secoh had been was already filled in, and there was no doubt now that both the horsemen and footmen were being pushed back towards the castle, faster and faster.

It's my fault! thought Jim, feeling cold inside. *I should have kept us all in the castle, in spite of the damned eagerness of all of them to get at the enemy. We might have stood them off there. An unusual, heavy snow might have come to drive them off—a dozen things! I let myself get carried away, too—*

But Hob was suddenly in front of him.

"M'lord! M'lord—they need us. Can't we go now?"

No! thought Jim, furiously. *Not the blood of these on my conscience, too. . . .*

However, now there was Angie before him and just behind Hob—who was now down on his small knees with thin arms held up in supplication.

"Let them go if they want," Angie was saying, in a clear, strong voice. Behind her a little way was Carolinus, with a strange, hard look on his face.

"Let them go!" echoed Carolinus.

"Don't ever kneel to me!" snarled Jim, yanking Hob to his feet by one of the upraised arms. "Go then—all you hobs—if that's what you want!"

Hob turned, and in one dive was into the fireplace and gone up the chimney. They heard his voice calling something brief but not understandable, and an answering wave of shrilling voices so numerous as to seem to make the castle tower itself vibrate.

"Look!" said Angie.

Jim, who had turned his eyes from what was outside the window, turned to it again.

"Open the gates!" he cried as soon as the shrilling died down and his voice could carry clearly to the gatekeepers. The heavy windlasses that operated the two massive leaves of the gates began to creak, bringing them open, and the equally heavy bar was jerked up. But the stream of hobs were not waiting for a way to be opened. They were heading for the battlefield above gates and curtain wall alike, on wreaths of smoke, and with a brown, thick cloud of it rolling across the ground before them.

The cloud and the hobs thronging behind it came to the goblins and hid the goblin front lines. The hobs dived into the smoke and were lost to sight, and the smoke spread to hide all the area where fighting was going on. The shrilling of multitudes of high voices rose, those of hobs now added to those of the goblins. Together they rang in the heads of those in the castle, seeming to threaten deafness—certainly to those humans fighting on the ground.

The footmen and horsemen emerged from the smoke, retreating, taking off their helms and coughing or otherwise struggling for breath as they reached clear air. They streamed toward the opening gates. The dragons above, their wings still aflame, had with instinctive caution stopped diving, though they still circled overhead, interestedly watching.

By now the great gates were wide open. The human fighters straggled in through them, swearing, still coughing and sneezing, their eyes streaming. When all were inside, the gates started to close, then stopped with a jerk.

No order to stop them had come from Jim or anyone else in the tower.

. "Close the gates!" shouted Jim. "The hobs can come back in over them."

The gates began to ponderously creak shut again.

But there was no sign of the hobs retreating. The smoke still hid their battle with the goblins. Swirls of momentarily clear air showed fleeting glimpses of hob or goblin bodies in one heaving mass—clearly, under the smoke the battle was still continuing furiously. Jim, Angie and Carolinus continued to watch through their opened windows, and a faint, acrid odor from the smoke now reached even to their nostrils, as well.

Jim found his teeth clamped close together.

Hob! he called mentally, finally, desperately. But the hob who had always responded instantly to his calls all these years did not answer.

Jim started to pace up and down, unable to stand still.

"I can't stand this any longer!" he said at last. "I've got to see what's going on there!"

"Jim! Don't you go there!"

"Have to," he said between his teeth. "Aside from the fact I'm going crazy up here, they're part of our army, and I've got to find out how the hobs are doing. Unless magick can help me see from here, somehow. Carolinus, is there any way to—"

"See through that smoke cloud from this distance?" said

Carolinus. "None I know of. Get down in the cloud and I can help you see. You'll still have to look through the smoke, but you'll be able to see better than anyone else at the same time. But I don't know if I can let you go."

"You can't stop me—" Jim began, and then felt something he had never known and never expected—he felt his mind seized. Not all of it—his thinking and his physical body was still under control—but some part of it that was concerned with his control of his magickal energy was now held in an immovable grip. He could not remember, nor even conceive, of how to handle the energy to put it to use. He was suddenly magickless.

"There's a counter to this," said Carolinus, almost sadly. "You'll learn it once you're accepted into the Collegiate. But until then, you've no way to get loose. You're the surety for all the magick the Collegiate lent you through me. If you die, there's no hope of ever recovering it. If you live, you will pay it back somehow. It may take you a hundred years, unless you win the day here and save the King—in which case the debt will simply be written off. Otherwise . . ."

Angie said nothing. But the expression on her face approved of what Jim was hearing. But in spite of the hold on him, Jim's wits were still operating.

"On the other hand," he said between his teeth, "if you keep me here, when if I went down to see the situation, maybe I could make sure of saving the King after all—the blame'll be yours, not mine. Do you want to spend a hundred years yourself, paying it off?"

"It wouldn't take me a hundred years," said Carolinus, with the sad note in his voice now plain, "even if the Collegiate didn't write off the debt in my case. Jim, believe me, it's my best judgment you don't go."

"And mine!" said Angie.

"For all that's sensible. Angie!" cried Jim, close to raving. "I'm warded! Nothing's going to happen to me!"

"How do you know? That smoke is magic—hob magic. Maybe there's something about it that could make your ward vanish somehow! Something you can't imagine! Couldn't that be so, Carolinus?"

"It's possible," said Carolinus.

Jim found his jaws so tightly clamped that it was a struggle to part them enough to speak.

"I've got to go!" he said.

Angie said nothing. For a long moment, neither did Carolinus.

"God help me," Carolinus said then—the second time Jim had ever heard him say anything religious, profane or otherwise. "If it comes to that, I'll pay off the debt myself. A human can only do what a human can do, using his best judgment, and in this case the judgment is yours, Jim."

Jim felt himself released.

"Good!" the word shot out of him.

"You're only in half-armor, Jim!" said Angie—a last, desperate protest.

Jim was suddenly in full armor, using his own magick, and belted and sworded.

"Throw me my helmet. Where's my shield?"

"I'll get them—" Angie was already in motion towards the lesser press, or cupboard, where Jim's armor and weapons were kept apart from their ordinary clothing. "But you've only a mail shirt on."

"With a quilted vest under it, and a ward around me! I'll be all right, I tell you, Angie!"

But she had already handed the helmet to Carolinus, who was raising it to place it on Jim's head, and Angie held up the heavy wooden shield for him. He ran his left arm through the nether strap and grasped the forestrap strongly in his fist.

She kissed him hard. He stood, impatient to be off.

"I love you," she whispered in his ear.

"And I love you!" he growled. "Work what magick you

can for me with the smoke, Carolinus!" he said. His mind was totally free—sharp and clear. A second later he had moved himself to the ground below in the very center of the battle.

He found himself in turmoil, among hobs and goblins, involved with each other in no sort of order. The air was thick not merely with smoke but dust. The shrilling of high voices, here in the midst of them, was unbelievable, though it was becoming less even as he stood there. But Carolinus had indeed managed to give him better vision. Jim could see through the combination of smoke and dust for some twenty feet in every direction.

"Hob!" he called—and realized that his voice did not even carry five feet in this racket. He magickally changed to his dragon-throat, lungs and vocal chords—adjusting his armor to contain the added size of his upper body—then changed his mind and made his body completely over into that of a dragon, and his human armor vanished.

All the goblins within sight of him scrambled to get away. The hobs they had been fighting, with no chivalry at all, cut them down with their reaping hooks, from behind.

For the first time Jim recognized how well-adapted for this fight the hobs had been. Clearly they had known their enemies better than he. Honed razor-sharp, and used as the hobs were using them, in a quick chopping motion, their blades slashed through the goblins' spears just behind the gleaming head. Then a second slash would follow the first, at a goblin throat or the back of a goblin neck. The curved, keen, reaping hooks were deadly at close quarters. Jim watched the fights around him as he searched for Hob—his hob.

Plowing over the ground with the awkward gait of a dragon, he saw more than one hob decapitate a goblin spear, then, stepping closer to his enemy, with one more sweep of his hook, take off the head of that enemy.

"Hob!" he kept calling. At the same time he was desperately sending out a mental summons. But there was no answer to either, and the thought that Hob could already be dead—his and Angie's hob—grew and became a coldness within him. Suddenly he wanted to kill goblins himself, with a very savage, personal desire that was like a hunger in him.

He turned himself back into a human, in tribute to Hob. If he was going to kill goblins, he would do it as Hob had gone to do it—as what he really was, and no other.

For the first time he paid real attention to the shrilling around him. Both hobs and goblins were shouting at the tops of their voices as they fought and died. But now that he listened closely, he heard the difference between them.

The essence of the noise they were both making was so similar that it almost seemed the same. But the rhythms of the two sets of voices were different. The goblins' shouting was an unending roar on a single note. But that of the hobs was more of an ululation—a continually repeated up and down between no more than two notes—strangely reminding him of the unforgettable Welsh anthem *Men of Harlech*. Pride and triumph, and something unkillable, rang in it.

If the hobs were losing, if their numbers had been cut down drastically since their first contact with the spears of the goblins, the sound of their voices still had that strange ring of victory in it. If they were dying, they were dying in some effort that brought them great satisfaction as they fell. As Brian might have said on a like occasion, this was a battle that in itself was worth dying for.

"By God!" said Jim to himself, unheard in the tumult around him. If the hobs could do it, he could! He would find his own hob, alive or dead, and stand over his body, killing any goblins who attacked him, until in their numbers they put him down, too. What was it that Hob's dream of his own end had been—that he would be found with a ring of his foes killed about him? Jim could do that much for him.

It was a mad decision on his part, like something from a legend. But, by Heaven, he would make it come true for Hob. Watching Hob's kind at work, he had learned how to fight the poisoned spears. But it was not time to stop searching yet. Dead or just dying, Hob must still be somewhere here under this cloud of smoke.

Jim forged forward into the melee about him, still more occupied with finding Hob than killing goblins. They, on their part, finding a human still alive, but discovering that spears that got past his shield and sword either slid off or broke on contact with the ward encasing him, mostly dodged out of his path as he went. So he searched through the melee . . . almost as if he moved among shadowy figures in a world of noise, smoke and dust.

Why hadn't he thought to ward Hob?

The thought stuck with him. The easiest answer was a purely personal one. He had never really planned to send the hobs into this battle at all, sure that they would inevitably be slaughtered like helpless baby animals. He had been wrong. But admitting that to himself didn't let him off the hook, nor did the fact that he could never have asked Carolinus, let alone gotten from him enough wards, to protect all the hobs. But *his* hob, who had created this hob army, could and should have been protected, if only for the possibility that Jim might have needed him, somehow, out here on the battlefield. . . .

It began to dawn on Jim that he had covered a good deal of ground out here by this time, and suddenly a new, ugly thought gripped him. He should by this time have seen the small form he searched for. Could he have passed by Hob, lying dead or badly wounded, and simply not recognized him? All hobs looked much like sculptured duplicates of each other.

Or did they?

He stopped to look at a dead hob, who had taken a spear through his throat that was still there, though there was no sign of the goblin who had killed him. A terrible, choking death, but the hob's face was not contorted, but serene. Facial muscles relaxed, Jim told himself, but, no, there was something more there than that. A look almost of satisfaction, of something successfully done—it was not the face of his hob . . . he reminded himself, that was what he had stopped to look for. He leaned his head down, close to the dead face.

It was definitely not Hob's face. Suddenly he realized he would have known that at a glance. But what made it not Hob's?

He studied it.

It was broader in the chin than Hob's, and perhaps the face itself was a bit longer than Hob's. He remembered now that Tiverton hob had given the impression of being slightly more burly all over than Hob, and his face had matched that appearance, being more square. It came to Jim that over the time they had spent together, he had unconsciously memorized Hob's features, and he would no more have mistaken Hob for some other hob than he would have mistaken Angie's face for that of some other woman.

He went back to his searching. But now, for the first time, he thought the battle seemed to be winding down. The combatants were not so thickly pressed together, and he realized that he could no longer make out the shrilling cry of the goblins. The ululations of the hobs were drowning it out.

Even as he recognized this, he saw a goblin before him doing a strange, weird thing. He was sinking into the earth as if it had no more supporting power than water. As Jim watched, the goblin reached out to seize a nearby goblin corpse, a goblin already dead, and pulled it down out of sight into the earth with him. By the time Jim got to where the two of them had been, they were gone.

Gingerly, with his toe, he tested the bare soil where they had been. It was perfectly solid—ordinary, bare, foot-packed dirt, like all the rest of the cleared area, where before today some rough tufts of grass had been plentiful.

He stretched up to his full human height and looked all around him. The dust and smoke seemed to have cleared to the point where he could see the castle gates and front part of the curtain wall, looming indistinctly like the lower cliffs of some mountainside.

—And the hobs were now streaming back toward the castle, riding wisps of smoke. Those unhurt were carrying some dead hobs, or others only wounded, some with goblin spears or parts of spears sticking in their bodies. They were moving, their ululation more like a song than ever, and proceeding—not towards the great gates that now waited, open, but sailing in smoke over the walls. A few other dead hobs, and the dead of the slain goblins, still were visible, scattered on the field under the thinning smoke, but the last of the living goblins had disappeared into the earth. Some words of Hob came back to him: "—they even eat each other."

In moments, there were none left to be seen alive above on the field, hob or goblin, and the dead goblins left behind were not strewn evenly on the ground, but here and there in little piles or mounds of dead, as if they had gone down after putting themselves back-to-back for a final stand. Their dead faces still stared fiercely up at the now-darkening sky, for the red sun was finally out of sight below the trees beyond.

The smoke had all but cleared, and the dust was settling fast. Jim could sweep the whole battlefield area with a single glance now. Suddenly, it seemed a very small place for so many dead to lie.

The dead hobs still left among them were few. Sweeping his eyes over all, Jim felt suddenly sure that none of the hob dead he could see was his hob. But something very like a superstition would not not let him believe that until he found Hob and was made sure of what had happened to him, beyond all doubt.

He began to investigate the small piles of dead goblins.

There was the body of an occasional hob among them, but he had almost exausted the piles left to be examined when he heard, off to his left, something very like a cross between the sound of a mewling kitten and a string of purely human swear words.

He left the pile he had been examining and started at a run to the one from which the sound came. He reached it in seconds.

At first glance, there was nothing to be seen but dead goblins. Still, the sound came in small bursts from underneath them. He pulled off the goblin bodies, and there was Hob, his eyes closed, with no less than three broken-off spears piercing his body and covered with blood.

Gently, very gently, Jim picked him up in his arms. Hob opened his eyes and looked up into Jim's face.

"They're supposed to be in a ring around me," he said crossly, in a voice hardly above a whisper, "not in a pile like this! Where's my sword?"

Jim found it on the ground, where Hob had been lying. It was also covered with blood. Still holding the light little body, he picked up the small sword and pushed it softly into the scabbard still hanging from the belt at Hob's waist.

"Solar!" he told himself harshly, and spoke with his mind—*Carolinus, if you're watching me*—

But Carolinus had anticipated the rest of the message, and Jim was at once back in the Solar, with Carolinus still looking at him with no expression on his face at all, while Angie was running towards him, arms reaching out to him and his featherweight burden.

"Jim! she said. "Are you all right? Give Hob to me!"

"No," said Jim. "The spears are still in him! I don't want to jar him, passing him about. Where can we lay him down?"

"On the bed," said Angie.

"Blood—" said Jim.

"Cold water takes it out! Put him down there!"

Jim lowered Hob to the bed.

"You could give me a hand!" snarled Jim at Carolinus over his shoulder. "These spears—"

"Look," said Carolinus calmly. Jim looked back at Hob and saw that both spears and wounds had vanished.

"I don't know how much blood he's lost. I think—I hope—that's mainly goblin blood all over him," said Jim. "Have you got any way of telling how much he's lost? Knowing that'd give me time to find out what else needs to be done—keep his heart going—or whatever—"

He broke off, suddenly having trouble getting air into his own lungs to speak with. He felt the helpless, almost panicky, feeling he had felt the first time he had experienced the out-of-control magick he had earned at the Loathly Tower. It had been only a few months after that fight, and the magickal energy he had unknowingly earned there had started changing him into dragon shape, whether he wanted that to happen or not.

Abruptly, without warning, he was whirled down and away into unconsciousness.

Chapter 41

Jim blinked his eyes open—almost immediately, it seemed to him.

But he had been undressed and put under the covers of their bed in the Solar. Looking further, he saw a wintry morning light flooding in through his familiar windowpanes.

"M'lady! M'lady!" a familiar, excited, high-pitched voice was calling out, only inches away from his ear, at the edge of the bed. He turned his head to see what he had already guessed. It was Hob, all right.

"Hob," he croaked, with dry vocal chords, staring at the pointed little face, "you're all right?"

"Oh yes, m'lord. How is m'lord?"

"I'm all right, of course!" In fact, Jim did feel all right. Just very rested and becoming more awake by the minute. "What am I doing in bed here? I've got to get up!"

"No, you don't!" Angie was suddenly beside the bed. "You stay right where you are."

"Why should I stay right where I am? It's a fine day. I couldn't feel better."

"You stay where you are, because you've had another relapse—or lapse, or whatever it is—from overdoing the magick. I warned you. Everybody's been warning you, to take it easy; and instead you go right into the middle of a battle, and for all I know, hacked right and left—"

"Never a hack! I don't think I even drew my sword ... well, maybe I did, but just to scare off the goblins."

"Well, the point is, you managed to get yourself all worked up, or this wouldn't have happened."

"What did I do, then, sleep all last night through?"

"You slept three days!"

"Three—" Jim stared at her "—days?"

"That's right. You've lain there like a ... well, you've just lain there, not moving. I was thinking we'd have to turn you over every four hours so you wouldn't get bed sores!"

"Bed sores? Don't be ridiculous! In fact, this whole business—what're you so worried about anyway? Three days—"

"Now calm down."

"I am calmed down. I'm cool as a cucumber—"

Carolinus suddenly loomed up beside Angie, looking very stern and tall.

"Jim!" said Carolinus. "You have to start taking this matter seriously, that's all there is to it. Every time you push yourself into collapse, as you've just done once more, you're weakened, and likely to do it again, that much sooner, the next time you let yourself get exited. Stay calm, as Angie says. Rest when necessary, and you'll get over it.

It's your magickal energy kicking back at you. You've been told that. You have to train it out of that habit, so that it finally forgets how to do it. It'll take time."

"But—" Jim was beginning.

"No buts! *Magick accomplished is NOT reversible.* You know that—it's in the copy of the *Encyclopedie Necromantic* I had you swallow! You somehow stole raw magick from the continuum to get everybody out of Tiverton. Now it's done—and you're stuck with paying off the cost of it! It'll take patience and time."

"How much time?"

"Who knows?" snapped Carolinus. "A year—maybe four? Though the more often you can use your magick without pushing yourself into this sort of collapse, the more you'll strengthen. But do exactly the opposite, and you'll weaken—it's that simple."

"How'm I supposed to know far I can use my magick—"

"I don't know! Never had it myself, though I've seen others with it. Everyone's different. The only thing you can do is err on the side of caution, and try not to get sensitive about things."

"I'm never sensitive!" said Jim.

"He's one of the most sensitive people alive!" said Angie to Carolinus. "People don't know it, but he is."

"People including himself, apparently."

"I am not, repeat, not sensitive—any more than any other man."

"Now there you're wrong," said Carolinus. "Angie's right. In any case, sensitivity is necessary to the use of magick, and in my experience you're definitely sensitive. You won't be able to change that. You'll just have to live with the capacity, and try to keep it under control."

"In *this* world?" said Jim, before he could stop himself.

Carolinus seemed to swell and stand even taller.

"No doubt it's a far, far better world where you come from!" he said. "No doubt everyone there is as sensitive as you are, and you're used to being handled with soft silk gloves. Well, this isn't your world, and no doubt this one's not a patch on what you're used to. But it's the world we live and die in, and we like it as it is! I'm sorry it can't be changed to suit—"

"I didn't mean that at all!" cried Jim.

"—your own particular wishes and feelings. It's a different world, a hard world in many ways, and if you want to live here, you've got to take its hard parts like everyone else and adjust to them, not expecting it and everyone in it to adjust to you!"

"That isn't what I meant, Carolinus—Mage!" Jim almost shouted.

"Carolinus, now *you're* getting him worked up," said Angie.

Carolinus lowered his voice. "I suppose so."

Jim lowered his. "I know," he said earnestly, "that it's up to me to do the adjusting—I've known from the start. I think your world is one hell of a fine world. It's just that people, Naturals and animals all think differently here. I'm trying to fit in. I'll keep trying. And I'll do my best to keep my—" he winced internally at the word "—sensitivity under control, if that's what it's got to be."

"Believe me, it is." Carolinus turned away and paced up and down the Solar a couple of times. When he came back to Jim, he was almost smiling.

"Well," he said, "I think maybe you ought to get up, now that you clearly understand. No point in keeping him in bed, Angie. He'll never recover lying there and stewing. He's got to get up and go out around other people to test his limits with them."

"Good!" said Jim, throwing off his covers and standing up. He had been in Carolinus' world long enough to pick up some of the general indifference about casual nakedness—and to understand its balancing concern with being dressed exactly right for certain necessary occasions. He looked down at Hob, cross-legged on the floor by his bed, then at Carolinus. "Hob's really all right, then?"

"And there you go, first crack out of the box!" said Angie.

"Oh, I think concern like that's not dangerous, Angie," said Carolinus. "It's normal—up to a certain point. Watch Brian, Jim. He takes everything in stride, while saving his strength for the moment it's needed. Yes, Jim. Hob lost some blood, as you noted, but no serious amount. These hobs recover quickly—don't know how they do it without rest and food, though, and Hob doesn't know either."

"It just happens, Mage," said Hob in an apologetic voice.

"All right, then," said Angie. "Jim needs food—after three days without—and some clothes. And I'll make you some tea while you're dressing, Jim." She lifted her voice so it would carry through the door. "Servant here!"

"Yes, m'lady?" said the servant, nipping immediately into the Solar.

"What do you want, Jim?"

"A meat pie!" said Jim, suddenly ravenous. "A whole meat pie, but one without all those extra crazy spices—" he glanced at Carolinus and might have blushed if he had been capable of it—"though if they don't have a plain one handy in the Serving Room, a seasoned one will do."

"Don't worry," said Angie. "Plyseth knows your tastes. See to it," she added to the servant, who nipped out again, in her hurry not quite closing the door behind her. They could hear her feet pattering away around the curve of the corridor to the stairs leading below.

"So, Jim," said Carolinus, not moving from where he was as Jim went to the wardrobe to get his clothes and begin dressing. "That's that, and you needn't worry about the Accounting Office. After the victory and your saving the King, there'll be enough left over from reimbursing the Collegiate members so you'll have a fair supply of magick left in your account."

"Good. Do you think they might be back?"

"The King and his entourage? Highly unlikely, though he praises young Edward and you for winning."

"It was the hobs who won," Jim said.

"He—the King—knows it like everybody else. But the garlands go to Edward—and you; more to Edward, naturally."

"Naturally," said Jim. A small, sour note crept into his voice. But that was only momentary. "What I wanted to ask, though, is will the goblins be back?"

"That I doubt very much, at least in your lifetime—and possibly mine as well. Like most primitives—and primitives they are, in spite of their magic, though why there should be any reason primitive Naturals, or any other kind of primitive people, should have any less access to magic than the rest of us, even if that access does stop at the animal level. But that's because of the innocence of animals—I mentioned that to you. No, I don't expect them back, any more than I expect to find one of them qualifying for membership in the Collegiate."

"Would they take in a *goblin?*" called Angie from the fireplace.

"Certainly!" said Carolinus in a surprised tone, half turning to her. "Why not?"

"Well," said Angie, "as you say, they're Naturals, for one thing, and for another they hardly sound as if they could subscribe to the Collegiate ideas of using magick only for defense. I could probably think of a lot more reasons, but those two should be enough to start with."

"What sort of other reasons?" asked Jim.

"They'd have to become civilized, and kindly, of course, and show other developments," said Carolinus. "I only meant to say that their simply being Naturals wouldn't bar them from membership, since they clearly, with their poison spears, are already working deliberately with magic, not just invoking it by instinct."

"So you really think it might happen?"

"Possibly, under the conditions I just mentioned. Not in the immediate future, of course." Casting a thoughtful eye on Hob, still seated cross-legged by the bed and watching them, he went on, "—but that's hardly a reason for considering such things at this stage of history. And now I must go."

He did.

Well," said Jim, a small time later, finishing up an unusual amount of only mildly overseasoned meat pie, hurried for once to the Solar while it was still hot, not merely lukewarm, "that hit the spot."

He wiped his lips with a snowy napkin, and took a good-sized swallow of mingled wine and their special boiled-and-cooled water to wash it down, and sat there, feeling a flash of gratitude toward the castle's unfailing inside well.

"Ready to go back to bed?" said Angie.

"I am not. I feel like a billion dollars, with food and drink in me. I've got to talk to the Prince before he learns I've been mobile for hours and haven't yet got in touch with him to congratulate him on his victory."

"Jim! He knows you did it, not him!"

"The hobs did it—though we humans all had a piece of it, as I told Carolinus. But Carolinus is right. He was the commander-in-name. It's his victory."

"I don't know why he doesn't turn purple from embarrassment, being congratulated by you."

"Why should he, as Carolinus might also say? The rules of this period have him owed congratulations."

"Fine rules," said Angie. "*Servant, here!* Oh, there you are. Clean this table—and this time shut the door as you go out."

The servant began to clean up, beaming her approval at Jim out of a young, thin face under unruly blond hair and above one of Angie's old gray working dresses. Food and drink were considered one of the best medicines in the world for any physical problem. She carefully left the wine and water pitchers on the table.

"Take—" began Angie.

"No," said Jim. The servant left, the pitchers stayed. She thoroughly agreed with him. He was showing almost no signs at all of the wine he had drunk so far. More would only be good for him.

"Tell me something," said Jim, as the door closed, stretching his legs out comfortably but carefully enough not to kick Angie's, which were now underneath the table opposite him, "do you think it was young Edward that sent Joan up here with the idea of the footmen going first?"

"I know it wasn't. I did."

"You?" Jim sat up straighter in his chair, putting down his glass wine-cup, one of the King's that the monarch had left behind.

"Of course. Edward knew nothing about that, and it seemed to me an idea you should be considering."

"Well, it was a good idea," said Jim slowly. He picked up his glass again, but merely held it in his hand. "It just didn't appear to me she might have thought it up herself. She can't have had any experience of battles."

"What would you have thought if Geronde had suggested it?"

"I'd have been more ready to believe her, of course!" said Jim. "But Geronde's defended her estate—with Brian's help—and grown up in the company of men who've fought battles."

"Joan's whole life's been spent in the company of men who've fought battles: the King, people like Chandos at his court, her two husbands. Her experience has been full of busy fighting men—when she was growing up and ever since. Her first husband, Holland, is a professional soldier to this day. Her present husband, Salisbury, is fighting in wars all the time."

"True."

"Of course it's true. And she hasn't been deaf and blind all these years."

"No. You were right. She was right."

"Thank you. Or, I mean—forgive me. But I hate to see someone like her ignored just because she's female."

"This is the fourteenth century."

"But you aren't—forgive me again. I'll leave it alone." She blew him a kiss over the table. "All right?"

"You idiot!" he said tenderly, "Forgive you for what?"

"Good."

They looked at each other lovingly over the table.

"Not now," said Jim. "As I said, I've got to congratulate the Prince. Oh, tell me something else. Is there anything out of the last three days I ought to know, before I go around talking to people?"

"Just that we're finally all ready for the wedding, day after tomorrow. Starting tomorrow, neighbors will begin to come in, now that the goblins are gone. It turns out most of them—neighbors, that is—followed our lead to set up a Nursing Room, so their deaths from the plague were held down some. But a lot of them fought here with you. Those who didn't won't want to miss the wedding."

"Isn't it pretty soon, though? We just finished the battle."

"Geronde did say she wasn't going to take the risk of putting it off a day longer. She even spent part of yesterday praying in the chapel—that if there was some kind of a curse on her getting married, would God please take care of it, this time."

"Poor kid," said Jim.

"Yes."

"Well, then—do you know if that scar on her cheek is worrying her, about how it'll look at the wedding?"

"Not that I know. Long ago she'd have done what everybody does here about something that can't be helped—just live with it. Why do you ask?"

"I just wondered. And the mother terrier, and her pups?"

said Jim, getting up, ready to leave. "I don't see them here."

"The pups are all down with Master Huntsmen now—"

"He survived the plague?"

"Never caught it."

"Well, good," said Jim, out of a sense of duty. Master Huntsman then would go on being a thorn in Jim's side— not that Jim would have wished the plague on him just to get rid of him. But he was the one person in the castle who thoroughly disapproved of Jim—since Jim had a strong dislike of hunting for the mere sport of it, which was unnatural according to the Master Huntsman's standards. The two beliefs, clashing, poisoned every contact between them.

"I should say he's got all the pups but one, that is," said Angie. "I took one in to show it to little Robert, and he fell in love with it. So I thought he ought to keep it. It can be his dog. I told him he had to be very careful handling the little thing, or we'd take it away from him."

"And he understood you? He's still awfully young."

"Oh I think he understood enough of it. He's getting older. Anyway, I told his nurse to watch out for the pup while Robert's still so young. It can grow up with him."

"Yes," said Jim, but for a moment remembering an unhappy day when he was half-grown, finally faced with the fact that the puppy that had been given to him when he was very young did not have a life span as long as his.

I tend to forget, he told himself, going out into the corridor to begin his search for the Prince, *how much the unfailing love of a dog means to you when you're young, and the words to express your troubles are not on your tongue yet. It's like magic—maybe it is magic, part magic anyway—*

"Oh, by the way," he added aloud to the servant and man-at-arms on duty outside the door, "do either of you know where in the castle His Grace, the Prince, is right now?"

He had thought of simply moving himself magickally to where young Edward might be, then remembered that it might pop him suddenly into the room shared by Edward and Joan at a time where they would not be expecting intrusions and would not welcome it.

"No, m'lord," said the man-at-arms righteously. He had been on duty five hours already, and he hoped that his lord would notice this indication that he had never left his post for a moment. "But it was said to me by a servant that His Lordship's Grace was in the Great Hall a half hour since."

Jim winced internally. It was not the mixing up of "his Lordship's" and "Grace" into one title—servants faced with an unfamiliar rank made sure they were least likely of mispeaking by tacking together as many titles as might apply. It was a fact that, although the Prince had been in Malencontri for some time, his title was both so high a one and, therefore, not one ordinarily required to be used by the staff—so it was not surprising the man-at-arms had got it wrong.

Actually, Jim found he had a real liking for the Prince— in spite of the other's flashing, on-and-off, sensible-and-wild reactions. He went down to the Great Hall and, as promised, found him there with Brian, both just ending a large second breakfast.

"With your gracious permission, may I join the table?" Jim asked the young man. The Prince beamed.

"No one could be more welcome!" he said. "By all means, sit, Sir James, and congratulate us on a good morning's luck. A stag of ten!"

Brian made a slightly embarrassed noise in this throat.

"If you will permit me, Your Grace," he said, his love of truth, Jim recognized, overcoming ordinary manners for a moment. "I don't think the beast had quite ten points to its antlers."

A shade of haughty displeasure darkened the Prince's face for a moment, but vanished immediately to let his sunny expression return.

"No doubt you are right, Sir Brian," he said. "I am not

the hunter you are, and I must confess I did not look as closely at our kill as I should have. Your Master of Hunt, Sir James, says you take the hounds out yourself but rarely?"

"My magick," said Jim hastily. "Your Grace understands . . ."

"Oh—of course."

The fact was, Jim had never taken them out alone, and dreaded the days when he would have visitors who would expect a hunt. But for the huntsman to tell the exact truth about his lord's hunting patterns to a mere visitor—Prince or not—was beyond the villainy of even that disgruntled master.

However, Jim was seated now, and Brian had just filled a mazer with wine and pushed it to him—all wine, of course. There was water on the table, but it was not his and Angie's boiled version. Except when the servants knew he or Angie would be there, the table featured water straight out of the castle well. The servants themselves were immune to whatever the well might contain, and never thought of boiled water for themselves. Jim had risked it on important occasions—but this was not one.

He lifted the mazer—possibly fourteen English ounces of uncut wine—and held it up to the Prince.

"I came to congratulate Your Grace on your glorious victory over the goblins!"

"Hah!" said the Prince, as Brian also lifted his glass to join silently in the toast. "That is greatly kind of you, James. I could never have done it without your assistance, the help of the Mage, the strong right arm of Sir Brian on my un-shielded side, and the arrow-work of Master Daffyd ap Hew-hooya—damn these Welsh names! No Christian can pronounce them!"

"The Welsh are also Christians, of course, Your Grace, if you will pardon me for saying it."

"No doubt. Nowadays, anyway. Wild savages before that

in Roman times, I understand. But you are quite right to remind me, James. There are good men among them and Daffyd is one of them. I needed you all to do what little I could do. Yes, dammit, but I must also give praise to those magnificent hobs! Who would have thought they could fight like that with those farm tools? Did they suffer much, James? Did they lose many of their number in the winning?"

"I believe a good deal less than we expected, Your Grace. They had one advantage, after all: that of knowing their enemy."

"Yes, the same blood and bones and such, I understand, James? Cousins to the goblins, in fact?"

"Yes, Your Grace."

"But how different! Loyal to their King, hardly able to contain themselves until they were let at those pernicious goblins—but what you say about knowing your enemy is indeed a great advantage. I do not know how often the good knight Sir John Chandos drummed that into me as I was growing up."

"A great war captain and knight," commented Brian.

"There is none to match him—a gentleman of piety and honor. Except my father the King, of course."

"Of course, Your Grace," said both Jim and Brian, burying their faces in their mazers.

"I remember him so well—I believe I told you this, once, James, how I saw him trying on the armor he was to wear later at the sea battle of Sluys. I was very young at the time, of course, but I thought then that I had never seen, nor have I, a more perfect vision of a King and warrior!"

The Prince was no longer looking at the other two, his mind elsewhere. He recovered suddenly.

"But, James," he said, "I understand you, yourself, were wounded in the battle. It was said you had been unconscious these last three days. I have never seen so many long faces among the servants of any gentleman. What was the wound—and how did you come about it?"

"It was a—magic wound," said Jim uncomfortably. "It left no body mark."

"Ah, that explains why you are are up and well again so suddenly. I am relieved to hear that. Would you believe it? Neither I nor any of the gentlemen with me were wounded by the goblin poison spears! I thanked God for that, even as I was praying you might recover from your wound. Perhaps my prayers helped to gain you some small intercession from on High."

"I've no doubt of it, Your Grace."

"Well, the main thing is you are once more on your feet for the wedding. I and the Countess will be staying for it—and even my father has said he will attend. I understand a stage and proper chair is being built for him to observe. They can be moved just before the wedding, in case of snow or other."

"Barring a change in the weather, Your Grace," said Brian, "or a pickup of a northly wind, I believe it should be quite pleasant—for this time of year."

Just above freezing, that is, Jim told himself. He and Angie would put on the layers normal for that sort of occasion. Good Lord! Come to think of it, he knew nothing about the wedding, except for Angie's few words, and now the Prince's.

"You remind me of my duty, Your Grace," he said. "If you might excuse me, there are many matters concerned with this wedding that I need to be about."

"By all means, by all means, James!" said the Prince. "We all know a host's work is never done until all his guests are in bed—in bed, hah!"

The last sound was more a chuckle than an exclamation. The Prince, Jim knew, was thinking of the time following the banquet after the wedding, when the newly wedded pair would be escorted upstairs to their bedroom by the more important members of the wedding party, who were supposed to witness the consummation of the marriage, to make it legal.

Happily, in practice, this meant merely watching the curtains drawn around the bed and listening for whatever sounds might come from within. Only the Solar would be large enough to hold the qualified observers in this case, thought Jim glumly. That meant he and Angie would bed down in their clean sleeping bags on the floor of the much smaller room which Brian and Geronde had been occupying.

He had forgotten all about that. No morning tea, none of the comforts he was used to, and they probably would not get back to their proper quarters before late, the following day. And Geronde would probably take her time, and have a sort of hen party. . . . Jim put it from his mind. There were other, more important things to be dealt with, right away. Blast those three days of being out of action! However, both he and Brian laughed dutifully at the Prince's humor. Jim stood up.

"I will hope to see you at supper, Your Grace, Brian. Anon, then."

"Anon," said the other two, and Jim walked off.

Chapter 42

He had been more embarrassed at offering young Edward congratulations on his victory than Edward himself had been to receive them. Brian, the original truthful individual, was completely unafraid to be absolutely honest with everyone, and he had undoubtedly had no discomfort in giving his congratulations. To his fourteenth-century mind, that was probably only what Edward deserved, simply for being there at the head of the armored contingent on horseback.

It would not have occurred to him that saying the words might bother Jim. But it had. Jim was not comfortable with sophistry.

At any rate, the usual cheerfulness of Brian and the casual acceptance of the bootlicking compliment by Edward had finally gotten to Jim. He had to get away from them, for the moment anyway, and there were, indeed, urgent matters in hand. Very urgent. Maybe any single day was too short a time to catch up with things undone, but Jim's conscience always troubled him in situations like this.

There were no two ways about it. He was perfectly aware that Carolinus had stood over him during his unconscious period as devotedly as Angie, and the senior Mage must have essentially cosigned his own magic fortune to get the contributions from the rest of the Collegiate. But now he must be asked for one thing more.

And Carolinus was always busy. He would not be happy to be disturbed by Jim now—least of all for a favor undoubtedly requiring a good deal of effort and personal leaning on fellow Magickians. But it had to be done.

Alone at the foot of the tower stairs, Jim sent a diffident thought in Carolinus' direction—the magical equivalent of a very gentle knock at his door.

Er—Carolinus?

What? shot back the answer.

I need to talk to you. Something very important!

NOT NOW!

I'm afraid . . .

Very well! It's important, is it? Come then! You've got two minutes to convince me of that!

Jim transferred himself immediately to Carolinus' little cottage with the ever-blooming flowers about the self-raking gravel path to his door—which opened before him.

Carolinus stood in the middle of the cluttered ground floor's single room, glaring at him. Ecce, the sibyl Jim had last seen leaving the cottage in tears, was perched now on the Mage's scrying glass, which he never used, being beyond needing it to see and hear at a distance. Ecce's gossamer wings were drooping, but she smiled at Jim.

"Forgive me, Ecce," said Jim, "for interrupting like this—"

Ecce gave a faint wave with one tiny hand to signal it was all right.

"But I *am* sorry—" Jim was going on, when Carolinus broke in.

"Enough of that. Your problem: quick!"

It was not possible to make an impassioned plea in a few brief words. Jim did his best.

"Geronde has a scar on her face. You may recall that we spoke of this some time ago? I want to get it removed before her wedding, day after tomorrow."

There was a long moment of awful silence. Carolinus stared at him.

"I remember," said the Mage. "You wouldn't, I suppose," he went on in a tired voice, "prefer a palace on the Loire with a thousand servants and the wealth of Midas in its storage rooms?"

"No," said Jim sincerely. Ecce flew to Carolinus' shoulder and tried to smooth out the grim lines in his cheeks with those tiny hands of hers, each no more than the size of a petal of a lily-of-the-valley flower, stroking his set forehead with her gauzy wings.

"I know you said you would want to consult with certain Eastern magicians," Jim went on. "But I don't know if you've had time to do that, what with everything that has been going on—"

Carolinus threw up both hands. Ecce began to sing to him in a sweet little voice, a singing that was all tune and no words.

"It's all right, Ecce. I'm all right," Carolinus' voice changed to a momentary tenderness. "I won't fly off the handle."

Ecce, looking happier, winged back to the scrying glass. Carolinus turned again to Jim.

"I believe I told you that after all these years—don't you know it's impossible to heal a scar that old? Impossible for you, for me, for . . . anybody!"

Jim concentrated on that slight pause before the word "anybody."

"But I thought you suggested there might be someone who could do it?"

"Of course. Certainly!" said Carolinus, cuttingly. "Why not try Merlin?"

"I'd ask him," said Jim stoutly. "Believe me, I'd ask him in this case. But you know as well as I do it'd be no use. He'd never stop his work to do anything so simple and having to do with the present, rather than the past or future. Besides, the last time I heard from him, he told me never to bother him again."

"Wise man. A very wise man!"

"And there's no one else, no other who could . . . ?"

Carolinus hesitated, and Jim knew he had him. Like Brian—but under an entirely different set of principles— Carolinus could not bring himself to tell a direct lie.

"There must be a magician somewhere who's looked into removing old scars," said Jim.

"Of course there are!" exploded Carolinus, and Ecce flew to him again. "Several! No, no. It's all right, Ecce." Carolinus' voice had become weary again. "I'm going to have to handle this first before we have any quiet time to ourselves. Will you forgive me?"

Ecce sang what was plainly a reassuring melody, and flew from his shoulder to the door, which opened considerably before her. In a small flash of wings she was gone, and it closed again behind her with a soft click of the latch.

"Go home!" said Carolinus to Jim. "I'll have to talk to several of my colleagues who've found an interest in that kind of magickal work. I'll be in touch with you as soon as I've found out if it's possible or not."

"Thank you," said Jim, humbly. He transferred himself back to Malencontri—absentmindedly, back to the foot of the tower stairs.

Luckily, there was no one approaching him on the level, or coming down the stairs. Not that his sudden materialization would have upset anyone, particularly not the servants. But it probably would have started a round of speculation. Where had he been? What had he been doing?

He hesitated.

What were the other matters he had wanted to look into down here, anyhow? They boiled down to seeing how the old Master Carpenter was standing up to all the work he had to do since he had risen from his sick bed, and finding how the Nursing Room had been getting along. He had the impression that the plague was fading away to some extent, at least from Malencontri.

Much as Jim had a fondness for the grumpy, aged carpenter, the Nursing Room—concerned with the well-doing of a number of people—took precedence over just one. He headed for it, accordingly.

At first glance, as he entered it, he saw that most of the beds were now empty. His spirits rose, just as a terrier who was certainly the mother of the pups he and Angie had brought from Tiverton came rushing up to him, tail going like a metronome run mad, and two other terriers—probably from the kennels of the Hunt Master—after a few warning barks at the intrusion of an obvious stranger, came rushing behind her, tails also awag, eager not to miss out on someone so very obviously a friend.

He patted, stroked and spoke to them all for a moment before going on toward the dais. It was empty, except for the tent that had been put up originally around his own sickbed when he was a patient there.

On the chance there might be someone inside it, he

mounted the dais and pushed his way in thorough the untied front flaps. May Heather was inside, seated at her desk, evidently having moved herself there to minimize calls for attention from the invalids still in the room.

"M'lord!" she jumped up from the books she was working on. Clearly, she had not only mastered the numbers Angie had started her on some time since, but writing as well. She curtsied, very expertly now, he noticed.

"Mistress Nurse," Jim replied. She almost gaped and did stammer in her response.

"Mistress . . . Nurse, m'lord? I be—I am still apprenticed to Mistress Plyseth in the Serving Room!"

"At present. Your Mistress there will have to agree to release you from that apprenticeship, of course, but I'll ask her to. In any case, are you *not* Mistress here?"

"Here I certainly be so, in a way, m'lord—" said May, throwing upper-class servant's English to the winds in her astonishment and gratitude. She had not done that in years. "But Mistress . . . I never thought."

It was understandable, thought Jim. As far as he knew she was not yet fifteen years old. But, as he and Angie had discovered, she was tough, brave, honest, unusually intelligent—and had a mind of her own.

"Don't think!" said Jim in his most authoritative, lordly voice. "I have said you are Mistress of this room, therefore you are its Mistress. Do you question me?"

"Oh no, m'lord!" cried May, delight in her voice. "Thank you ever so much, m'lord. Bless you, m'lord!"

"Come, come, enough of this. To important matters. Give me an account of things as they stand now here in the room. I seem to notice more empty beds."

"Yes, m'lord." She gestured towards the paper on which she had been writing. "Some sadly dead, m'lord, but less for our numbers of sick than other poor people elsewhere. A goodly number recovered. I have written down their names and the days of their death or leaving here in health—"

"Oh?" said Jim. "Did my lady tell you to do that?"

"No," confessed May, suddenly uncomfortable. "It just seemed the right thing, like. Did I do wrong?"

"It was well thought of, Mistress." May beamed. "And looking at your papers, I see it was well done."

"Oh, m'lord!"

"But go on. You must have other things to tell me."

She had. The extra opium and pipes the hobs had brought had worked a miracle in easing the patients' suffering. "— and it gave them strength to sleep, m'lord. . . ." Five, actually *five*, had walked out well in one day! Almost no sick ones had come in this last week. The servants of the neighbors who had come with armor and horses to fight the goblins had said their lords had followed Malencontri's example, and had done well by their lights—but none so well as Malenconti in curing sick ones.

The terriers had been a blessing, too, being devils on any rats who dared show their selves in the room by night or day. ". . . But m'lord's little bitch was the best!" May had kept a tally of their kills, and the bitch was six rats ahead of the best of the other two. They would all insist, though, in carrying a dead rat proudly to show it off to the patients or her. Still, they were dear little things—hark, if m'lord listened, he could hear them now at the tent flaps.

May stopped talking, and in the silence, Jim could hear the faint scratch of clawed feet on the boards of the dais— and the almost as faint whimpers right outside the flaps.

"They wish to come in to m'lord, here," May said. "But of course I taught them never to stick nose inside. Oh, yes, and His Grace, the handsome young Prince, paid the room a visit once—"

"He did?" Jim stared at her. "But surely there were only servants and armsmen among the patients, once Master Carpenter was gone?"

"Yes, m'lord, not a Master or Mistress, let alone any gentlefolk—who in any case would be in the tent here! Our sick ones were main proud to see him—something to remember all their lives—and he spoke to them, too!"

Jim was privately astonished. Young Edward had revealed another unexpected side to his character. The way he had of talking about the servants as if they had neither ears nor feelings, when they were standing less than ten feet from him, hardly signaled the sort of noble who would visit a roomful of sick commoners. It was a good mark for his character. Perhaps this was one reason why the Collegiate was so bent on keeping his father alive—at least until the Prince was adult enough to be King.

"Well," said Jim, "that's fine, May. You've done a great job here. I've got to go, Mistress."

"Thank you, m'lord," said May happily behind him,

He stepped out through the tent flaps; and the little female terrier, who had been waiting all this time for him, swarmed over him, wagging her tail as if she would wag it off, licking any reachable area of uncovered skin about him, and wriggling with the desire to convey how much she loved him. The two males, who probably had been waiting also, pressed forward, trying to shoulder the female aside in their eagerness to prove their own loyalty and affection for this human, who was certainly a pack-leader among all the other Masters, here in this great stone kennel.

Going out the entrance to the Nursing Room, Jim found the little terrier leaving with him. Sternly, he ordered her back. Ears wilting, she obeyed.

He went to the Master Carpenter's shop, in the castle's unroofed courtyard, noticing with approval that the great gates were once more closed and barred. He stepped inside, gratefully escaping the chilly wind that was finding its way here, even inside the castle walls. There would be a hard freeze tonight. He hoped the weather would not worsen for the wedding, due to be held on the steps to the chapel, which had its only entrance also on the courtyard.

He glanced at the chapel's closed door as he passed. There was no fireplace in it. No heat inside there, either.

Going back through the carpentry, he heard the hoarse, angry voice of the carpenter raised.

"—and don't touch the end of the chair arms until I can get to them, myself, d'ye hear! The grain in the wood needs to be dealt with properly. You hear me?"

The old man was plainly in a temper. He was standing by a thronelike chair, plainly being constructed for the King to observe the wedding. Enduring the tirade patiently were two men in their twenties, whom Jim recognized as his top journeymen, whom the old man had once recommended to Jim as perfectly capable to take his place.

The carpenter was still going on.

". . . The grain is everything. The grain is all!" Still shouting, he turned enough to catch sight of Jim. "—and if you don't believe that," he went on in exactly the same tone of voice, "ask your archer friend. There's a man who knows the grain in a piece of wood—" His voice dropped suddenly to a more proper tone in which to address his overlord, though anger still rang in it. "M'lord! May I be of service to you?"

"I just dropped by to see how you're getting on," said Jim.

"As well as I can with short time, dull tools, with—it'll be Heaven's mercy if I can get it done properly in time. I can't work as fast as I used to—but I'll have it done, I'll have it done—m'lord. It's the leopard heads to be carved on the ends of the armrests that have to be done just right. The grain—"

"Did someone say the King had to have leopard heads on the ends of the arm rests?" said Jim. "I can look into it, and maybe, with the time so short, I can have them changed to plain ends." The leopard, Jim knew, was a necessary part of the royal arms.

"No one had to say there had to be leopard heads. Of course there must be. Flog me if you will, m'lord, but I would not shame this castle and you by giving the King a chair having plain ends to his arm rests!"

The idea of flogging the elderly, highly respected carpenter, or anyone of the Master or Mistress level, was so far-fetched—let alone the fact that Jim had all but successfully dodged the necessity to flog *anyone* since he and Angie took possession of Malencontri—that he merely stared at the carpenter.

"—And your coming down, and coming down, to ask how the chair is coming won't finish it a whit sooner, if I do say so right out, my lord!"

This was going too far, even for the carpenter. Jim had to stop it before it damaged his authority among the servants. The ears of the two journeymen were plainly wide open, even if their faces remained studiously without expression.

"Master Carpenter!" he said, in a deliberately hard voice. "This is the first time I've seen you since I visited you in your sickbed in the Nursing Room, and I only came by now to make sure you were on your feet. Keep your voice down and speak to your lord properly!"

Long years of training took over in the carpenter.

"Forgive me, my lord!" he said in almost meek tones, as far as his ordinary rasping voice would permit it. "I beg on banded knee the mercy of your forgiveness. I was angry with these two here, and forgot myself. It should never be said I failed in my proper service to my lord—"

"That's enough!" said Jim, embarrassed to hear the old man grovel. "I know you have troubles, and you bravely rose from your sickbed to do your duty here. For that you have my forgiveness. But this must not happen again."

"I promise my lord it will not. It would be ill if I failed to honor the King properly, but worse if I failed to honor my lord."

"We will forget it," said Jim. "Now, how are you feeling?"

"Quite well, m'lord. Thank you."

"How are you feeling, I said?"

"I have some small pains from age, and stiffness of the hands, but no sign of sickness, since your lordship reminded me of my duty in the Nursing Room. I bless your lordship for doing so. I am happy to be back among my tools and wood."

The last words came with an earnest ring of truth.

"I am satisfied to hear so. Continue with your work."

Jim left the carpentry with mixed feelings—satisfaction that he had handled the situation right and unhappiness that he had been forced to lower the boom on the carpenter, whom he admired. He suspected the "little pains" and "stiff hands" were a great deal more than that, and his railing at his journeymen was simply a way of denying the limitations. Servants, Jim thought, were growing old around him. The carpenter with his troubles, Plyseth with what was undoubtedly severe arthritis in her legs.

James! said the voice of Carolinus unexpectedly in his head. *Go right to the Solar. I have a Magickian who may be able to help you with a scar removal. We will meet you there at once!*

An uneasiness he could not push away woke in Jim. Carolinus, Kinetete, Barron—all invariably addressed anyone, even Kings, by their most private names. Carolinus had almost never called him James, since the first moment they had met.

Chapter 43

Who— Jim began to ask Carolinus.

Son Won Phon. He made an unusual effort to come with me quickly because of the urgency of the matter. The least you can do is come quickly, yourself.

Then Carolinus was no more in mental contact with him. The uneasiness in Jim deepened. Carolinus had known he must contact Son Won Phon. That explained his earlier hesitation.

Son Won Phon was the Magickian who some years back had challenged Carolinus—very much his superior—to a Magickian's dual over Jim's use of Oriental magic which had not been taught to him by a qualified Oriental Magickian. Since then, Jim had heard Son Won Phon had advanced rapidly in rank, also that he would be the Observer for the Collegiate in its determination of whether to admit Jim from the apprentice ranks into Collegiate membership as a fully qualified Magickian. Son Won Phon was at least three fully qualified ranks above Jim by now.

Jim translated to the Solar. Angie, he saw, was not there, which was a relief. If things got rough or sticky, he would just as soon tell her about it later, than have her present and required to listen. Carolinus and Son Won Phon were there, though.

He turned his gaze on Carolinus and the brilliantly red-robed Magickian with him. It was, Jim recognized almost against his will, the most remarkably happy red he had ever seen. Carolinus was, as usual, wearing one of his old robes, looking as if it had been rescued from the trash basket.

But the red robe of the Oriental Magickian clothed a man with a face of no particular age, strongly boned and with something close to a stern look about it. And now that Jim saw the man up close, Son Won Phon's body struck him as being unusual for that of a Magickian. The man was a good inch or so shorter than Jim—who had been above average height even in his own future world—but his body was heavy and very powerful in appearance. A physically strong body, that at the same time gave the impression of being a remarkably controlled one.

There was no sign of impatience or tension about him. The kind of man who was unlikely to be disturbed by any challenge or threat, secure in his own faith that he could handle whatever came. The face from which his gaze met Jim's was serene.

"Son Won Phon, my apprentice, of whom you know," said Carolinus. "James, you have the pleasure of being named to Son Won Phon, an A-plus member of the Collegiate."

"I'm honored," said Jim, "to meet a Mag—"

Carolinus suddenly went into a coughing fit. Standing a little behind Son Won Phon, he glared at Jim.

"—honored to meet a Mag*ick*ian of your reputation and rank," Jim hastily corrected the word "Magician" before it could escape him. He made his best formal bow to the visitor.

"Do not offer any obeisance to me," said Son Won Phon, in a startlingly deep and resonant voice. "I agree strongly with the reply given one of your earlier English Kings, Richard the First, commonly called the Lionheart. At a council of fellow Kings on one of your early crusades, he so forgot himself that he began to issue orders, rather than offering counsel to those with him. I believe it was the aged King of Hungary who rebuked him, saying, 'You know, we are all equals here.' We in the Collegiate, which you may join one day, know that no one of us is above the others."

"I understand," said Jim.

"As of now, of course, you are only an apprentice. I believe your Master-in-Magick addresses you as Jim, and in tribute to the several remarkable accomplishments in the magickal realm, I shall do the same. I understand there is someone with an old scar on her face, and you have a great desire to see it removed before her wedding—the day after tomorrow, I believe?"

"Yes, Son Won Phon," said Jim. "It's beyond me, of course. Could you possibly—"

"I cannot say certainly," said Son in his deep voice, that seemed to set some piece of glassware in the Solar to ringing slightly. "There are several of us in the Collegiate who have investigated the removal of old scars and related matters. You will have to give me particulars about the age of the scar and the way of her coming about it."

Jim did. When he had finished, Son Won Phon was thoughtful for a long moment.

"It may be possible. There is no certainty to anything that long in place, for what must be removed or altered is not a fresh wound, which you may have already learned to do yourself—"

"He has," said Carolinus dryly.

"—but it is growth of the individual's body that heals such wounds over time, and in destroying the scar, we must destroy some of that, too. This comes very close to the prohibition of our Collegiate against taking offensive action, for first must all scar tissue be removed, then the original open wound closed cleanly and magickally. It has proven successful in some cases, not in others, and so far no reason for the different results has been discovered. You understand—" he glanced at Carolinus "—there will be a heavy cost involved?"

"Actually," said Carolinus, still dryly, "Jim can pay you out of his own account, after his saving the life of the current English King—to the great relief of all of us—by his recent *coup de main* against the aggressive goblins from Deep Earth."

"Ah, yes," said Son Won Phon, and surprised Jim by

adding, in a tone of simple regret, "I beg you will accept my apologies, Jim. Of course I had known of and been overjoyed by that recent valuable feat, as every Magickian in the Collegiate has been. Like the rest, I am deeply grateful for your success in preserving Edward on the throne. I was in error in even asking such a question. I pray you forgive me."

He said this seriously, without any apparent self-consciousness, and without losing any of his aura of personal power and authority.

"Of course, Son Won Phon," said Jim, floundering slightly. The point of payment seemed too tiny a matter for such elaborate courtesy—particularly to an inferior like himself. But the Eastern Magickian was going on.

"In any case, I would have wished to do it. It is an interesting case. You may leave it in my hands. Mage, Jim, will you forgive me if I now depart?"

"Certainly," said Carolinus. Jim, unsure of how to respond or whether Carolinus had not spoken for both of them, made an inarticulate sound in his throat. Son Won Phon disappeared.

Jim stared at the space where he had been, and turned on Carolinus.

"Is that all there is to it?"

"It is," said Carolinus. "You didn't expect him to let you involve yourself in his magickal process, whatever it is?"

"No, no . . ." said Jim, "I was just surprised to see the Magickian was Son Won Phon; I thought he would want to know more about it, before he went to work."

He had, though—had hoped to watch what Son Won Phon would do. But if that wish had seemed possible earlier, clearly there was no hope of it now.

"Son Won Phon is the most capable in the Collegiate in this specialty. But no Magickian is going to let you look over his shoulder as he works," said Carolinus. "Would you?"

"Certainly," said Jim, staring at the Mage. "What harm could it do?"

"Hah!" said Carolinus derisively, and vanished in his turn.

Troubled, Jim went to the fireplace and tried to make himself a cup of tea. While he was struggling to get the kettle swung over the fire where it would best have a steady heat without covering the kettle's bottom with soot, Angie came back in.

"Did you tell May Heather she was elevated to the rank of Mistress?" she asked.

"Certainly."

"Did you forget completely she's still apprenticed to Mistress Plyseth in the Serving Room, and no more than a day over fourteen or fifteen if she's that? Plyseth will have to be asked, first."

"She'll be told, not asked. I'm the lord of this castle. I can promote someone to Mistress or Master if I want to."

Angie looked at him with concern.

"You don't have to snap my head off," she said, but in a voice more worried than anything else. "What's the matter, Jim?"

"Sorry," he said, "I didn't mean it the way it sounded."

"It's not that," she said. "It's just not like you to talk so. What's bothering you, Jim? Tell me. Are you all tired out again?"

"No, no."

"Well, something's wrong. Here, let me at that kettle before you set the place on fire, pumping on those bellows. Turning the fireplace into a blast furnace's not necessary. You go sit down—or lie down, if you find yourself feeling like it. I'll bring you a cup of tea."

"Here you are," she said, minutes later. He was in the bed, but sitting up against the headboard when she brought him the steaming cup and sat down on the edge of the bed beside him.

Jim took the cup and sipped gratefully.

"I guess I was a little wound up," he said.

"Tell me."

"Well, I've wanted to magically do away with that scar on Geronde's cheek before her wedding if I could, for a long time."

"Jim, what a wonderful thought! That's why you asked me about that before?"

"Not as easy as it sounds, it seems. I wanted to surprise you. I thought I could do it myself, but I can't. So I asked Carolinus, and he said it was practically impossible, but there were some Magickians in the Collegiate who'd looked into the problem; he's not one of them, but he'd see about getting one to help. So he did."

"That's terrific!"

"Not quite. The specialist Carolinus brought here just before you got back was Son Won Phon."

"Not that Magickian who's been out to get you all along, and fought the duel with Carolinus over you?"

"Yes, but maybe no. I mean Carolinus told me it wasn't a vendetta. I mean, I may've been wrong about that. Carolinus says he's simply the soul of principle and would as soon condemn himself as anyone else."

"He doesn't sound like it."

"Well, I don't know now," said Jim. "As I say, he came and it was the first chance I'd had to meet him. He wasn't what I'd thought. Maybe Carolinus was right. Anyway, he's going to try fixing Geronde's scar. There're evidently problems with scars because they aren't like healing a fresh wound. You have to destroy what the body's grown to close the wound, and that's attacking a living part of another human being—against the rules of the Collegiate. Sometimes it works, sometimes it doesn't, no Magickian knows why."

"Jim," said Angie, "why don't you just tell me everything, from the time he first showed up until the time he left?"

Jim did.

"I don't know about him now, either," said Angie, nipping at her lower lip with her teeth. "But you say he struck you as honest?"

"Yes, he did."

"Well, then," she said, "there's no harm in letting him try, is there? He might as well go ahead. If he does, tremendous. If he doesn't, that's that."

"You're right, of course. God!" said Jim, looking at her gratefully. "It's good to have you to talk things over with, Angie!"

"That's one of the things I'm here for," said Angie, leaning forward to kiss him. "How do you feel now?"

"Much better," he said, setting down the empty teacup on the bedside table. "You're right. It was still bothering me a bit. You know, I think I will take a small nap."

"Good," said Angie, "you do that. Sleep's what's good for you right now."

He lay down on the bed, and sleep folded in over him immediately. He had a vague memory of Angie pulling up a bed cover over him, and then nothing—not even dreams.

He slept until the next morning.

He came to slowly. Judging by the sunlight through the windows, it was late morning, and Angie was not in the Solar. He lay there in a sort of delicious peace, coming to the full surface of consciousness. Sometime during the night she must have undressed him and got him fully under all the covers—none of the servants would have dared to— although it was standard practice for a knight or lord who'd drunk too much. But a Magickian—that was different.

Lazily, he tried to think of what he should be getting up and busy at, but he could think of nothing. Blessed nothing at all! He snuggled down under the covers and closed his eyes, willing himself back into the cozy well of sleep. But he did not sleep. Instead he gradually became more awake, and as he did, he began to think.

This was the next day. Why hadn't he heard from Son Won Phon—or at least from Carolinus—before this? A delicate magical—or even magickal—operation would not need what Jim's future world had needed in the way of time. With magic you could either do something or you couldn't. Essentially, you commanded it to happen, and if you knew what you were doing, it happened. Otherwise it didn't. In either case, you knew almost immediately.

He became rapidly more awake, and the emotion in him about Geronde's scar began to rise. He was astonished at the power of it, greater than his concern with the goblins. But that had been a case of instinctive survival. Necessity, not emotion, had been on his mind. But this determination that the scar should be gone at last was driving him like a storm wind at his back. No doubt it came from the years during which he had told himself he would fix it but had actually done nothing—and now time was short.

He got up from the bed abruptly and dressed. When that was done, he called Son Won Phon, the same way he was used to calling Carolinus and Kinetete.

Son Won Phon!

There was no answer. He tried again, putting extra energy into the call, on the chance that the lack of an answer came from the fact Son Won Phon was probably on the other side of the world. He was wading recklessly into the magic he had just earned in defeating the goblins, but that didn't matter now.

Son Won Phon!

No response. When the other got his message, he would, in effect, be hearing those words in Jim's voice, know who was calling him and realize the urgency behind the intrusion. But there was no reaction.

He tried calling twice more, in each case with less hope. No reply.

Jim braced himself. If Carolinus did not answer either, he would try Kinetete to see if she could help him get some news from Son Won Phon. She was a woman and might understand better how much a successful result to the operation would mean to Geronde. If even she was no help, or the answer from Son was bad news, he'd . . . he did not know what he'd do, but he'd keep trying on his own.

Carolinus!

Awake, are you, now, Jim? Carolinus' words sounded silently in his mind, with a foreboding kindliness to their tone. *Son's with me now. Stay where you are. We'll be with you in a moment.*

Remembering the unmade bed, Jim called in the servant to tidy up the Solar. While she was doing this, Jim paced the floor. As usual in such cases, the wait seemed to stretch out as if it would last until doomsday. The servant finished, curtsied and left. Jim reminded himself that Magickians— senior Magickians—had a bad habit of not paying attention to how prompt they were. But they always showed up eventually . . . the thought did not help.

Finally, Carolinus and Son Won Phon appeared.

"Here we are, Jim," Carolinus said. "Knowing how important sleep is to you right now, we didn't want to disturb you until you were fully awake." The treacherous kindliness in his voice, all wrong for him, was still there. "Son Won Phon will tell you of his efforts," he wound up.

"Jim," said Son Won Phon, "in this case, the necessary magickal process failed. I regret it extremely, and wish there was more to be done. But there is not. If all had gone well, as I hoped, Geronde would have woken up this morning with her disfigurement gone. She did not."

"I see," said Jim bleakly.

"As I say, I wish there was something further I could do. But the magick normally works immediately if it is going to work at all. Neither I, nor any of the other Magickians who have looked into this problem—some of much more exalted rank than I—have been able to understand why it succeeds in some cases and not in others. The magick is identical in the cases of both failure and success."

"Is there anything in common about either the failure or success?" said Jim desperately. "Something about the time the magick is used, the age or condition of those it's used on—anything at all in common with that separate group of failures that you don't find in the successes?"

"I do not understand you," said Son Won Phon.

"I'm wondering about the conditions under which the magick has to take effect—for example" he said, suddenly remembering something, "could the successes have all been people who as a group were more *innocent* than the failures—in the sense that animals are innocent and therefore immune to magick?"

"I see what you would suggest," said Son Won Phon. "Let me run over in my mind the cases I have personally known."

There was a long moment of silence in the Solar.

"No," the Oriental Magickian said, breaking the silence at last. "There is no group difference such as you suggest, and I can think of nothing else that would divide those in whom the magick fails from those in which it does not fail."

"It happens, Jim," said Carolinus. "Happens to the best of us. Sometimes magick does not work."

"In any case," said Son Won Phon to Jim, "I must leave now. As I say, I regret extremely not being able to be useful to you in this matter. There will be no charge, of course."

"No," said Jim. "I'm going to pay you anyway, as far as I can in magical energy, at least. I don't have a great deal of worldly goods to pay for such—"

"I regret," said Son Won Phon, "but I will not accept payment in any form from you. At the risk of disagreeing with the Mage—although I would assume it would be simply in the way he would seem to phrase his objection, if he should—my answer would be I feel you are not quite ready to accept the result in this case, and you would be quite right in not doing so, though I have little belief in your being able to improve upon what I failed to achieve."

"I didn't mean—" Jim began.

"It makes little difference what you meant," said Son Won Phon. "I simply warn you against unreasonable expectations. If you should by rare chance be successful in trying further yourself, knowledge of your solution would be greatly welcomed by all who have searched for the answer. Each of us who work with magick know that every other worker has his or her own way, which may give an answer when all others have failed. As a Magickian superior in rank to you, permit me to remind you that it is never magick itself that fails, but the Magickian who uses it. Therefore I have done nothing for you and no pay is due. Other Magickians may deal otherwise. That is up to them. I do not. Farewell, Apprentice Jim."

He was gone.

"He can be a prickly fellow sometimes," said Carolinus. "But it's a good idea just to accept the way he wants to do something. He lives by his own code, as all of us must."

"I follow you," said Jim, not quite truthfully. "But I can't help remembering someone said where I come from—said it a very long time ago, I think: 'There's nothing so dangerous as a completely honest man.' Or words to that effect. I hate to think he's the one who's going to observe me and report on me to the Collegiate before the rest will accept me into it—as you said has to happen."

"You'll do well," said Carolinus. "Don't concern yourself with that, Jim—not with that nor with Geronde's scar. Everyone did their best. Put it out of your mind. Just don't make any mistakes when you're being observed."

"Hah!" said Jim. "As if that was easy!"

"It's not easy. But you have to do it, now of all times. So do it."

"Don't worry," said Jim—adding, entirely untruthfully, "I've almost forgotten about Geronde's scar already."

"Good!" said Carolinus, and vanished.

Jim looked at the empty place where his Master-in-Magick had been. He had just lied to Carolinus. Lied in his teeth, and Carolinus was an old friend. What chance would he have of living up to Son Won Phon's expectations?

But none of that mattered. His mind could no more give up searching for a way to get that scar off Geronde's face, impossible as that now seemed, than Saint George could have turned his back and walked away from the dragon, or for that matter, than the dragon could have turned and left. Their battle could well be legendary—though not in this world, he reminded himself; in this improbable world it could well have been sober truth.

That was beside the point. Inside Jim, wrath was kindling. So Son Won Phon had failed. So, judging by Carolinus' reaction, he would never have shown him how his scar-removal magick worked. None of that mattered.

Jim was not a person of instant fighting reflex. If someone without warning threw a punch at him, he might dodge the blow, if he could, but instead of hitting out himself automatically, he was more likely to ask his attacker, "Why did you want to do that?" It was simply built into him to act so.

Usually, not until he saw the second blow coming would fury wake in him, and he would begin to fight. After that, of course, he often stood a fair chance of winning, since his fury would keep growing as he fought, until he no longer noticed being hit. But that delay of his could be suicidal, in this world, he reminded himself. Slow to reply could mean a dead James Eckert.

So, give up the idea of getting rid of Geronde's scar, as Carolinus had said, a duty which had been a burr in his conscience ever since he, Brian, Danielle, Dafydd and Aargh had not rescued her in time to keep her face from being cut?

Hell, no! She and Brian had been forced to wait too long to marry—and the actual marriage process meant too much to both of them. They had loved each other too deeply and too long not to deserve the most he could do for them!

Chapter 44

How much time did he have? Jim asked himself.

The wedding was tomorrow noon, and would take place on the steps of the chapel, to be followed immediately by a celebratory Mass inside. If the scar was to be gone, it would have to be gone before Geronde came out for the ceremony. He mustn't just make it disappear in the middle of the day, when everybody could notice its vanishing.

Local people would be quick enough to wind up calling it a miracle anyway, but he wanted them to give the credit to the wedding, the Mass—any number of things, just so they didn't suspect that magic and he had anything to do with it.

The only really practical time for it to disappear was overnight, when Geronde was asleep and didn't know about it herself until morning.

All right, he had time, then. Ignore the fact that Son Won Phon would not let him know how he had tried to do it. He was used to figuring magic out in his own way, anyway.

In fact, Carolinus had always left him to figure things out by himself—the equivalent of throwing him into deep water to teach him how to swim. No two Magickians, Carolinus had insisted from the start, made identical magicks the same way—that much was true. But it had been some years before Jim began to understand this was not the standard way of training apprentices in magick.

The usual way was to make them learn simple spells by

rote, and then practice them until they began to experiment on their own and develop the first elements of their own unique artistry. Possibly, that was the reason even experienced Magickians like Son Won Phon did not offer to share their methods.

So, he was free to follow his own, personally worked-out, pattern of learning how to do something he wanted.

First find the roots of why the magic hadn't worked on Geronde, he told himself. Son Won Phon had suggested a reason when he told Jim that if magick failed, it was never the fault of the magick itself, but of the Magickian.

There must be two groups of patients after all, in spite of the senior Magickian's denial—one for whom the magic worked, one for whom it didn't.

All right then, what divided the failures from the successes? It couldn't be the magick alone, because Son Won Phon would be using the same technique each time—otherwise he'd quickly have found out what worked and what didn't.

That meant the difference had to be in the people he was working with. What could be different between scarred people? It had to be something about their individual natures—or characters.

But everybody was different from everyone else. It had to be some difference that the successful patients had in common.

Well, what made the strong differences between people in this time? Their capacity to love was certainly one. Angie had it in large amounts. Geronde had it probably almost as—no, be fair—equally as much as Angie, but in her own way. Aside from the fact that it also varied from person to person, the very word was used differently here and—as had occurred to him as he watched those moonlit drifters trudging westward, some nights past—it had a much wider use in this time and place. It could mean sexual love, but it also could mean a great many other relationships. Men here, for example, would use the word readily, where men in Jim's time in many cases avoided it—using "like" instead.

Women of course had no such inhibitions, now or in the future. "Love" to them primarily meant strong affection—a strong bond, with someone or something.

Very strong affection was capable of being as strong as Faith. Strong enough to do the impossible, sometimes. Almost all enduring religions had claimed love as part of what should be possessed by their worshipers.

And the strongest loves were often for children or Faith. Faith and Love were cousins, even brothers—or sisters—in the happiest people.

He needed help.

"Hob!" he called to the fireplace. "I need you!"

There was only a few seconds' wait before Hob appeared in the fireplace, unconcernedly walking out through the blazing fire that was now being kept lit, twenty-four hours a day, as winter came down on them.

"M'lord?"

"I need you to help me understand some things."

"Me, m'lord?" said Hob, and his voice rang with delight. Then caution set in. "But I'm only a hob."

"That's why."

"Oh!" Caution had given way to mystification.

"You told me sometime before the battle that the tenants and serfs with a cross on their doors were quite safe from the goblins, but a cross on the gates here at Malencontri wouldn't protect us at all."

Hob writhed with a touch of embarrassment and ended up standing on one leg.

"It was just that you're a Magickian, m'lord. You remember that was what the Mage was telling you before the battle."

"Exactly!" said Jim, and Hob's leg came down. "And because being a Magickian made me no longer an innocent, the castle could be attacked. What made the cottagers innocent when I wasn't?"

"Well, they . . . they believed the cross would keep them safe, so it did." Hob hurriedly added "—but I don't mean that they're any way better than you, m'lord, or even any great or good human. They just believed."

"Like animals? Animals are immune to magic. They're innocent, too."

"But it's a different sort of innocence with animals, m'lord! Animals can't smell, see or taste magick, so they just don't believe in it. Instead of believing, they don't believe—at all. To them, it can't be there, so it isn't."

"The cottagers have faith, you mean, and it keeps them safe, and the animals have no faith so that's what keeps them safe. Let's try it from another angle. What happens to a goblin that tries to get into a house with a cross on it?"

"But m'lord, they never would try. They know it's no use."

"*Why* is it no use? How do they know it'll never work? Try to imagine one trying to get in a door with a cross on it. What if he tried to rub out the cross? Could he get in then? What would happen, exactly?"

"He just couldn't!" said Hob strongly. "He couldn't touch such a house—and he could never, ever touch a cross itself to rub it out. He just couldn't. Even I can't touch a cross. Has m'lord something he can write a cross on that can be rubbed out? I'll show you."

Paper was beginning to be made and used near the end of the medieval period, and Angie used it for her accounts of Malencontri's expenditures, income, items and food stored—and so forth. It was a thick, brownish-white paper. The ink Angie used would be indelible on it, but chalk should show up on its darker surface. . . . Jim rummaged in Angie's desk, careful not to disturb her filing system, and came back to the eating table with a sheet and a piece of chalk.

He laid the paper on the table and drew a small cross on it.

"All right," he said to Hob, "show me."

Hob came to the desk and poised a slim finger over the just visible white cross.

"See, m'lord," he said to Jim, "*I'm* not afraid to try to touch it, the way a goblin would be. That's because they just use magick for hate things; but we hobs use our magick for loving things, like making children laugh, or taking them for a ride on the smoke when they're lonely or unhappy. We found loving everyone and everything—except goblins, of course—was much happier, and then we found that it let us get into houses and chimneys, too. We could live with you humans and be even happier. So it was all in the way we were different from the goblins to start off with."

Love, and Faith in Love making the magical difference for them, thought Jim.

"Except that when I try to touch the cross—" Hob was going on.

Hob leaned on his thumb, still poised in the air over the cross Jim had made, with all his small weight. But his fingertip would not make contact with the paper.

"I think," he said, apologetically, "it won't let me touch it because I'm just a Natural, and I've got magick, too."

"All right," said Jim, brushing the chalk away just to see if he could make the cross disappear, now. He could.

"I believe you," he went on. "But a goblin wouldn't even be able to touch any of the house if just that one cross was there?"

"No, m'lord. Even if he dared."

"The cross sets up a sort of ward, then?"

"If m'lord will forgive me," said Hob, a little timidly, "I think the two things aren't the same at all. I can't say why, but I'm sure they're different."

"But for people to deal with Faith, at all, they have to be innocents. But we humans aren't innocents."

"If m'lord will forgive me again, I don't think humans have to be all the way innocent—just in certain things. Maybe some humans have a sort of innocent faith part."

Jim thought of some of his cottagers who were not at all innocent in certain aspects of their lives. On the other hand they were innocent about the cross protecting them from goblins—and that innocence had protected them. Come to think of it, the same thing was true of the knightly class. Innocent in some things, decidedly not in others—except for the rare ones like Brian, who was actually, Jim told himself, touchingly innocent in a remarkable number of ways.

That was probably the reason moral decisions always seemed so clear-cut to Brian. Jim remembered being amazed, when he had first encountered Brian, that the other man seemed to be capable of what Jim at first thought of as double-think—such as understanding his King was a drunk and not overloaded with moral scruples, but at the same time revering him, and being ready to die for him as someone anointed by God and above all ordinary men. Brian seemed to find no conflict at all between the two points of view.

But it was not double-think at all. It was a matter of two equally valid, different things. Brian did not *love* the King, but he had unlimited *faith* in him, as chosen to rule and destined to be obeyed by all Englishmen.

It was one of the vast differences in attitude behind the same words and the same facts, as they were accepted in the fourteenth century and in Jim's twentieth.

"And," Hob was saying, growing even braver, "being part innocent doesn't happen with animals, at all. They're all innocent clear through."

"Right!" said Jim.

He thought he knew what was needed to get that scar off. It would require finding the Love and Faith he needed from somewhere—but in unusual quantities. Beyond that, it would only be a matter of creating the necessary concept in a form he himself could believe, to have the power to do the work.

It struck him that this must bear some relationship to the making of real miracles, in which the ordinary human apparently was always reported as asking Someone above him or her to cause it to happen.

But was he in any touch with any such Someone? There was no hoping to find that kind of Faith in himself—he did not have it. But close at hand he had at least one other human person who might have.

"Hob," he said, "do you happen to know where Brian is, right now? Is he in the castle?"

"Not right now, m'lord," said Hob. "He and Lord Dafydd went out with bows to hunt."

That was Brian, of course. He could never sit still for more than a few minutes. He had to be active at something.

"Do you want me to take the smoke and go looking for him, m'lord?"

"No, that's all right. I can find him myself, and you shouldn't call Dafydd a lord where anybody but Brian and I can hear you."

"Yes, m'lord. And I never let anyone know he's a Prince."

Jim winced.

"That's in another land—"

"Yes, m'lord. The Drowned Land. But I know he doesn't want anyone but you and Sir Brian to know—and I'll never let them know!"

"I wish you'd just forget it completely," said Jim. "You aren't supposed to know. Daffyd wouldn't be pleased to learn you did. When did you find out, anyway?"

"The time we were in the Drowned Land, on our way to Lyonesse. I was riding on your back under your mail shirt, as I always do."

"Well, try to keep it out of your mind. Don't even say it

to the Lady Angela or me. That's safest. You can go now.
Thanks—"

His last word was out before he thought. He was always
forgetting that in this time, words like that were used very
rarely indeed. Your inferiors wouldn't dare praise you in
any way—that would be presumptuous, as suggesting that
they had some kind of equality with you. Your equals
wouldn't because doing so might suggest they were admitting your superiority over themselves—and your superiors
never praised you if they could help it, for fear of giving
you a better opinion of yourself than was good for you.

"Wait!" he added hurriedly. "You have to understand
something, Hob. I'm glad you mentioned Dafydd's secret.
But you must understand how important it is you never
mention it, particularly to Dafydd. He'd have no choice but
to think I'd broken my word not to tell anyone."

"Oh, m'lord!" Hob clasped his hands together. "I'll let
him cut me into little pieces before I made a sound about
any of this!"

"I don't think Dafydd'd go that far, but I'm glad to know
you'll stay silent."

"I will! I will!"

"Good. You can go now, then. I'll set about finding Brian
in my own way."

Hob went back up the chimney in one swift motion.

Jim flopped on his back on the newly made bed and vi-
sualized Brian in his mind. The image was not clear. He
tried instead to visualize Brian's surroundings at the moment. It was a matter of making himself see what kind of
surface Brian was on and expanding from there. Carolinus
had a much quicker way of finding people he decided to
visit. Jim had been with him on occasions when Carolinus
had decided they two should go somewhere, and immediately they were there.

Jim made a mental note to look into a faster method for
himself, and went back to putting together what he wanted

to say to Brian. Meanwhile, in his mind's eye the woodland scene where Brian now sat was taking form.

Brian was in a small glade, no more than a dozen yards in length, entirely surrounded by old elms and an occasional oak. It would have been a pleasant little place in the warm summertime, when the leaves were out, but now only a few brown tokens of the summer still clung to the otherwise naked boughs. All there glistened with moisture. The air would probably be close to a freezing temperature.

Brian's hunting clothes were on his back, his sword hung at one hip, his quiver of arrows at the other. His bow was on his shoulder. No armor. He was seated on a very old, large elm that had finally fallen after a long, long life—as usual blithely ignoring the weather. He was sharpening the point of a boar spear he had probably brought along just in case—a short spear with a crosspiece halfway up its blade to keep the boar, once speared, from pushing himself all the way up the metal shaft to savage the spear-holder with his tusks.

Only Brian would go out hoping to encounter a full-sized male boar alone—and without at least dogs, a mail shirt and some leg armor.

Dafydd was not with him. They had spread out, no doubt to increase their chances of finding some rabbits—that, Jim told himself, was a break for him. He needed to talk to Brian alone. Dafydd, of course, would fade away into the woods at the slightest hint that the situation was one that would call for a private talk between his two friends. But it was embarrassing to let him know he was not wanted, close as the three of them had always been.

Brian! Jim called to his mind. Brian immediately forgot all about the boar spear, lifted his head alertly and looked around as if he expected to Jim to materialize out of the surrounding forest. *I need to talk to you about something important. Is now a good time?*

"Certes, it is!" said Brian aloud, at the same time involuntarily sending the thought Jim-ward. "Where are you?"

"At Malencontri. But I'll be with you in a minute—or two," Jim added, remembering it would be cold out there and he was dressed for indoors. He got up hastily, found the lined leather jacket Angie had made for him to wear under his shirt of mail, and put it on.

He also added the mail shirt itself and his knight's belt with sword and scabbard—more because Brian would ask why he wasn't wearing them if he showed up without them than for any practical reason.

As Brian and many of his kind thought, no knight went outdoors without his sword, at least—temperature up or temperature down.

It annoyed Jim slightly. Carolinus could show up before Brian in these same forest surroundings, wearing only one of his old red robes, and it would never occur to Brian that the Mage should have dressed otherwise.

Jim transferred himself to Brian's glade. Brian rose to his feet at the sight of him.

"Had a chance at a large buck," he said. "Magnificent beast, but too much distance between us for me to make sure of bringing him down with one arrow. Wound him only and he could run for miles. Dafydd wasn't with me—had gone after rabbits. Rabbits! He could have brought the stag to earth in a wink, stone dead. But we aren't short of food anyway."

"That's just it, we may be," said Jim. Dafydd had once privately explained to him that he should understand Brian was actually over-bowed, like many who did not really understand the bow. He insisted on using a bow with an eighty-pound pull, when he should actually be using a seventy-pound one—or even a sixty. Eighty pounds threw his aim off, which was why he was less than expert with that one weapon, compared to the way he handled all others.

But a sixty-pound bow was considered a woman's weapon; and seventy pounds for striplings. And even worse,

Danielle, Dafydd's wife, daughter of an archer, pulled an eighty-pound bow with authority. Brian would be embarrassed and offended by a change to a lighter bow, so he compromised by getting as close as he could to very large targets.

"Short of food, James?" Brian was saying now. "And winter just starting?"

"Maybe," said Jim. "Angie's checking supplies now. Remember how many people we've been housing and feeding. Thank heaven the hobs don't eat."

"Wonder how they do it," said Brian, who stuffed himself at every opportunity and never gained weight.

"I don't ask, and they don't know themselves."

"Trolls eat like wolves."

"I know. But Naturals are all different in some way. Forget that, Brian. I've something more important to say."

"France talks of war?"

"No. More important than that. This concerns Geronde, and I'm going to have to swear you to secrecy about this present talk of ours before I go on. Above all you must never tell Geronde of it."

"James! I cannot promise blindly to keep something secret from Geronde, my wife before God—as she will be tomorrow!"

"A miracle may depend on your doing so."

Suddenly very serious, Brian crossed himself.

"On my soul should be it, then. Geronde! What is it, James—don't torture me with these preliminaries."

"These preliminaries—never mind, Brian," said Jim. "In a word, I have a feeling she may be touched by a miracle this coming night!"

"A miracle!" Brian almost shouted the word. "A—a good miracle?"

"One I think she would desire only second to this marriage finally to you."

"What—"

"It only may be. Note, I only say it may happen. But if it does, she will wake tomorrow without the scar de Bois put on her cheek."

"That scar?" Brian's voice trembled. His eyes filled with tears. "Oh, James, she would wish that more than anything on earth! I was remiss, James—I have been very very remiss! I have had time to do it, but I should have hunted down that Hell-bound bastard and carved him into fishbait—I should have insisted on standing in for you when he challenged you before Malencontri, that time we dealt with the rogue magickian Malvinne. I should have—"

"Never mind what you should have. None of those things would have erased the scar. This may."

"Of course. Of course—De Bois may yet be alive for me to find him. But James . . . I hardly know how to ask. Do you have a hand in this possible miracle? I mean—with your, your—"

"Me?" said Jim. "Reassure yourself, Brian! I can swear truthfully in my turn that none of my magick will have a part in this!"

"Then it will be a true, holy miracle?"

"It may be," said Jim thoughtfully, "I don't know. In spite of the imaginings of men like myself, it may be. Remember though, Brian, the word that it will happen is *may*, not *will*."

But Brian did not answer. He had fallen to his knees on the dark carpet of damp, fallen leaves, already rotting from the rains of the past weeks. He bowed his head, closed his eyes and folded his hands together, pressing them against his lips. His lips moved slightly. He was silently praying. Jim stood and waited.

"Come, James!" said Brian; suddenly getting to his feet with clear eyes and a strong voice. "We must hurry back to the castle. I must pray in the chapel all this afternoon and night that this miracle may come to pass!"

"Wait!" said Jim, standing where he was as Brian turned and started striding off through the glade. "Come back! I'll get us both to the castle in no time at all when I'm through telling you about this. Geronde must never know that I told you anything. A long vigil in the chapel, the night before the wedding, is bound to make her curious—"

"Why?" Brian stopped and turned, staring blankly at him. "I am a knight and have my own duties to God, and prayers are privy—sacred. She would never ask—as I would not ask her."

Brian came back.

"I must do something," he said. "I cannot just wait for a miracle as wished for as this one, meantime doing nothing to show my desire and thanks to God for it!"

"That's what I've still got to tell you, and I haven't had the chance yet," said Jim. "This miracle will depend on what you yourself do—and what you must do will take all your heart, all your soul and courage!"

"Only tell me what that is!" Brian's eyes were shining in the watery sunlight.

"You must now," said Jim slowly and as seriously as he knew how to do, "spend the time between now and this coming morning with only this in your mind. Miracles are not to be questioned. Avoid giving away any hint of what you know and feel to Geronde. Do not look at her scar more than you ordinarily would. But at the same time never doubt for an instant that the miracle will come to pass. Believe with all that is in you that all of her face will once more be untouched, and never give in to the desire to look and see whether the miracle has happened—in short, your faith in it must be beyond all doubt!"

"I shall do it," said Brian simply.

They looked at each other for a second, and then Brian spoke again, almost gaily, in the sort of voice Jim had heard from him when he was about to go into battle.

"But now take us back by your magick to Malencontri, without further delay, James. I must be about my doing."

Chapter 45

Back at Malencontri, Jim felt like taking a nap but didn't dare for fear he might sleep all night. It was just as well, for the minute he and Brian appeared in the empty great hall—its three huge fireplaces blazing away, but so far not taking much chill out of the large, uninsulated space—Angie captured him.

"There you are!" she said. "Hello, Brian, any luck?"

"I had a chance at a buck. Magnificent beast, but there were too many branches in the way of an arrow."

"Too bad," said Angie. "We can use any extra food we can get, with winter all ahead of us."

"So James explained to me. But you know, James, Angela, there is extra food and to spare in other castles like those of your neighbors who have lost many more of their people to the plague than you have. They can hardly refuse to share, when you have given them a victory led by a Prince of the Blood, and under the eye of the King himself—a victory to be sung of."

Jim and Angie stared at each other. Then they both turned to face Brian.

"Brian!" said Angie. "Do you really think they'd contribute? Of course I know Geronde would share Malvern's store with us, but the plague touched as lightly there and at Smythe Castle as it did here, and the most she could give wouldn't see us through."

"Certes!" said Brian. "Your other neighbors can well afford to help. Just ask them. Common neighborliness requires their generosity in addition to everything else."

"Never thought of that," said Jim.

"Neither did I," said Angie. "But, Jim, I need you—right now. We're going to take May Heather to Mistress Plyseth and see how she feels about releasing May from being her apprentice—it was your idea."

"As for me," said Brian, "I must be about other matters. I will mention it to Geronde, who can spread the word among tomorrow's guests. See you at supper, if you are not so occupied with this business of Mistress Plyseth you miss that gathering. Bit of an appetite, myself."

He walked off towards the stairs.

"Come on, Jim!" said Angie, with the firmness of a chatelaine secure in a matter where her authority must be recognized, even over the lord of the castle.

Jim had been staring after Brian. He had seemed so much his usual unconcerned self, within a few minutes of committing himself to something that Jim could not conceive of enduring. Was it just that Brian was taking his coming night in the chapel lightly, after all? No, Brian never would—never could—be so indifferent about pledging his soul to an ordeal Jim could imagine only too clearly, knowing the chapel as he did.

No. It was his own, rather wonderful, way of facing whatever lay before him as an ordinary matter. Not with fatalism—far from it—but simply as a duty to be done.

"Coming . . ." said Jim vaguely, and turned to follow Angie on her way to the Serving Room. They found Gwyneth Plyseth, Mistress there, seated in a chair padded with cushions, watching a slip of a young girl in a whitish dress practicing putting plates into the warming oven for the noontime meal—here, always called dinner.

"—No, no," she was saying to the girl as they came in. "How many times must I tell you! Put the food on the plates and then warm plate and food together—m'lady! M'lord!"

She made an effort to struggle to her feet.

"Sit!" said Angie. "We've just come to tell you something. May Heather's work in the Nursing Room has been so well done we wish to make her Mistress of it. That means we must ask you to release her from her apprenticeship to you."

Gwyneth began to cry. She did not burst into tears as a younger woman might have done. Instead the tears simply began to streak down her gray, lined face.

"Oh," she said, brokenly, "I knew this day would come. May was such a comfort to me, and I was only waiting to see her back here again. So quick to understand. So good to remember! And now you will end up making her Mistress here in my place!—in this Serving Room where I have worked so long!"

She rocked slightly back and forth in her chair, weeping.

Jim melted. Angie, however, was made of sterner stuff.

"Nonsense!" she said. "You're Mistress here. You'll stay Mistress here as long as you can give orders. Who else knows what must be done in this room as well as you? How could we ever do without you? Now, you know that!"

Gwyneth snuffled a little and wiped her tears away.

"But May—" she began.

"May will simply come here for a few hours a day to courteously pass on to your new girl what she knows, and help her to do things that would force you to get up from your chair. May's domain is only the Nursing Room, no more."

"Bless you, m'lady—m'lord! And will she beat this new one for me? I'm afeared it's too much for me, though she's nowhere the strength of that devil—begging your pardon, m'lady, m'lord—that very good May Heather. Oh! they don't make apprentices like they used to when I was a girl!"

The new girl looked terrified.

"As for beating, we'll see," said Angie. "You know I don't greatly approve of beatings, just to help make the apprentice remember the right way to do something. I've told May what to do. But, as one Mistress to another should, she will, in all things outside my orders, listen to your wishes in this room. She understands that."

"Bless you again, m'lady. I will give up May, as apprentice, then, with a much less regret. But it is heartwarming of you to still want old bones like mine here. But I would, if God is so good to me, to die in this Serving Room where I have spent so many years."

"Knowing you, you undoubtedly will, still making sure everything is done right," said Angie. She turned to the new servant in the room. "What's your name, girl?"

"Alaine, m'lady, dotter of Will-below-the-Mill, so please you," squeaked the girl. "Ee found me a place here, so's I'd might be not get the plague, so please you." She made an awkward stab at a curtsy.

"Well, be a good girl, Alaine," said Angie, "and May'll treat you kindly."

"Oh, thank you, m'lady!" said Alaine, looking greatly reassured—but not completely. She had heard those words before.

Jim and Angie left, moving towards the Nursing Room.

"Gwyneth and the other old hands are like sled dogs," said Angie after they had walked a little distance. "If one of a dog team breaks a leg and you have to cut her out of harness, she'll run alongside on three legs, trying to still be on the team—did you know the carpenter got up from what looked like his deathbed and went back to work, and is literally flourishing?"

"I do," said Jim. "He almost bit my head off earlier today when I dropped by his shop. He was telling off a couple of his journeymen and simply included me in the list—ah, May, there you are."

"Yes, m'lord, so please you. Will you grant me a moment to put this rat in the slop bin?"

"Certainly," said Jim, and May went off to do it. She was back in the moment she had mentioned.

"Begging your forgiveness, m'lord, but holding rats is bad luck. The little terriers are wonders at killing them, but they will never learn to take them to the bin, alone."

"Hah! Yes," said Jim, in full knightly voice, "my lady wishes to give you some new orders."

Now it was May looking—not alarmed, but cautious.

"Mistress," said Angie—and May's expression relaxed into happiness, "—I'm glad to see so few patients, since I've got an extra duty for you. Idle hands are the Devil's instrument, you know."

"Indeed I do," said May, crossing herself and curtsying at the same time, so that all Superior powers might be equally honored. "I will gladly—"

"It is simply that Mistress Plyseth has a new apprentice named Alaine," said Angie, "and when you have an hour or so to spare, I'd like you to drop by the Serving Room and teach her some things Mistress Plyseth herself now finds difficult to do. You are, of course, a Mistress yourself now, and Mistress Plyseth understands that your helping her is a courtesy on your part—you are in no way under her orders; though, as more youthful than she is, you will defer to her in manners as a younger Mistress should."

"Yes, m'lady."

"One other thing. You know my views on beating apprentices to make sure they remember what they're taught?"

"Indeed, m'lady!" said May.

"I have reminded her of them, so you need only follow her views as you think best. I would not give this advice to most young Mistresses, but you are not afraid of learning new ways."

"I fear nothing, m'lady" said May, stoutly—it was literally true, Jim knew.

"But I will give it to you, because I think you have the wits to use it to advantage. The truth—though it's rarely known—is that an apprentice will learn more and quicker if she or he loves you, rather than fears you. That's because loving you makes her want to be like you, enjoy learning, and be eager to do it right to please you."

May's eyes lit up, but then she looked somewhat doubtful.

"But are they not then tempted to get up to pert or naughty tricks, m'lady—pardon my presumption for suggesting it. One might even sometimes be a bit—" May was plainly remembering her apprenticeship to Plyseth "—stubborn?"

"Well, if they're into anything like that, you'll have to use your own good judgment. But try to gain their love and keep it. That may make it so no beatings at all are necessary."

May's eyes grew big. But, of course, she did not argue—which Jim knew she had never hesitated to do when she objected to something.

"I will, m'lady. But you and m'lord can make people love you; I don't know if I can."

"Try."

"I will, m'lady. I really will."

Jim and Angie left, heading for the tower stairs that would lead them to their own large and comfortable room.

"In fact, I believe you saved his life, ordering him back to work that way," said Angie as Jim shut the door behind them—*Ah, peace,* thought Jim. Angie would be speaking of the carpenter, once more. She did that occasionally, after a gap in the original conversation, and he could hardly be irritated by it—she had probably caught the habit from him. He was often lost in his own thoughts and forgot that the person he was talking to had not shared them.

"Well, we'll see," he said, heading across the room and sitting down on the bed—to his own surprise. He had meant to sit down in one of the padded chairs, but his body had automatically steered for the bed.

But the bedding and bedstrings upholding it felt good. Friendly and good. He stretched out on his back.

"I thought so!" he heard Angie saying. "What've you been getting up to that would gear you up more than you should be geared, now? No, forget about answering that. Just let yourself sleep."

"I can't," he answered. "With guests here we ought to make an effort to show up for dinner."

"Why?" said Angie. "If it's sleep your body needs? Didn't Carolinus tell you to let yourself rest whenever you felt like it, and eventually, suddenly, this sleepy business would stop—but until then, don't fight it?"

"Something like that . . ." said Jim groggily. "But . . ." He could not think what he was going to say.

"Hey, wait!" he heard Angie's voice as if from some distance. "Let me at least get you undressed and under the covers—"

But he heard no more. He was already gone into deep, deep unconsciousness.

It seemed only a moment later that Angie was shaking him. Morning sunlight was once more shouting through the windows of the Solar.

"What? What . . ." he managed to say.

"It's the last thing I wanted to do to you, the way you are now," Angie was saying. "But you've just got time to get to the chapel steps before Brian and Geronde make their appearance."

"Appearance . . . ," he echoed, bewildered, his still half-asleep brain refusing to make sense of this.

"The wedding, Jim. Their wedding. I'm part of Geronde's wedding party, and you're part of Brian's. We can just make it, if you start dressing now and don't waste any time."

"Why didn't you rouse me before this?" he demanded, suddenly awake and sitting up. He jumped out of bed, abruptly realized he was naked, and at the same time noticed that Angie was wearing a remarkable, new, russet wool robe he had never seen on her before. She also seemed to have gained weight slightly since he fell asleep. It was unbelievable and hard to tell, but it looked like it.

"Come on," said Angie. "I've got your clothes all laid

out on the foot of the bed. Come on, now, I'll help you into them!"

"I can dress myself," growled Jim, and proceeded to do so, becoming more and more astonished at the layers of clothing she had laid out.

"Why all this?" he demanded, but putting them on, anyway.

"It's cold outside."

"Not this cold, actually?"

"You'll find out."

"All right," said Jim. "But I could just as well ward us against cold."

"And what would happen to your ward when we went into the chapel?"

Of course . . . all magic would vanish on the threshold of a consecrated area. And the unheated chapel would not easily shed its stony coldness, despite being packed with all those who could get in.

The chapel was the same temperature as the courtyard—an icebox this time of year. It had not been built with a fireplace, for the simple reason that such would need to be ablaze more than twenty-four hours before the place was used—stone walls, stone floor, stone roof.

"Well, I'll wear my fur-lined winter cloak," he said, "instead of all this."

"No, you won't," said Angie. "You're in Brian's wedding party. No cloaks for the wedding party."

"Why that?" cried Jim.

"Because it's Geronde's wedding and she wants it that way. Now will you get dressed? I let you sleep to almost the last moment."

He dressed, meanwhile catching up on his own thoughts. Waking suddenly like this, his mind had been numb. These Olympic-class sleeps he'd been having lately were so deep he lost track. He had planned this morning to get hold of Brian quietly and early, to ask him about the scar.

Now, he had lost all chance to do that. But, he remembered, as one of the groom's wedding party—along with Dafydd—he was to be with Brian all through the process of the marriage on the chapel steps, even if talking in the chapel was out.

But outside would be a problem, too. Brian was not always the most patient of men, and the antagonism between him and his treasure-hunting, future father-in-law had reached a new high, all the more in that it had never come out into the open between them, so far. But there were few of the Somerset gentry present who did not know of it.

If Sir Geoffrey de Chaney should even mutter something unintelligible, but possibly offensive, during the wedding, it would be well that Brian had his two closest friends beside him, to whisper a calming word or two in his ear, to keep him from challenging de Chaney to say it aloud.

Even a less-than-audible sound from de Chaney could set Brian off. A raised eyebrow might do it. Jim would have to choose his moment to ask about the scar, carefully.

Then he remembered that, of course, he'd be seeing Geronde's face for himself. Probably earlier than he'd have a chance to ask Brian about it. He cheered up. These problems only required being patient.

He finished dressing and the two of them went downstairs. A few of the neighbors were dodging the weather and helping themselves to the food and drink on the *table dormant*, set up for just this occasion. With a cheerful word or two, Jim and Angie hurried past them—as official members of the proceedings, it would surprise no one that they had no time to be hosts. He and Angie went out the door at the far end of the hall into a stiffer wind than Jim had thought possible, even from the amount of extra clothing Angie had laid out.

The chilling breeze was probably coming from what was currently a stormy North Sea, its damp, icy air mounting the curtain wall and sweeping down into the open courtyard.

Many of the neighbors, all cloaked, were already there. Even the King, bundled in furs, was there on a small platform, sitting above the crowd in the new armchair with the leopard heads, now finished, at the end of the arm rests.

Jim remembered that his royal self was not officially supposed to be present. Jim, like everybody, had been briefed to address him—only if highly necessary—as Sir Jack Straw, an obvious *nom d'etat*.

And there was Brian, with Dafydd already beside him, in the small clear space at one side of the steps. Neither was cloaked. Brian was wearing a startlingly white, silk, furlined cote-hardi with tight blue sleeves above blue hose. That cote-hardi was something he would never have wasted money on himself. It would have been Geronde's choice and purchase. Dafydd's hose and jacket were both forest green—clothes that did not violate the sumptuary laws against common men dressing above their class, but worn with that strange elegance Dafydd seemed able to achieve with everything he wore, handled, or used.

Everybody was standing, waiting. One necessary person was not there.

"Where's Geronde?" Jim asked Angie.

"I don't know?" she said. "I'll go find out."

She vanished back into the Great Hall. Jim went on to join Brian, taking the opposite side from Dafydd.

Brian was looking both grim and tense. Unusually so. It was obviously not the moment to begin asking him about Geronde's scar. Also, Jim would just as soon not even Dafydd should suspect Jim's part in the attempt to remove it.

But, with the moment so close, now, Jim found his need to know like an ache inside him. He discovered himself praying internally, an unusual activity for him.

But he could wait, he told himself. Geronde would be coming out in a few minutes.

"Damned bastard!" growled Brian, under his breath.

"Easy, Brian," he murmured. "Easy! What did he do?"

"Nothing," Brian muttered. "He just keeps standing there and staring at me as if I was a cockroach in his pudding! That's what's so maddening about it."

"Things will start and then he'll have to pay attention instead to what's going on. Ignore him."

"Not by-our-Lady easy!" answered Brian. But he deliberately looked away from de Chaney to stare instead at Malvern's Steward, who had already mounted importantly to the second of the three steps to the chapel door, proudly carrying a roll of parchment in his left hand.

There was a sudden stir in the standing, watching, cloaked crowd. Geronde had just appeared out of the door to the Great Hall, Angie and Danielle with her. The crowd stared.

She was wearing a lady's version of the same male-fashion cote-hardi Brian and Jim were wearing—a garment interestingly called, Jim remembered, a Hell's Window.

The cote-hardi was sleeveless, showing her lower arms tightly clothed by the sleeves of a rich, dark blue gown, trimmed with white silk. The Hell's Window also had slits down each side to reveal more of the gown; and a wide belt was worn low around her hips as a knight's belt was worn. It was also made in the same way—a belt of joined plaques—not of steel plaques, but lacy silver ones enameled in floral designs.

The Hell's Window was also open in front to show a row of tiny buttons down the front of the dark blue dress; and her golden hair was completely loose—it would be put up only after she had become a married woman.

Jim looked eagerly at Geronde's face. He saw no scar. Belatedly, he remembered that the left-handed de Bois had, of course, slashed her right cheek.

To get to the chapel, Geronde and her party had necessarily turned left when coming out of the Great Hall door, so the side of her face with the scar was still hidden from where Jim stood with Brian, at the far side of the steps. Only when Jim got a look at the right side of her face would he know.

It was a comforting explanation. But in spite of its reasonableness, he felt a small, cold, sinking feeling inside him. For one thing, those who could now see the right side of her face were not acting as if they could see anything different about her. The eyes of all—particularly those of the women—were all on her clothes. Jim pushed the whole question sternly from him. In time, he would see.

Geronde, Angie and Danielle came to the right side of the steps and halted there. The priest from Geronde's castle came out of the chapel door, pulling the hood of his white alb up to cover his head.

He was the only person there, besides those involved in the wedding, who could not indulge himself in a cloak. He was wearing only the alb for outer garment, but presumably, Jim thought, like everyone else he must have extra clothes beneath it. With the tonsure on his head now covered, he looked, more than anything, as a representative of Holy Church addressing a group of pilgrims about to go on a pilgrimage.

"We are here gathered together," he said now, in clear baritone voice—and the crowd stilled its busy murmurings about Geronde's clothing and their probable cost and style. "—to witness the marriage of Sir Brian Neville-Smythe and Lady Geronde Isabel de Chaney. We will now hear the reading of the marriage contract."

He stepped backwards a little to put the closed door of the chapel at his shoulder blades, to cut off the wind from circling around him quite so cruelly.

The Steward moved to the center of the second step and unrolled the first six inches of his scroll, holding it at arms length, and began to read loudly.

Chapter 46

What the Steward read began with a long screed written in English, but also in heavy legal language, understandable but ornate.

It began by naming the parties involved, their ancestries and social positions, and the financial arrangements concerned with the marriage, at the present moment and in case of certain future developments. From there it descended into particulars of these matters and the basis upon which the contract had been drawn up.

The visitors in the courtyard wrapped their cloaks more tightly around them, pulled their hoods over their heads as far as they would go, and listened in silence.

It might be, thought Jim, that a fair share of them were actually interested in this long declamation, hoping to learn something more than they already knew of Geronde's prospects and Castle Malvern's worth and wealth.

But Jim himself paid little attention. He found his attention was all on Geronde; and he had been mentally sending a message to turn her head enough to let him see her other cheek.

She did not oblige.

In spite of his keen desire to see for himself, the worry he had been struggling to keep out of his mind stayed with him. Had Brian's determination to do what Jim had suggested yesterday, failed? Jim's theory had been that if the right conditions could be arranged, Son Won Phon's magick could still take effect. But what if he had been wrong? Or— there was an ugly possibility that Son Won Phon's magick could already have lost its power to effect a change; magick spells unfulfilled did not hang around for long, he already knew that. . . .

Most special magicks like this either worked without delay, or did not work at all. The power of this one might have been gone in only a few hours, if not less. If he had failed in his theory to make it work . . . if it didn't, what should he do—what could he do? He would have failed to achieve what he had hoped, and worse than that, raised expectations in Brian that could not be fulfilled.

A great wedding present, he thought unhappily, for two of his best friends on their long-awaited wedding day.

He felt the cold certainty of failure growing in him. To fight it off, he told himself that years of practice, conscious and unconscious, had made Geronde expert in unthinkingly hiding the marred side of her face from the gaze of others. But the thought did not seem to help.

—A sudden interruption in the Steward's reading, sudden unexpected words from Brian, and following movements by everyone on the steps jerked him out of his thoughts.

Like most people, Jim was capable of listening to and watching something while engaged in his own thoughts. But it took him a moment now to reconstruct what the Steward had just said, and what had happened.

The Steward had just been reading off the number and descriptions of personal keepsakes and love-tokens from Brian that Geronde was bringing with her to the marriage, and which would now legally belong to Brian, but which actually they would now share together.

The reading had included a little ceremony in which a few coins on a plate were passed from Geronde to Brian, as token of the fact she brought all she owned and would own to him. But then the Steward had gone on to announce an entirely unusual addition. . . .

". . . including," he had said, "those small gifts most loved and prized by Lady Geronde Isabel de Chaney, which Sir Brian Neville-Smythe hath made her from time to time, but any of which he may ask back from Geronde de Chaney at any moment, and instantly be given them as surety for her evermore undying love and faith in him—"

At that moment, Brian had unexpectedly spoken, in a firm, carrying voice that silenced the Steward by both its unexpectedness and its authority.

"Then I do chose *now* that which I latest gave her!"

It was that announcement that had brought Jim fully back to what was taking place, and he now saw its results:

Geronde's hand darted in through the right-hand parting of her Hell's Window, to draw forth—with effort—a sausagelike, leather-wrapped bundle. It was apparently weighty, for she used both hands to hold it out as Brian took a step forward to relieve her of it. Out of the ranks of her wedding party, her father took two lunging steps forward—but found the diminutive form of Geronde blocking his path. Brian went one step only back to his original position, handed the bundle to Dafydd and stood waiting.

The sausage had to be, Jim knew, the capful of gold pieces donated by the Prince and won by Brian when he had been champion of the tournament held as part of the Earl of Somerset's annual Christmas party. Brian had given it to Geronde for safe-keeping—she planned to use it for rebuilding Smythe Castle, and trusted not even Brian with it until this could be done.

Until she was married, all Geronde had was theoretically the property of her father, who had been trying to get his hands on that small fortune ever since she had gotten it. The control of Malvern Castle and its lands, however, had long been in Geronde's hands, and the servants and men-at arms were *her* people—enough so, at least, after the long absences of her father, that he was unable to use force to take the gold from her.

And if Sir Geoffrey had indeed tried to take the gold, Geronde was prepared to use any means, including violence, to resist—and all the people of the castle would have backed her up. Stranger things had happened in the fourteenth century.

Her father's legal rights were one thing. His coming up with financing for the law, or to muster an armed force to enforce it against a daughter who held the present power, was quite another. Geronde might be a stern Chatelaine, but she was a beloved one—followers would take a strong ruler over a weak one any day: the chance of personal survival was better.

So Geronde had held the money safely, but there was a problem looming in the necessary marriage contract. Unless she could legally return the gold to Brian, she and he could be liable under law in the future if Sir Geoffrey should regain the wealth by trying to take back his legal property.

But now Geronde had found a way to pass the money back to Brian, legally—and before witnesses. Sir Geoffrey's face was suddenly ugly.

Brian's face, however, Jim saw, had lost all of its previous grimness and tension. It was relaxed now, almost cheerful, looking steadily into the eyes of Sir Geoffrey. This day had finally served up something he was used to. He could have been posing for a statue that was to have the words *Come and get it!* engraved on its pedestal.

Sir Geoffrey stood still. He, Brian, nor anyone else watching was wearing sword or even dagger on this happy occasion. But even if both Sir Geoffrey and Brian had been armed, Geronde's father was twenty-six years older than Brian—and, worse, he was carrying half again that number of pounds in unseemly fat. Even shorn of these differences, no one there would have considered him a match for Brian.

The frozen, silent moment stretched out. In spite of his disadvantages, it was not impossible that Sir Geoffrey, as much a child of the fighting upper class of this historic time as any man there, might have thrown himself at Brian anyway, in a blind fit of rage, but already the spectators had begun to give up hope of that and were beginning to whisper among themselves over the excitement of a possible scandal. From his fur nest within his chair, the King himself

(Sir Straw) was looking at the group on the steps with stern disapproval.

Still meeting Brian's eyes with an expression now of undying hatred, Sir Geoffrey also took a long step back, and the Steward, obviously badly rattled, took up again the reading of the wedding contract.

Eventually, to everybody's relief, it ended. The priest turned and started leading the wedding party and all the other favored guests into the chapel where they were out of the wind and their own body warmth would soon moderate the cold of the small, crowded place. He, himself, dodged into the cubbyhole which was the sacristy, and closed its door behind him.

Brian and Geronde, with the two wedding parties— Brian's and hers—had been first to follow into the interior of the chapel, where the only daylight came from a window over the door, made up of the same sort of small, uncolored, six-inch square glass panes which filled the Solar windows. The only other illumination was from the two candles on the altar, those in the hands of two acolytes, and a few more around the walls.

In this dim space, Geronde's loose golden blond hair caught the yellow light of the candles, making her seem to light up the dusky interior of the chapel just by her presence. She and Brian went directly up to the first of the three steps to the altar, with their wedding parties behind them, followed by a little space, and then the crowd of favored neighbors filling the rest of the chapel to its open door. Beyond the door, crowded even closer, were the less-favored visitors—outside, but closely listening.

All this gathering parted like a sea to allow the King, still on his chair and dais, to be carried in to a place right behind the wedding parties—its bulk, incidentally, forcing some of the furthest neighbors already inside, back out beyond the door.

Meanwhile, those still inside were taking off their cloaks

and folding them into pads they could kneel upon. Actual pads had already been placed for Brian, Geronde and the members of the wedding parties. Jim stared about him, his eyes adjusting to the dimness of the chapel interior.

He had seen it in all its disorder and with the dirt of the years when Sir Hugh de Bois and his men had owned Malencontri—its walls stripped of anything religious and valuable, the glass of the window above the doorway knocked out, its frame empty.

He had also seen it some days ago, swept, cleaned, empty, its altar scrubbed and the broken-out windowpanes replaced with the cheaper, uncolored squares it presently held as a temporary measure.

But only now was he seeing the little chapel properly refurnished, a bronze cross on the wall above the altar— itself hardly more than a narrow shelf, its inner edge fastened to the wall behind it. To Jim's left, there was a carved Madonna, with the Christ Child in her arms, freshly painted and gilded—no doubt rescued from who knew what dusty corner.

Under the bronze cross two candles in two tall bronze candlesticks burned upon the altar. The two youthful acolytes in their dark robes, standing each at an end of the altar, also carried lighted candles.

In the dusky chapel, this candlelight fell on the beautifully worked frontal of the altar cloth. Angie had mentioned some weeks back that Geronde had had it worked for her wedding in the close stitch called *opus anglicanum* ("english-work" said Jim's mind, automatically translating the Latin name). This after her attempts to duplicate that highly professional work herself had reduced her to tears. In tiny close gold and white stitches, the frontal showed two kneeling angels facing each other with a golden cross between them.

Those behind the wedding parties were holding their folded cloaks ready for use; and whispering or murmuring.

Brian and Geronde were alone on the first of the three steps
up to the altar—all else present, including the wedding parties, shared the level floor.

The priest came out of the sanctuary, having taken off
his alb. He was now in his white chasuble and stole. He
crossed himself.

"In Patri nomine et spiritu sancti . . ." he said, and began
the service. Jim heard the Latin words in a strange double
fashion at first.

It had not happened that way when he had been in this
world's France. There, for some reason undoubtedly magical, but which he had yet to fathom, everyone had seemed
to speak the same language he had encountered in England.

The same thing had happened when he and Brian were
in the Holy Land. People who must be speaking Arabic had
also seemed to Jim to speak the identical language he had
heard in the two northern countries. But in Dafydd's legendary Drowned Land, the local language had been unintelligible.

Here and now, however, he heard the words in Latin,
which he had understood from his studies before he came
to this world, and his mind automatically translated them
into the upper-class fourteenth-century English with which
he was now familiar. In just a short time, however, the two
different versions blended together in his head and understanding was automatic.

But the priest was now well into the form for Solemni-
zation of Matrimony, and Jim found himself wondering how
closely the guests behind him were following it. It came to
him that probably all of them were familiar enough with
the ceremony, even if not with Latin, to follow what was
being said.

But Jim's mind rode along on the sonorous sound of the
Latin. After the raw air in the courtyard and the businesslike
marriage there—before that the battle and his sickness—
now there was a general happiness that Brian and Geronde

were united at last . . . the warmth and the solemn ceremony gradually enfolded him in an unusual feeling of peace and comfort. He no longer felt himself merely a spectator from another time, but one of those who belonged here at this moment.

It rang a long-time forgotten memory of a Sunday in a little church of a small community of retirees in Canada, when his father had briefly considered giving up his work and settling there.

It had been fall, and on that Sunday the service had been one of old-fashioned Thanksgiving. The church had been filled, mostly by the local people, and those parishioners were generally in middle age, or older. The men were mostly retired, living with their wives on small pensions; they often owned small properties from as little as half an acre to two acres, fertile farming land on the Fraser River delta. They had followed the time-worn English custom of making-do on the pensions, together with what they had saved and what they could grow, in their later years.

What was sharpest in Jim's memory was their singing of the harvest hymn—

> Come, ye joyful people! Come!
> Raise the song of harvest home!
> All is safely gathered in.
> Ere the winter storms begin. . . .

There had been a great and real unity in joyfulness and heartiness in the chorus of their voices. It had rung an echo in young Jim that had stayed with him all these years. Innocent as he had been then of the daily struggle to survive, it had come home to him clearly that they were each singing of real things—each giving thanks for the bounty of root and vine, vegetables and fruits, they had sowed, raised and harvested, to eke out their slender resources through the coming winter months.

There was something similar now in the atmosphere of those who had jammed into the chapel—and those clustered outside at the door. Jim at last realized why Geronde had been so determined to have a Mass to follow her marriage. The marriage itself was hardly more than a commercial transaction. This, here and now, was what gave the achievement of marriage all of its real meaning and memorability.

Jim tried another glance at Geronde, but still he saw only the unharmed side of her face. The other side was still turned away from him.

Behind, he heard those who had been able to crowd into the chapel, stirring and occasionally whispering to each other. They fell silent as the priest, facing the altar and the crucifix above it, began a fresh paragraph in Latin.

For a moment his conscious attention had been lost in memory. For a moment the Latin was not understandable. Then he was caught up by what was being said, and he was following it once more. The priest was already into the first of two blessings on the married couple—this one a blessing on the bride; in the heightened atmosphere of the chapel, the music of its words caught all his attention.

"... *respice propius super hanc famulam tuam* ..." the priest was saying. "... look in Your mercy on this Your handmaid who is now joined in wedlock and implores protection from You. May the yoke of love and peace be on her ... may she be dear to her husband like Rachel, wise like Rebecca, long-lived and faithful like Sarah ... *doctinis caelibus erudita.* May she be well taught in heavenly lore. May she be fruitful in offspring ... may they both see their children's children to the third and fourth generation, and reach the old age they desire. Through the name of Our Lord."

The priest went on to the consecration of the Host, and the congregation seemed to hold its breath as an acolyte rang a small bell three times. They continued in the same powerful concentration as the priest prayed, unheard by them, to consecrate the bread. He knelt on one knee, holding it, then rose, facing the altar and lifting it up at arms-length for an extended moment, that the people might see it. He placed it in a small golden dish on the altar, knelt again, and turned to the consecration of the wine in a silver chalice.

The audience breathed once more as the wine was consecrated. The wine was out of sight in the chalice, but the bread was the visible, living miracle they had been waiting to see.

The priest then partook of the wine and bread himself, and after, gave it in turn to the acolytes. Finally, he turned to give the consecrated bread to Brian and Geronde as they knelt on the steps.

Only they received it. He turned his back once more, ate and drank what remained of the wine and bread, that none of the consecrated Host might be left over, then washed the chalice that had held the wine.

He gave one more blessing specifically to the bride and groom. Then, facing the congregation, he said a single brief prayer and, making a sweeping sign of the cross, said the final words of the Mass.

"*Benedicat vos omnipotens Deus, Pater et Filius et Spiritus Sanctus.*" ". . . May God almighty bless you, the Father, the Son, and the Holy Spirit. Amen."

The Mass was over.

It was almost with a sense of shock that Jim realized there was no more to be said or done, and they were all about to leave the chapel. He turned about with the rest of the wedding party to wait for the few moments it took for those who had been behind them to clear the way by getting out of the chapel door.

He saw some of the women softly crying, and was startled—though by this time he should know better than to be so—by seeing an almost equal number of the men weeping quietly as well. The moment of the lifted bread had been one of great emotion, and males of this time gave free vent to their emotions—all emotions.

Outside, finally, at first the new, low, wintry sunlight, shining directly in his eyes, blinded him. So, half-seeing, he blundered forward to join the others in both wedding parties, now mixed together as they moved toward the Great Hall door and the wedding feast waiting for them there.

Abruptly he realized that now, for the first time, he was next to Geronde on a side that enabled him to see the cheek that had been hidden from him until now.

He glanced quickly at it.

The scar was still there, clearly sunlit, still on her face.

Chapter 47

The Great Hall echoed with high voices and good cheer. After the emotional solemnity of the Mass, this was the happy time of celebration of the marriage, in a joyful clamor of voices and clatter of spoons and eating knives.

Silent at the High Table with Brian and Geronde, Jim felt sick.

"What is it?" whispered Angie, at his side.

"Tell you later," he whispered back, and made a heroic effort to smile, drink and talk happily like everyone else.

To cover up the way he was feeling after seeing the scar still there, he made an effort to fall into conversation with the priest, next to him at table on his right. Manners required he should do so anyway. He had never seen the priest before today, and he now discovered the other was to be addressed as "Sir William," a courtesy title required by the fact that he was not a member of a particular religious order—for whom the name of "Father" was reserved.

Sir William had the chair next to him, on the other side from Angie. The man of the cloth was between him and

Geronde, with Brian just beyond her. Somewhat to his surprise, he found the priest to be an unusually intelligent, obviously highly educated man, only a little older than Geronde.

Out of his ecclesiastical robes, Sir William was dressed like a scholar, in a houpeland—a sort of ancestor of the loose, long academic robe Jim was familiar with in his own time, with wide sleeves.

He was a lean, calm man, who—as had Jim himself under the different circumstances of the future—had originally intended to teach at the university he had attended. But he had found the call of religious service stronger. He had been ordained by the Archbishop of Oxford and, after getting a letter from Geronde, who had heard of him through friends and written, had taken up his duties at Malvern.

William had been attracted by the position and found his attraction justified. In addition to his priestly duties, he acted as a secular advisor, and someone for Geronde to talk to and learn from. He could be useful in a multitude of concerns with the staff and guests. He liked his religious duties as castle priest, dealing closely with an ever-changing household of servants and men-at-arms.

Although ordained by the Archbishop of Oxford, as he explained to Jim, he was, of course, now responsible to the Bishop of Bath and Wells, and would remain so as long as he was in that Bishop's diocese.

Their talk took Jim completely out of his preoccupation with Geronde's still-existing scar—until he found his attention pulled away by their early loss of the King—Sir Straw—who had been seated at the table's far end. During the wedding outside, the King had been steadily drinking hot mulled wine, brought him by a servant, as an additional specific to deal with the cold and windy day. During the Mass, of course, there was no drinking—even by a King. But once in the Great Hall with the food, he had made up for lost time.

In earlier years his capacity had been legendary. It was still respectable, but age had nibbled away at it for some decades now. So at the table he had become sleepy and had needed to be escorted by his knights up to his suite of rooms—undoubtedly, literally carried up the long flight of steps—accompanied and watched over by both the Prince and Joan, who slipped away from the table to go with him.

This gave the others more room to spread out in the empty chairs, and since this was Brian and Geronde's—in particular Geronde's—hour of glory, those two were in no hurry to call their dinner over and leave.

A couple of hours later, however, when the arrow slits in the walls of the hall were showing nothing but darkness outside, the dinner had reached the point where it began to seem sensible for Brian and Geronde to retire to the Solar, their first-night bridal chamber, in preparation for those who would crowd it to witness their bedding. The uproar in the hall was at a proper pitch and the general mood was just about to exceed a safe level of merriment. Brian and Geronde slipped off to their wedding bed.

"Slipped off," of course, was a polite way of saying it. Everyone in the Great Hall had been watching and waiting for this moment, and after a short, decorous wait, a cheerful, mostly male, more or less inebriated tail of visitors followed up the steep tower stairs. The least drunk among them made their ascent on the outside, unprotected end of each step, to make sure those less steady on their feet did not spoil the occasion by the splash of a body on the stone floor, far below.

Carried candles lit up the interior of the tower and created dancing shadows, and the tower itself was full of echoing voices. Jim had been in witnessing groups like this before, at several earlier weddings—he had little choice in the matter, since he was expected to be a leader, due to his rank and the fact that Malencontri was the only real castle in the district. Some of the better-off neighbors had homes that could generously be referred to as castles by their friends—strongly fortified, but small compared to Malencontri—but none owned the equivalent of Malencontri's tall, encircling curtain wall.

Therefore, Jim believed he knew what to expect.

When those who were not too drunk had been admitted to the Solar, even that room was jammed by the number who wanted to be among the obligatory witnesses to such an important bedding. A burly neighbor was acting as door guard to keep those too gone in alcohol from entering.

Those excluded, however, were allowed to crowd about beyond the open door, and tried to raise their voices above those within. All this Jim had seen before. But this time he noticed a distinct difference.

The jokes were more restrained—less barbed, less skirting the edge of bawdiness. They were, if the word could be made to apply, almost "gentle." It was perfectly true that this witnessing of the bedding of the just-married couple, required by Church canon law for a legal marriage, was effectively licensed, and there was nothing to stop them from being downright rowdy if they wished. True, not all such witnessings were so; at some everybody behaved with decorum—sometimes even with forbidding solemnity.

But these were country gentry. They had grown up with many of the ways of their own tenants and servants, whose behavior at a marriage ceremony had its roots in pagan times, when from start to finish this was an occasion for unbridled fun. At a time in which the most often-quoted phrase Jim heard from his staff was "*Old* ways *are* best!" there could be a strong tendency to let themselves go.

But not this time. They had taken their time—or rather the more sober ones leading, including Jim, had taken their time—forcing a slow climb of the stairs. So when they all finally entered the temporary bridal chamber, Brian's wedding finery was piled loosely on a chair on one side of the

bed, while he himself was out of sight behind the tightly
drawn bed-curtains.

The temporary little tent in which Geronde had been
helped to disrobe by female servants was standing with its
flaps wide open to show that not only was she through using
it, but that she would be in bed, out of sight behind the bed-
curtains with Brian now. Even her wedding garb had been
put away by servants, who themselves were no longer in
sight.

The witnesses did not take this amiss. It had happened
before in their experience. But to Jim's surprise, when the
usual loud-voiced witticisms began to fly, they were all—
without exception—no worse than what the fourteenth century would consider parlor jokes, quite fit for mixed company among the gentry.

In fact, they were almost too gentle. Jim, in the front rank
facing the bed, began to worry that this was a disarming
tactic before some country-style sort of prank was to be
sprung on the newlyweds. Secretly he activated his dragon
hearing, far more sensitive than his human ability in that
respect, and strained over the noise around him to hear if
anything like a prank was being suspected by Brian and
Geronde.

It took him a few moments to focus down on whatever
sound might be coming from inside the bed-curtains.

"What . . . ?" Brian was whispering groggily.

His falling asleep was not unexpected to Jim, seeing that
his friend—at Jim's instigation—had ended by spending all
the previous night at vigil in the chapel. He would naturally
be overwhelmingly sleepy after that, particularly with food
and drink inside him.

"Forgive me, sweeting," Geronde's whisper answered,
with a tenderness Jim had never heard in her voice before,
"I didn't want to wake you—"

"Nonsense!" Brian's whisper was stronger. "Awake now,
and should be. What is it, my honey-love? Do you—"

"Not yet . . . but I don't weigh enough to make the bedstrings creak by myself. That is all Holy Church requires, you know, and they will not leave until they hear it. I want to be alone with you."

Jim abandoned his dragon hearing, embarrassed at having spied on them, but glad he had done it. If there had been some prank in prospect as he had feared, he could, forewarned, have nipped it in the bud.

He was no Sir William, with the weight and powers of the Church behind his words. But he was a magickian, and a small show of warning magick would have been enough to halt any pranksters in midstride, reminding them he was there, and it would go ill with them if they tried what they were thinking of doing.

Inside the curtains, Geronde evidently allowed the witnesses' jollity to continue to flow for about another five minutes. Then the bed strings gave an audible creak from inside the curtains, the joking faded off, and the witnesses began to make a relatively decorous departure, again with the more sober ones herding any tempted to linger.

Jim was the last one out—in fact, he was the only member of the wedding parties present—Angie had not come along, and neither Dafydd nor Danielle had followed the crowd—it was his duty to be so. Outside, the corridor was empty, except for the on-duty servant and man-at-arms.

He headed down to the room that had been Brian and Geronde's and was the temporary residence for Angie and himself tonight.

It was a small room after the expanse of the Solar. But because he was who he was, another pair of on-call servant and man-at-arms were standing outside its door. And when he stepped inside, he found that an affectionate, or perhaps very rank-conscious, Malencontri staff had done their best to make the little space as Solar-like as possible for their lord and lady.

The room shone with cleanliness. Somehow they had

found—or, thinking ahead—had built a larger bed for Angie and himself. A wardrobe from the Solar was crammed into one corner, and a brisk fire was blazing merrily, with the long arm of a hob set up next to it and the kettle in which their tea was normally boiled singing to itself.

Best of all, Angie was already there. Unfortunately, so also was Joan of Kent. The two of them had clearly been sitting there, talking. In courtesie, however, Joan should now rise and withdraw.

"Oh, Jim," said Angie herself, rising from her own chair to meet him. "Joan's been waiting for a chance to speak to both of us—but mainly you. Do you want some tea?"

Jim did want a cup of tea, but not to drink while in conversation with anyone but Angie, and then only to settle all else he had been eating and drinking at the banquet just past.

"I guess not," he said. "I'm glad to see you, Lady Joan."

But Joan was already on her own feet now and coming towards him.

"Jim, dear Jim!" she said, warmly, "we have been at our baptismal names for some time now, you and I. Will you take it amiss if I now address you in the most closely familiar form of your name? Surely, on this last occasion only I might venture on that liberty?"

Jim was about to make some stiff, polite, very definite refusal, but it stuck in his throat.

"It's good of you to want to do that," he said, "and believe me, I appreciate it. But if you'll forgive me, in all this world there is no one but my wife—excepting magickians like Carolinus, who are a class apart—who calls me 'Jim,' and I'm the only one who calls Angie, Angie. But if you would greatly wish it, at this moment . . ."

"No, no. I understand, James," said Joan. "Of course! How could I not? I will not intrude. You shall always be 'James' to me; in my mind as on my lips."

"That's all right . . ." began Jim, feeling guilty, but she interrupted.

"Forgive me," she said, "but my time is short. What I have come to tell you is that Edward and I must be leaving Malencontri early tomorrow morning—perhaps before you would be up. The four of us may never meet again in our lives, and so I must quickly to my reason for coming here. I was waiting to speak to you one last time. There is something you should know. I have already told Angela, but I wished to tell you myself what I have to say. It is a matter of great joy to Edward and myself, and we have you to thank for it. Can you guess what it is?"

"No," said Jim, honestly.

"Edward and his father are reconciled at last! Indeed, the reconciliation was more on the King's side than Edward's, though both had been at fault, and it took both to come to one mind together again. But we have you and Brian and Dafydd—all of you at Malencontri, our dearest friends—I may say that, may I not?—to say our thanks to you for it. But most of all to you, dear James, and most particularly for putting Edward in command of your force against the goblins, so that the victory redounds to his credit."

"There was no other real choice," Jim said, somewhat awkwardly. "As a matter of rank—"

"Let us not talk of that. You let him *lead*, which was what mattered—to him *and* the King. You did not send him out with a personal guard around him to protect him from the brunt of the battle. That, above all, was what made his father love him. Certes, Edward, at fifteen years of age, had proved himself against some of the best of the French. But Cumberland's lies had all but convinced the King that Edward had been guarded and led by Chandos and others, throughout the chevauché into France."

"Oh, yes," said Jim.

"But now!" Joan went on triumphantly, "Old Edward stood in your castle and saw his eldest son, his heir, the

next King of England to be, leading as such a one should—
leading and winning. This, added to the fact that you and
Brian and Dafydd had accepted him as a friend and companion; which the King already had remarked—that Edward
had also been accepted into the company of close friendship
with two known paladins—put the seal on a very different
image of his son, to his eternal happiness."

"Well . . ." Jim looked looked a little desperately at Angie
for some words to assist him. But she was still standing
silent, leaving it to him. "I'm glad it all turned out as you
say."

"And so are we all!" said Joan happily. "So are both of
us, Edward and I, and do not believe that he will ever forget
what you have done for him. That is not his nature."

"I still think you give me too much credit—" Jim was
beginning clumsily, but Joan went right on, paying him no
attention.

"Mark my words!" she said. "I do not mean to tell you
that all is now mended forever between father and son.
Cumberland will not yield easily in his efforts and his am-
bitions, and King and son will unconsciously give him op-
portunities. Those two hotheads, both aware of what they
are, and both always initially convinced they are right, will
find reason to fall out again. But the King is not the wine-
soaked fool that too many take him for. He puts up with
Cumberland because Cumberland is so useful to him.

"He is no longer the young man he was when I was a
little girl at court with Edward," she said. "In those days,
his father would never have allowed Cumberland so much
liberty; now he lets the man win from him in small matters.
But if that Earl should ever seem to oppose him in some
dangerous way, he would crush him like a cockroach, without warning, under his foot."

"Are you really sure of that?" Jim said, remembering how
the King had needed to be assisted from the table, only a
short time since.

"I am more than sure. I am certain. Remember, I have known Old Edward from my childhood upward. I know him now. He has been a good King—good for England—and a word from him can bring all England to his banner. He has always played the great lords against each other, so that they might not unite dangerously among themselves. Oxford has not survived this long as almost Cumberland's equal by his own wits and power alone—though he may think he has. Never the King forgets he is King—and that Cumberland may only say and try to do what he wishes. No effort of his will ever erase from the King's memory the sight of Edward leading the charge against his enemy from your castle. There is a great love between the two of them, though neither will admit it, and Old Edward did not have the chance to see his son with his own eyes in action in France, if you will remember! Now, is all your doing!"

Joan broke off abruptly.

"—So, buss me now, James and Angie," she said briskly, "for I must go. My Edward has overdrunk tonight, it being the night it is, and will be no help. I have things to get ready before the morn and will need what sleep I may get."

Jim and Angie both bussed—kissed—her farewell. Jim had always been embarrassed by this, the medieval custom of everybody kissing everybody else, and it made it no better that Joan was as attractive as she was and Angie was standing there watching. But he kissed Joan, and she kissed him whole-heartedly back, kissed Angie, and went out the door.

"God keep you both!" she said as she disappeared.

"You, too," Jim called after her, almost wordless himself by this time. The door shut behind her, and he turned to Angie.

"Why did you let this happen?" he asked.

"Because I thought she deserved the chance to tell you what she did, and because I wanted to see how you'd react."

Jim grinned at her suddenly.

"Did I pass the test, then?"

"You did," she said. "With flying colors."

"Good."

"Good, but expected. I knew you would. Now, why don't you get into bed? I'll make your cup of tea while you're doing that."

"There's nothing I'd like better," said Jim. He got started taking off his wedding finery. There was something almost sacramental about that end-of-day cup of tea, he thought, watching Angie finish the making of it.

She gave him his cup, and he sipped on it, waiting for the tea in it to get down to the exact temperature he liked. She proceeded to get ready for bed herself, put out all the candles in the room, except the one on the table at Jim's side of the bed, and climbed in beside him.

"The day's over," she said, taking his now-empty cup away to put it on her bedside table, before snuggling up to him.

"And thank Heaven it is!" he answered her.

He blew out the remaining candle flame beside him. In the darkness he could smell the last smoldering of its wick. Beside him, nestled against him, Angie was already breathing slowly and deeply—already asleep. Her day had been a long and hard one.

Without warning, all the unhappiness over his failure to get rid of Geronde's scar came back over him in a rush. Why had he let this drift the way he had? Why hadn't he gone to Carolinus right away while the wound was fresh? Of course that was before he understood what magick could do here. But if he had just thought, he would have gone to Carolinus anyway, simply because he was the only one in this world who might help.

The self-accusations poured blackly in on him. But before they could drag him down to their uttermost, lightless depths, sleep took him, also.

Chapter 48

Jim slept like a log. Like a sodden log sunk to the ocean bottom three miles below the sea's surface. He had done a lot of sleeping lately, but he could never remember sleeping like this.

He woke, not recognizing where he was for a second. But the mists cleared rapidly.

Somehow he was back in his familiar bed and his familiar Solar—moved while he was dead asleep, obviously. It was late morning again, and he came all the way to consciousness.

He felt extraordinarily good, for some reason. The big things—the great things—were now all under control. They had won the battle, the goblins were gone. The Prince and Joan would probably have left by now—happy. The King would be leaving, also happy—according to Joan. The wedding had gone off without a hitch, and Geronde had gotten Brian's gold back to him, legally.

It was like the morning after a long-awaited family reunion—especially joyous, but over. The only bad part of the moment was that Angie was already up and gone. He wanted to tell her how well he felt, and he would have liked her there to make his first tea of the day . . . and now, of course, he must call in a servant—no, anything but that, it would taste like dishwater and spoil this marvelous day—or make it himself, and he had never managed to make it as well as Angie did.

But why not? Good practice for him! In the long run maybe he'd learn how she worked the daily miracle. He bounced out of bed and swung the long, darkened metal rod of the hob, with the kettle on its end, in over the heart of the flames that would bring on a hard boil in no time at all.

While he waited for it to do this, he pulled on a comforting old red, foot-length gown that had served him for several years now as a lounging robe, and sat back on the bed. As he did, the door opened. Angie stepped in, closing the door again tightly behind her without waiting for the servant to do it. Her hair was somewhat disheveled.

"Where—?" he began, but that was as far as he got.

"I've been helping Joan, and seeing her and Edward off!" she said. "Back in a minute. Robert's nurse thinks he's ailing with a cough! Maybe nonsense, but—be right back!"

Reaching for the door behind her to go out, she checked before opening it.

"I saw Geronde. Her scar's gone—say nothing to anybody! Be right back!"

Then the door had opened and slammed shut again. She was gone before he could say a word.

Scar gone?

How?

—No. NO! he told himself, the day cascading in ruins around him like a smashed window.

He wouldn't even think about what Angie had just said until she got back. That, on top of everything else that had worked out so well, was too unbelievable to trust.

One thing at a time—one thing at a time—he repeated to himself, trying to gather the shards of his earlier happiness back into being. But it would not be gathered. Forgetting all about the tea, he sat back with his shoulders against the high, hard backboard of his bed, Angie's news forcing its way into his thoughts.

Scar gone? How could it be—this late? It was against all his building belief that raw magic was a natural force in this world, a stuff from which humans could make things happen—but only if they knew how to capture it—or if they could go into some unnatural high gear, as he had done in the end, at Tiverton. Was there another, freak, unconsciously magic-controlling person in the castle??

The scar vanishing now was completely against everything he had ever taught himself—against all the knowledge of Carolinus, or even the scar-experienced wisdom of Son Won Phon. Also, it was absolutely, completely, against his own theory that had led Brian to spend his pre-wedding night in the chapel—more than Jim had ever expected him to do, but something, of course, he should have expected, knowing Brian's commitment to anything he had decided to undertake. He did nothing halfway, but all with all his heart and soul.

Morever, Son Won Phon would not have told him his magick had not worked—nor left—if he had thought there was the smallest of chances of it still working.

Ugly possibilities jumped to Jim's mind. What if Angie's news was right, but the change was only temporary? What if in a few days, or even after a few months, the scar came back—ruining all Geronde's happiness at losing it and giving her back all her original sorrow?

Above all—what if it had been his own attempt to help, *on top* of Son Won Phon's magick, that caused the scar to go and then return? He would never forget—never be able to repair what he had done. He was only a half-baked apprentice magician, after all, for all his proud theories based on the logic of a time six hundred years later.

The thought was unbearable.

And how could he explain to Angie—as he undoubtedly would try to do, sooner or later—that he was responsible? Tell her because he could not bear the burden on his conscience any more?

She would be shocked, of course—though she would hide it, and try to comfort him, telling him he had intended well, and in any case no one could do anything about it.

He could imagine her saying, if the scar came back,

and in spite of the fact Geronde was her best friend, "She got over it once. She'll do it again." And of course that brave little mite would. She had all the courage in the world. But, God, women for all their capability for gentleness and love, could be shockingly hard at times in practical matters, or if something else—children or husband or some other thing, had priority for them—sometimes hardest on their own sex.

He remembered May Heather—a ministering angel to those in the Nursing Room—saying to him about the hazing of little thirteen-year-old Lise, ". . . Got to have some of that in life, m'lord. . . ."

Or was it simply a trait men did not have?

No. As always men and women were not all that different; men could be hard among themselves as well. He remembered the time, a few years ago, when he was relatively new to this world—when he, with Dafydd and others, including some of Jim's men-at-arms, had driven off a gang of sea raiders who had come ashore, as sometimes happened, to sack Brian's half-ruined and lightly defensible Smythe Castle.

The trained and armored fighting men had waded through the unarmored, untrained pirates, though they had been double in number.

Jim, himself—also untrained then, but carried away by the fight and feeling invulnerable in his mail and helm—had been driving before him a lank ruffian with no more than a long knife, thinking that winning this sort of battle was a snap, when his opponent unexpectedly kicked him—up under the lower edge of his mail shirt, directly in the groin. Suddenly he had been bent over double with pain, and the lank pirate had escaped safely, just about as the rest of the raiders decided to flee. Brian had come hastily to see how he had been wounded. But when Jim told him, this tried-and-true comrade burst into uproarious laughter, slapping Jim heartily on the shoulder.

"Never fear, lad!" Brian had shouted, in the middle of his laughing. "Wilt not die of it!"

Jim grinned, remembering—and in spite of himself felt somewhat better. Brian had been right, of course. A kick in the privates was nothing in a fight when swords and knives were out—nothing at all in that sort of a day's work.

Jim also remembered that after a first burst of anger, he had not really been upset at Brian's lack of sympathy, even then. Annoyed by it, yes; but not upset. Dafydd, and Danielle who had also been into the fighting—there were no glass curtains for women when lives were at stake, in these centuries, and face it, Danielle was certainly a better knife-, and probably a better sword-fighter than he would ever be, while as an archer she was simply and plainly forever out of his sight—both Dafydd and she had both been in easy earshot of Brian's words and the laughter.

But somehow Brian's response was part of what men were, and were expected to be—in any time.

No, that kind of reaction among the people of this time had not gotten under Jim's skin.

But he realized now that there *was* something, much more recent, that rankled in him—the unexpected, apparently total absence of feeling in all the men, from the King down to Brian himself, at the deathbed of Sir Verweather. They had uttered words of forgiveness as if engaged in some ritual, but to Jim's ear there had been no actual emotion or true compassion for the dying man. That had gotten under Jim's skin.

He had not expected, by now, to feel that way.

But with women, with all their demonstrated capability for gentleness and kindness, hardness came as a shock, the first time a male encountered it. Not that he had even seen or heard Angie—

The door burst open again, slammed behind her, and she was back.

"Just as I thought!" she said, charging into the room. "Nothing at all. False alarm! No temperature, forehead cool, happy and gurgling—what are you doing, boiling the kettle dry?" She was about to swing the kettle off the flames, when she hesitated.

"Were you trying to make yourself some tea? Was that it? There's enough left in the kettle for one cup anyway, and it's all ready to go. Want me to make it? Jim, you don't look—is something wrong with what I said?"

"No, no . . ." he said quickly. "Just something else. You see—but it's all rather complicated. Would you make a cup for me, please? There's sort of a tangle, but with some tea in me, I could probably explain it better."

"Of course!" she said, and looked at him worriedly. She took the kettle off the hob. "You sit right there. Don't move. Just stay the way you are."

"I won't," he said. "It's just that magick can be tricky stuff—"

"Don't try to tell me now. Just sit there and breathe quietly. Relax, we've got all the time in the world. You can tell me after you've had your tea."

"I keep trying things, that's the trouble—"

"Sit. Breathe. Don't move! Don't think!"

"Yes," he said, on the breath of a heavy sigh, and stopped trying to talk.

But he could not help thinking.

If only he'd asked Carolinus before talking to Brian, told one of the three best Magickians in this world what his theory was first. But now there was no way to mend it. Son Won Phon's magick had been balled up, and once magick was twisted, there'd be no way of straightening it out—

"No!" he shouted, suddenly joyous—and found Angie handing him a steaming cup.

"I'm wrong!" he babbled at her. "I forgot—"

"Don't spill the tea!"

"Right!" he said, still happily. The scent of the tea rose to his nostrils. *Oh blessed cup!* somebody had called it once. He sipped. It was magnificent, and not too hot to drink fast. He gulped.

"It's all right!" he said, beaming up at Angie and handing her back the empty cup. "It's absolutely all right. No hurry now. You tell me first—what was this good news you came charging in with?"

"You're sure you're all right?"

"I am now. You tell me."

"Little Robert's not sick at all!"

"Yes—yes. But about Geronde . . ."

"Geronde!" Angie shouted. She almost slammed down the empty teacup on the bedside table by her right hip, spun around and headed for the food and drink wardrobe. "Geronde's scar's *gone!* This is a celebration! I'm going to have a cup of tea, too! Do you want another?—No. Wine! Wine for me, anyway!"

She opened the door of the wardrobe. "How about you—now? Wine?"

"Yes, me too," he said, almost closing his eyes with happiness. Memory had come to his rescue just in time to keep him from pouring incorrect bad news all over Angie.

Blessed cup be hanged—*blessed words* were what fitted this moment. Carolinus' words when the Mage had been lecturing him on how he'd have to rest whether he liked it or not, because he couldn't do anything else about his sleeping. Jim took a quick mental glance at the passage in the tiny, shrunken tome within him that at normal size was too heavy to lift. Once he had had to cough it up to full size to consult it. Now he could read it with nobody else knowing what he was doing.

There the words were, just as Carolinus had quoted them: *Magick accomplished is NOT reversible.*

Hah! If the scar had vanished, no power on this earth, or any other, could bring it back. It was gone, destroyed, disintegrated forever.

He had been prepared to rain on Angie's happiness over Geronde's miracle, for no good reason. Of course! It burst on him now like the sudden rising of the sun after a black night. He had been right! Logic was back in its proper place. Neither Son Won Phon with his magick, nor he with his theory, had been wrong.

It had been Son's magick acting as a necessary trigger, no doubt. But after that it really had needed the *Faith* and *Love*—in that order—that had worked the actual miracle. Brian's vigil in the chapel, and all his and Geronde's years of yearning, were what had made the magick work. The happiest moment in both their lives. Their wedding night!

"They've loved each other so long!" Angie was saying, over by the wardrobe, pouring wine into two of the King's tall, forgotten, wine glasses, "and now this, to wind up a perfect wedding! She just woke up this morning, and it simply wasn't there! Can you imagine it—"

She broke off suddenly, looking wisely at him.

"But it was you who did it, wasn't it?" she said.

"No," he answerd, happiness like a bright day inside him. "It wasn't me at all! It was Brian and Geronde. They did it."

"Brian and Geronde?" Angie echoed, standing by the wardrobe with the two filled glasses and staring at him.

"That's right," he told her. "By themselves. Bring the wine and join me, over here." She came with a filled glass in each hand. "That's right. Give me the glasses and I'll hold them while you go around the other side, so you can come and sit down next to me . . . fine. Now, here's your wine and I've got mine."

She looked at him narrowly, taking the glass from his hand, however.

"Comfortable?" he said. "All right, then. I'll tell you all about it."

So he did.

Historical Note

The marriage of Edward, Prince of Wales and heir to the English throne of Edward III, to Princess Joan of Kent, was one of the rare love matches among royal marriages, which were normally dictated by politics.

It completed a lifetime of affection, dating back to their having been children together at the court of Edward III, father of the Prince, and it was a marriage which had needed a papal dispensation to be possible—since the two were first cousins.

Joan, eventually to be called the Fair Maid of Kent, was born in 1328, daughter of Edmund Plantagenet, Earl of Kent; and by that birthright she would later become Countess of Kent. Sir Jean Froissart, the leading chronicler of the Hundred Year War between France and England, and of the fourteenth century in which all these people lived and died, would write of her as, *"la plus belle dame de tout le roiaulme d'Engletterre, et la plus amoreuse . . ."* ("the most beautiful lady in the kingdom of England and the most loving . . .").

The marriage to Edward was her third; the Prince had never married. Their wedding came when both were in their thirties, a late date for the first marriage of a Prince who was in line to be King. But the two were first cousins, and circumstances, as well as the Canon Law of the Church, had kept them apart until then.

Young Edward, called the Black Prince for no provable reason—perhaps because he wore a black jupon over his armor on some prominent occasion—never ascended to the throne of England. His father outlived him. But beginning with the *chevauchée* (invasion) of France that led to the English success at the Battle of Crécy, during which he was knighted though only fifteen, and until his death, he compiled a good record as a military commander.

Joan's first marriage came at twelve years of age. She married Thomas Holland, a young professional soldier, in a secret, but legal, marriage *per verba de praesenti*, as the Canon Law of the Church described it.

Holland left to fight at the sea battle of Sluys, and then went on to gain fame in the war against the Tartar invaders of Prussia. Meanwhile, Joan's relatives, now worried about her physical and mental growth, decided to marry her off to William Montague, who was eventually to become the Earl of Salisbury. Holland—now Sir Holland—on returning, confronted Montague—now Salisbury—and demanded the return of Joan to him. Salisbury refused.

Joan was a Plantagenet of royal blood, so any case brought to make Salisbury give her up had to be brought to the papal court, at that time located in Avignon, in southern France. The cost of such action was for a time beyond Holland's means—until, at the siege of Calais, he captured the French Count d'Eu, an aristocrat for whom the King of France would give Holland in ransom 89,000 florins.

Now well off, in 1349 Holland was able to get the papal authorities to issue a Papal Bull, a ruling that Joan was indeed his wife and must be yielded to him. The couple would be married for another ten years, and would have several more children before his death—Joan had already had other children fathered by both Holland and Salisbury.

Holland continued his distinguished military career, becoming one of the twenty-four knights that could be named to the Round Table, an English honor created by King Edward III and the Prince in imitation of the legendary table of King Arthur. The group would eventually come to be called the Order of the Garter.

Holland was eventually appointed captain general of all English positions in France and Normandy. But soon after that he died. A secret marriage by Joan to the Prince followed.

The King had been keeping other marriage plans in mind for his son and heir, and was angry on hearing of the secret marriage. But he relented enough to petition the Pope to free the Prince and Joan from the penalties of excommunication, to which their marriage as first cousins would otherwise condemn them, according to the Papal Canons.

Since the Papal Bull had ordained that Joan's marriage to Holland was the valid one, following his death the banns for her marriage to the Prince could be published, and a quiet, if official, wedding was held. Joan and the Prince would go on to have two sons. The younger became Richard II of England, his older brother having died by then.

The Prince himself died in 1376, of an infection contracted some years earlier during an expedition to Spain. Joan died in 1385. She had directed that her body be laid, not with that of the Prince, but with her first husband, Holland. As our history goes, however, her son by the Prince, Richard II, was later deposed by the usurper, Henry IV, and murdered. Moreover, another of her sons, John Holland, Duke of Exeter—along with her grandson, Thomas Holland, Duke of Surrey—was killed for opposing King Henry.

As Froissart would mention, regardless of the fact that she was the most beautiful and loving woman in England, all of Joan's immediate descendants were unlucky.

GORDON R. DICKSON

The winner of two Nebula Awards and four Hugo Awards, Gordon R. Dickson is one of science fiction's most popular authors. His Childe Cycle, including novels such as *Dorsai!*, *The Final Encyclopedia*, *Young Bleys*, and *Other* is one of the cornerstones of modern SF. He lives in Minneapolis, Minnesota.